CHILDREN OF THE GLENS

CHILDREN OF
THE GLENS

Gwen Kirkwood

This first world edition published in Great Britain 2004 by
SEVERN HOUSE PUBLISHERS LTD of
9–15 High Street, Sutton, Surrey SM1 1DF.
This first world edition published in the USA 2004 by
SEVERN HOUSE PUBLISHERS INC of
595 Madison Avenue, New York, N.Y. 10022.

British Library Cataloguin   Kirkwood, Gwen

Kirkwood, Gwen   Children of the
    Children of the glens   glens / Gwen
    1.   Country life - Sc   Kirkwood
    2.   Agriculture - Sc
    3.   Scotland - Socia   F   :tion
    4.   Domestic fiction
    I.   Title   1482754
    823.9'14 [F]

    ISBN 0-7278-6122-0

Typeset by Palimpsest Book Production Ltd.,
Polmont, Stirlingshire, Scotland.
Printed and bound in Great Britain by
MPG Books Ltd., Bodmin, Cornwall.

It is February, 1962. Conan is now married to Fiona Sinclair and they have taken in Lucy as their own daughter. The story continues following the lives of Ross and Rachel's children and grandchildren and commences with a family gathering to celebrate the coming of age of Ewan and Lucy in Lochandee Village Hall.

One

Rachel felt an unexpected shiver tingle down her spine. Why? she wondered uneasily. Subconsciously her gaze was drawn to the slender, swaying figure of one of the young women from the teacher-training college. Rachel had always had an uncanny instinct where the welfare of her family was concerned but she was not given to dramatic flights of fancy. She gave herself a mental shake. Still a frisson of unease lingered.

This was a happy occasion: a gathering of family and friends in the familiar surroundings of Lochandee Village Hall. They were celebrating the coming of age of her youngest son and her granddaughter, Ewan and Lucy. They had been born within a couple of weeks of each other and a joint celebration had seemed a good idea. They were both at colleges in Ayr and consequently had several mutual friends.

It had been a shock when she first discovered that Lucy was her granddaughter, the child fathered by Conan, her eldest son. Conan himself had never dreamt his wild moment of passion – kindled by his impending departure for the RAF – had resulted in the birth of a little girl. Lucy was almost twelve years old before her mother, Beth, had confided in anyone. Even then she had only divulged her secret because she knew she was dying. She had not wanted to leave her child alone, unprotected and without a mother's guidance. She had been beset with fears that the close friendship Ewan and Lucy shared might blossom into a deeper relationship as they grew older. She dared not take her secret to the grave leaving Lucy unaware that her real father was not Harry Mason, the man who had adored her. Harry had died suddenly

1

and Beth's grief had been deep and sincere, but she had been glad he had never suffered the heartbreak of discovering Lucy was not his child. He had never known that she had committed that single, fateful act of infidelity with his young friend, Conan Maxwell. Beth had worked at Lochandee and Rachel had known her most of her life. She had valued her help as a maid, but friendship and mutual respect had grown over the years.

We must have been blind not to see the family resemblance, Rachel reflected now, as she had done many times in the past. She watched with pride and pleasure as Ewan and Lucy circled the floor together, smiling, radiating the warmth generated by long-standing friendship and shared memories. Yet even in the family, their true relationship was rarely mentioned. Rachel supposed it was what was known as a skeleton in the family's cupboard. Thankfully it did not seem to have affected Lucy. She had grown into a pleasant, well-adjusted young woman, working hard at her music and her teacher-training course, eager to fulfil the dream Harry Mason had cherished for her future.

Lucy was kind and thoughtful too. It was her kindness that had prompted her to invite Gerda Fritz-Allan, the girl with the curtain of long blonde hair, who was not one of Lucy's own particular friends, but who had recently joined a study group at the teacher-training college. All the others in the group had already been invited to the party, and Lucy had felt it would be unkind to leave her out.

The girl had a rare beauty and Rachel frowned now, wondering why she should have such an uneasy feeling about her. Was it her affectedly child-like voice and fluttering hands that irritated? She put such silly whims out of her head, thinking they would probably never see Gerda Fritz-Allan again after the young people returned to college tomorrow.

Rachel felt her heart swell with pride as she turned her attention to some other members of her family as they joined in the dancing: Bridie, her only daughter, and Nick, a son-in-law who had earned her respect and her affection. They

2

danced well together, as they did most other things, including their singing and their work at Lochandee. Other young couples began to dance – Ewan's fellow students from Auchincruive agricultural college and Lucy's friends from Craigie teacher-training college. Rachel sighed. They all looked so happy and carefree. She hoped life would continue that way for all of them in a world free from wars.

Her eye was caught by Conan and Fiona. What a handsome couple they made, but what a pity they had not been blessed with children of their own, Rachel thought. They had been married seven years now, and Conan would be forty in May. Fiona was thirty-seven. Secretly Rachel was still a little in awe of her daughter-in-law. She was such a clever and capable young woman, and she had proved a great asset and partner to Conan, helping him build up his business to a whole fleet of touring coaches. She kept their home beautifully too. She had excellent taste and the new extension to their house had made it a good investment as well as a desirable residence. Far more importantly, Fiona had been a wonderful stepmother to Lucy. She would always have Rachel's heartfelt gratitude for that, and yet she almost envied the closeness of their relationship. They were more like sisters, in spite of the years between them.

'Why are ye frowning, lassie? You'll spoil your bonnie face.'

Rachel looked up at the sound of her husband's deep voice and her heartbeat quickened. Even after all these years, Ross's smile still had the same effect on her.

'I'm scarcely a lassie any more.' She chuckled. 'Watching all these young folks really makes me feel my age.'

'Och, we're as young as we feel, and you're as lithe as any o' them. I'm not sixty until November, remember, and I only feel half of that when I see that wee dimple in your cheek. Come on, let's show them how to dance. Some of the youngsters these days dinna know how to begin.'

'I know. Ewan was warning me that the second half of the party will be music to suit his generation. Rock and Roll, or something, he called it.'

'I think it's some sort of jiving they do nowadays. All the more reason for us to enjoy this half. Listen, they're playing the Pride of Erin Waltz.' He drew her on to the floor and Rachel felt her spirits rise, her fears and apprehensions forgotten, at least for the moment.

A couple of hours later Rachel, Bridie and Fiona cleared the remnants of the buffet meal away into the small kitchen at the back of the village hall.

'Well, they certainly enjoyed that!' Fiona exclaimed. 'I thought there were mountains of food, but it's nearly all gone. I could never cook like you two,' she added with a wistful sigh.

'Och, Fiona, there's nothing to cooking when you've done it all your life,' Rachel reassured her. 'You can do so many other things that I've never heard of.'

'Yes, like organizing.' Bridie grinned. 'I'd never have thought of setting the food out as a buffet, but it all worked splendidly.'

'Mmm. We'd never have managed to feed so many at a sit-down meal.' Rachel nodded agreement. 'Bridie, your father and I are going home as soon as we have seen Lucy and Ewan cut the cake. I got the impression Ewan thinks their friends will relax and enjoy it better if we are out of the way. I hope they'll not get too boisterous,' she added anxiously.

'Don't worry, Mum.' Bridie smiled. 'I think they only want to play some of that rowdy music that Dad calls a "hell of a din". Fiona and Conan will keep an eye on them. We'll stay on for a while, but I expect the twins will be ready for bed long before the finish.'

'I'm sure they will. After all, they're only seven. But it was good to see them joining in the dancing. Your father is sure they have inherited a good sense of rhythm from you and Nick. He says Alicia can sing beautifully.'

'Mmm. Max isn't bad either,' Bridie reflected. 'I wish we still had a choir at the kirk for him to get some practice. Nick thinks we should send him for piano lessons but I'm afraid of sickening him like Dad did with Ewan.'

'Oh, it wasna your father's fault!' Rachel protested. 'Ewan simply didn't have any musical ability and he didn't want to be bothered. All he has ever wanted to do is farm Wester Rullion.' She smiled, the dimple flashing, making her look younger than her fifty-seven years. Almost a mischievous smile, Bridie thought affectionately. 'He can't wait to finish at the college and get on with breeding a cow good enough to beat your Lochandee herd.'

'Oh! That's what he thinks, is it! Nick and I will give him a run for his money then. We got a lovely little heifer calf from the Star family last week.'

'Well, Ewan seemed well pleased to get a brand new tractor for his birthday present,' Fiona remarked, joining the conversation as she deftly packed away the remains of the food.

'I'm afraid we were needing one anyway,' Rachel said ruefully. 'The old Ferguson had packed up, despite Nick's skill at keeping the machines in order. We did get Ewan a decent watch for something more personal, though.'

'Well, according to Conan, Ewan's over the moon about the tractor.'

'I overheard that beautiful blonde girl saying she thought it was a queer sort of a present.' Bridie chuckled. 'She thought he wouldn't get much pleasure out of a thing like that. I gather she doesn't know much about farming, or she'd realize what an essential piece of equipment it is for someone as keen as Ewan. Are you and Dad taking him into partnership now he's reached the . . . er . . . age of discretion?' she asked.

'We had intended to, but your father says he will wait until Ewan leaves college and learns what real farming and hard work are all about!'

'Oh, I can just imagine that!' Bridie laughed. 'Anyway that will only be another six months now. Ewan's course finishes at the end of June, doesn't it?'

'Yes, but one or two of his fellow students are talking about going abroad before they settle down.' Rachel frowned.

'And you think Ewan might join them?'

'He says not, but we'll wait and see. He seems younger for his years than you and Conan did at twenty-one. I suppose the war made you both grow up too quickly. Ewan's still impressionable. There's no telling what distractions he might encounter.'

The three of them made their way back into the main hall but Lucy waylaid them at the door.

'Bridie, we're just trying to persuade Nick to give us a song but he says he needs you to sing with him.'

'I'm sure your friends will not want to listen to our kind of music, Lucy.'

'Of course they will. I could listen to you both singing all night.'

'Yes, so could I,' Fiona said. 'Do sing, Bridie.'

'All right, if you and my father will accompany us, Lucy.'

They sang a couple of Scottish songs, then Ewan called out, 'Sing us some of the more modern songs, please, Bridie.'

'What about "*Que sera, sera*"?' Nick asked. 'Isn't that appropriate for all you youngsters on the threshold of life?'

'That went down well,' Bridie said in surprise. 'What about the one that young American lorry driver sings for the last one?'

'Elvis Presley? "Wooden Heart"? OK.'

When the song drew to a close they were greeted with enthusiastic calls for more, but Gerda Fritz-Allan did not join in. She was bored by someone else being centre stage. She wondered what had persuaded her to accept an invitation for a visit to the country when she could have been enjoying herself at a dance in Glasgow. Then she saw Nick stepping lightly down from the little stage and taking his small daughters gently by the hand. Margaret was shy but Alicia loved to sing, and Lucy added encouragement and softly played an accompaniment while they sang 'How Much is that Doggie in the Window?'.

Gerda was standing behind Fiona and Rachel. 'For God's sake,' she muttered. 'I didn't think I was coming to a Sunday school party!'

'I'm pleased not everyone thinks like she does,' Rachel whispered to Fiona as the applause burst forth spontaneously, making the twins shyly lower their heads.

6

'One more to finish, then we'll leave you all to dance the night away,' Nick announced. 'How about "I Could Have Danced All Night"?' He and Bridie shared a special smile, which Gerda did not miss. The song was one of their own favourites.

They left the platform to loud applause as the bandleader struck up the dancing again, announcing a ladies' choice to get the ball rolling. Bridie was astonished when the girl with the long blonde hair made a beeline for Nick – but then he was a fine figure of a man, she thought proudly, especially in his new fitted jacket with the split at the back. It accentuated his firm, muscular figure and his long legs. Even so, he was considerably older than Ewan and his friends. Nick and Conan had already joined the RAF when Ewan was born – a big surprise to everyone, not least their parents.

As soon as the dance finished, Nick extricated himself and crossed the floor to where Bridie was waiting with the twins. He was frowning slightly.

'There's home we'll go now.' Bridie raised her eyebrows. She could always tell that something had upset or excited Nick when he fell back into the Welsh lilt of his youth. Walking to the car, he said quietly, 'A flirtatious piece, that one is. Too much experience, she has.' Bridie nodded, knowing he meant the girl called Gerda Fritz-Allan.

'I think she's from the city,' said Bridie. 'Fiona says she lives with her father. She doesn't know whether her mother is dead or whether they are divorced, but I got the impression Fiona felt she needed a mother's guidance. Perhaps she's had a go at flirting with Conan.' She grinned. 'Maybe she fancies older men, especially handsome, married ones . . .'

'Flattering me, are you, girl?' Nick chuckled softly and squeezed her hand.

'Why are you two holding hands?' Margaret asked innocently as they reached the car and turned to wait for Nick to unlock it. 'Hurry up Daddy, I'm frozen.'

'So am I,' echoed Alicia.

'Well, sweethearts, it is February and we did tell you to wear your scarves and gloves,' Bridie reminded her small daughters. 'But you did look very pretty in your red velvet dresses.'

'Yes. Grandpa said we were the best-dressed young ladies at the party, except for Granny,' Margaret said solemnly.

'Blondie wouldn't have been too pleased to hear that,' Nick whispered in Bridie's ear. 'Thought she was the bee's knees, she did, in that revealing black dress. Far too old for her it was, in my opinion.'

There was a hard frost overnight and, as Bridie had feared, some of the dairy equipment was frozen by morning. It had to be thawed out with kettles of boiling water before the milking could begin.

'Thank goodness for the Aga and plenty of hot water,' she muttered, stifling a yawn and wondering what time the party had ended.

'I'll take the big kettle and thaw the dairy pipes if you can get the milking machines on,' Nick volunteered.

'Thanks, Nick. Sometimes I'll bet you wish you'd never seen Lochandee.'

'Oh, I don't know, it has its compensations . . .' He gave her a wolfish grin and slipped an arm around her waist. 'Like when I'm tucked up in a nice warm bed with this soft little bottom to cuddle.' He gave her rear end a gentle pat.

'I thought you'd had enough of that sort of thing last night, Nicholas Jones,' she retorted with mock severity.

'A–ah, there's never enough I get of you, cariad.' He gave an unexpected yawn. 'It's a pity cows can't milk themselves on Sundays, though.'

It was later than usual when Bridie finally returned to the house, the milking finished and the cows fed and cleaned for the day. The telephone was ringing.

'Hello?' she answered breathlessly.

'A–ah, Bridie, I was just about to hang up. Have you had a bad morning with frozen pipes?'

'I'm afraid so, Mum. How are things at Wester Rullion? Are you very tired after the party?'

'Not too bad. Ewan was up and out at the milking parlour with your father and Peter, but his friends are just surfacing so I'm waiting to dish up their porridge and cook bacon and eggs for those who want it.'

'Mmm, that makes me hungry. We haven't had ours yet.'

'I mustn't keep you then. I just thought Fiona might need a helping hand. The girls want to see round the farm with Ewan's friends. I'm not sure whether it's the animals or the boys that's the attraction,' she added with a laugh. 'Anyway, Conan is bringing them over here in about an hour and he says he is taking the whole lot of them back to his place for lunch.'

'Gosh! Fiona will be busy with all of them to feed.'

'Yes, I know, but Conan thought it would save time. It gets dark so early and it looks as though it will be hard frost again. He says the bus doesn't hold the road like the Land Rover does, so he wants to get them back safely and in good time.'

'Mmm, I can understand he'll not want to be too late on that road in the dark if it's icy. I'll go over and help Fiona then. Nick will pick up the children from Sunday school and bring them over there. Does she want any food? I could take some apple pies out of my freezer. You'll have to get one, Mum. They're wonderful for all sorts of things.'

'I'm sure they can't be as good as fresh pies though,' Rachel said doubtfully. 'But I expect Fiona will be glad of any contributions.'

'I doubt if Ewan's friends will know the difference,' Bridie said drily.

'Maybe not. I cooked a big piece of ham to feed the boys, so I said I would slice it up and send it back with Conan. Fiona sounded grateful for that. It's strange that she is so capable when it comes to making big decisions and dealing with all sorts of crises concerning the business, yet catering for a group of hungry students seems to worry her.'

'Yes, maybe I should persuade Fiona to invest in a deep freeze then, so that she can fill it up at leisure and always be prepared – even when her mother-in-law comes to tea!'

'Oh, Bridie! I'm not that bad, am I? I don't criticize,

9

and I've always thought Fiona makes Conan an excellent wife . . .'

'I was only teasing, Mum.' Bridie chuckled. 'When the time comes, I just hope Ewan gets a wife who fits into the family circle as well as Fiona does.'

'Yes.' Rachel sighed happily. 'I often think how lucky we are, your father and I. I felt so proud of you all last night.'

Fiona had worried about the sleeping arrangements for ten young women and only three bedrooms, but Lucy had assured her they were all used to making do with sleeping bags when the occasion demanded.

'We'll toss a coin to see who gets the beds,' she had said cheerfully, but by mutual consent the girls had all agreed that Gerda Fritz-Allan should certainly have a bed. She was still new to their group and they were somewhat in awe of her beauty, her fragile air and her expensive clothes. It just didn't seem fitting to ask her to rough it as they were prepared to do.

They had thoroughly enjoyed the party and were now looking forward to rounding off the weekend with a walk in the crisp, frosty air.

'It's such lovely countryside,' one of the girls remarked. 'You're really lucky, Lucy.'

'I know, I love it too.' Lucy smiled. Only Fiona noticed Gerda's grimace of distaste, and felt a surge of relief. The girl was not one of Lucy's special friends, so they were unlikely to see her again, especially if she didn't like the countryside.

'Do we have to go looking at animals and trailing round a muddy farmyard?' Gerda demanded, as though to confirm Fiona's opinion of her.

'Even if ye dinna want tae see the farm, Gerda, I'd hae thocht ye'd wanna hae anither wee flirt wi' the birthday laddie,' one of the girls said in mock astonishment. She gave a wicked wink to one of her friends. 'Ye'll no' want tae miss checking oot Ewan's inheritance,' she drawled, knowing full well her exaggeration of a broad Scots accent always annoyed Gerda.

'Inheritance?' Gerda frowned uncertainly. 'What inheritance? You talk as though he's a laird, or something.'

'Well, so he is. Laird o' his ain wee patch, anyway.'

'Of course Ewan isn't a laird!' Lucy intervened quickly, alarmed by the sudden flare of interest in Gerda's pale-blue eyes. 'Betty's only teasing.'

But Betty grinned unrepentantly, unaware of the seeds she had unwittingly sown in Gerda's mind.

Two

U sually Gerda's questions would have exasperated Ewan in a very short time, but he was flattered by the interest she was showing in himself and in the farm. He knew most of his friends were attracted to her, so he basked in her undivided attention, answering even her stupidest questions with patient tolerance. He was aware of Lucy's eyes on them, amused, then amazed, her eyebrows raised incredulously. He knew exactly when her amusement turned to irritation and even contempt, and he felt uncomfortable. Lucy was usually the least critical of people.

Surely no one could be so ignorant of country life as to believe a chicken popped out of an egg the moment it was laid, Lucy thought. Even more ridiculous was the prospect of bulls producing milk just as cows did. She wanted to ask Gerda if she would expect a man to suckle babies as well. And surely everyone knew a cow had to have a calf before she produced milk. These were things Lucy had known all her life, having spent most of her childhood with Ewan at Glens of Lochandee. But she knew Gerda did not lack intelligence. Was she pretending? Was she trying to make a fool of Ewan?

Lucy could barely conceal her irritation as Gerda continued to cling to his arm, gesticulating dramatically, exclaiming in the high-pitched little-girl voice she often used to gain attention. She had hoped that her best friend, Christine Greig, and Ewan would hit it off over the weekend. Chris was so knowledgeable about farming and the life it involved.

Lucy and Chris had become friends as soon as they started at Craigie Teacher-Training College. They were both country girls with common interests. Chris was great with animals and children, but she was quiet and rarely made the most of her own abilities. She had three older brothers who teased her unmercifully and a mother who was continually harassed from caring for her family and her house and poultry. So people had to take Chris as they found her, and impressionable young men never seemed to look beneath the surface, Lucy thought with a rare flash of anger.

'What they see is what they get with me,' Chris would say, grinning merrily when the other girls tried to persuade her to use eyeshadow and mascara for their Saturday night dances.

'I would much rather have attended the agricultural college than trained as a teacher, but Mother insisted I must have a career that had nothing to do with farming,' she once confided to Lucy. 'I couldn't stand to be with a man who expected me to look like a film star all day.'

When Lucy had embarked on her career, she experienced a world far removed from the village of Lochandee and the farm and the garage. She had been grateful for Fiona's guidance, her advice on clothes, the discreet make-up she wore and the expert way she styled her curly hair – even the way she walked and talked to suit the occasion. These things had given her confidence and an air of calm, even when she was feeling as quivery as a jelly inside.

Lucy had visited Chris's family often because their farm was only ten miles south of Ayr. She had frequently heard Mrs Greig comment: 'Three lads to be put into farms is more than enough. Our Chris needs to get hersel' a good job and earn some money. I dinna want her tae marry a farmer. It's all work an' no play.' Chris had reluctantly bowed to her mother's wishes, but Lucy knew her heart was as much in farming as Ewan's was.

Ewan showed everyone round the milking parlour and the dairy. The huge tank not only held all the milk, but also kept it refrigerated until the milk tanker arrived to take it to the creamery. Chris was genuinely impressed and interested. Her parents milked their cows in a byre and the milk was collected in ten-gallon churns that had to be carted to the end of the road every day in readiness for the milk lorry. She wanted to ask Ewan all about the various tubes and lines and how it all worked, but Gerda clung to him like a limpet.

'My brothers would love to see round here,' she murmured to Lucy. 'It must make the work a lot easier.'

'Yes, I suppose it does,' Lucy agreed. 'I know the local farmers all think Ewan's father was very far-sighted when he decided to go for a milking parlour and cubicle house instead of building a byre. There are quite a few springing up now. Bridie still milks her cows in a byre at Glens of Lochandee though. You'll have to come to stay for another weekend, Chris, just the two of us, then you can see everything. Bridie reckons she can give her cows more individual attention in a byre, but I've heard her say she thinks it would be better if they didn't need to be tied by the neck all winter.'

'Mmm. I can't believe that Ewan's cows are allowed to just wander freely around the shed and feed themselves at the silage pit. Don't they ever fight?'

'Sometimes, but you'll notice they've all had their horns removed so they can't do so much damage to each other.'

'A–ah, yes, of course. I thought there was something different about them. I don't suppose Gerda would know they'd ever even had horns!'

'I'm sure she wouldn't. I wonder what's making her show such an interest. I can't believe it's genuine. She hates anything remotely smelly and she can't stand the smallest bit of mud.'

Chris gave her friend a knowing look and was about to tell Lucy exactly why Gerda was interested in Ewan and his farm, but Lucy was frowning and did not catch her eye so Chris kept her opinion to herself. No doubt Gerda would soon lose interest in all things country, including Ewan. Even if the novelty lasted a while, surely Ewan would see she was only feigning interest.

But in this she was wrong. Gerda made it her business to quiz Ewan's closest friends on his prospects as a farmer. Of all the girls they knew, Gerda was the least likely to make

14

a farmer's wife, so they exaggerated his assets at every opportunity, teasing her unmercifully, never dreaming that Gerda would take them seriously. She could see Ewan as a future country gentleman, provided he had a wife like her to lead him, she thought secretly.

After their tour of Wester Rullion, Conan shepherded them all into the coach and back to Rullion Glen for lunch.

'We'll come over in the car and join you,' Ross said. 'We'll need it to get home for milking.'

Fiona, with the help of Bridie and the twins, had already set out huge bowls of soup, with crisp, buttery rolls and a selection of cold meats, to be followed by apple pie and cream. The crowd of young folk chattered happily as they ate.

'This has been the best weekend I've had since I started college,' one of the young men announced. There were cheers of agreement, but all too soon it was time to leave. Lucy turned to hug Fiona.

'You've given me a lovely birthday weekend, Fiona. I can never thank you for the way you look after me,' she said huskily. She turned to Conan and hugged him too. 'Thanks for laying on the transport and chauffeuring us all around, Conan.' She bent closer and whispered mischievously, 'And thanks for being such a generous daddy.'

'Och, you!' Conan gave her an affectionate pat on her neat little rear. They rarely mentioned their real relationship, and Lucy knew he still found it difficult to accept that he had fathered a child when he was little more than a teenager himself. It had taken her some time to get over the shock too, but now she liked to tease him occasionally. Conan knew that was down to their deepening affection, but above all he knew he had Fiona to thank for helping Lucy to come to terms with all the shocks and changes in her young life.

When they were all seated on the bus, Gerda lost no time in leaning forward and poking Lucy's shoulder.

'I say, it's a bit off to call your parents by their Christian names, isn't it?'

'I don't think so.' Lucy frowned, irritated by Gerda's sharp finger and probing stare. She seemed to take a delight in delving into things that did not concern her.

'They are Lucy's adopted parents, as you know very well,' Chris said abruptly.

'Even so . . .'

'Oh, for goodness' sake, Gerda! I knew both Conan and Fiona long before they adopted me. Anyway, Fiona is more like an elder sister to me than a stepmother.'

'I suppose it would make her feel old if you called her Mummy. So. . .If they are only your adoptive parents, you're not really Ewan's cousin, are you? The two of you always seem very . . . er . . . close. I wondered if there was something going on between you. . .' When Lucy made no answer, Gerda persisted. 'You look quite like each other. At least, I've sometimes thought so, but then I thought you really were related. I couldn't help wondering . . .'

'Ewan and I were practically brought up together,' Lucy snapped. 'We've always been the best of friends, and I hope we always will be. Now, will you sit back in your own seat and stop poking me in the back?'

Chris gave her a sideways glance and winked wickedly. She bit back a smile in case Gerda should see, but out of the side of her mouth she whispered, 'She's jealous.'

'Heaven forbid Ewan should ever be tempted in that direction,' Lucy muttered.

'Mmm . . . I can just imagine her tottering out to feed the chickens in her red toeless shoes with the three-inch heels.' Chris grinned.

As the cold weather of February turned to spring and onward to May, the countryside burgeoned with new life and the scent of blossom filled the hedgerows. Ewan longed to be back home at the farm but instead he worked hard at his studies. All he wanted was to gain his diploma now that he was so near to finishing his course. He was looking forward to helping with the crops and to working with the fine Friesian herd that his father had built up at Wester Rullion. Although they sometimes argued when Ewan wanted to change to more modern methods, he was grateful for his father's wisdom and experience.

He realized how fortunate he was to be able to return home to Wester Rullion with the prospect of farming it himself some day. Several of his fellow students were seeking employment, but some were going home to work with elder brothers, and wondering whether they would ever get a chance to farm on their own.

Although he did not feel his age, Ross knew that he was not as fit as he had been when he was twenty-one, or even a decade ago. He was looking forward to having Ewan around to share some of the responsibilities and the decisions. Most of all, he hoped he would take over some of the increasing piles of paperwork attached to their pedigree herd. All the calves were black and white and each one had to be carefully sketched and coloured in with its respective markings. Then the sire and dam and grandparents, plus their registration numbers, had to be done in duplicate and submitted to the breed society within a month of the calf's birth. It was not a side of farming that Ross enjoyed and the older he got the more he resented it taking up his valuable time and energy. Rachel dealt with all the farm accounts and paid the bills and he was grateful for that. Sometimes she relented and helped him sketch the calves and fill in the pedigrees, but it was not a chore she wanted to add to her own busy life on a regular basis.

'I'm getting older too, you know,' she remarked from time to time, when she felt her husband needed a gentle reminder. 'These days there are no maids to help in the house as there were before the war, and I like things to be clean and tidy for when the milk recorders arrive.'

Every month a young woman came to stay at the farm overnight – sometimes two nights when there were a lot of cows for milking. She weighed the milk from each cow at the evening milking and again at the morning milking, recording the results in ledgers and calculating the records for the month. In addition she tested the butterfat from each animal, using special Gerber tubes, alcohol and a portable

17

centrifuge. These records were an essential requirement for a pedigree dairy herd. At the end of each lactation the records helped with the selection of the best breeding animals, as well as adding value to a cow and to her progeny in the sale ring.

'You could get rid of the hens – then you would have more time to do the pedigrees,' Ross suggested on one occasion when he was particularly exasperated with the amount of paperwork.

'Get rid of my poultry!' Rachel was indignant. 'They pay for the housekeeping and for Peter's wages, as well as the petrol. Besides, I like having the chickens and hens, and it's better not to put all our eggs in one basket . . .'

Ross exploded with laughter and his ill humour vanished.

'You know what I mean,' Rachel chided, but the dimple at the corner of her mouth could not be hidden. She grinned at him. 'Seriously, Ross, what if we had another outbreak of foot-and-mouth and lost all our cows again?'

'Don't even think about it!' Ross growled in mock horror.

'No, it's too terrible to contemplate, I know. But about the pedigrees – I'm sure Peter would help you with sketching the calves and filling them in if you asked him. He's proved himself capable of most things we've asked him to do since we took over Wester Rullion, and he's conscientious.'

'Aye, you're right there. I've never regretted taking a chance with Peter. I'm glad he decided not to return to Poland when the war was over. And he keeps his wee cottage as neat and clean as a new pin too.'

'Yes, it would have been nice if he'd met a suitable girl for a wife, but he seems content with his garden and his vegetables in the summer and with his wood-carving in the winter.'

'Aye, a wife might have led him astray. Did he tell you he was thinking of buying a second-hand car for himself?'

'No. He's never mentioned that to me. I did hear Conan telling him he could get a new Mini for just under five hundred pounds now that the chancellor has cut the purchase tax.'

18

'It's still a lot of money,' Ross said gravely. 'Peter was just asking Conan for advice. I think he's keeping a look out for a bargain for him.'

'Maybe he'll go out more if he gets a car.'

'He might. I think I'd better wait for Ewan to come home and take over the pedigrees. He's familiar with most of them already.' He smiled reminiscently. 'I reckon there's going to be some healthy competition between Wester Rullion and Lochandee when Bridie and Ewan start showing and selling in the same ring at pedigree sales.'

'So long as it stays as friendly rivalry it will be all right.' Rachel grimaced. She did not welcome the idea of a family feud between her daughter and her son. 'Anyway, half of Bridie's cattle are still pedigree Ayrshires. She's loath to change over to Friesians completely.'

'I know.' Ross grinned down at her and his eyes crinkled at the corners. 'And I suspect you agree with her,' he teased.

'We–ell. . . Yes, I shall always have a soft spot for a good Ayrshire cow, and if you would admit the truth, I suspect you do too, Ross Maxwell.'

'They take a bit of beating for appearance, but we have to think about the economics these days, and the Friesians do give better yields and eat more roughage. I'd hate to get too complacent, but I reckon we have been jolly lucky that things have gone so well for us since we bought Wester Rullion. I never imagined we would get the loan for the land paid off in record time. It's a great relief.'

'Well, so far the government have made sure we get a fair price for our produce since the war, even though they say the price of food in the shops is the lowest in Europe.'

'It's government policy to pay us a subsidy to encourage home production and keep the cost to the consumers in check at the same time,' Ross mused. 'The idea is that the workers will be less likely to strike for higher wages if they can afford to eat well.'

'I suppose that's what Mr Macmillan meant when he said we've never had it so good.' Rachel nodded. 'But from what Fiona says, people want to be able to afford more than just food and clothes these days. She says some of the holiday-makers book for next year's holiday as soon as this year's one is over. Perhaps we should think about having a little holiday once Ewan comes home?'

'A holiday! We . . .' Ross stopped suddenly and stared at his wife, his keen glance searching her face. 'You're not feeling ill are you, Rachel?' he asked anxiously.

'No, of course not, silly! I just thought it would be nice to have a few nights away together, just the two of us.' She sighed wistfully. 'We've never been on holiday. Conan says the people who go on his buses really enjoy seeing all the sights and having their meals set before them every night.'

'I think I'd be bored to tears riding around on a bus all day,' Ross scoffed. 'And so would you. Now I'd better go and start the milking. The parlour has made that job a lot easier, so we should be thankful for that.'

'It has,' Rachel sighed, 'but the milking still has to be done twice a day. I don't suppose they'll ever invent cows that can come and get milked themselves!'

Over at Glens of Lochandee, Nick's thoughts were running on similar lines to his mother-in-law's.

'I wonder whether your mother and father will take a holiday from the farm when Ewan comes home from college,' he said as he and Bridie walked behind the ambling cows, bringing them in from the field for milking. 'I think your mother has looked unusually tired recently.'

'I can't imagine my father on holiday,' Bridie said, 'but I'm sure it would do them both a lot of good if Conan could persuade them. By the way, did I tell you Lucy has been offered a job at a school in Ayrshire when she finishes college?'

'No! Are Fiona and Conan disappointed she'll not be working nearer home?'

'If they are they would never say so,' Bridie mused. 'Fiona says that lovely blonde girl has been pestering Lucy to invite her down for a weekend, but they're not particular friends. I think she irritates Lucy a bit.'

'No wonder! Irritate me she would, that one. Dramatic she is.'

Bridie's eyes widened. Nick was not normally given to criticism, and a return to his Welsh accent always reflected his feelings. 'I thought all men automatically fell for beautiful blondes.'

'Not this one, bach.' He stepped closer and slipped an arm around Bridie's waist. 'All the woman I'm wanting, you are.' He squeezed affectionately and she laughed up at him.

'I'm glad to hear that, for I've no intention of letting you go, Nicholas Jones. Let's see, how many years have we been married now?'

'September 1949 it was. Thirteen years this year and not a single regret have I had.'

'That makes two of us then. I think Fiona and Conan are well matched too, in spite of their resistance when they were younger. I just wish they had had children of their own . . .'

'Maybe they don't want any. They work so hard at the business. I believe that's Conan's baby.'

'Yes, he's always been ambitious, I know.' Bridie sighed. 'And they do everything together. That wouldn't be possible if they had a family – not the travelling part anyway.'

'So is the blonde beauty coming down to stay then? I must say, I prefer Lucy's friend from Ayrshire – Christine isn't it?'

'Yes, Christine Greig. Her father bought a Lochandee bull at the Castle Douglas sale a few years ago. He said he wouldn't mind another if it was going cheap!'

'A satisfied customer then.'

'Chris has three brothers all keen on farming. Lucy told me they are trying to rent another farm a few miles away. I have a sneaky feeling that she has a soft spot for the eldest brother, Donald – Don for short.'

'She'll not be thinking of getting married until she's established herself in teaching though, if I know Lucy.'

'I shouldn't think so. She's a sensible lassie, and she listens to Fiona's advice. Conan is thinking of buying her a wee car of her own if she passes all her examinations. I think they both miss Lucy's lively company about the house. And her music of course. Perhaps they think she'll come home more often if she has her own transport.'

'I expect Ewan will be wanting a car of his own as well then. The pair of them were always like twins – except for the music of course,' Nick reflected.

'I hope Ewan has grown up enough not to want everything that Lucy gets.' Bridie frowned. 'Anyway, he will be living at home and I suppose he'll use Father's car when he needs one.'

A little while later Nick was helping Bridie fasten the chains that kept the cows in their own stalls along both sides of the long byre.

'I wonder why Gerda Fritz-Allan wants to come down here again.' he said. 'She didn't seem like a country girl to me.'

'I don't know. She and Lucy are not exactly bosom pals.' Bridie frowned. 'I don't think she has a very happy home life. Her mother went off with someone else when Gerda was eleven. She was killed in a cable-car accident soon afterwards. Apparently her father spends most of his time at his office. That's what Lucy told Fiona anyway. I think she was feeling mean for not wanting to invite Gerda for another weekend.'

'There's kindly, she is, our Lucy,' Nick said warmly. 'But she's not a bit like the blonde siren.'

'No–o. I think Ewan must be feeling sorry for Gerda as well. He's been putting on the pressure with Lucy to invite her down once the exams are over.'

'Sorry? Feeling sorry is it!' Nick gave a mocking guffaw. 'That's not how I'd describe Ewan's feeling for Miss Gerda Fritz-Allan, from what I saw of them!'

Bridie frowned, but she didn't reply. Nick was a shrewd judge of people and situations, but in Ewan's case she fervently hoped he was wrong.

22

Three

'You don't seem too sure about bringing Gerda Fritz-Allan home with you when college finishes, Lucy,' Fiona suggested when she telephoned to finalize the arrangements for clearing Lucy's possessions out of her college accommodation.

'We–ell. . .' Lucy frowned at the receiver in her hand. She was talking from the payphone in the corridor and one never knew who might overhear.

'Has Ewan anything to do with it?' Fiona asked.

'He's keen to have her down again,' Lucy admitted. Fiona guessed by her tone that the whole idea had been Ewan's. 'But sometimes I do feel a bit . . . well, sorry for her. I've been so lucky to have a home with you.'

'Och, away with you.' Fiona laughed softly, but her voice was a little husky and she was touched. 'We're the lucky ones.'

Lucy was still considering her own good fortune as she and Gerda carried their suitcases up the stairs at Rullion Glen.

'Lucy, you don't know how lucky you are to live in such a lovely house.'

'It wasn't always a lovely house.' Lucy chuckled. 'You should have seen it when it was just a poky little flat tucked on to the end of the garage. Conan and Nick built it up from nothing but a bare piece of land after they came home from the air force. They worked terribly hard.'

'Did they fall out?'

'No. They just wanted to do different things, so they each took out their share and went their separate ways. Nick has

23

done very well with his own business. He has more trade than he wants sometimes with his livestock transport. His real love is repairing machines and adapting them, seeing how they work – and of course spending time at Glens of Lochandee with Bridie and the children. He couldn't have done that if he'd stayed in partnership here.'

'No, I suppose not. The Conan Maxwell Coach Company must be getting well known. I'm always seeing coaches on the road.'

'It expanded quite fast after Conan and Fiona got married I think. They work so well together.' Lucy sighed. If ever she got married she hoped she would be a real partner to her husband as well as a wife – and hopefully a mother.

'A–ah but I expect Fiona knew she was on to a good thing when she married him,' Gerda remarked smugly.

Lucy's irritation returned at the thinly disguised bitchiness in her tone. 'Neither of them knew what the future held then,' she said sharply. 'They've both worked jolly hard. Fiona used her own money to expand the business and she built the original house so that we could all live here, near the garage. The land used to be part of Wester Rullion, so that's why they named the house Rullion Glen. They only extended it fairly recently and made the garden.'

'If you say so.' Gerda shrugged. 'But your foster-mother, or whatever she is, certainly looks after herself. I mean, the clothes she wears for a start. . . You never see her in anything cheap or shabby.'

'A–ach!' Lucy choked in disbelief. 'I reckon that description fits you even better than Fiona, and at least Fiona earns money to buy her own. Besides, she needs to be smart and efficient when she's dealing with a whole lot of men. She says they judge her by her appearance, but they never seem to expect us to have brains as well.'

'Some of us have brains!' Gerda corrected grimly. 'I don't know what possessed me to train as a teacher. The long holidays, I suppose.' She stifled a yawn. 'I can't say I'm looking forward to keeping a class of spoiled brats in order. My old man says he's supported me long enough.'

24

'Well, you'll be independent once you get a salary,' Lucy said cheerfully. 'I'm sure not many of the children are spoiled brats. I'm really looking forward to teaching. I love younger children.'

'Maybe that's because you've been pampered yourself,' Gerda muttered with more than a hint of jealousy. 'You don't know how lucky you are.'

'Oh, but I do,' Lucy said fervently. 'I never forget how much Conan and Fiona have done for me, and still do.'

'My mother went off and never even said goodbye. I don't think my father cares whether I'm in the house or not. He's always working – or so he says,' she added darkly.

'I'm sure he must care,' Lucy said, 'or he wouldn't buy you all those lovely clothes. You have twice as many as anyone else at college. And jewellery too.'

'Oh!' Gerda screwed up her small nose. 'I think he just buys me those things to ease his conscience.'

'His conscience?'

'Well he must feel guilty, mustn't he? Mum wouldn't have gone off if he'd made her happy. Then I wouldn't have been left without a mother. It's his fault, so he has to buy me what I want to make up for it.'

Later on, the evening meal was barely over when the telephone rang.

'That's my kid brother wanting to speak to Gerda,' Conan said drily. His expressive eyebrows rose as he met Fiona's glance. 'He seems to be smitten by her,' he muttered when Gerda had left the dining room. Lucy bit her lip and Conan's eyes turned to her. 'Was it Ewan who persuaded you to invite her for the weekend?'

'Mainly.'

'Well, don't worry about it. He's old enough to know what he's doing. Just don't let either of them use you. If they try it again and you want an excuse, just tell them I need you to work in the office with the bookings . . .'

'Do you really?' Lucy's eyes lit up and Conan looked surprised.

'Do you want a holiday job then? I thought you'd want a rest before you take up your new teaching post in September.'

'But that's weeks away . . . Anyway, I want to earn my keep.' Her mouth set in the stubborn line that both Conan and Fiona had learned to recognize.

'Well I'd be glad of some help in my office.' Fiona said to them both.

'Right then,' Conan said with satisfaction. 'We're certainly busy enough with all the summer trips. There's always something being cancelled or rearranged. If it's not a hotel that's overbooked, it's a driver going off sick, or a coach needing an emergency repair. We could use someone with initiative to help over the busy time.'

'You really mean that? You're not just making a job for me?' Lucy said eagerly.

'I would really appreciate having you to help, Lucy.' Fiona smiled.

'Right then,' Conan said, assuming a stern, businesslike manner as Gerda returned to the room. 'You'll start work on Monday, Lucy. Nine o'clock prompt. There's no allowances for family when you're on my payroll. Don't you forget that, young lady.'

Lucy met his eye briefly and bit back a smile. 'Yes, sir!' she said promptly. 'You can rely on me.'

Gerda looked from one to the other and her dismay was obvious. 'Ewan was hoping I'd be able to stay a few days longer . . . Maybe until Thursday, or even until after next weekend. Surely you don't have to work during your vacation, Lucy?' She looked accusingly at Conan.

'Money doesn't grow on trees, young woman. If people want to eat, they need to work first. Doesn't your father tell you that?'

'Och, my father! He's aye lecturing about the cost o' things.' For a moment Gerda forgot her airs and graces and her native Glasgow accent became more apparent. A faint smile hovered on Fiona's lips. She had met several Gerdas in her life.

'Well, you may as well make the most of your weekend

26

then, girls. I will deal with the washing-up for tonight. You two can help tomorrow.' Her eyes rested briefly on Gerda's surprised face. It was clear that she had not expected to do anything other than enjoy her weekend. 'Has Ewan persuaded his father to lend him the car tonight?' Fiona asked pleasantly. 'Is he coming to take the pair of you into Dumfries?'

'Er . . . er, yes.' Gerda's eyes sought Lucy's, frantically trying to convey a message, but Lucy was busy collecting the dirty dishes to take to the kitchen. A little while later she went upstairs and found Gerda hovering by her bedroom door.

'Couldn't you pretend you have a headache, Lucy?' she said impatiently. 'Ewan will be here soon and I want to get changed.'

'Well, what's stopping you?' Lucy asked.

'Do you mean you intend to come with us then?'

'Mmm . . .' Lucy put her head on one side as though considering the matter. 'We–ell, I can see I shall be very welcome as a third . . .'

'But . . .'

'Don't worry, Gerda.' Lucy grimaced. 'I think I really would end up with a headache if I had to watch the two of you mooning over each other all evening. There is just one thing though . . .'

'What's that?'

'Don't involve me in any of your schemes, and most certainly don't expect me to lie for you – either of you.' Gerda's colour rose under her pale skin. Lucy's eyes narrowed. 'I mean it, and you can tell Ewan that too. I would never lie to Mr and Mrs Maxwell, not even to cover up for Ewan. I've too much respect for them.'

'Respect! They're stuffy old fogies!' Gerda muttered angrily. 'Ewan says the whole family goes to church on Sundays, and they're insisting he must be home before midnight! They only agreed to let him have the car because they think you're going as well.' Turning on her heel, she flounced off to her own room.

Lucy sighed. What an exciting weekend this is going to

be, she thought morosely, wishing she had accepted Chris's invitation to spend it with her family in Ayrshire. At least she and Don would have had some time together then, even if only to help him finish hoeing the turnips or start on the hay.

During the summer holidays, Gerda twice wangled an invitation to stay with Lucy. On both occasions she used the excuse that she was lonely because her father was away on business, and Ewan added his own persuasion.

'I'm surprised she doesn't try getting a job for the summer,' Fiona commented.

'I don't think Gerda likes work. The trouble is we don't really have anything in common except the course we did together,' Lucy admitted. 'I've never heard her mention missing her father before though. In fact, I didn't think his job took him away from home.'

'I expect it's an excuse to invite herself here.' Fiona nodded. 'But this time we'll leave her some chores to do.' She smiled. 'After all, we both know she's just using us. It's Ewan she really wants to see. I do hope he gets rid of his moonstruck blinkers soon, for his own sake.'

'Oh, so do I!' Lucy agreed fervently. She had a feeling that when it came to Gerda, for the first time in their lives Ewan would not want her opinion, and her stomach gave a sickening lurch. She wished she had never invited Gerda to her birthday party.

Four

Rachel suspected Ewan and Lucy had quarrelled and she guessed it had something to do with his increasing obsession with Gerda Fritz-Allan.

She had believed Ewan's main ambition in life was to farm at Wester Rullion and to breed even better Friesian cattle than his father had. She couldn't believe he had become so infatuated with a girl like Gerda who had no interest in animals, or farming, or in the countryside at all. She had looked forward to welcoming Ewan's wife when the time came, just as Alice Beattie had welcomed her to Glens of Lochandee when she was young and newly married to Ross. Rachel's heart sank and she felt cold all over at the thought of the beautiful blonde girl becoming such an important part of her family. If only Gerda did not have such a superior and sophisticated air, such a petulant mouth and dramatic manner. If only she had some character, some substance.

It was the middle of harvest and the last week before the new school term started. Reluctantly Rachel had given in to Ewan's pleading and invited Gerda to stay at Wester Rullion for the few days before she started her teaching career.

'They're far too young to be serious,' Ross grumbled. 'And we're far too busy with the harvest. It looks like we're encouraging them if we invite her to stay here.'

'I think Lucy would agree with you. I suspect they have quarrelled over her refusal to invite Gerda down again. Anyway, Ewan reminded me that he is twenty-one now, and we were even younger when we got together,' Rachel said unhappily. 'And I've always said we would welcome his friends.'

'We were already living under the same roof and we had both been working since we were twelve years old. Our circumstances were different,' Ross insisted stubbornly. 'Neither of them have earned a penny yet.'

'Everyone is so busy, my dear,' Rachel said, doing her best to inject some warmth into her voice. She felt a hypocrite because she could not feel any warmth in her heart when she looked into Gerda's cold blue eyes. 'Please make yourself at home. We have to make the most of the good weather to get the harvest in. Ross – that is, Ewan's father – thinks it will break soon and he's usually right about such things.'

Gerda sniffed. A common countryman couldn't possibly tell what the weather was going to do. She had expected Ewan to be at Lockerbie station to meet her, even though he had told her where to get the bus. She had felt annoyed all the way to Wester Rullion, but her anger had given way to a feeling of triumph and satisfaction when she saw the surprise on his mother's face as she stepped out of a taxi. Rachel had been more dismayed than surprised, especially when the girl asked where she could find Ewan so that he could pay the taxi driver. In the end Rachel had paid the man herself, but her heart was troubled. It was better that Ross shouldn't know about such extravagance.

'So where is Ewan then?' Gerda demanded petulantly.

'He's driving the tractor. I expect he warned you he would be baling straw if the weather was good.'

'Oh, he mentioned something about harvest, but surely he can stop for the weekend now I've arrived.'

'They barely stop long enough to eat, I'm afraid. He'll not be back at the steading until dark. They all work as long as the daylight lasts when the weather is so good. If you'll bring your luggage I'll show you to your bedroom and make you a cup of tea. Then if you'll excuse me I must go and bring in the cows ready for milking. You can come with me if you like, dear,' Rachel suggested uncertainly. She had never before met a young person who made her feel as awkward and unsure as Gerda did. The girl stared at her as though she had taken leave of her senses.

'Bring in cows? Me? Not on your life.'

'Very well. Make yourself comfortable while I attend to things outside. I have the eggs to collect and the hens need their afternoon feed. You wouldn't like to . . .'

'No, I would not.'

Rachel sighed as she left the house and called for Tess, the ageing collie. The dog rose languidly in the afternoon heat and trotted at her heels. Rachel bent to pat her head.

'You're always ready to help, aren't you, lassie?'

Tess wagged her tail, knowing she was being praised. As they walked down the leafy lane towards the pasture a wave of relief washed over Rachel. Gerda's presence would have brought a strain to the blue and gold of the late summer afternoon. She breathed in deeply, relishing the scents and sights of the hedgerow. The blackberries were ripening fast now, already hanging in luscious, glistening clusters, ready for picking to make bramble and apple jelly. Ewan and Lucy had always helped her to gather brambles from the hedgerows. She wondered whether Ewan would help this year. He loved home-made jam.

The whole world seemed to be still, as though waiting for something. Even the leaves barely rustled. The gentle cooing of a wood pigeon added to the soporific effect and Rachel felt herself relax for the first time in days. She had not looked forward to Gerda Fritz-Allan's visit and it troubled her that she should feel so inhospitable towards any of Ewan's friends – especially one who was clearly so important to him. She had made an extra effort to make the guest bedroom clean and pretty. She had cleaned and swept and washed, and she had done more baking than usual, hoping that the girl would find something to please her.

'The house is always clean and tidy, lassie,' Ross had remonstrated. Rachel smiled to herself now as she walked along between the hedgerows. She was fifty-eight, but Ross still called her lassie when he was being affectionate, or when he was concerned about her.

Walking along, she pondered Ross's suggestion to buy a freezer chest for storing food. Bridie had told him it would keep beef and lamb fresh for a year and that her scones and cakes would keep for months. Rachel frowned, wondering whether the food would be safe to eat afterwards, but Ross had seemed quite enthusiastic.

'The man who supplied the tank for storing the milk says his firm has sold quite a few to farmers' wives.' But he hadn't told her how much these new contraptions cost. She frowned. After a lifetime of careful budgeting, Rachel found it impossible to accept that they could live comfortably now that they had paid off the Wester Rullion land and built modern buildings to house the dairy herd and a parlour for milking them. It was hard to believe that a chest run by electricity could be better than the cold slab in the pantry or the little refrigerator where she kept the milk and butter. But it would be wonderful if she could bring out scones as good as freshly baked ones without having to bake every day. Maybe she would consider it.

She swung open the field gate and called for the cows. Most of them looked up and began to move towards the open gate, knowing it was nearly milking time. A few lay still, chewing their cud contentedly, while one or two were intent on snatching a bit more grass to chew while they waited for their turn to go into the milking parlour. Rachel was still amazed at how quickly the cows had learned the new routine of the parlour instead of finding their own stalls in the byre. They had their own order of precedence too. Old Star was always the first in to be milked, with Belle a close second. They were the oldest cows in the herd and the rest followed them as obediently as a class of children under the supervision of a strict headmaster.

Tess began to move slowly around the stragglers, urging them to follow the herd, yet knowing instinctively that she must not hurry them when their udders were full of milk. Rachel leaned on the gate and looked up at the sky. She was sure this good weather would not last much longer.

'Wouldn't be surprised if we have thunder, old girl,' she

murmured, bending to pat the dog as the last of the cows ambled through the gate. Tess looked up at her with trusting brown eyes. She hated thunder. She rarely came into the house but whenever there was a storm she would scratch urgently at the door and dart under the scullery table the moment someone let her in, cowering there until the storm died away.

As they walked slowly behind the herd of cows, Rachel whisked ineffectively at the flies and dust that inevitably surrounded the animals in the summertime. She broke a branch from a nearby elderberry bush and wafted the offending insects away, wondering whether they really disliked the smell of elderberry leaves, or whether it was just one of those stories she remembered from her childhood. Most of the farmers who brought their horses to be shod at her father's blacksmith's forge had adorned their bridles with a bit of elderberry when the flies were biting. It was just as well Gerda had not come, Rachel thought. That beautiful blonde hair would have been coated in dust by now.

Ross was waiting for her at the gate into the farmyard. He smiled gratefully.

'I wondered whether you'd have time to get the cows in for me when you had yon lassie to entertain.' His blue eyes crinkled at the corners and the appraising look in their blue depths deepened the colour in cheeks already flushed with the heat of the afternoon. Even after all these years Ross could still make her pulse race, and she knew he still found her attractive. They had been so lucky to have each other, to work together as they had and still be in love. She had always felt Bridie and Nick shared the same sort of union and she was truly thankful. She had once believed Conan was too proud and independent to have such a deep and loving relationship, but as the years passed she had come to realize that Fiona was the perfect partner for him in every way. She brought out both gentleness and respect in him. Rachel hoped it would be the same for Ewan one day.

'The flies are really biting today. I think you may be right about a thunderstorm. I asked Gerda if she wanted to come but it's just as well she declined,' she said, brushing away the flies with the elderberry branch.

'Aye, I've seen her. I asked if she would like to make us a cup of tea until you returned with the cows.'

'Oh good, I'm sure she must be ready for one and I—'

'Good? It's not good at all. She said she didn't know where anything was and in any case she hadn't come here to be a servant!'

'Oh dear!' Rachel stared at Ross's face in dismay. She knew by the furrow between his brows and the grim set to his mouth that he and Gerda had not got off to a good start. 'I suppose she's just not used to country ways,' Rachel soothed.

'Well I hope Ewan soon realizes that. He needs a wife who will support him, not somebody to be good for decoration and nothing else.'

'Times are changing, dear.' Rachel sighed. 'A lot of wives have careers of their own now and they don't necessarily give up work when they marry as they did before the war.'

'I get the impression she's not even keen to follow her career. Anyway, it's different for farming folk. A man still needs a wife who will understand when his work comes first, lend a hand when he needs one . . .'

'I know, I know, dear. But not every woman is cut out for milking cows and feeding poultry. You—'

'I'm not saying she needs to milk cows these days, not with milking machines and parlours,' Ross conceded, 'but there's still a lot a good woman can do to support a man, inside as well as out. I'd certainly expect her to keep accounts and make the meals and rear the poultry and clean the eggs . . . Aye, there's plenty to be done. I can't imagine Ewan will want to come in and start cooking his own breakfast if he's been up since five o'clock milking cows, can you?'

'Do you think he's serious about Gerda then?'

'I don't know, but I think she sees farming life through very rosy spectacles if you ask me.'

'Time will tell,' Rachel murmured. 'Did you have a drink of tea then? I sent a basket out to the field. I thought you would have it there.'

34

'Oh, I did, but I could have drunk another one and I thought the lassie might be glad of one herself. I was trying to be sociable and make her feel at home, but I didna get much response.'

The men worked on at the harvest long after the milking was finished. The storm clouds were gathering and the rumble of thunder could be heard in the distance. After the milking, Ross had hurried back to the field, taking with him a basket of rolls and scones to keep the men going until they finished for the day and could sit down to a proper meal. Rachel and Gerda had eaten together but immediately afterwards the girl had draped herself across the settee in the living room and turned on the television.

The rumble of thunder was growing louder. Rachel grimaced. She hated storms. As a child she used to think it was God riding his chariot across the floor of heaven. She had always thought He must be very angry and she hoped his chariots would not fall through the floor and kill them all. Even now her imagination ran riot when the thunder seemed to be right overhead. A sudden flash of lightning made Gerda come running through from the living room.

'Where's Ewan? He should be here. I hate thunder . . .'

'I know, dear. They will all be in soon.' Rachel was standing at the kitchen door, just as anxious to see the men and their machines safely home. 'There's the rain coming,' she said, watching the first huge drops plop into the dusty yard. Another crash of thunder drowned out her words and Gerda screamed. Tess made a dart for the house, tail between her legs, head down. Her damp coat brushed against Gerda's long, bare legs and she aimed an angry kick at the collie. Rachel frowned.

'This is the only time poor Tess comes indoors. She's petrified of thunder. We think it is loud enough but a dog's hearing is far more acute and sensitive than ours.' She watched Tess squeeze beneath a low table and she went over to pat her gently. 'Poor lamb. You feel safe there, don't you? It'll soon pass.'

Gerda watched scornfully. How could anyone call a dog

a poor lamb? Rachel moved back to the open door where the rain was now splashing on to the tiled floor of the back porch. She didn't like to feel shut up inside when there was thunder. Another terrific rumble sounded above their heads.

'I think you should turn off the television now, Gerda. I believe it can conduct the lightning or something . . . A–ah, I hear the tractors coming home. Ewan will be here soon.'

'About time too . . . Oh, my gawd! See that bloody lightning. It's forked. That's bloody dangerous!'

'Ye–es.' Rachel stared anxiously through the arrows of rain, vaguely conscious that she preferred Gerda's native Glasgow speech, even with the expletives. 'A–ah, the men are all in from the field.' She sighed in relief. 'I see them sheltering under the barn beside the tractors . . .' She broke off as lightning lit the sky and Gerda screamed. Rachel put an arm around her slim shoulders, trying to offer comfort, but the storm was a bad one, far too close for her own peace of mind.

The rain slackened briefly and the three men ran across the yard to the house. Ewan and Peter, long-legged and young, covered the distance in no time, and tumbled laughingly into the porch, shaking their wet hair from their eyes like a pair of young puppies. Rachel handed them each a towel but her eyes were fixed on Ross a few yards behind them. He would be sixty in November and he was still lean and fit, but he was no match for a son of twenty-one. The rain was pelting down again, faster than ever.

'Where's young Billy?' she asked as Ross stepped into the porch beside her.

'We came home by his cottage and dropped him off. Thanks, lassie.' He grinned at Rachel as he accepted a towel, rubbing vigorously at his hair, still thick and dark except for a few silver streaks above his ears. 'Phew! That's better. Peter had better wait here a while. He'll get drenched just running to the other end of the steading.'

'I have some soup heating on the Aga and there's a beef casserole with dumplings in the oven. Change your clothes while I set them out.' She moved through to the large kitchen.

36

Ross followed on his way to the stairs but his eyebrows rose when he saw Gerda perched on Ewan's knee, her arms draped around his neck.

'Peter, you'll eat with us tonight,' Rachel said firmly.

'Oh, no, Mistress Maxwell . . .' Peter rose to his feet.

'I insist. Just for once.' Rachel smiled and pushed him gently back on to the kitchen chair. 'You're much too independent, laddie. It's late and you'll be too tired to start cooking after such a long, hard day.'

'But you've kept us well supplied with the harvest baskets at the field . . .'

'Och, nothing but sandwiches and scones and a bit o' apple pie. Now you need a proper meal. Anyway, you've all earned it and there's plenty.'

Peter bit his lip. He always tried not to take advantage of the kindly folk who had given him work and a place in the world. He often thought he was the most fortunate man alive to have found a family like the Maxwells when he was a young prisoner of war. He was lucky too with old Mrs Forster. She had given him lodgings in the old farmhouse and mothered him as though he was the son she had lost. Peter had missed her terribly when she died, but Mr Maxwell had agreed he should take over the house, and Mrs Forster had left him her meagre savings and her furniture. Now he had a home with a lovely garden to call his own and he asked for nothing more.

Suddenly Peter almost jumped out of his chair. A terrific thunderclap exploded overhead. Gerda screamed and clung even more tightly to Ewan. The electric light sputtered and died.

'Oh well, at least the meal is cooked and ready to eat,' Rachel said philosophically. 'I think there is still enough light left for us to manage.'

'It's creepy!' Gerda protested.

'I'll get a candle,' Ewan offered, drawing her arms from his neck. 'I'm a bit damp.' He laughed ruefully, shaking the legs of his trousers away from his skin. 'How about you, Peter?'

'Just a bit. I'll probably be worse before I get home.'

His dark eyes twinkled. His hair had dried into a mass of black curls, Gerda noticed. She had barely looked at him earlier. After all, he was just a labourer and she didn't think Mrs Maxwell should even have invited him into the house. Now she saw that he was a handsome man, even in his working denims. Moreover, he had an air of aloof pride, a certain dignity which she felt was out of place for a man in his position. She frowned. She would soon bring him to heal and keep him in his place when she was in charge at Wester Rullion.

They were halfway through eating their meal when Tess scrambled out from her refuge, barking hysterically.

'Poor dog, she's terrified,' Rachel said, pushing back her chair and moving to soothe the shivering collie. The back door was still ajar and the porch floor was wet but Rachel preferred it that way. As a child someone had once told her that if the devil got into the house with the lightning he needed a way to get out. She knew it was silly but she had never been able to dispel the feeling that it was safer to leave the door ajar. Now the dog seemed to share her fear as she darted to the open door and back towards her, barking furiously, gazing up at her with anxious brown eyes, then darting back to the door, as though beckoning her to follow.

'He's mad!' Gerda muttered, picking desultorily at her food.

'Come into the kitchen then, old girl,' Rachel soothed, reaching for the dog's collar, but Tess darted to the door, then back to Rachel and back again to the door in a frenzy. Ross frowned and set down his knife and fork reluctantly. The beef and dumplings were delicious and he was hungry at the end of a hard day's labour.

'I think she's trying to tell us something,' he said.

'Yes,' Peter nodded and followed Ross and the dog to the door. They peered through the driving rain but there was little to be seen except rivulets washing through the farmyard and gutters overflowing.

'Thank God we got the straw baled and the stacks

covered,' Ross said fervently. 'Any corn not cut will be flattened by this lot. Come on in, Tess.' He bent to grasp the dog's collar but she refused to budge from the doorway. Her ears pricked up. She looked at Ross, whining in agitation. 'I wish I knew what you were trying to tell me, old girl . . .'

'Anybody would think the bloody dog could talk,' Gerda muttered with contempt, but Ewan did not smile. He was not even looking at her. He was sitting up, tense and alert, his eyes on Peter.

'What is it? Can you smell something?' he called, watching the man wrinkling his nose.

'Fire! Yes, I think Tess smells fire!' Even as he spoke he was pushing his feet into his wellingtons, dashing into the farmyard, oblivious to the pouring rain. Halfway across he turned to yell: 'The barn! It's the barn. Struck by lightning . . .'

'We left the tractors there!' Ross shouted. He and Ewan were already pulling on their own boots.

'There's four calves penned in there as well,' Ewan gasped as a tongue of flame leapt into the leaden sky.

'Phone the fire brigade, Rachel,' Ross called as he followed the two young men down to the barn.

'Ross! Be careful! Oh, please be careful . . .' Rachel's voice trailed away as she ran to the phone, her face ashen.

Gerda was still sitting at the table. She grimaced and pushed away her plate. Some weekend this was turning out to be. She had had every intention of forcing Ewan to make a major decision.

Rachel dashed back into the kitchen, pulling on her coat, her feet already in her wellingtons. 'The fire brigade is on its way. Phone Bridie. If the fire spreads . . .' She caught her breath on a half sob.

'What's her number?' Gerda asked sullenly. Rachel called the number over her shoulder.

'Ring Conan too. The numbers are on the yellow card.'

Nick answered the phone. Gerda was pleased to have someone to talk to and she chatted away without urgency.

'Were you phoning for anything in particular?' Nick asked,

puzzled. Gerda usually showed little interest in anyone except Ewan.

'There's a fire outside. It's the lightning.'

'A fire?' Nick didn't think he'd heard correctly.

'Yes. Mrs Maxwell asked me to tell Bridie. Don't know what she can do about it though.' Gerda shrugged carelessly. 'She's phoned the fire briga—'

Suddenly there was another loud crash and the phone seemed to jump out of her hand. The line was dead. Gerda began to whimper with shock. Ewan had no business rushing out and leaving her on her own. She lifted the candle to go back to the kitchen but a sudden gust blew out the flame. She swore and groped her way back to the big cooker. She was still standing there in the gloom, clinging to the steel rail, when Bridie, Max and the twins burst into the house twenty minutes later.

'For goodness' sake, why are you in the dark, Gerda?'

'The candle went out.'

'Well, there's matches on the shelf there.' Bride reached for the box herself, as well as a second brass candlestick that was gleaming dimly in the gloom. Impatiently she lit them both. 'Where's Mother?'

'Outside I expect.'

'She's out there? We followed the fire engine in. Nick's gone to help. I'll go and bring mother in. I pray to God they can stop it spreading . . .' Bridie's face was white but as she glanced at the table, still littered with dirty dishes, she frowned. 'They'll all be soaked to the skin and cold. Fill up the big kettle and put it on the hot plate.'

'Which one is that?'

'Max will show you. Girls, help Gerda clear the table and wash the dishes, please. Then—'

'Hey, I'm not here to take orders!' Gerda protested. 'Or to scivvy—'

'Then you should go back to where you came from,' Bridie snapped, her face strained with worry. 'I'm going to find Granny and Grandad. Margaret and Alicia, you know how to lay the table. Be good. No, Max, you can't come with me. It's not safe.'

'But, Mum . . .'

Bridie waved away his protest and hurried outside. The thunder seemed to be further away now, but flames were leaping into the sky. The rain was still lashing down and Bridie prayed silently that it would stop the fire spreading. Another car drew up.

'We saw the fire! What's happened?' Conan demanded urgently.

'Thank goodness you've come,' Bridie said. 'Will you keep Max indoors please, Fiona? And get some order into the kitchen if you can? Everyone will need hot drinks, but Gerda is useless. I'm going to bring Mother in.'

'She's out there?' Conan gasped incredulously, immediately loping away without waiting for a reply.

'I'll come with you, Bridie,' Lucy said. 'Maybe I can help with something if there are animals to be moved, or whatever.'

'OK, Lucy. You might be better at persuading Mother to come in than I am. Ah, here's someone else come to help,' she said gratefully as she recognized a neighbour's car.

Rachel was struggling valiantly with the ropes that had been used to make a temporary pen for four young heifer calves. They were not quite old enough to be turned out to the fields, yet they had needed the fresh air during the recent humid weather. Ross had made the pen in the open-sided barn, but it was one of the poles supporting the roof that had now caught fire.

Ross, Peter and Ewan were busy trying to get the tractors and machinery well away from the flames and Rachel fervently wished she had brought her penknife. At last she managed to loosen one side and she yanked the gate open. The calves did not understand. They refused to move from their huddle in one corner. The smoke was thickening and Rachel coughed violently, her eyes streaming as she tried to usher the animals to safety. She could no longer see the figures of the men through the dense smoke but she knew there would be an inferno if any of the tractors caught fire. All she could do was stick her fingers into the mouths of

41

two of the calves and coax them out of the pen as they sucked. It was the only thing they understood.

She had rescued three calves and was just going back for the smallest when she heard Ross shouting her name. He was rushing towards her, just a few feet away. Rachel frantically blinked her streaming eyes. There was an almighty crash. She gasped in horror. Ross was lying face down. A thick beam was pinning him there, across one arm and leg. Everything seemed to happen at once. Rachel screamed as she struggled to Ross's side and tried to lift away the beam. Then Conan was beside her, dragging her away.

'Let me go! Your father is trapped. He'll be burned alive! Please God . . .'

'Leave him, Mother. Nick and I will carry him. Get out of here. Now!'

Reluctantly, Rachel obeyed. She knew Conan and Nick would do their best to get Ross out. She remembered the calf but she could barely see it in the smoky darkness. Then she felt it nuzzling against her and she thrust her fingers into its mouth, pushing it as quickly as it would move to join the other three outside in the open field. Behind her she heard Conan and Nick and saw that they were carrying Ross between them.

'We'll lay him out in the open, well away from the fire,' Conan decided.

'Ross! Oh, Ross,' Rachel cried and ran to kneel beside him. 'You can't leave him here! We must get him inside . . .'

'No, Mother. He's hurt. Better not to move him any more until we know how badly. Go back and phone the doctor—'

'No! I can't leave him!' She turned at a slight tug on her arm.

'Come, Mrs Maxwell, I'll help you back to the house. You must help me find blankets to keep him warm.' Lucy's voice was calm and firm. Rachel went with her as meekly as a child and Conan had never been so proud of his daughter as he was then, amidst the smoke and danger. Bridie took Lucy's place and knelt beside her father.

'Can you hear me, Father?'

'Aye . . . Can't move my leg . . .'

'No, I–I think it's broken. We darena move you until the doctor comes. Lucy has gone to fetch blankets . . .'

'Where's Ewan? Have you seen Ewan?' His voice rose urgently.

'Ewan will be fine—'

'No! He couldna get his new tractor out. Tell him to leave it . . . Not worth his life . . .'

'The firemen are getting things under control,' Bridie said, trying to sound reassuring. 'I don't think it will spread to the house now, or to the cattle sheds.'

There was no reply. Bridie saw that her father's eyes were closed. His breathing sounded laboured.

Five

Dawn was breaking by the time the firemen were ready to leave, and even then two of them were left to keep watch in case the smouldering timbers should be fanned into flames again.

The ambulance had arrived promptly, considering the stormy night, and Bridie watched anxiously as her father and Ewan were carried to the waiting vehicle. They were both too shocked and in pain to protest, but Rachel had only agreed to go because she couldn't bear to leave her husband and son. At the hospital the doctor had checked up on her breathing and insisted she should stay in hospital, at least for the remainder of the night. Bridie could scarcely wait until morning to phone for a report.

'We are keeping your mother in for observation, but she will probably be allowed home later today,' a nurse had informed Bridie briskly. 'Your father has a fractured fibula and we think he has fractured a bone in his arm. Unfortunately the doctors are unable to operate as he is suffering from smoke inhalation. Dealing with his breathing is our first priority. Meanwhile we have given him something to ease the pain.'

'And Ewan? My brother?'

'He has sustained a nasty burn on his forearm but he will probably be allowed home after the doctor has seen it again tomorrow.'

'At least they are all alive.' She sighed with relief as she turned to face Fiona and Conan. 'Nick, I think I should stay here to help Peter with the milking. Then there's the calves to feed and the hens to attend to. He can't do everything himself – the poor laddie must be as exhausted as we are.'

'Milking time already, it is,' Nick reminded them wearily. 'I'll tell Emmie and Frank what's happened when I get back to Glens of Lochandee. I'll give them a hand with the milking before I go to the garage. Shall I leave the children here?'

'We may as well let them sleep,' Bridie said, nodding. 'I'm glad you were here to take charge inside, Fiona, and persuade the twins to go to bed.'

'I'm glad I was able to help,' Fiona said simply. 'The men appreciated copious quantities of hot tea once they had things under control.'

'Not to mention sandwiches and toasted cheese,' Lucy said wryly, stretching her arms above her head and smothering a yawn.

'Yes, thank goodness you thought to bring some bread, Bridie. That freezer is a blessing sometimes. I just hope everything else will turn out as well.' She looked at Conan.

'You'll let us know when there's any news, Bridie? We'd better get off home now and snatch a hot bath. How about you, Lucy? You worked hard. We were proud of you.'

'Perhaps I should wait here if Bridie is helping Peter with the milking. Someone ought to be here in case the twins wake up. Anyway, Mrs Maxwell might need someone to bring her home.'

'Yes, Lucy, you're right,' Bridie agreed with relief. 'But you should try to have a nap while you can. Where's Gerda by the way?'

Fiona raised her eyes heavenward. 'She went to bed,' she said flatly.

'When?'

'Oh . . . more or less as soon as we arrived. But it's probably just as well,' she added wryly. 'Your seven-year-old twins have more idea about setting to work than Gerda has. They were really good, and so was Max, once he accepted that he couldn't go outside.'

'Oh dear.' Bridie sighed. 'You'd have thought Gerda would be anxious about Ewan at least. Still, you never know, this may have put her off the idea of living in the country,' she suggested hopefully.

As the weeks passed, Ross chafed against his inability to work. The corn harvest was all in safely but there were still turnips to lift. He continued to grow them for winter feed, in addition to the pit of grass silage. He was reluctant to cast off the old methods in spite of Ewan's arguments that turnips were out of date and silage was easier to handle.

'I know Bridie still grows turnips and hay at Glens of Lochandee, Father,' Ewan argued earnestly, again and again. 'But she still has her cows in a byre. When you have a milking parlour and cubicle shed you should move on to more modern feeding methods.'

'Turnips are damned good feed and it's a good crop this year,' Ross insisted. 'So it's up to you and Peter to get them in and properly stored. Gerda will have to get used to farm life if she's as set on marrying you as she seems to be.'

Ewan flushed. Since the fire he had been tied to the farm due to his father's incapacity, but his parents seemed to have accepted Gerda as his special friend and she now came down to Wester Rullion most weekends. He knew they didn't think she was suited to the life of a working farmer. In his heart he knew they were right but he wanted her, he needed her, his body ached for her. She excited him as no other woman had. He had said this to Gus, one of his college friends, but he had only given a mocking guffaw.

'How many women do you know at your age, Ewan?' he had asked. The answer was none, but he knew he longed to make Gerda his and she had made it clear that marrying her was the only way he was going to get her. It troubled him when she refused to accept the demands of farm life and the time needed to care for the animals. She railed continually because he had to work at weekends.

'We're not all lucky enough to be teachers,' he would say, laughing. 'The cows don't leave on Friday nights and come back on Monday mornings as your pupils do.'

Patiently he tried to explain that life was more hectic than

46

usual at Wester Rullion while his father was incapacitated. The situation was aggravated because they had a lot of cows calving to increase their winter milk supply. The price was better than for milk produced in summer, but it meant longer milking times and more calves to rear and this routine work was the same on Saturdays and Sundays as every other day.

Ewan had never known either of his parents to be ill, and he now began to realize how hard they both worked. Since his father's illness, his mother had spent more time indoors keeping him company. Although she still fed the newly born calves, she left the older ones to him and Peter. She usually fed the few pigs that they still kept, and she always attended to the hens and pullets. She regarded them as her particular responsibility. They depended on the sale of her eggs to pay Peter's wages and to give Ewan spending money, as well to pay for the household expenses and petrol for the car. This left any profit they could make from the cows and sheep for more major expenses like buying cattle cake and maintaining and renewing machinery, buildings, fences and drains, as well as buying in the seeds and lime for the spring crops.

Ewan had been proud to show his college friends around Wester Rullion and he knew some of them had envied him. His father kept the whole farm clean and tidy and well maintained. Every spring the buildings were thoroughly cleaned and limewashed and the wooden doors freshly painted. Moreover, his father was coming round to the idea of using more fertilizer as a regular routine on the grassland too. Ewan knew this was partly due to his own reports from college lectures, but he was beginning to appreciate that his father must have had to adapt many times during his lifetime to accommodate the changing demands made on farming.

'You're young and impatient, laddie,' his mother would remonstrate when he thought his father would never see his point of view, or make the changes he considered modern. One thing Ross and Ewan still disagreed upon was the use of chemical sprays. Ewan insisted that, according to his college lecturers, this would soon be the only way to grow

47

cereals. But Ross remained wary, and stubbornly refused to use them.

'A few thistles in the corn will do you no harm. That's all part of harvesting,' he would retort.

Ewan had argued that there were other weeds besides thistles that spoiled the yields of the corn. Secretly he sometimes felt a bit overwhelmed by the decisions his father had to make. Every year there were more regulations coming into force to control the quality of food sold to the public. Even poultry-keeping was changing. There was talk of fierce competition from businessmen who knew nothing of traditional farming methods. They were intent on breeding hens that would lay eggs for 360 days of the year. The idea was to keep these hens in tiny individual cages and feed and water them via conveyor belts.

Where his mother looked after three hundred hens at Wester Rullion, these men would have three thousand or more. Where his mother had six wooden huts dotted around the farm steading and paddock, these new methods would house them all in one large building. His mother had laughed at the idea of a hen laying an egg almost every day of the year. She simply couldn't visualize hens being kept in cages all day, being fed and watered at the touch of a button on a timer switch, instead of scratching around in the earth.

'It's unnatural,' she insisted. 'How could they lay eggs or stay healthy if they never have any fresh air!'

Ewan was not so sure, but he didn't argue. His mother knew as well as anyone how farming had changed since the war.

During his time at college Ewan had listened to innumerable lectures and discussions concerning modern trends in farming. Some of the lecturers believed the public wanted cheaper and cheaper food and that the majority of people didn't care how it was produced. His father, on the other hand, believed the cost of food to the consumer would go up if the discussions concerning a European Common Market bore fruit. Higher prices to the general public would mean demands for higher wages, he maintained, and that would lead to spiralling costs for everything. Ewan smiled, knowing how opposed his father was to any marketing agreement with Europe, especially since it would mean restrictions in trade with commonwealth countries and possibly an end to New Zealand lamb and butter.

Ewan had tried to talk to Gerda about his way of life, the future of farming, and the changes that were coming to them all, but she was all in favour of cheap food.

'Why should I care how you farmers produce food? I'd have more money for clothes if I didn't have to pay so much for food and digs. Just think, Ewan, we could go away at weekends, instead of slaving away milking cows. We could go abroad in the winter . . .'

He had just laughed at her. She was like a child sometimes with her wild enthusiasms and he wanted to give her the moon if it would make her happy. She simply didn't understand that cheap food didn't mean that cows only needed milking five days a week. If anything it would mean breeding cows to give more and more milk every day.

Ross often sat in brooding silence, his eyes watchful. Rachel worried about him. He had never been a moody man, but then he had never been so confined to the house as he had been in the weeks since harvest and the fire, as his broken arm prevented him hobbling around on crutches. He questioned Ewan constantly about the cattle and the sheep. Peter was also summoned to answer questions, but usually the pair of them ended up with a lively discussion on woodwork, or some other topic that was nothing to do with farming. Rachel warmly welcomed Peter's visits, assuring him that they were both happy for him to come in whenever he had time to spare.

Rachel had always known when Ross was hatching some plan or other and she was almost certain there would be changes made as soon as he was up and about again. She prayed that his plans would not upset Ewan, or the fragile peace that existed whenever Gerda came to stay.

A few days before Christmas Fiona telephoned.

49

'Lucy rang us last night,' she said excitedly. 'She asked me to tell you that Donald Greig has asked her to marry him.'

'Lucy? To marry? So soon?' Rachel echoed faintly, and saw Ross sit up straighter, listening intently.

'They're not getting married for another eighteen months but Donald has bought her an engagement ring and she wanted to tell us. They mean to have a quiet wedding sometime in the summer of 1964, after Lucy has completed her probationary teaching. She sounds so happy and excited.'

'And so do you, Fiona.' Rachel smiled. It was unusual for Fiona to show her feelings so clearly.

'Yes, well we're both pleased for Lucy. She has known Donald almost since she started college. Chris invited her to stay for a weekend with her parents and I suspected there was a mutual attraction between Lucy and Donald from the beginning.'

'Yes, you could be right. Chris seems a nice girl. I hope the rest of the family are the same.'

'So do I,' Fiona echoed fervently. 'I did wonder whether Mr Greig might be a bit . . . thrifty though,' she said carefully.

'We're all thrifty. Do you mean a bit mean, Fiona?'

'Perhaps. I don't really know, of course. Just one or two comments Chris has made occasionally. I expect the Greigs have had to be careful with three sons wanting to farm and Chris to be educated. We're sorry that Lucy will not be settling nearer to us, but Conan says it will not take us long to drive up to Ayr in the car.'

'Didn't Lucy mention the Greigs were hoping to rent another farm?' Rachel asked. 'Has it materialized?'

'Yes, I think that may have precipitated the engagement. The laird has agreed but only on condition that the tenant lives there and occupies the house. Lucy says it's very dilapidated but the laird has promised to do some basic repairs. Don is going to live there on his own until they get married.

When Rachel broke the news of Lucy's engagement to Ewan he smiled widely.

'Well, that's no surprise. Don Greig never looked at any of the other lassies after Chris introduced him to Lucy. He came into Ayr most Saturday nights to take her out. I'll phone and congratulate them after supper.'

Rachel nodded, aware that Gerda had greeted the news with a scowl and a tightening of her mouth. Was she jealous?

'Did you know Donald Greig, Gerda?' she asked gently.

'Of course. We all knew him. I don't know what Lucy saw in him, or in his sister,' she added waspishly. She shuddered with distaste. 'You should have seen how rough her hands were, and her fingernails were always broken.'

Rachel resisted looking down at her own work-roughened hands. She said nothing.

Gerda had made it clear that she intended to spend the Christmas holiday at Wester Rullion. Rachel was surprised that she was leaving her father on his own, but she thought perhaps he had other friends – maybe even a woman friend. Gerda revealed very little about her home life.

'There's only one shopping day left, what with Christmas Eve being a Sunday,' Gerda announced when she arrived at Wester Rullion. 'So Ewan will need to take me Christmas shopping tomorrow.'

'I've already done my shopping,' Ewan protested. 'And I've a lot of extra work to do to get everything organized for the holiday. We only do the essential work at Christmas. It'll be like three Sundays in a row this year.'

'Sundays!' Gerda exploded. 'You always work on Sundays, even though I come to see you. Sometimes I wonder why I bother!' She pouted.

'We only do the milking and feeding and the mucking out,' Ewan said. 'You wouldn't expect us to leave the animals to starve, would you?'

'It wouldn't bother me,' she said, shrugging.

Ewan had not thought about getting engaged yet, but when they went shopping the next day, Gerda made straight for the jeweller's shop. He soon realized that an engagement ring was exactly what she had set her heart on.

'You're just wanting to keep up with Lucy,' he teased, but Gerda was furious at such a suggestion.

'I don't need to keep up with anyone, but if she can get engaged so soon after leaving college, then so can we.'

'A–ah, but there's a difference. Don is five years older that we are and he's been working since he was sixteen. His father wouldn't let him go to agricultural college. He said he needed him to work at home.'

'What difference does that make?'

'It probably means he's earned a bit more money than I have,' Ewan said drily. 'Anyway, we should have consulted your father . . .'

'Oh, Ewan, don't be so old-fashioned. He'll not care.'

'Well, I should have discussed it with *my* parents then. After all, it will affect them if we get married and—'

'Ewan Maxwell, I've given up my Christmas holiday to spend it on your bloody farm – with you! The least you can do is forget about your family and buy me a decent engagement ring.' Ewan's brow darkened. She knew he loved the farm and the farming way of life. Before he could argue she purred softly, 'You have to prove your intentions are honourable when you keep pestering me for . . . you know what!' She fluttered her thick, dark lashes provocatively and edged closer, hugging his arm against the rounded softness of her breast. He felt the familiar stirring in his loins.

'Oh, all right then. There's loads of time before we need to discuss serious plans. Let's go inside and see if they have anything I can afford that pleases you.'

Rachel was surprised when Gerda flashed the diamond ring in front of her nose the moment the two of them returned from town. She glanced anxiously at Ross but he didn't seem as surprised as she was.

'We–ell now,' he said slowly. 'So you're keeping up with Lucy, eh? It will be a long engagement, I suppose . . .' He caught the venomous expression in Gerda's narrowed eyes and broke off, his eyes moving to Ewan.

'Oh we're not getting married for ages—'

'The wedding will be at the end of June,' Gerda said, cutting Ewan off. She flashed a beaming smile. 'Ewan doesn't want to wait, do you, lover boy? We've no need to wait as long as Lucy. I'm quite willing to give up my career for Ewan. If we have the wedding at the end of June we shall have the long summer holiday in front of us.'

'You might.' Ewan grimaced. 'I shall probably be making hay by July.'

'You will need a place to live before you make serious plans,' Ross intervened firmly. 'I imagine that's your first priority.'

'But surely you and Mrs Maxwell will be mov—'

'There's a cottage coming vacant,' Ross cut in abruptly. 'Ewan, did young Billy tell you the laird is planning to sell off the cottages where his parents live?'

Billy Smith lived quite close to Wester Rullion and had recently come to work for Ross after leaving school.

'No, he didn't mention it,' Ewan said, puzzled. He had expected his father to be angry and present them with a list of reasons why they couldn't possibly get married yet. Indeed, he felt that things were getting a bit out control.

'A house would be a good investment for the future. If we could buy the one next to the Smiths for a couple of thousand it would be big enough for the pair o' you. That is if you really are planning to get married so soon, Ewan?'

'I hadn't consid—'

'What sort of cottage?' Gerda demanded belligerently, her eyes straying round the big farm kitchen as though already making plans for it.

'Well of course, it's your decision, laddie,' Ross said.

'It's my decision too!' Gerda shrieked. 'What sort of a cottage are you talking about? I'm not going to live in any old shack'

'Oh, the cottages aren't shacks!' Ewan said, almost impatiently. 'Billy's home is quite comfortable. I've seen it.'

'Well it's that or nothing,' Ross said firmly, looking Gerda in the eye. 'If you take my advice you'll both wait a few years before rushing into marriage.'

'We don't want to wait, do we, Ewan?' Gerda fluttered her eyelashes at Ewan and moved closer to him.

'Well, if that's the way it has to be we could probably get a grant to modernize the cottage,' Ross mused. 'They have large gardens at the back, a relic from the time workers all kept a pig and a few hens and grew their own vegetables.'

'As Peter still does,' Rachel said.

'Yes he does, but I was thinking about the future,' Ross said. 'When . . .' He glanced wryly at Ewan. 'When you've both earned some money, and can afford it, there would be plenty of room to build a garage, or an extra bedroom for your children . . .'

'Children!' Gerda screeched. 'I see enough kids at school every day. I don't intend to have any squawking little brats of my own.'

'Well then, a small cottage should suit you fine,' Ross said and closed his mouth firmly. He was well aware what Gerda Fritz-Allan had had in mind. He'd seen her glancing critically around his home many times. He'd had plenty of opportunity to observe her during his convalescence and in his heart he hoped fervently that Ewan would see her true colours and change his mind, but he had no intention of alienating his son by thwarting his plans outright. It was Ewan's life. It had to be his decision and even Ross admitted that Gerda was a beautiful girl. He just wished he didn't feel so uneasy about her.

Ross had never spent so much time in the house in his life before. It had made him appreciate Rachel's hard work more than ever, but in contrast it had shown him how lazy and often sullen Gerda was. He suspected she wanted the best from life but with the minimum of effort on her part. He had noticed the way her mouth drew into a thin line whenever her plans were thwarted. Now he watched her glowering at Ewan, clearly longing to state her opinion, while he seemed quite oblivious to her displeasure.

'That's a splendid idea,' he said now. 'Thank you, Father, for . . . well, for understanding, and for being prepared to help us find a place to live.'

'Do you think your father would like to join us and share your news, Gerda?' Rachel asked. 'Or perhaps he knows already?'

'No.' Ewan flushed. 'I didna know myself until we went to town so . . .' He grinned at Gerda but she returned his look with an angry scowl.

'Then you must tell him immediately. Ask him if he will join us. We don't want to leave him out. We'll have a family gathering to celebrate. Ask him to come on Boxing Day, if he is free, and he could stay overnight.'

'He'll never trail down here to the countryside,' Gerda said ungraciously. 'I'll tell him we're engaged next time I phone.'

As soon as they were alone she turned angrily to Ewan.

'Why did you agree? You needn't think I'm going to live in a poky little cottage!'

'We shall be as happy as a pair o' skylarks.' He chuckled, seizing her around the waist and swinging her round gleefully. 'I never thought they'd take our news so calmly, let alone help us make plans for a place of our own. I can't wait!' He kissed her passionately.

'Well I can!' Gerda pulled away from him. 'I'm not going to live in any horrid little hovel . . .'

'Oh, Gerda.' Ewan laughed merrily. 'We'll do it up like a wee palace. You'll not know it when it's finished. Father always makes a good job of things once he starts. You'll enjoy choosing your own furniture and colour schemes. You know how you enjoy shopping for new things.'

'I thought we'd live in this house. After all, you're the farmer now . . .'

'You'd better not tell Father that!' Ewan chuckled. 'I hope he has plenty of years left yet. He's still the boss and he still makes the decisions, so you'd better keep on the right side of him.'

'Humph.' Gerda pouted. 'I still think you could have suggested that they move out and let you take over.'

'Oh, I expect they'll move when they're too old to work.' Ewan shrugged. 'Meanwhile, I'm glad Father is still in charge.

It'll give us a few years without so much responsibility. It's the Young Farmers' Christmas dance tonight. How about getting into your slinky red dress so that I can show you off and make the lads envious?'

Gerda looked at him and her eyes brightened. There was nothing she loved more than getting dressed up and going dancing. Ewan was a handsome partner too, and she loved it when he showed her off to his friends.

'But before you make plans for tonight, I want you to phone your father. I don't think we should keep him in the dark. It makes me feel uncomfortable. Anyway, it was good of Mother to invite him, so the least you can do is pass on her invitation.'

No one was more surprised than Gerda when her father readily agreed to come to Wester Rullion on Boxing Day, and even agreed to stay overnight.

As soon as the festive season was over, Ross made an appointment to see Jordon Niven, the solicitor who handled all his family's legal affairs and who had given him sound advice over the years. He did not confide his real reason for seeing his lawyer and Rachel assumed he was arranging the purchase of the cottage, and perhaps enquiring about a grant.

Ross had no wish to worry Rachel with his own misgivings. In his heart he felt that providing a home for Gerda and Ewan might be the least of their problems. Yet the girl made Ewan happy, and what more could he ask for than a lifetime of happiness for his youngest son. Moreover, he and Rachel had taken an immediate liking to her father when he had visited Wester Rullion to celebrate the couple's engagement.

John Allan had spoken frankly with Ross and Rachel, telling them that he owned his own wee house but he was not a wealthy man. He had put aside money to provide Gerda with the sort of wedding he believed she would want, but he had little else except his works pension. He confided that he had only moved into a blue-collar job ten months ago. Previously he had been a welder in the shipyard where

56

he had spent all his working life. This had been something of a surprise considering Gerda's version of her father's employment.

They had appreciated his honesty and sincerity, but had both sensed there was more he wanted to say. He had an air of weariness that had aroused Rachel's sympathy and concern. Several times, when he thought he was unobserved, Ross had caught him shaking his head as though in despair. Ross could not know that the older Gerda got, the more John wondered whether she bore any relation at all to himself. He knew her mother had been an outrageous flirt, but he had adored Gerda as a baby, spoiled her as a pretty toddler and indulged her as a demanding teenager. But he could no longer deny her selfishness and discontent that reminded him so painfully of her mother. It had destroyed their marriage, and had ultimately taken her life.

When Ewan had started at college they had paid an allowance into his bank for textbooks, fees and a little extra for pocket money. He had never overstepped his budget. The arrangement had continued in the months since Ewan had come home to work, except that Ross had promised to make him a full partner in the farm and he knew it was in his own interests to plough back any spare cash into the business. He had the use of the car as well as his food and clothes. Ewan had his own dreams for the future and until recently they had all centred around Wester Rullion and the pedigree herd. Ross knew most of the farmers treated their sons in a similar fashion, though some accepted the old ways more willingly than others.

Ewan seemed content, but Ross accepted that this arrangement would have to change once his son had a wife. The time had come to make him a partner as he had promised. He was a good son and a hard worker, so why, Ross wondered, did he feel so wary about giving him half of the land and stock on Wester Rullion? It was what he and Rachel had worked for since the day he secured a bank loan and bought the run-down farm. They had worked hard together and put everything they could back into the land and the buildings until it was one of the most fertile and modern farms in the county. When he died, the whole farm would be Ewan's. But there was also Rachel's future to consider.

Ross would have liked to talk over his plans with Fiona, but she was part of his family now. It would be unfair to involve her in such judgement. When she had worked for Jordon Niven, before her marriage to Conan, Ross had taken her advice on more than one occasion and he valued her common sense and wisdom.

'What's worrying you, Ross?' Rachel asked softly as they lay side by side in their big bed the night before his appointment with Jordon Niven. 'You're twitching and turning. Why are you so restless?'

'I'm not worrying – well, not exactly,' he said slowly. 'I need to make plans for the future. It's time to make Ewan a partner in Wester Rullion. He'll need a bit more money every month when he marries. But I worry about your future too.'

'You don't need to worry about me! I have my hens and—'

'But when we're too old to look after hens, and milk cows, Rachel, we shall be dependent on Ewan to support us . . .' Ross frowned in the darkness. He prized his independence and he had never considered his own mortality or infirmity until the fire. The doctors had warned him the smoke inhalation had damaged his lungs and he would have to take care. He wasn't afraid for himself, but he worried about Rachel being left on her own. He couldn't explain his uneasiness. He couldn't imagine Gerda being very patient with an old lady, even one who had worked all her life for the benefit of her family. 'Almost everything we have is tied up in the farm. We'll need to use some of our capital to buy one of the Bevendale cottages and do it up for Ewan and Gerda.'

'I'm sure Ewan appreciates you're giving him a fine start in life. He'll see we're all right if ever we need him.' Rachel chuckled. 'After all, we've taken good care of him all these years. Everything we've worked for at Wester Rullion has been for Ewan. He'll not forget that. Surely you've no fears on that score, Ross?'

'No–o. Not really, I suppose, not as far as Ewan is concerned anyway.' He frowned in the darkness. 'At the market I heard a couple of farmers discussing pensions for their old age. It sounded like a good idea, but we'd never heard of pensions when we were young. Anyway, there was never any money to spare. We put it all into buying land and then improving it.'

'Surely you've no regrets, Ross?'

'Not so long as I can always take care of you, Rachel. I could never have managed without you. You know that, don't you?'

'We've been fortunate indeed, Ross.' She laid her cheek against his broad shoulder. 'So fortunate to have each other. So there's no need for you to worry about silly things. You've done well for all our children. Go to sleep now or you'll be falling asleep in Mr Niven's office. It's always as hot as an oven.'

Ross paid several visits to the lawyer's offices over the next few months and he considered his advice carefully.

'You seem to have some doubts, Mr Maxwell. Do you feel you can't trust your younger son?' Jordon Niven frowned. 'You have every reason to be proud of your family and the way you have brought them up.'

'Yes, I am.' Ross nodded. 'And I'm pleased you've managed to buy the cottage and arrange the grant for modernizing it. We shall have to keep on at the builders or it will never be ready in time. The wedding is at the end of July.'

'Yes, but I sense you have other reservations about the future.'

'I don't know. Ewan and his future wife are so young. I wish they hadn't been in such a hurry, but, as he keeps reminding us,' Ross gave a wry smile, 'we were just as young. I'm just not sure Gerda understands what farm life is like. I don't think she realizes how we have to budget for the rainy days. Her father admits he spoiled her and I get the impression she believes farmers who own their land are made of money.' Ross grimaced. 'The only time we're worth anything is when we die, unless we have no sons and can sell up to retire.'

'I can't see you retiring, whatever your circumstances, Mr Maxwell.' Jordon smiled. 'If she is an intelligent woman, Ewan's wife will realize her living depends on keeping the land, surely?'

'I'm not sure she understands anything at all about farming, or about living in the country. The only thing I am sure of is that Ewan is besotted with her. She makes him happy, and she certainly wants to marry him, so who am I to judge?'

Jordon Niven put his fingers together in a pyramid and frowned thoughtfully. 'Leave it with me,' he said at last. 'I think I may have a suggestion to make regarding the land, but I'd like to discuss it with my father first.' He grinned suddenly. 'He may be retired but he likes to be consulted occasionally, especially when the interests of his former clients are concerned.'

'Very well, but meanwhile you will draw up the papers to put half the business in Ewan's name? Then draw up my will leaving the rest of the Wester Rullion business to him when I die. I've promised it will be his since he was a schoolboy. He never wanted to do anything else but farm. He is the opposite of Conan.'

'You're sure about your will?' Jordon Niven asked with a frown.

'Yes, for the present anyway. I suppose I can always rearrange my affairs as time goes on . . . You don't think of taking a wife yourself, Mr Niven?' Ross asked curiously. He had known the young lawyer since old Jacob Niven first took him into partnership. 'I expect your father would like to see grandchildren.'

'Your son, Conan, stole my ideal woman, right from under my nose.' Jordon smiled disarmingly. 'Fiona has everything – a good brain as well as looks. She's a great asset to any man, but she always kept herself aloof. I don't know how the Maxwell charm succeeded in breaking down the barriers when I failed.'

'Aye, Fiona's a fine lassie. She has helped Conan a great deal and they always seem happy together. We're thankful for that.'

'But you're not so happy about young Ewan's choice of wife?'

'I don't know. I just don't know,' Ross said slowly. 'They seem too young to be settling down for a lifetime. Neither of them has any money, but they have plenty of ideas for modernizing the cottage – so long as I'm paying,' Ross said drily.

'A–ah, then you should give them a set sum – reasonable but not over generous. Then leave it to them. Insist they must get their priorities right. Don't be persuaded to hand out more if they run short. I see a lot of problems over money in my business. In my opinion a man is better off without a wife, than with one who can't budget her money.'

'Mmm, that's not a bad idea . . . The sooner they realize I don't have a bottomless purse the better. Well, Ewan understands that anyway, but he's in love and he wants to give Gerda the world. Maybe I'll take your advice.'

'You may not be very popular if they overspend on the wrong things and end up sleeping on the floor because they can't afford a bed.' Jordon Niven grinned wickedly. 'But it is a lesson better learned early. Perhaps you can see now why I have never taken a wife myself. Most women would find me much too hard, I fear.'

'Maybe you're wise,' Ross smiled.

'Maybe. Come back and see me in a week. I'll give you my advice for dealing with the Wester Rullion land and let you have my father's opinion – though we may not be too popular with your son, or your future daughter-in-law.'

Six

When Ross told Ewan and Gerda he had opened an account for them with the money they could use to modernize and furnish the cottage, Ewan was overwhelmed by his parents' generosity and support, and even Gerda seemed satisfied.

'Just remember that's all you're getting, in addition to the grant,' Ross warned sternly. 'If you don't budget for the essentials you must make do until you've earned enough to pay for the rest yourselves.'

'You've been more than generous, Father,' Ewan said happily. 'Gerda will enjoy choosing the furniture and curtains and things, won't you, sweetheart?'

'I shall, but I've no intention of scrubbing out after the filthy workmen.' She looked defiantly at Rachel. 'You'll have to get someone else to be your slave.'

'Well, that's between you two now. Paying someone to do your work will all be part of your budget. It's up to you how you spend it,' Ross said. Silently he thanked Jordon Niven for that bit of advice. Gerda had made it clear already that she had no intention of helping with anything to do with the farm, not even the poultry. She called the hens 'feathery fleabags'.

She would be leaving her Ayrshire school at the end of the summer term, and she had talked of giving up her teaching career altogether. Ewan had persuaded her to apply for jobs at two village schools near Wester Rullion so that she could complete her training. She had seemed surprised when she was offered one of the posts but Ross got the impression she was not thrilled at the prospect. He suspected

Ewan would not find his beautiful bride the easiest of people to live with. If only he could have been persuaded to wait until he had more experience of life. But did the young ever listen to advice? He shook his head, his heart heavy. He sensed Rachel's foreboding too, but they had already offered their opinion and they knew they could not run their children's lives. Ewan was a man now – young and not worldly wise perhaps, but old enough to make his own decisions.

'We wondered whether you would like one of those new washing machines as a wedding gift from us?' Rachel asked.

'One that does everything?' Gerda asked, her pale eyes gleaming.

'I think they do,' Rachel said uncertainly. 'Fiona says you just put the clothes in with washing powder, then you switch it on and leave it. You don't need to rinse the clothes or put them through the ringer as I do. Fiona is thinking of getting one herself because her twin tub keeps breaking down. Then you just hang the clothes out on the line to dry when the machine stops.'

'Doesn't it dry them as well?' Gerda frowned. 'I thought that's what automatic meant. After all, if I'm working at school all day I shall not have time to mess about with Ewan's dirty farm clothes.'

'All day?' Ross teased with a chuckle. 'We've done half a day's work in the milking parlour before you start at your school, lassie.'

Gerda scowled. She was never quite sure when Mr Maxwell was teasing and when he was criticizing her.

'Your father has been extremely generous, Gerda,' Rachel said to smooth away the tension. 'You'll be able to buy other things to make everyday work easier.'

'You know how much my father is . . . is giving us?' Gerda's blue eyes widened in surprise and swivelled accusingly to Ewan. But she had not told Ewan the exact amount. She had no intention of telling him. She had her own plans for that money. After all it was supposed to be *her* wedding, she thought defiantly. Her father must have told Mrs Maxwell in one of the letters they exchanged. She wondered what else he had said.

She had never mentioned the furious quarrel she'd had with her father, not even to Ewan. Apparently John had been saving up for years to give Gerda a traditional wedding with all the trappings her heart desired. It was to be his final gift to her, and she knew he really meant final this time. She shivered inwardly as she recalled their heated exchange.

How often she had dreamed of herself in a beautiful gown and veil, sailing down the aisle of a church crowded with admirers, but she had certainly never envisaged her father's friends and neighbours being a part of that crowd. She had been dismayed when he told her all the people he planned to invite – neighbours from the Avenue where she had been brought up.

'They're common! I'm not having them at my wedding!'

Gerda had been unprepared for the anger that had darkened her father's brow, the purple that had suffused his thin face, then drained away to leave him ghostly pale. She had never seen him like that before.

'They are my friends – and yours,' he said very quietly, very distinctly.

'They're loud, and when they're drunk they're . . . they're just slobs and—'

'And they have hearts of gold. How do you think I'd have coped all these years after your mother cleared out, leaving me nothing but a pile of debts and a four-year-old bairn?' He almost snarled in contempt. Gerda was shocked by the change in the mild little man she had always known. He even seemed taller now as he drew himself up. 'Well? Who looked after you when I went to work? It was May McBurnie. She's been more of a mother to you than your own mother ever was – even when she was here. Who did the washing for us? Who cleaned the house? Have you forgotten how May slaved after you, and the tantrums you threw when you didn't have a clean white blouse every day and you wouldn't wash or iron a single thing for yourself, even when you were old enough? Well? Have you really forgotten our real friends?

Where d'you think I'd be while you're away at college, spending every penny I can earn on your clothes and your pleasures? Who would I have talked to every evening without Jim and Willie and the rest o' my friends?'

'They may be your friends, but they're certainly not mine!' Gerda snapped. 'And it's my wedding. *Mine*, Father!'

'Oh aye, and who's to pay for it?'

'You, of course. It's your duty as my father—'

'Duty? You know nothing about duty! Or loyalty!' He almost spat the words at her. 'Anyway, I've often wondered whether I am really your father, or just the silly bugger who was landed with you. Your mother played the field but I never knew what a whore she was until a few years ago.'

'You shouldn't speak ill of the dead! You can't mean that.'

'Can't I? I've often searched for a bit of me in you, a resemblance to my mother, or my father, or even my sister Ginny – God rest her soul. But I've seen nothing in you to remind me o' any o' them. You're your mother's bairn all right – her looks, aye, but ye've inherited all her sullen discontentment now you're a grown woman. Only God knows who sired ye.'

Gerda sat down heavily. She was stunned by his outburst. This was the man she had thought adored her, the man she had twisted around her little finger all her life.

'So,' he said more calmly, 'who are you going to invite to this grand wedding o' yours? We've no close relations left since Ginny died. Where are all your fine friends? I've never met any o' them . . .'

Gerda opened her mouth to answer, but who were her friends? She hadn't kept in touch with any of the girls she'd known at school. Those she had known at college were just fellow students. Lucy had befriended her, but in a rare flash of honesty Gerda admitted she had only used Lucy to capture Ewan. Slowly she closed her mouth. Who would she invite to her wedding to fill the church? And anyway, which church? Neither she nor her father attended church. Tears welled up in her blue eyes. John Allan turned away. He had never been able to resist her tears, but this time he could not – would not – deny his own friends. That would be like Peter denying Jesus Christ before the cock crowed.

In the end he relented, but only so far. There would be no wedding without his friends and neighbours. If Ewan agreed to a civil ceremony he would give them the money he had saved to pay for her wedding. It would help to furnish their new home. Gerda had stared at him as her dreams melted away. When John Allan admitted he had saved a thousand pounds for her wedding day she was astonished. So he really had planned to give her a grand send-off. For the first time genuine tears filled Gerda's eyes, but she was the one who turned aside. They were tears of self-pity.

Ewan had been shocked at the idea of a wedding that was not in church. In the end it was Rachel who found a compromise after an exchange of letters with John Allan, who then agreed to come down to Wester Rullion for a night. The wedding ceremony was to be held in the Lochandee Kirk that Ewan had attended all his life. Their parents would be the only people present, except for Ewan's friend Gus, who had agreed to be his best man and witness. Reluctantly Gerda had asked Lucy to be her witness, and even more reluctantly Lucy had agreed. In her heart she knew she was only doing it for Ewan. Twice they had quarrelled when she had tried to persuade him not to rush into marriage with Gerda, although they had never had a serious quarrel in their lives before.

After the wedding they were to have lunch in a hotel near Lockerbie, for which John Allan insisted on paying.

Bridie was surprised and saddened that Ewan was not to be married with all his family and friends around him, whether in Glasgow or Lochandee, and the twins were bitterly disappointed that they could not be bridesmaids.

'Conan and Fiona had a quiet wedding and they are supremely happy,' Rachel reminded her. 'Apparently Gerda does not have many relations and her father feels they'll probably make better use of the money if they put it towards their home. Neither of them have worked long enough to have much in the way of savings.' After her first conversation with John Allan Rachel guessed this was only part of the truth, but she liked Gerda's father so she had not asked questions. 'He may be right, you know, Bridie. All the pomp and ceremony in the world will not guarantee a lifetime of happiness.'

Ewan's thoughts were preoccupied with the cows he was getting ready for the Dumfries Show and as it drew nearer he became relieved Gerda was not planning a big wedding. Her demands on his time seemed endless as it was, and there was so much to do at Wester Rullion in the summer – even without preparations for the show. He had agreed to most of her plans, but he had insisted the wedding must not be arranged until after the show. He had great hopes of winning at least one class this year. The rivalry between himself and Bridie was friendly but Ewan longed to prove himself as a first-class stockman and he was determined to have his cows in superb condition. Each evening after milking he and Peter haltered them and walked them round and round the yard to train them in readiness for the show ring. It took a lot of time and patience and Gerda grew more and more exasperated with this evening ritual.

'It will only be for another week,' Ewan told her, but she would not be placated, and she absolutely refused to do any of the cleaning at the cottage. Instead she had asked Billy Smith's mother to do it. As she had always done when she felt resentful or neglected she went on shopping sprees, oblivious to the fact that their budget was dwindling rapidly and the builder and the plumber still had to be paid. They had worked extremely hard to please her and to get the cottage finished in time for the wedding.

Ewan was dismayed and angry when he realized how much money had been drawn from their account.

'You'll have to stop buying things until we have paid the tradesmen,' he insisted.

'We have to have carpets and a bedroom suite,' she said sullenly.

'We'll manage without a carpet in the bedroom if we can't afford one,' Ewan said. 'And we'll leave the front room empty for now. Why did you buy all those mirrors and ornaments, Gerda? And those carvings you asked the joiner to make for the built-in cupboards?' He looked around the hall and up the narrow staircase in exasperation. 'I can't see where the money has gone.'

'Oh, don't worry so much!' Gerda said impatiently. There was no way she could tell him she had spent forty-two guineas on a radiogram if he was going to be like this. 'I've chosen the carpet for the sitting room. We need a good one for our best room so I've bought a lovely thick Axminster. You'll love it when you see it. And the three-piece suite was a bargain at about seventy-one pounds.' Ewan opened his mouth to protest but she snapped accusingly, 'You were too busy to come with me last weekend so it's your fault if we've overspent.'

'Gerda, you'll have to cancel them. You must have realized we don't even have enough left to pay the tradesmen.'

'A–ah, but you don't know how these things work, Ewan. We can get them now, but we don't have to pay everything immediately. There was this lovely salesman in Simmons. A handsome, dark-haired young man . . .' She looked archly at Ewan but he was frowning and only half listening. She raised her voice in anger. 'He has arranged everything especially for me. I've paid a deposit on the big items of furniture and the carpets. It's only two shillings in the pound. Then we pay the rest over two or three years . . .'

'You've what!' Ewan stared at her in disbelief, but he could see she was deadly serious. 'We don't do that sort of thing, Gerda! You'll have to cancel them. We don't buy things until we can pay for them. You end up paying twice as much as—'

'Of course you don't!' Gerda snapped. 'I'm not stupid. It's only a shilling in the pound.'

'That's five per cent. You're paying more than the goods are worth! Don't you see . . .

'For goodness' sake, Ewan, that's not much to ask!'

'It's twenty pounds extra if you spend a hundred pounds. How much did you spend, Gerda?' Ewan looked at her, saw her guilty flush and his heart sank. 'Well,' he sighed heavily, 'we don't work that way at Wester Rullion, and at a guess I'd say your father doesn't buys things until he can pay for them either. You'll just have to use his money to pay the Simmons account. We'll try to save and put it back as a nest egg for you, as I expect he intended.'

'Indeed I shall not. I've used that money to buy a dress for the wedding and some clothes for our honeymoon.'

'What honeymoon?'

'A–ah, that's a surprise.' She fluttered her eyelashes and edged closer. 'Very romantic, although you're the one who should be planning romantic surprises for our honeymoon.'

'And how do you know I haven't?'

'You haven't, have you?' Gerda asked, her eyes widening.

'I'd planned to have a few days on our own, touring down south. Father says I can borrow the car.'

'Oh that's all right then. Nothing that can't be changed. We're going to Paris, lover boy.' Her voice deepened huskily and she trailed her fingers down his cheek, down his neck, and down inside his shirt, pressing her body along the length of his until she felt him respond as she had known he would. It was a heady sensation to discover she had such power over men. As a child tears had always worked with her father but the power she was discovering as a woman was far more exciting. She would soon wean Ewan away from the old ways of Wester Rullion and his parents.

'Your father must be sitting on pots of money!' she said softly against his cheek, her lips moving tantalizingly close to his. 'You'll have to tell him we need a bit more.'

'No!' He jerked his head back, looking down into her lovely face. She bewitched him. 'Father has been more than generous to us already. We must cut back. Farmers don't have money to throw away on fripperies, even with the guaranteed prices and the marketing boards. We still—'

'Who do you think you're kidding!' Gerda scoffed. 'Don't take me for a fool, Ewan. I can read, you know. I read in one of your farming papers – *Scottish Farmer*, I think it was – that an Aberdeen Angus bull had sold for sixty thousand guineas! One bloody bull! You've got lots of bulls at Wester Rullion, so—'

'Oh, Gerda!' Ewan half laughed, half groaned in despair. 'That was a pedigree Aberdeen Angus from a famous herd with excellent breeding. Even so, I can't see how he was worth all that myself, but ours are nothing like that kind of value.'

'Oh, don't give me that, Ewan. I don't believe it. Isn't that why you're spending all this time preparing your cows for the Dumfries Show? Isn't that why you're so desperate to beat Bridie, so that everyone will want to buy them?'

'We–ell, it helps a bit if you win . . .'

'There we are then. You'll just have to sell a bull or two.' She reached up and kissed him full on the mouth, a lingering, passionate kiss, as she twined her arms around his neck. She didn't want any arguments, at least not any that prevented her getting her own way.

Even to herself, Gerda would never admit she was jealous of Lucy. It was Lucy's close friendship with Ewan that had first drawn Gerda's attention to him, and made her determined to win him away from Lucy. She hadn't believed the two really were only friends, and even now she sometimes wondered when she saw them together. She knew Lucy was determined to complete her two years in teaching and gain her parchment before she married Don Greig, and it pleased her to learn they were only planning a small family wedding too. She couldn't have borne it if Lucy had a big affair. In her heart Gerda still yearned for a fairy-tale wedding with lots of admirers and herself as the beautiful bride.

She was determined about one thing: her own house would be a palace compared to the old barn of a farmhouse where Lucy and Don Greig would have to live. Don was staying there by himself because the landlord had insisted that the tenancy depended on the place being occupied. The previous tenants had been elderly, old-fashioned and reluctant to change anything. Consequently the house did not even have piped water, electricity or a water closet. Gerda had overheard Mrs Maxwell telling Bridie that the landlord's promised improvements consisted of little more than having a hot water system and bathroom installed in the house. The news filled Gerda with smug satisfaction. Her little cottage would be far superior to anything Lucy would have if Don had to make any other improvements himself. His father had refused to spend money on the house and had insisted on controlling everything as one business along with the Greigs' Home Farm. He was sending twenty cows for Don to milk along with some sheep and one of his tractors, but Don would get a wage instead of sharing the profits.

Mrs Greig had insisted on buying paint and wallpaper to make the place more habitable for Don, but it was Lucy and Chris who spent most of their weekends scrubbing and painting. Gerda, gazing around her own newly decorated home, with the expensive flock wallpaper in the small dining room and the heavily embossed paper in the sitting room, gave a smirk of satisfaction. She had lots of ideas that would make Lucy's home look like a slum in comparison.

The day of Dumfries Show arrived and Ewan got up at the crack of dawn to get the milking finished and set off for the show with the five animals he had selected for various classes. He and Ross had disagreed on his choice of two of the animals, but in the end his father had agreed that it should be Ewan's decision now that he was a partner, and because he had worked so hard to prepare the animals. Gerda simply couldn't believe Ewan was serious when he told her they were to be shampooed from the tips of their tails to the end of their noses on the day of the show.

'Well we do trim their hair first,' he said seriously. 'And they will probably need to be washed again when they arrive at the show. After that someone needs to stand guard and wipe their bottoms if they make a mess, and keep polishing up horns, if they have any, and brushing their hair to keep them smart.'

'You're pulling my leg!' Gerda said accusingly.

'I wish I was!' Ewan grinned wickedly. 'But no, I'm serious, Gerda. It's a lot of work presenting cattle at their very best, honestly. I'm hoping you'll come to the show a little later. Mother has packed a huge basket of sandwiches and scones and flasks of coffee and tea. If you come to the cattle lines you'll see us all there. And if we win plenty of prizes you could lead one of the cows around the main ring for the parade, if you like.'

'Me? Lead one of those huge smelly beasts? I hope you're joking, Ewan Maxwell!'

'I wasn't, actually . . .' Ewan frowned and hid his disappointment. He thought Gerda would have enjoyed parading a prize animal around the ring where everyone could admire her, as well as the animal he hoped she would be leading. 'Even the twins can lead a cow around the ring,' he told her. 'All of Bridie's family help on show days. In fact, Max is getting as keen as Bridie. I hope we can beat them or the young wretch will never let me hear the end of it.'

'I don't understand what all the fuss is about.' Gerda pouted. 'I hope you haven't forgotten we're supposed to be getting married in less than a week.'

'As though I would forget that!' Ewan chuckled. 'It's the most important day of my life. . .well, after today!' His eyes twinkled and he ducked his head as Gerda swiped out at him. 'You will come to the show, Gerda, won't you? I want to show you off too.'

'But I thought we were going to the show dance at night?'

'So we are, but it doesn't take you all day to get ready. Besides, I'd like you to understand what it means to me, showing the Wester Rullion cattle. I'm really proud of them.'

Seven

E wan's pride and joy was boundless when his favourite cow won the overall dairy-breed championship, beating one of the Lochandee Ayrshires into reserve. Bridie was unreserved in her congratulations and she hugged him warmly.

'You've done well, little brother,' she teased. 'I thought you'd be showing the heifer out of the Star family. Is she out of condition?' she asked.

'No–o.' Ewan grimaced ruefully. 'Father preferred her. We were third with the Jenny heifer, so I expect he'll say we would have won that class too if I'd listened to him. He could be right, I suppose, but we've had a good day.'

'You certainly have.'

'Can't you two talk about anything else but cows?' Gerda demanded, tottering to Ewan's side and clinging to his arm.

'You'll get used to it, Gerda.' Bridie laughed. 'And at least you'll have two silver cups to show for all Ewan's effort. They'll look lovely in your new house. I'm quite envious.'

'But you have to keep cleaning them with that awful polish,' chirped Alicia.

'It makes your hands all dry and nasty.' Margaret nodded.

'You two are just jealous,' Ewan teased, aiming a playful fist at them. They grinned back at him, nodding vigorous agreement.

'We'll beat you next year though, Uncle Ewan,' Max threatened with an irrepressible grin. 'Hey, did you see Peter has won a cup in the crafts classes with one of his marquetry pictures?' he asked. 'It's a ship done in all different woods.

73

It's great. I heard a man saying it was really good and he wondered whether he could commission one.'

'What's commission mean, Dad?' Margaret asked.

'The man would like Peter to make one specially for him,' Nick told her. 'I just had time for a quick look at the pictures and the walking sticks, but I thought Peter's was outstanding.'

'I didn't have time to go round,' Bridie said regretfully. 'Did you enjoy the craft tent, Gerda?' she asked, trying to include her and banish the impatient frown from her lovely face.

'I didn't look.'

'Oh. I thought you might have enjoyed that sort of thing.'

'I prefer the stalls where you can buy things. What's the use of goggling at other folk's stuff? I bought this. Look.' She held out a brown leather handbag, beautifully embossed and hand-sewn.

Bridie's eyebrows rose. 'It's lovely,' she murmured, and wondered how Gerda could afford such an expensive accessory when there must be lots of things they needed for their new home. 'I hope you're both coming back to Lochandee tonight for supper. Mother and Father are coming, and Conan and Fiona. I think Lucy and Don will be there too, but Don has to get back to Ayrshire tonight.'

'All right.' Ewan nodded eagerly. 'It will be good to see Lucy and have a chat with Don—'

'We can't,' Gerda intervened. 'We're going to the show dance. You promised, Ewan.'

'That doesn't get going until about ten o'clock, unless times have changed since I was young.' Nick chuckled. 'Plenty of time to join us for a meal before you go. Anyway, Bridie has some wedding gifts for you, haven't you?'

'Yes,' Bridie agreed. 'Do come.'

'No!' Gerda stared challengingly at Ewan. 'I've suffered the talk and preparations for your bloody show for weeks. I've had enough. We'll go back to Wester Rullion and get ready for the dance.'

Bridie looked down at the crestfallen faces of her children. They loved family gatherings and above all they loved

Ewan. He and Lucy had so often teased and played with them. She looked up at Ewan and saw the disappointment in his eyes too.

'We'll come another time,' he said, smiling ruefully.

Everything about Gerda and Ewan's wedding was expensive, from the bride's cream lace dress, to the veiled hat and bouquet that she had insisted upon, even though the wedding was not a traditional grand affair. She had made an appointment for studio photographs, and the lunch had so many courses Rachel could not even nibble at the last three. She hid her doubts and concentrated on Ewan's happy expression. She was glad Ross had been so understanding about the honeymoon in Paris.

'I hadn't intended to leave you and Peter for more than four days, Father,' Ewan had explained, 'but Gerda arranged a surprise honeymoon in Paris. It would mean being away ten days if we go . . .'

'Oh.' Then, after the faintest hesitation, Ross nodded. 'You must go if it's all arranged. Aye.' He sighed. 'You only get married once. Things are different now to what they were in our day, but there's no doubt you'll have to settle down to plenty of hard work when you get back.'

'You're sure you can manage?'

'We managed well enough until you left college, laddie!'

'Yes, but that was before the fire, and you were fitter then.'

'Fitter? I'm like a new man after all those weeks of sitting around the house,' Ross growled, but they all knew this was not true. 'Peter and I will manage fine. The hay is all in and the first cut of silage is in the pit. We'll starting mowing the second cut ready for you coming back if the weather is good. That should just be about the right stage.'

'All right.' Ewan grinned in relief and gave his father a friendly thump. Rachel often watched the two of them discussing the farm, the crops, the breeding of the cattle. It was their life and they loved it. She was thankful now that Ewan had been born in their later years, although it had been a shock at the time to find she was expecting another baby when Conan was already old enough to fight for his country.

So after the wedding they waved Ewan and Gerda away with goodwill, and John Allan set off back to Glasgow immediately afterwards. Suddenly the day seemed flat.

'Your turn next, lassie,' Ross said, turning to Lucy.

'Mmm, not for a year though. It seems ages away.'

'It will not be long in passing,' Rachel comforted her. 'Beth and Harry would have been proud that you have done so well and waited until you have finished your teacher training, Lucy. No one can take that away from you, lassie, and things are changing now, even for farmers.'

'Aye, they buy fancy washing machines and vacuum cleaners, then they spend half the week curling at the ice rink.' Ross nodded, tongue in cheek. 'At least you'll bring in some money if you are teaching children.'

Lucy laughed. 'I suspect Don's father hopes I shall bring in some money and be able to help Don milk the cows as well. That might be possible in the summer holidays, but during term time we have a lot of preparation to do for lessons.'

'I'm sure Don will understand that,' Rachel said.

'Oh, he does. And he knows I love the children.'

'Aye,' Ewan's friend Gus chipped in. 'He was real jealous of me being best man today.' He grinned. 'He needn't worry though, I like my freedom. I don't envy Ewan being tied down with a wife. I can spend enough money myself without needing the help of someone like Gerda.'

Gus laughed but Rachel had an uneasy feeling there was criticism beneath his banter. 'Ewan was saying you plan to go abroad,' she remarked.

'Yes. I'm bound for Canada for a year. I leave in a fortnight. Well, Lucy, I'm ready to set off home now. Do you want a lift back to Ayrshire and that jealous swain of yours?'

'Did anyone ever tell you you're mad as a hatter, Gus?' Lucy laughed. 'But yes, I would like a lift back, since you brought me down here.'

*   *   *

Ewan enjoyed the experience of visiting Paris, but he was eager to get home when they landed at Dover. He was astonished when Gerda seriously expected they would take several days touring around on the way back to Scotland.

'We have to get back. I said we would be home tonight,' he insisted. 'Father and Peter will have the grass cut ready to start making silage tomorrow. Anyway, we have the car. I expect they will be needing it.'

'I don't see why. Your mother does all her shopping from the vans. I never knew there were so many butchers and bakers and grocers. She even has a fish man to bring her fresh fish.'

'Well, that's what they do for a living. It's their business. They are pleased to have new customers. I expect they'll call on us as well, once they know we are settled in at the cottage.'

'They needn't bother! I shall go to Dumfries and choose my own shopping. I do think you ought to tell your father we need another car now you are married, Ewan.'

'Oh, I don't think we can afford two cars,' Ewan said in alarm. He was beginning to feel Gerda's demands were never-ending. He frowned as he remembered her father's advice just before they said goodbye. He had been deadly serious. Ewan glanced at Gerda in the seat beside him. Her full red mouth had a sulky droop and there was a tiny frown between her eyes.

'Cheer up, sweetheart,' he urged, patting her knee gently. 'It'll be good to get home and have peace in our own wee house.'

'Will it?' she asked sullenly. 'Maybe for you it will. I can't see what difference it will make if we just have another night or two on the way up north.'

'No, Gerda.' Ewan's tone was firm. 'I promised to be back to work by tomorrow. That's the end of it.'

Gerda's scowl grew and she set her mouth in a sullen line. She was beginning to realize Ewan was not as easily swayed as she had thought, nor as her father had been. Ewan had genuinely enjoyed Paris, especially visiting the gardens and the Louvre. He would have stood for hours looking at the pavement artists or watching the world go by from the outdoor cafés. Gerda was surprised to find Ewan so interested in art and history and she had grown bored with sightseeing. She wanted to be part of the nightlife of Paris. She had enjoyed dining late in the evening but Ewan had grumbled about being hungry and the fact that even a cup of coffee was expensive.

But it was not just the sights of Paris that had caused minor disagreements. Gerda knew their honeymoon had not been the greatest success. She was Ewan's wife now and he did not expect to have to buy her favours each time he wanted to make love to her. Nevertheless she kept up a sulky silence as they drove mile after mile.

Ewan seemed content to concentrate on his driving, at least until they had left the busy roads behind. Eventually they stopped for an early lunch and he smiled and chatted pleasantly. Gerda realized she could either sulk or return to normal but whatever she did, Ewan was not going to change his mind, nor was he going to make any effort to humour her. She looked at his profile.

'You're just like your father,' she muttered involuntarily. Ewan looked down at her, his dark brows arched in question. 'Oh, never mind,' she said impatiently. 'Let's eat. I'm famished.'

'Suits me.' Ewan smiled. 'That was the general idea. Why did you say I was like my father just now?'

'Stubborn. I can just imagine him being the same.'

'It's not being stubborn, Gerda. It's keeping my word. I said I would be back and I shall. My father would never let anyone down if he could help it. That's why so many of the neighbours come to him when they need help or advice. I hope I'm as well respected when I'm his age.'

'But you still argue and disagree with him.'

'We don't argue.' He laughed. 'We discuss things and sometimes we have a different opinion. I suppose it's because I'm a different generation.'

*   *   *

78

Ross was pleased to see Ewan back. He hadn't realized how much work and responsibility his son had taken over in the year since he left college. Worse, he had been dismayed to discover how much less fit he was himself after all those weeks without physical work, and how breathless the dust made him when shaking out straw to bed the calves – such a simple task, yet it had left him wheezing for breath, his heart thumping.

Peter had already mown the grass ready for silage and it was wilting while waiting to be gathered into the pit.

'I'm glad you're home, Ewan,' Ross greeted him. 'We need you to drive the silage chopper. Even young Billy is eager to get on while the weather holds.'

Ross did not enjoy silage making himself. He was getting too old for changes and modern methods with new, ever more complicated machinery.

'Nick has promised to come over tomorrow and lend a hand on the buck rake,' he told Ewan. 'But he would like us to send Peter over to Lochandee to give them a hand when they start the harvest.'

'That's fair enough,' Ewan agreed and began to ask questions about the cows and the farm.

'For goodness' sake!' Gerda snapped in exasperation. 'We've only been away five minutes. Nothing much can have changed in such a short time. Let's go home. You've kept saying that's what you wanted.'

'I am home. The farm is home. You go down to the house, sweetheart. I'll not be long. You still have some wedding presents to open. I want to see Peter's gift so that I can thank him properly when I see him.'

'Oh that! You went on enough about it before we went away. It won't be anything much. He's just a labourer.'

Ross frowned and looked into Gerda's pale blue eyes. He took a deep breath, but before he could say anything Ewan intervened, his own mouth tighter than usual.

'Whatever it is that Peter has given to us, it was probably chosen with great care, from what I know of him. We shall both thank him for it. I'm sure he would appreciate a short letter from you, just like everyone else.'

Gerda scowled but she did not reply as she flounced out of the house.

'I think Gerda's a bit tired after the long journey,' Ewan said, proffering a feeble excuse on her behalf.

'Mmm . . . well I think she is in for a surprise. I've seen Peter's gift and it's beautiful – quite unique in fact. I'd be proud to own it.'

'That's praise indeed!' Ewan said in surprise. 'I'll go and see for myself as soon as you've given me all the news.'

When Ewan arrived at his new home an hour later Gerda had not opened Peter's neatly wrapped parcel, nor the two small parcels that lay beside it on the new settee. Instead she had opened one of the suitcases and was trying on a pair of new red shoes with ridiculously high heels. She also had on a very short, very straight skirt, which was obviously new too. He had not been round the Paris shops with her, and now he shook his head. She'd already bought a pile of new clothes for their holiday. Gerda's father was right – she just couldn't resist buying more.

'I'll open Peter's parcel, shall I?' he offered.

'You're more interested in Peter's bloody present that you are in me! How d'you like my new outfit?' She twirled around, swaying this way and that between him and a long mirror at the end of the hall.

'You look fine. Gerda, I do wish you wouldn't swear . . .'

'Swear? Good God, Ewan, that's not swearing. You wait until I really get started. And at the rate you're going that will not be long!' She strode through the door and snatched Peter's parcel out of his hands and flung it back at the settee. But she didn't throw quite far enough and it slid on to the floor. Ewan's mouth tightened and he bent to pick it up and carried it into the kitchen to open it at the table.

He stood and stared at the picture in silence for several minutes. He couldn't believe his eyes. Gerda strutted in to see what had caught his attention.

'Well!' she sneered. 'You'll see what I mean now. Some wedding gift your fine Peter has bought us. It's home-made – a bloody picture made with bits of wood.' She gave a hollow laugh. 'Well if you think that's going to hang in my house you can think again. You can stuff it in the rubbish bin.'

'Gerda!' Ewan was horrified. Before she had joined him he had felt tears prick the back of his eyes. He could visualize the hours and hours Peter must have worked, painstakingly cutting out each tiny shape and contour. He must have designed the picture himself, for no one else could have captured Wester Rullion like that. 'See the ripples in the sky,' he said softly. 'The darker shape of the hill in the distance, the golden sheen of a harvest field.' His finger reverently traced the beautifully inlaid pieces. 'And the farmhouse, the exact outline, and the steading . . . It must have taken forever just drawing it all out – and then to find so many different woods, so many grains and shades,' he said incredulously.

'For goodness' sake!' Gerda snapped. 'It's rubbish. He's made it himself, I tell you. It's certainly not hanging in my house.'

Ewan turned to stare at her. He felt cold fury bubbling up inside him. He wanted to shake Gerda. He wanted to knock some sense into her silly little girlish head. He forced himself to breathe in deeply, several times. Stupidly, Gerda took his silence for acquiescence. She reached for the picture.

'I'll put it in the bin. He'll never know . . .'

'You're a heartless snob!' Ewan shouted, and his fingers tightened on the frame of the beautifully polished picture. 'You haven't even looked at it properly. Have you any idea of the hours Peter must have spent – no, not hours, months and months! That took a lot of loving care, and he did it especially for us. My father is right – it is unique.'

'I'm not a snob! But I'm not having that bloody monstrosity in my house. And—'

'This picture will leave this house only over my dead body.' Ewan's face was white. His eyes were narrowed slits, and they gleamed more green that blue in his anger.

Gerda stared at him. 'D–don't look at me like that! You frighten me, Ewan . . .' She began to whimper and her eyes filled with tears. Ewan ignored them. He looked at his wife and wondered how she could look so beautiful and yet have no soul.

'You have no soul,' he said aloud. 'I don't understand how anyone could fail to appreciate the skill and love that Peter has put into that picture. We shall hang it on the long wall in the sitting room. You wait and see – all your friends will admire it.' Ewan was calmer now, his voice even again, but Gerda recognized the thread of steel in it. She would not dare defy him, at least not yet. This was their first real quarrel. He could hang his picture, but she would see to it that he paid for his outburst.

In November, news of President Kennedy's assassination rocked the world. It was announced on radios and televisions in every nation. Rachel was busy ironing when her radio programme was interrupted to make the announcement. The shock upset her more than she would have believed. He had been so young and handsome, so vital and full of energy, with a lovely wife and a young family, and everything to live for... He was a leader, strong and trustworthy. He had not given in under the pressure of the Cuban crisis. He had stood his ground with confidence, and with the most powerful nation in the world behind him, trusting him to make the right decisions. Another war had been avoided. Who could possibly take his place? Rachel almost felt like she had known him after seeing him so often on the television. She felt shattered and alarmed. She prayed fervently that the peace of the world would not be threatened now that he was gone. She thought of the words of the poet Robert Burns:

> Man's inhumanity to man
> Makes countless thousands mourn!

How true. Rachel switched off the iron and went outside to find Ross, to share the news and seek his comfort, as she had always done when she was troubled.

Eight

As Rachel had predicted, the months passed swiftly and it seemed no time before preparations were being made for Lucy's wedding to Don Greig.

'I can't believe Chris and I – and Gerda too, of course – will soon have been teaching for two years,' Lucy said, shaking her head in disbelief.

'You've lost weight, lassie,' Ross told her, eyeing her with affection. 'Have you been working too hard?'

'We've been pretty busy. I wanted to get most of the rooms made habitable,' Lucy admitted, 'and there's only Don in the house so he has to do his own cooking as well as the work outside. He has fifty cows to milk now, and another twenty to calve before mid-September.' She smiled at Ross. 'Of course, it would be a lot easier if he had a lovely modern milking parlour like yours, but there's no hope of that. Even the byres are a bit old-fashioned and inconvenient, but I think he will be able to improve them in time. He does have a woman from one of the cottages who washes the milk cans and keeps the dairy clean, but she has a large family so that's all she can manage. It's all Don can pay for – or rather all that his father considers necessary. Mrs Greig is sending a hen house and some of her pullets over as soon as we get settled after the wedding.'

'You'll have a little bit of money for the house then, lassie, if you have to give up the teaching,' Rachel said. 'I don't know what I'd do without the egg money.'

'That's what Don's mother intended,' Lucy said ruefully, 'but his father has other ideas. He says the hens will have to be fed, so any money must be pooled for the good of the family. He keeps reminding us that he has another two sons to set up in farms. He runs everything as one business so all the income goes to Home Farm and he pays all the bills from there. He gives Don an allowance, when he remembers, but it's little more than money for his food and clothes.' She frowned. 'I'm not meaning to criticize, but even Mrs Greig thinks it's not enough. She says I'll just have to keep a bit of egg money back and say nothing. I shall hate it if I have to be deceitful but I do feel sorry for Don. He works so hard and it is his brothers who benefit. There are two of them – as well as Mr Greig and a boy – and they only help Don when it's hay time or with the sheep shearing. None of them came to help with the turnip hoeing. They milk seventy cows but that's as many as their byre will hold so they are sending all the heifers to Don, and Mr Greig has started dealing in dairy cattle. He goes to market two or three times a week. Of course, they have a hundred ewes and Don only has forty.'

'Surely one of Don's brothers could lend a hand more often,' Ross said. 'It's only a couple of miles between the two places, isn't it?'

'Two and a half, to be exact.' Lucy grimaced. 'Don wouldn't like to think I was complaining, and I'm not really, except that I feel he works too hard.' She smiled wryly. 'Chris says her father has always been tight-fisted when it comes to parting with money. She says Jake and Willie take after him but Don and herself take after their mother. I must say, Mrs Greig does what she can to help Don.'

'I'm glad to hear that,' Rachel said with some concern. She couldn't help wondering what sort of life Lucy would have.

'There's a boy who comes to Skeppiehill during the holidays and at weekends, and he wants to work on a farm when he leaves school. Don says he's a good help already but Mr Greig refuses to give him anything for working. Mrs Greig gives the boy a few shillings from her egg money every now and then, and sometimes a dozen eggs for his mother, to encourage him to keep helping Don. His name is Richard

Green. As a matter of fact, his elder brother Adam is a dairyman on a big dairy farm about ten miles away. It's not far from the school where Chris teaches, and they have become very friendly. In fact they're more than friends, but Chris's father doesn't approve. He says Adam has no prospects.'

'Some of the good dairymen earn more money in a year than many farmers,' Ross commented. 'I expect Mr Greig thinks Chris should marry a farmer.'

'Yes, he does. Adam has ambitions to be a farmer himself, even if it is only a smallholding, but Mr Greig doesn't want to hear about his dreams. He doesn't know Adam already rents three small fields from a neighbouring farmer. He and Chris have bought four pedigree heifer calves between them. They plan to sell them as heifers, after they have had calves.'

'Good for them!' Ross whistled. 'They'll get another four calves to rear if they're lucky, then.'

'Yes, Adam is really keen on his stock. You would like him, and so would Ewan. He studies the Friesian pedigrees and the sale catalogues and he knows all about the Wester Rullion and Lochandee herds. Mrs Greig and Don know about Chris's plans but she doesn't talk to her father about them any more. She feels a bit bitter because she can't even take Adam home. He's trying to buy a couple of dilapidated cottages with some outbuildings so that they can house the calves in the winter, and they plan to get a pig and some hens. If he can get the cottages at a reasonable price, he and Chris hope to get a grant to renovate them. I think they will get married eventually but Chris knows that wouldn't please her father at all, so no one mentions it.'

'All right.' Rachel smiled at Lucy. 'We'll not say a word out of place when we meet Mr Greig at the wedding, shall we, Ross? Are you listening?'

'I shall be Mr Tact himself,' Ross promised. 'Is Christine bringing her boyfriend to the wedding, Lucy?'

'Yes, would you like to meet him?'

'I would indeed.'

'Shall I arrange to seat him at your table then? He would

enjoy the chance to hear about your herd. He'll not know many people except Chris.'

'Then we'll look after him,' Rachel promised.

'I . . . er . . . I haven't mentioned Don's father to Fiona or Conan – I mean about him being a bit . . . er . . . mean,' Lucy said suddenly, and her cheeks flushed guiltily. 'In fact I shouldn't have talked so much to anyone . . .'

'Don't look so worried, lassie.' Rachel laid a comforting arm around her slim shoulders. 'We shall not breathe a word and anyway, it does you good to confide sometimes. I'm sure things will work out for you both eventually.'

'Aye, and we can understand both sides.' Ross nodded. 'Sometimes I feel we keep Ewan on a tight rein, but he gets fifteen pounds a week and that's a lot more than Peter – and more than we've ever taken for ourselves.'

'Don would think he was rich if his father paid him half of that every week!' Lucy said incredulously.

'Well Ewan's a partner now and he'll have to learn to share the responsibilities and decisions before long, including doing the accounts . . .' Ross frowned. 'I'm just not sure he and Gerda are ready for that yet. The lassie seems to spend money like it's flowing past her door. Still,' he shrugged, 'I suppose she earns it herself so there's not much I can say. We bought a little van so that we should have two vehicles between us but she's not satisfied with that arrangement. She's bought a brand new car of her own. She didn't get it through Conan, or take Nick's advice either, so she must know what she's about.' He winked at Lucy. 'You teachers must earn even more than I thought, lassie. Now I'll need to go and do some work or Peter will be looking for me.'

As Ross walked away he didn't see Lucy's wide-eyed surprise. She knew Gerda was no better paid than she was herself, and she certainly wouldn't have bought a car. She knew she was lucky that Conan had given her hers for her twenty-first birthday.

'Come and have a cup of tea, lassie,' Rachel said and ushered Lucy into the big cosy kitchen. 'Conan said he would be over this afternoon – about three, he thought.' She glanced at the old wigwag clock on the wall. 'He'll be here in time for tea, so I'll set out some scones and a bit of ginger-bread. They're still his favourites, I believe?'

'Yes, I shall have to ask you for some of your recipes.' Lucy smiled. 'Don loves home-baking.'

'Ah, here's Conan now. You're just in time for tea, laddie, as I should have known you would be!'

'Of course.' Conan grinned. 'I wanted a word with Father too. Will he be in for tea?'

'He'll be back soon when he sees your car.' Rachel frowned. 'He's trying not to eat so much of my baking. He thinks if he puts on weight it will make him more breath-less.'

'Weight? Father?' Conan laughed. 'He's as lean and fit as he ever was . . . isn't he?'

'Yes,' Rachel said seriously. 'But don't you see, he must feel short of breath or he wouldn't be thinking about it? Anything with dust aggravates his lungs since the fire. Ewan and Peter do their best to keep him away from those sort of jobs, but I expect he does things automatically because he's done them all his life.'

'Mmm, I see what you mean.' Conan nodded. 'And knowing Father he wouldn't take kindly to being wrapped in cotton wool, or being told he should keep away from his animals.'

'No,' Rachel agreed. 'I'm learning to accept that there may be some risk to his health, but he has to have some pleasure from life too, and farming has always been his joy as well as his work – especially the cows.'

Looking at her grandmother, Lucy couldn't suppress a small shiver. She knew how deeply Ross and Rachel loved each other, and how much they would each miss the other's companionship when the inevitable parting came, but they were relatively young and she prayed they would have many years together yet.

'Anyway,' Rachel said, briskly changing the subject, 'you said you wanted to talk to Lucy about the wedding . . .'

'Yes, I do.' Conan flushed. 'But I meant to lead into the

87

subject tactfully.' For a moment both Lucy and Rachel saw the vulnerable uncertainty of a small boy with his hand caught in the sweetie jar, and both laughed aloud. This was not the Conan Maxwell, successful young businessman, that they both knew.

'It sounds ominous.' Lucy chuckled. 'You'd better tell me now.'

'All right, but don't take offence or argue until you've heard me out.'

'Agreed,' Lucy promised solemnly, but her green eyes, so like his own, twinkled.

'Well Fiona and I know how independent you like to be, Lucy, and we respect you for it. We also know you didn't want us to spend a small fortune on a big wedding for you and Don. We agreed to that, mainly because we believe it would send all the wrong messages to the miserable soul of your prospective father-in-law and—'

'Wh–what did you say?' Lucy gasped.

'Sorry! Sorry!' Conan held up his hand. 'It's just the impression he gave us when we had a talk, but maybe he's just . . . well . . . careful. Anyway, we've arranged for a marquee to be erected in the small paddock at the bottom of the garden at Rullion Glen. Fiona has got it all organized with caterers and decorations and heaters in case the weather turns cold—'

'Oh, but—'

'Hush.' Conan held up his hand to silence Lucy's protest. 'Fiona is really enjoying organizing it. In fact, Lucy, I want you to know what a lot of pleasure you have brought to both of us. Fiona has no other family at all, as you know, and she thinks of you as more than her daughter; she regards you as a sister and friend. Whatever she does for you, I can assure you she probably gets more pleasure and satisfaction than you do. So don't hurt her by being too independent, or too proud to accept her generosity. She thinks this may be the last time we shall be able to do anything for you, once you have a husband. Anyway, now that the wedding is to be in a marquee it will not matter if you invite a few more guests than you intended. If Don's brothers want to bring their girl-friends, for instance, and the two cousins Don often mentions . . . So, you're happy with all that?'

'Well, yes. In that case I'd like to invite Carol too. She was such a good friend to Mother when we were all at Lochandee. And Wendy and Joanne too. Mother often said how she loved them when they came with Carol as young evacuees, but . . .'

'But nothing. I'm glad you thought of them. Carol and your mother helped each other a lot during the war. Right, that's the reception then. Now, we know Don can't get away from the farm for more than a night, so Christine has an idea. Her boyfriend has agreed to take a few days of his own holidays and milk the cows for Don. We're just tagging on a few more days to his wedding day. It's probably the last holiday either of you will get for years. Fiona and I want you to make the most of it. I've booked you into a hotel in Jersey. You fly from Manchester. One of our drivers will take you down to the airport, so it's all arranged.' Conan was talking quickly now, anxious not to let Lucy interrupt or have time to consider.

'B—but . . . I don't know what to s–say,' Lucy gasped. Then suddenly she was in Conan's arms. 'Y–you've both done so m–much for me already,' she stammered, trying to brush away the tears.

'No more than you deserve, lassie,' Conan said huskily. Watching them, Rachel wished with all her heart that Conan and Fiona had been blessed with other children, but it was not God's will, and at least they were supremely happy with each other.

'Er . . . there's just one more thing, Lucy, but this is supposed to be a surprise. I'm giving you warning so that you don't refuse it. Fiona wants to buy you something special for a wedding present, something you would not buy your-self. I know you might think it's an extravagance, but please, please accept it. It's what she wants to do. It was her own idea.'

'But. . .' Lucy looked puzzled. 'I already know. Fiona told

me you're buying us one of those automatic washing machines and I can't tell you how much it will be appreciated—'

'No, lassie.' He looked across at Rachel. 'Mother and Father want to buy that for you, the same as they bought for Ewan and Gerda.'

'Oh!' Lucy turned open-mouthed to look at Rachel. 'That's such a big present . . .'

'We wanted to make you and Ewan just the same, lassie, just as you've always been in our eyes.' Lucy knew they were talking about relationships and love as much as wedding presents and her chin trembled. Rachel simply opened her arms and hugged her. 'We wish you all the happiness in the world, Lucy.'

'Am I to hear what this special gift is then?' Lucy asked tremulously.

'No, that really is Fiona's surprise.' Conan grinned. 'All I ask is that you accept it and don't argue about it being too much. She would never buy anything she couldn't afford, but you know that, lassie.'

'Yes.' Lucy nodded. 'But I'm really intrigued now.'

'Did you know that Bridie and Nick and the children want to buy you a deep freeze?' Rachel asked. 'Bridie thinks they're wonderful. She keeps trying to persuade me to get one too.'

'Everyone is being so generous . . .'

'Ewan wanted to buy you a vacuum cleaner but Gerda refused. She said you probably wouldn't have any carpets to clean.'

'Well, she's right there.' Lucy smiled ruefully. 'We shall get some eventually. Meanwhile, Don and I have made a huge rag rug for the kitchen from everybody's scraps. I remembered how mother a–and H–Harry used to make them. And I've made two rugs with wool ends for our bedroom. I got a huge bag from one of the woollen mills for three and sixpence and they look really nice in shades of pink and blue and green.'

'I'm planning to have one of those wall-to-wall carpets

90

for our sitting room, like Gerda has in all her rooms,' Rachel said suddenly. She caught Ross's look of surprise. He had heard no mention of such plans. She sent him a green-eyed warning and a small frown to signal that she would tell him more later. 'If you and Don wouldn't mind having a second-hand one, you're more than welcome to ours...'

'Your rust carpet with the lovely border?' Lucy said in surprise.

'Yes.' Rachel nodded quickly. 'I think a carpet fitted from wall to wall would be warmer for our old bones – not so many draughts round the edges, you know. Of course, Don may not want my second-hand offerings...'

'Oh, Don wouldn't turn his nose up at a gift, and I've always liked the warm rusty colour. Are you sure? We would have to pay...'

'Indeed you will not, lassie,' Ross intervened quickly. He understood what Rachel was about now. They all knew how fiercely independent Lucy was. He was all in favour of her getting the carpet. 'Just you ask Don if he will cart it out of our way or we shall end up with an attic full of junk.'

The twins could scarcely contain their excitement as the wedding drew near. They were to be bridesmaids, along with Christine, and they had new dresses almost down to their ankles in a beautiful pale blue. Lucy was borrowing Bridie's wedding dress but it had needed a few extra tucks since she had lost weight. In the end Lucy had invited most of the girls who had been at college with her and they were all bringing their various partners.

'It will be almost like a college reunion,' Chris said excitedly. 'What does Gerda say about the wedding growing bigger and bigger?'

'I have hardly seen either Gerda or Ewan,' Lucy confessed. 'But she'll know most of them so I expect she will enjoy seeing them again.'

'You don't really believe that, do you?' Chris scoffed. 'The only person Gerda enjoys seeing is her own reflection in the mirror – unless she's changed since she married Ewan, of course. I wonder if he's still as besotted with her.'

'I expect he is.' Lucy chuckled. 'It's barely a year since they were married.'

In fact, Gerda could still drive Ewan wild with desire when she set her mind to it. She had a slim figure with curves in all the right places and no one could deny that she was beautiful with her long, silver-blonde hair, her blue eyes and finely boned oval face. When she heard that most of the people she had known at college would be at the wedding, her first reaction was jealousy that Lucy was to have a proper celebration.

'You'll be the belle of the ball in the dress you wore for our wedding,' Ewan told her.

Gerda's pale eyes narrowed thoughtfully. 'Yes, I will...' But she would not be wearing a dress she had already worn. She would have a brand new outfit; in fact she would go to Glasgow or Edinburgh. A new hat and gloves and a handbag all to match, she would have, as well as some new shoes. Perhaps she should have her hair cut too...

'Ewan, you should let your hair grow and have a style like the Beatles,' she said aloud.

'I'm not some teenage pop idol!' He laughed.

'Well you could at least try to be a bit more modern.'

A few days later Gerda was filled with resentment. She could barely wait for Ewan to come in from the hayfield, but when he did he was hot and tired, ready for his evening meal and then bed. But Gerda had not prepared a meal.

'I thought you would have had it in the hayfield with Peter,' she said sulkily.

'Oh, we had sandwiches at six o'clock but that's three hours ago and I'm ready for my dinner.'

'Well you'll have to make do with bread and cheese then. That's all there is.'

'What did you get a freezer for if you've nothing in it?' Ewan asked irritably.

'Don't you snap at me. You didn't tell me your parents had given Lucy and Donald Greig a carpet as well as buying them a washing machine for a wedding present.'

'They didn't buy her a carpet. Lucy is just taking the carpet square that Mother had in her front room.'

'They didn't offer us a carpet! She's not even part of the family.'

'Of course she is,' Ewan said wearily. 'Where's that bread and cheese you were getting?'

'Get your own! She's only adopted. Why should they give her a carpet and not us? You went on and on about the money I had spent and—'

'Well you did spend far too much! We're still paying most of my wages every month for the things you bought, and we shall still be paying for them this time next year. Anyway, you wouldn't have accepted a carpet square from my mother even if she'd offered it to you.'

'You're dead right I wouldn't!'

'Well then? What are you going on about, Gerda? I'm tired and hungry. It's been a long day.'

'It's the principle of the thing. But you've always stuck up for Lucy, haven't you? You can't see past her. It's a wonder you didn't marry her yourself,' Gerda taunted.

Ewan frowned. Several times he had been on the point of telling Gerda that Conan was Lucy's real father and that he was really her uncle, but something always held him back. In some way he felt he had to protect Lucy from Gerda's spite, and his family too . . . There ought not to be secrets like that between a man and his wife, but he knew instinctively that Gerda would use such gossip at every opportunity. He wondered whether Lucy had confided in Don and Christine and their parents.

In fact, Lucy *had* told Don about her true parentage. She felt there should be no secrets between them. As she had guessed, it made not the slightest difference to Don and so together they had told Christine and Mrs Greig one Sunday afternoon.

'Well, lassie, it's none of our business who your parents are.' Mrs Greig smiled reassuringly. 'All I ask is that you make my laddie happy and I can see you do that already. I reckon he's a lucky man.'

93

'Mmm. I agree with that,' Chris said, 'but I don't think you should tell Dad that Conan Maxwell is Lucy's real father. You know how funny he is about some things, and he would ask all sorts of awkward questions.'

'Aye.' Mrs Greig frowned thoughtfully. 'Aye, well maybe you're right, lassie. Maybe we'll just keep it between the four o' us then.' No more was said about it until Chris and her mother had departed, and then Don took Lucy in his arms and kissed her tenderly.

'You know how much I love you,' he said huskily. 'It wouldn't make any difference to me if the Devil himself was your father. I doubt if he'd be any tighter than my old man,' he added with a rueful grin. 'As a matter of fact I really like Conan and Fiona. They seem more like an elder brother and sister than prospective parents-in-law. I had expected them to be a lot older the first time I met them, at your twenty-first birthday party.'

'I couldn't have wished for a nicer couple if God had made them specially,' Lucy said with feeling, 'so I don't really mind who knows. It's just that we never talk about it in the family because it would have caused such a scandal locally.'

'It would still cause gossip if it happened now,' Don agreed, 'but I suppose everything was more strict in those days. Father often grumbles about young folk having neither morals nor manners since the war, so Chris is probably right about not telling him.'

'Well, you know your own family best,' Lucy acknowledged. 'You know when I went to the hospital to collect Mrs Maxwell after the fire, she introduced me to the nurse as their granddaughter.'

'Well so you are, and would be if Conan was your adoptive father – in a manner of speaking anyway.'

'I know, but ever since then there's been a difference . . . Just a subtle change – a firmer claim to kinship or something. I can't quite put my finger on it because they have both been kind to me all my life. Whatever it is, it makes me feel warm and . . . Och, I don't know.' She hid her face against Don's broad shoulder. 'I expect you think I'm crazy.'

'I think you're wonderful,' Don said huskily, stroking her chestnut hair with a gentle hand. 'And I don't blame Mr and Mrs Maxwell for being proud to claim you as their grand-daughter.'

Lucy looked up into his face and smiled. 'You always reassure me . . .'

'I can hardly wait until the wedding and I know you're really my wife,' Don said, his arms tightening.

Nine

It was a beautiful day in early July and Lucy looked almost ethereal as she moved gracefully down the aisle on Conan's arm followed by Christine and the twins, their dark, curly heads lowered shyly as they clasped their posies of pink and white rosebuds. The little Lochandee church was full and the village people crowded outside, waiting to see the bride and guests as they entered and give their good wishes to the bride and groom when they reappeared as man and wife. Most of them had known Lucy and her mother all their lives. Some of them even remembered her great-grandfather, old Mr Turner, and his bicycle shop, the man who had taught Conan about cogs and wheels and greasy hands.

The good wishes were many and they were sincere. Lucy had been overwhelmed by the generosity of these people when she arrived at Rullion Glen to find a room full of wedding gifts, large and small. Now she felt a lump in her throat at the warmth of their greetings and for a fleeting moment she wished with all her heart that her mother could have been here to see this day and all their friends. Her eyes were bright with love as she raised her face for Don's kiss on the steps of the church. The crowd cheered with delight, but Gerda did not smile. In her heart she knew she was jealous of Lucy's effortless popularity.

It brought Gerda satisfaction to know she was the most fashionably dressed of all the women at the wedding. She had already seen some of the young men eyeing her appreciatively and her fashionably short skirt showed off her shapely legs to perfection, especially with her new stiletto heels with their slingbacks. Knowing how much the Maxwells loved music, she knew the wedding reception would not be complete without some sort of entertainment. Surely Fiona would have organized a wooden floor for the marquee so that they could dance.

In fact Fiona had not only organized a wooden floor but she had arranged for a small band as well. The young fruit trees and bushes in the Rullion Glen garden were adorned with coloured fairy lights. She was determined that the whole affair should be as perfect for Lucy and Don as she could make it. Lucy still did not know what Fiona had bought for their wedding present. It was to be a surprise when they returned from their honeymoon and with Chris's co-operation it would be delivered and waiting for them on their return to Skeppiehill Farm.

The catering firm was first class. Conan had spared no expense and the drinks flowed freely. He knew most of the members of his own family would enjoy the evening with or without the beer and spirits, but he and Nick had seen more of the outside world and they had agreed that most of the younger men would enjoy free beer. What neither of them had anticipated was the amount of wine that Gerda and two of her companions would imbibe. The young men flocked around her, seeking every opportunity to hold her close, whether the dance was frenzied rock'n'roll or an old-fashioned waltz.

Soon after the bride and groom had departed, Bridie gathered up the tired twins and a reluctant Max.

'Och, young Max, we workers must go home to bed,' Chris told him, smiling. 'Adam and I must leave now if we are to be up in time to milk Don's cows in the morning.'

'But Dad's not coming home yet . . .'

'He's helping Uncle Conan serve the drinks and that's no place for youngsters like you, young man,' Bridie told him firmly.

Ross and Rachel, along with Mr and Mrs Greig, retired to the relative quiet of Fiona's lounge for a friendly chat, leaving the younger guests to dance the night away.

Eventually the caterers departed, leaving Nick to take one more tray of drinks to a noisy group at the far end of the marquee. Ewan, leaning against a tree near the entrance, reached out and lifted one of the glasses, drained it and reached for a second before Nick could pass on.

'Steady on, Ewan.' Nick frowned. 'You'll not know whether you're at the cow's head or its tail tomorrow morning. In fact,' he drew up his arm and peered at his watch, 'it is morning! No wonder your mother and father and Don's parents have all left.'

'Piss me 'nother.' Ewan slurred and lurched toward the tray.

'I think you've had enough. It's that wife of yours who is keeping the party going. You'll have to get her home. Mind you, she's no more fit to drive than you are. If you wait until I've taken this tray of drinks to that noisy bunch, I'll drive you home.'

'Doan wanna go h–home,' he hiccuped. 'Ger me 'nother.' He blinked foolishly at Nick.

'There's talking nonsense you are!' Nick said, consternation accentuating his Welsh accent. 'Drunk you are, Ewan. I will be getting the pair of you home right now.' Nick hurried away and found Conan in the kitchen brewing some coffee.

'There's young Ewan out there. Needing some of that, he is. Drunk and miserable, poor devil.'

'Bad as that?' Conan raised his brows.

'There's home I'm taking him,' Nick said grimly. 'That wife of his too.'

'Watch her then, Nick. The way she's carrying on tonight, she reminds me of some of the worst women who used to hang about the RAF camps.'

'Mmm, taken her jacket off she has for the dancing. Not much left to cover her. Her dress now, up it is where it should be down, and down where it should be up. No wonder, is it, our Ewan is drunk.'

'They could stay here for the night,' Conan said. 'We've plenty of room.'

'Better if I get them home,' Nick said darkly and hurried

away to get his car. He had no difficulty persuading Ewan to drink the coffee. He kept a firm hold of his elbow though to guide him in the direction of the car. Once he was safely in the back seat he went to fetch Gerda. She was enjoying herself in a wine-induced haze.

'Time you were going home, it is,' Nick said loudly in her ear. Some of her fellow dancers fell back a little.

'Go 'way.' Gerda brushed a hand at him as though he was a persistent fly. Nick was tired, and more than a little concerned for Ewan in his present state.

'There's leaving we are. Now.' Nick grasped Gerda's arm but she began to struggle, wriggling her hips as though going on with the dance. Irritably Nick waved to the band, indicating it was time to stop. 'Past midnight, it is, boys. There's coffee for you, and food, in the kitchen up at the house. You'll find Mr Maxwell there.' The band began to pack up. Gerda swore loudly and crudely at Nick.

'It's time we were all going home,' one of the men announced peaceably.

'Wish I was going home with you,' another one told Gerda drunkenly. She reached out an arm towards him but Nick caught her and held out the small bolero jacket that matched her tangerine dress and almost made it decent.

'Put this on. There's cold it is out there now.' Gerda shrugged it away.

'Please yourself,' Nick muttered grimly. He had never liked Gerda and tonight he almost hated her. He grasped her arm none too gently and half led, half dragged her to the car, ignoring her foul language and drunken hiccups. He pushed her in beside Ewan.

It was Nick who unlocked the cottage door and helped Ewan inside, before hustling Gerda after him. He gave her no time to protest or try out a drunken flirtation, something he dreaded more than her filthy temper.

It was cool inside the cottage and Ewan sobered up enough to throw off his jacket and help Gerda up the stairs. Automatically he washed his face, cleaned his teeth and drank a glass of water, unaware of his actions. Back in the bedroom

Gerda lay sprawled across the bed, singing tunelessly. He helped her undress, feeling all the thwarted passions of the day rising in him as her naked flesh was displayed. She made no effort to cover herself.

Astonishingly she responded with a desire that more than matched his own. In truth Gerda was as intoxicated by the admiration she had received during the evening as she was by the copious quantities of wine she had drunk. She didn't know, or care, whether she was making love with her husband, or any one of the young men who had been so eager to partner her. Neither did she raise any objections to Ewan's almost insatiable desire. In fact, she seemed more than ready to meet passion with passion.

A few days after the wedding, Bridie called in at Wester Rullion to have a chat. The children were enjoying the summer holidays and they had accompanied her, eager to see Ewan and follow him around as he worked.

'Nick said Ewan got a bit worse for wear after we left the wedding reception.' Bridie grinned. 'Has he quite recovered?'

'He has now,' Ross said darkly, 'but he missed the milking on Sunday morning. Peter went to call on him when he didn't turn up but he couldn't even make them hear.'

'We didn't see him until four o' clock on Sunday afternoon,' Rachel said, 'and he still looked dreadful. I'm surprised at Conan supplying so much drink,' she added reproachfully, 'especially now beer has gone up to two and a penny a pint.'

'Oh, Mum!' Bridie chided. 'Conan was doing his best to be the perfect host. He would expect his guests to know when they had had enough. I thought Fiona made a super job of organizing it all. I was quite sorry I had to leave so early but Alicia and Margaret were really tired – not that they would admit it, of course.'

'Children never do.' Rachel smiled.

'I had a grand talk with Chris's boyfriend, Adam Green,' Bridie said. 'He seems really keen on cattle and he knows a lot about the Friesian pedigrees. The four heifer calves he's bought are really well bred. Their pedigrees all go back to Adema 88. One of them is out of a first-class cow too. I told him I wouldn't mind buying a bull calf out of her. He seemed surprised. It's a shame he can't get a farm of his own.'

'Well his own parents aren't farmers and they have no money to help him get a foot on the ladder,' Ross said. 'I had a good talk with him and Chris, too. They deserve encouragement. Ewan and I would buy a half share with you if he breeds a decent stock bull, Bridie. You never know where he and Chris will end up if the right opportunity comes along. They're both prepared to work hard.'

'Yes, but Chris says her father would never help them,' Rachel said. 'He only considers his sons, apparently. I thought he seemed quite intolerant where Chris is concerned. He even disapproved of her bringing Adam to the wedding.'

'I got the impression he favours his youngest son. Jake, isn't it?' Ross frowned. 'He seems to have made up his mind that he's the one who will get Home Farm eventually. That wouldn't be so bad, but he doesn't seem to treat Don very fairly. Apparently Mr Greig deals quite a bit at local markets and he's started sending cows and heifers to Don's place if he hasn't a buyer waiting, but all the pedigree cows are at Home Farm and he leaves Don with the ones he doesn't want.'

'But I thought it was Don who was most interested in the breeding and the pedigrees when he was at home?' Bridie said.

'So I believe, and it was Don who did the milking and started grading up their own cows to pedigrees. When I mentioned that, Mr Greig just shrugged and said Don's day would come soon enough but he'd need to work for it. Meanwhile he's the boss and he'll make the decisions, he said.'

'Don couldn't work much harder from the sound of things!' Bridie said indignantly.

'No–o,' Ross said slowly, 'he'll not have an easy time. It's not much fun being landed with half a dozen extra heifers to milk without warning. By the time he's got them nicely quietened and settled down to milking, his father takes them off to another market to sell them on at a profit.'

'Oh! I'd hate that!' Bride said vehemently.

'Mmm. I gather Don doesn't like it much either, and it's only since they got Skeppiehill Farm that Mr Greig has dealt much in dairy cattle. Before that he just bought and sold sheep and a few bullocks.'

'It sounds as though Don and Lucy will have a hard time dealing with Mr Greig,' Rachel said. 'But I do like Mrs Greig. I think she'll do her best to see Don and Lucy get fair treatment.'

'I wonder what they'll all say when they see Fiona's wedding gift.' Bridie chuckled. 'I'll bet Mr Greig says it's a waste of money.'

'It's really generous of Fiona, and such a thoughtful gift too.' Rachel said warmly. 'Lucy loves her music and it would be such a pity to let all her hard work go to waste, especially if she has a family and has to give up teaching.'

'Aye.' Ross smiled. 'Fiona is a wise lassie. I wouldn't mind betting she's looking to the future. Lucy and Don may have a struggle while Mr Greig insists on controlling all the purse strings and treating Don like a labourer.'

'You think that's the reason for her choice of gift?' Bridie asked, puzzled.

'Oh, I'm sure she bought it because she knows how much pleasure Lucy gets from her music – and the lassie couldn't have afforded to buy a piano of her own, even a second-hand one. But she is qualified to teach piano and it crossed my mind she may be able to take a few pupils for lessons if she needs a bit of spare cash. I'd be surprised if Fiona isn't thinking along those lines.'

'A–ah, I see now.' Bridie nodded. 'Good old Fiona. Either way, I'm certain it is a gift Lucy will appreciate for life. She just loves her music.' She stood up and stretched. 'Well I'd better see what my offspring are up to. I have a feeling they will be telling Ewan we're going to beat him at the show next week. It doesn't seem like a year since he won the championship, does it?'

'No.' Rachel sighed. 'Time goes so fast these days, or seems to.'

'He hasn't had much time to prepare the cows for the show this year,' Ross said with a slight frown. 'I think I must be getting old or I'd have given him more help.'

'Oh, you can't blame yourself, Ross,' Rachel said quickly. 'Ewan has had Gerda to consider this year. But at least they seem happier and more settled since Lucy's wedding.'

'I expect Gerda is enjoying the school holidays too,' Bridie said. 'It is a pity she hasn't any interest in the farm. I'm sure they would have been happier working together.'

'Not everyone is as lucky as you and Nick, or me and your father.' Rachel smiled. 'But I must say it's a relief to see Gerda more content. I thought her father might have come down to stay for a little while, but they don't seem to keep in touch very often.'

Ewan also felt more relaxed and happy. Gerda was less restless, and she had not been on any more shopping frenzies since Lucy's wedding. He had no idea she had already committed her salary, as well as his wages, to various hire purchase agreements. Even her wedding outfit was to be paid off over the next six months.

Money, or lack of it, was not the only reason Gerda stayed at home. She felt content and relaxed for the first time in her life. She even pottered in the garden and experimented with her new cooker.

Even when Bridie won the championship at the Dumfries Show and Ewan did not even get reserve, Gerda felt none of her usual jealous spite. She smiled serenely at everyone. The twins responded by taking her hands and leading her off to see their favourite ice-cream van. She rather enjoyed being introduced as the young Mrs Maxwell of Wester

Rullion, and it was easy to be gracious when the men offered extravagant compliments about her appearance while the women viewed her slim figure and long blonde hair with envy.

Even when the long summer holidays were over and Gerda had to return to work, she did not resume her usual grumbling as Ewan had anticipated. He was delighted and went out of his way to help with household tasks whenever he could. Long days at the harvest meant this was not always possible, but Gerda remained placid.

It was a particularly cold day at the beginning of October and Gerda decided to put on a pair of warm trousers for her Saturday shopping trip into Dumfries. She had never got used to having her groceries and butcher meat delivered by the vans that came round all the farms. Gerda's one concession was to patronize the baker's van, which came round three times a week with fresh bread and scones and cakes. Recently she had developed a craving for fish and Mrs Smith was delighted to get it for her from the van, which called on Wednesdays, bringing fresh fish all the way from the east coast.

As Gerda tried unsuccessfully to fasten the waistband of her trousers that October morning, she was dismayed to find that she had put on weight since she last wore them in the spring.

'It's eating so much fish!' she wailed at Ewan, who was just finishing his breakfast. 'I've put on so much weight I can't fasten the waistband.'

'You look as lovely as ever to me,' Ewan reassured her, and he meant it. It was true Gerda did enjoy better meals these days, but she seemed so much happier and contented that Ewan didn't care if she put on weight. She still had plenty of curves to satisfy him. He grinned wickedly at her.

'Do you want me to help you dress?' he asked.

'That's all you think about, Ewan Maxwell.' She pouted prettily. 'How is it you're not rushing back to the farm this morning?'

'I'm going soon, but the rush is over for now. The harvest is all in and we haven't started the turnips yet. Anyway, I've already milked a hundred cows while you were getting your beauty sleep.'

'I must be eating too much,' Gerda muttered, returning her attention to the offending trousers. I'll go and change into a winter skirt.'

'It's not that cold,' Ewan told her. 'This is just a crisp autumn morning. The sun will get out soon and it will probably be hot by afternoon.'

'I shall be back by then and I can change into something cooler if it is.'

But Gerda soon discovered she couldn't button any of the skirts she had worn the previous winter. She had been eating more lately, and enjoying her food too, but she didn't want to get fat! Anyway, she couldn't afford new clothes. Her heart sank at the thought of all the money she owed to various firms. She would never dare to tell Ewan. She sensed his shadow in the bedroom doorway and turned to face him, still struggling with the button of her skirt.

'Don't look so distressed, Gerda,' he said softly. 'It's not the end of the world if you've put on a bit of weight. I love you like this.' He moved closer and ran his hand down the length of her body, drawing her closer. 'And I like you better still without your skirt, or any other clothes, come to that,' he said huskily, beginning to remove her blouse.

'It's not often you have time for this so early in the day.' She laughed throatily. 'You'll have to wait a second while I go to the bathroom. Must take my usual precautions, you know. . .' She broke off, staring at Ewan, her eyes wide with shock.

'Gerda! What's wrong? Are you ill?' He moved to draw her close again but she shrank away and sat down on the edge of the bed. Her face had drained of colour.

'It can't be,' she whispered faintly. 'I can't . . . I always . . .'

'Gerda! What is it? What's wrong? Tell me!'

Her eyes narrowed and she stared at him, but her mind was calculating dates. Suddenly she jumped up.

'I don't want a baby!' she screamed. 'I never, never want a baby! I won't have it! I tell you, I—'

'Gerda!' Ewan caught her flailing arms and sat her down again on the side of the bed. He turned her towards him. 'What's wrong? What are you trying to say?'

'It must be a baby! Don't you see? I haven't . . . I haven't had . . .' She began to cry. Tears rolled down her pale cheeks and sobs shook her body.

'Do you think you are having a baby, Gerda?' Ewan asked softly, incredulously, and there was no doubting the hope and happiness in his voice. Gerda stopped crying and stared at him.

'It's your fault!' she screamed. 'I told you I didn't want a bloody baby! Not now! Not ever! It's all your f–fault!' She began beating his chest with small clenched fists.

'Well if you are expecting a child, I should hope it is mine!' Ewan said, trying hard to stop the smile that wanted to stretch his mouth across his face. He felt a bubble of happiness inside him. Gerda had told him she didn't want a child but he had always hoped she would change her mind some day. She had asked the doctor for a birth-control pill and he had sent her to a family planning clinic, but after her first visit she had changed her mind about the pill. She had said there were other precautions she could use and she would see to it that there were no babies.

'Are you sure, Gerda? Are you expecting a child?'

'I d–don't know . . .' She had stopped fighting and screaming now and she flopped against him, her head under his chin. He could smell the scent of her silky hair. 'Oh, Ewan, I d–don't want a baby. I never want a baby. It's horrible. The thought of it makes me feel ill.' She grimaced and clung to him. Then she pushed him away, staring wildly into his face. 'I shall get rid of it. You can, you know. People do . . .'

106

'No, Gerda! No, you can't think of such a thing! Anyway, we don't know for sure. You must see the doctor.'

'I won't have it! I will not have a baby!' she screeched through gritted teeth. She began to pull clothes from the wardrobe, flinging them over the bed, the chair, the floor. 'See! Nothing fits me! Already I'm fat. Babies make you fat and ugly and horrible.'

She began to sob but when Ewan tried to take her in his arms and comfort her, she threw the hairbrush at him and picked up a glass scent spray. 'Get out! Leave me alone! This is all your fault. Get out!'

She threw the heavy glass bottle, but Ewan ducked in time and closed the door behind him. He was deeply troubled. If Gerda *was* expecting a child, surely such emotion couldn't be good for her. He went slowly downstairs. Supposing it was not a baby? What if it was something terrible? Almost without being aware, Ewan pulled on his wellington boots and made his way to the farmhouse to see his parents. His mother would know what to do to calm Gerda. Surely she would be able to help her.

Rachel listened attentively to Ewan's garbled account.

'I expect it's the shock if Gerda thought she couldn't have a baby . . .'

'It's not that she couldn't. She d–d . . .'

'Well for whatever reason, it seems to be a shock to her,' Rachel soothed. 'Would you like me to go down and talk to her? She may be wrong after all. But that could account for her appetite, her new serenity, and—'

'Serenity! She's anything but serene, Mother. She's talking of getting rid of it, if it is a baby . . .'

There was a catch in Ewan's voice and Rachel found herself wanting to hug and comfort him as she did when he was a little boy, but it was his wife who needed the comfort and support right now. 'You wait here,' she told him. 'Make yourself a cup of tea to steady you. I'll bring Gerda back with me if I can persuade her.' She pulled on a cardigan and set off down to the cottages. It was not far if she cut through the orchard and the small paddock, but by the time Rachel

107

got to the lane she saw the tail lights of Gerda's little car speeding away from her amidst a screech of tyres and a cloud of dust. Her heart sank.

'Please God, don't let her do anything foolish!' she prayed.

Ten

Gerda returned from town filled with anger and deep dismay. She blamed the doctor, she blamed Ewan, she even blamed his parents. She convinced herself that they wanted a grandchild, that they had wished this horrible fate upon her. Furiously she bought new winter clothes, running up her account to the limit in Binns before moving down to Buccleuch Street. She had long desired a fur coat. She was oblivious to the cost now. She had already opened an account in Barbours, one of the most expensive shops in town, but now she didn't care who would have to pay the bill. It would certainly not be her.

She knew Ewan and his family, especially Bridie and her mother, disapproved of running up accounts. Ewan had flatly refused to get one of the new American Express credit cards. He said he didn't earn the two thousand pounds a year you had to have before you could get one.

'You could tell them you do,' she had pleaded but he just shook his head emphatically.

Now she felt an odd feeling of triumph as she swirled in front of the long mirrors and drank in the well-dressed sales assistant's lavish compliments. The woman was experienced and knew exactly which customers could be influenced by insincere flattery. Moreover, she had heard of the Maxwells of Wester Rullion. Her brother-in-law had a small farm and she had heard him speak highly of them. Even so, she was taken aback when Gerda asked if she might try on the mink coat that had arrived that very week. The squirrel fur at four hundred pounds was expensive, but there was a world of difference between that and a mink. You could buy a house for that money.

'It is the only one we have had in. It is very expensive, madam,' the sales assistant murmured. She knew farm workers earned about ten pounds a week and she resolved to quiz her brother-in-law about the Maxwells. They must be very wealthy landowners.

'Yes, I know,' Gerda agreed. Suddenly she knew how she would use her hateful condition to her advantage. She leaned towards the woman conspiratorially. 'My husband is hoping for a son and heir,' she whispered, and patted her flat stomach. 'He is so delighted he would buy me the moon.'

'Then madam must certainly try the mink. It's two thousand, one hundred and ninety pounds, and ten shillings.'

Gerda winced inwardly but she heard the awe in the woman's tone, and saw the way she stroked the sleeve so lovingly. Having tried the coat she knew it was what she coveted more than anything else. What was to stop Ewan selling a bull to pay for it, she thought defiantly. God knows he had plenty of them. She thought defiantly of Bridie and Mrs Maxwell. Neither of them spent a lot of money on clothes. Their maxim was that if you couldn't afford a new dress, you made the old one do. Well, they all deserved to suffer, she decided resentfully.

'Perhaps madam would like a new hat to go with it? And we have a lovely calfskin handbag at fifty pounds. It would go perfectly with the mink,' the woman purred. Gerda readily agreed.

On the way home she argued her case for her wild spending spree. So what if she had run up a huge debt? Ewan deserved to suffer. Nothing could be as bad as her suffering, the humiliation of her slender waist expanding, the gross bulge that would distort her slim figure – not to mention the pain and degradation of giving birth. She shuddered with horror at this last prospect and almost drove into a ditch.

In the weeks that followed, nothing Ewan could say or do could make Gerda see reason. In desperation he sought Rachel's advice, thinking she might understand the ways of pregnant women. Rachel did her best to convince Gerda there was nothing to worry about, but her sudden outbursts, her foul language and uncontrollable temper surprised and dismayed her.

'Dear child, please try to be calm,' she said in consternation. 'You'll harm yourself, and your bairn.'

'I don't give a damn! I wish it was dead. The doctor refused to get rid of it . . .'

'Then think of your own health.'

'What the hell does that matter? I shall be ugly and fat and . . . and . . .'

'Of course you won't. As soon as the baby is born you will soon—'

'Shut up! Don't talk about it!' Gerda screamed and clamped her hands over her ears like a child. 'Why don't you go and tell Conan and his precious Fiona that you want another generation of Maxwells! That's all you're bothered about! That and whether we have another war and your darling boys have to go!'

'Well the world is rather a troubled place just now,' Rachel agreed. It was true she had mentioned her fears to Ewan when the Indonesian troops had invaded Malaya. A state of emergency had been declared. Britain, New Zealand and Australia had all agreed more defence and economic aid must be provided. 'Now there is all this trouble in Vietnam,' she said, speaking her thoughts aloud, hoping to channel Gerda's attention away from her own concerns. 'President Johnson declared that "the world must never forget that aggression unchallenged is aggression unleashed." I think it is a warning that war will follow.' Rachel trembled at the thought. She remembered the shock and devastation of the last war. 'If Russia and America go to war, the Americans would expect Britain to help, and people like Nick and Conan would all be required to sacrifice their lives once again.'

'Well, if people like me weren't forced to have babies there wouldn't be any people to fight!' Gerda shouted unreasonably. Rachel sighed. It was clear Gerda could think of nothing but herself.

111

'But you are keeping in good health, dear, aren't you?'

'What do you care about my health? All you're interested in is another Maxwell to carry on farming your bloody land! Get out! Get out!' she screamed.

Deeply troubled by such hysteria, Rachel left the cottage. That evening she sat down and wrote to Gerda's father, expressing her concern for his daughter's health and for their unborn grandchild. She pleaded with him to come and visit Gerda.

I will do anything I can to help, she wrote, *but Gerda will not confide in me. Perhaps she is frightened. Perhaps you can make her understand that childbirth is perfectly natural, and infinitely safer than it used to be. Please come if you can help her.*

John Allan wrote by return, thanking her but declining her offer of hospitality. He feared his presence would aggravate Gerda even further and Rachel's heart sank as she read the letter.

'He says her mother reacted in just the same way,' she told Ross. 'He says she was the most unnatural mother he ever knew, even after the baby was born. She never wanted to look after her. He says she seemed incapable of loving her. Poor Gerda. No wonder she is so distraught and so...so...'

'Selfish!' Ross finished the sentence curtly. 'Don't waste your sympathy on her, and don't you be worrying about her.' He had little patience with Gerda's histrionics. As far as her health was concerned she looked better than she had ever looked – positively blooming in fact if it were not for the sullen droop of her mouth. 'Let me see the letter.' He took it gently from Rachel's fingers and read on. 'A—ah.' He expelled a long breath. 'Even her own father is advising Ewan not to give in to her demands. He says that whatever he did, it didn't make her mother any more human. She just made more and more demands ... Poor Ewan! I fear he's married a siren if Gerda takes after her mother, and it sounds as though she does. He's already given in to her over—' Ross bit back his words, frowning. He hadn't meant to tell Rachel yet. He didn't want to worry or upset her.

'Given in over what?' she asked. 'He has to humour her at a time like this,' she reasoned anxiously. 'Surely you agree . . .'

'Not to the tune of paying nearly three thousand pounds for the debts she's run up – and all that on top of the money we gave them for the house. Ach, Rachel, I didn't mean to tell you so bluntly, but you would have had to know eventually. She hasn't spent all that money because of the baby. She hasn't known about it very long . . .' He turned to face his wife and saw Rachel's face had drained of colour.

'Three thousand pounds?' she whispered hoarsely. 'B–but I d–don't understand. She hasn't bought anything for the baby yet. I mean a cot, or pram, or . . . or anything.' She sat down heavily. 'Three thousand pounds!' It was three times as much as she spent on herself and Ross and keeping house in a whole year. 'That's far, far more than Peter earns in a year . . .'

'I know, I know.' Ross sighed. 'I didn't mean to blurt it out. Ewan was forced to tell me. It seems they've had letters threatening to send in the bailiffs.'

'What! B–but how? When?' Suddenly Rachel bowed her head and clasped her hands to her temples. She felt sick and dizzy. How could Gerda and Ewan have got into such debt? Ross had been more than generous. And Gerda had had her teacher's salary until recently. How would they manage without it? She had blamed Ewan because she'd had to give up her career. Even without her job she didn't do any of her own housework or cooking. She had employed Mrs Smith to go into the cottage three days a week and Ewan had to pay her wages. And now this . . .

'Please, Rachel, drink this . . .' Ross was kneeling beside her, holding a glass of water. His face, so close to her own, was filled with love and concern.

'B–but what shall w–we do?' she asked hoarsely. 'It's such a lot of money!'

'I've drawn it out of the money I was saving for our old age,' Ross admitted. He shrugged helplessly. 'I told Ewan I must tell you. He understands it must never happen again.

It *can't* happen again. But I don't think he knows how to deal with Gerda in her present state. He's thrilled to bits about the baby himself. I suppose that makes him more tolerant with her. He say's he'll repay us, but I can't think how . . .'

'We'll manage, dear.' Rachel reached up and stroked Ross's cheek. 'We're both in good health and so long as we have each other, we'll manage.'

'I know,' Ross said huskily. 'So long as we have each other,' he repeated. He shivered suddenly, looking down into Rachel's pale face. 'I couldn't live if anything happened to you, my love. We've been so lucky . . .'

'I know, I know. We'll get by.' Rachel got to her feet, but she felt suddenly old, old and very tired. Deep in her heart she know this was not the end of the problems Gerda would bring to them, and to their family.

The contrast between Lucy's new life and Gerda's could not have been greater. Don worked hard and without complaint, but his father's promise made their labours seem worthwhile. One day Skeppiehill Farm would be his, and the stock would be of his own choosing – fine pedigree cattle and a small flock of sheep for breeding. Stockmanship was Don's great strength and sometimes Lucy felt he ought to have been a vet.

'You seem to have an instinct, a sort of sixth sense where animals are concerned,' she told him. 'You sense they are falling sick almost before they do.'

'That's just regular observation.' Don grinned. 'I'm pretty certain Bridie and your grandfather have it too. Most farmers only call in the vet when the animals are already sick, so my sixth sense, as you call it, wouldn't have been much good. Anyway, farming is what I love, and what I've always wanted to do.' He hugged her. 'And I'm the luckiest man in the world to have a wife like you,' he said softly.

Lucy fed the calves and hens each morning before she set out for school, and she frequently helped him with the milking when she returned in the afternoon, especially during hay and harvest times when Don worked from dawn to dusk to get the crops safely in. Usually his father sent one of his brothers and a hired man over to help at such times, and Lucy made meals for them too. She often blessed the modern appliances that made her life so much easier. She clearly remembered the wash house and boiler at Glens of Lochandee where she and Ewan had helped to turn the mangle to ring out the clothes when they were children. Bridie telephoned occasionally for a chat and Lucy often expressed her appreciation to her, and to her grandparents, for the washing machine and the deep freeze.

As for the piano, it was pure luxury. Something she could never have afforded or justified to Don's father. It brought her the greatest pleasure. Time was precious but each evening before they went to bed she usually played for a little while, feeling the tensions of the day seeping away as she wove the magic of her music. Often Don would wash and prepare for bed then creep into the room and sit in the big armchair, sipping his glass of cool milk and listening contentedly. Sometimes he would request some of his favourite melodies. Greig's 'Morning' from *Peer Gynt*, and the tune he called 'The Trout' were two of his regular requests, but mostly he was content to just listen as the music rippled like a soothing balm, quieting his fretful thoughts and calming the stresses of his day, as it did her own.

It was Fiona who passed on the news that Gerda had given up her teaching job and was expecting a baby.

'I believe Ewan is having problems trying to keep her calm, but Conan says he's privately elated with the news.'

'Oh, I'm sure he must be,' Lucy said joyfully. 'Do please pass on our congratulations. Gerda always said she would never have a baby when we were at college, but I'm so glad she has changed her mind. She knew far more about birth control than any of the rest of us.' She chuckled. 'She always said she would take the contraceptive pill if she ever got married. I'm a bit surprised she changed her mind so soon, but I don't think she really enjoyed teaching.'

'Mmm, I don't know about that,' Fiona said dubiously.

'Apparently the baby is due about March. Nick has a theory that it happened after your wedding. He drove them both home that night because they were so drunk.'

'Oh well, so long as they don't blame us.' Lucy laughed, then more seriously said, 'I'm sure it will be for the best. Gerda will have a baby to love and care for instead of thinking so much about herself and how she looks and what she should wear.'

'I hope you're right, for Ewan's sake. Some people don't know how lucky they are.' Lucy heard the wistful note in Fiona's voice and changed the subject. She knew the greatest disappointment in Fiona's life was that she had been unable to give Conan a son, but it didn't seem to trouble him. More than once Lucy had heard him say what a disappointment he had been to his own father because he hadn't wanted to follow in his footsteps.

'If we'd had a son he would probably have wanted to be a farmer, and follow in my parents' footsteps instead of mine!' He chuckled. 'Then I'd have been as disappointed as my father was.'

Fiona had enough sense to know this was perfectly true but she still regretted her childless state. Lucy understood now that she was married herself. She longed for children of her own, certainly more than one. Although she had been an only child, she'd had Ewan as her constant companion and she had never been lonely. Even now she regarded him as a dearly loved brother. Fiona had been an only child too and she had once confided that she had often been lonely. As always when Lucy thought about children she worried about giving up her work. She earned considerably more than the allowance that Don's father paid them and she wondered whether he would increase it if she gave up teaching to care for a family.

She had mentioned this to Chris during one of their discussions.

'I wouldn't bet on it,' she had answered darkly. 'All Father thinks about is our Jake and Will and a farm for them. He was always harder on Don and me.'

Lucy and Chris had become even closer friends now that they were sisters-in-law, but it made Lucy uncomfortable when Chris spoke bitterly of her father. They were barely on speaking terms these days. He disapproved strongly of her friendship with Adam Green and it made Chris all the more determined to support Adam in whatever he decided to do. She loved him and she willed him to be a success, if only to prove her father wrong.

'We had an awful argument,' she confided on one of her visits to Lucy and Don. 'Father was ranting on, telling me I shall never be anything but the wife of a farm labourer with Adam. I told him that Adam is a well-respected stockman and that he earns twice as much as the pitiful allowance he pays Don. And that's only for looking after a dairy herd, not for having the responsibility of a whole farm, as Don does. Of course Father blustered furiously, saying Don has to make sacrifices now if he wants to farm on his own in the future.'

'Oh, Chris, you shouldn't quarrel with your father on our behalf,' Lucy said. 'Your mother is very kind . . .'

'I know she is. She feels as bad as I do that Don works so hard and gets so little to keep for himself. I don't see our Jake economizing much, and he has girlfriends galore. He's ruined! And Willie is nearly as bad now that Don and I have left home. At least I'm working for myself, but Don is working to support them!'

'Never mind, lass,' Don placated. 'We'll get by, you and Adam, Lucy and me. How about the four of us meeting up for the Christmas Eve dance in Ayr?' Don had turned Chris's thoughts away from their father and they all looked forward to the dance.

'I shall really miss all the family on Christmas Day,' Lucy sighed. 'We always had a family gathering. Mind you, I think Bridie will be making it this year. My grandparents are not getting any younger and I think Gerda makes their life more difficult with all her moans – at least that's what Nick says. Your mother has invited us to Home Farm for Christmas dinner. Will you be there, Chris?'

'Nope.' Chris pursed her lips into a determined line. There

was an unforgiving expression on her pleasant face. 'Adam's not invited so I'm not going either.'

'Come and join us on Boxing Day then,' Lucy urged. 'Fiona and Conan are coming up if the weather is OK. I think they might bring Max and the twins too. Max is longing to see round the farm with Don, and Alicia and Margaret always like an outing. I'm really looking forward to making little parcels for them to open.'

'That's because you're so good with children, Lucy,' Chris said warmly. 'But we'd love to come. Wouldn't we, Adam?'

'Yes, so long as you understand we'll have to be back for the milking.'

'That's all right. Don will have to milk anyway. I know the cows don't just dry up for Christmas, Adam.' She chuckled.

'Aye, well that's more than some of Chris's fellow teachers realize,' Adam said with a wry smile. 'They think I'm mad, getting up at five o'clock every morning, but I was forgetting you spent most of your childhood at Glens of Lochandee.'

'I did, and I loved it there.'

'Aye, and she can milk cows with the best o' folk,' Don said proudly.

'I expect that's why you and Chris get on so well.' Adam smiled at Lucy. 'You share the same interests.'

'Yes.' Lucy nodded gravely. 'We do. I can't help wondering whether Ewan and Gerda will ever develop interests in common. I think she's leading him an awful dance now that she's expecting a child.'

'He was a fool to marry her,' Don said with feeling. 'It was so out of character for Ewan, but he seems to have a blind spot where Gerda is concerned.'

The onset of morning sickness one February morning alerted Lucy to the fact that she was expecting a child. In spite of the discomfort and inconvenience, she and Don were delighted at the prospect, but they resolved to keep their secret to themselves as long as possible.

During the cold weather Gerda treated herself more than

118

ever as an invalid, often spending most of the day in bed, or lying on the sofa watching the new colour television she had bought. The result was a large baby, and coupled with her hysteria at the slightest pain, her labour was long and difficult, culminating in an operation to save the baby.

Ewan gave Gerda all his sympathy. He was delighted and deeply moved by the sight of his baby son when he first saw him through the glass panel in the hospital's special-care unit.

'He's a sturdy wee fellow,' the doctor assured him. 'We're just making sure he's all right but we'll have him out of here in no time. Your wife . . .' The doctor hesitated, frowning, choosing his words with care. 'She has not seen him yet. She . . . er . . . she says she doesn't want to see him. It does happen sometimes after a traumatic birth, but . . . well, we would like to be sure there will be someone to keep a close eye on both mother and child when she gets home. Of course, that will not be for about ten to fourteen days and hopefully her natural mother's instinct will have overcome the experience of giving birth by then, especially when she holds him in her arms.'

'Y–yes, I'm sure it will,' Ewan said uncertainly. How could he tell this kindly doctor that Gerda had made up her mind she didn't want anything to do with the baby? She was adamant that she would not feed him herself. But in spite of his worries over Gerda, Ewan was filled with pride and deep satisfaction at being a father. 'We have a very good neighbour who helps my wife around the house,' he assured the doctor, 'and my parents live near too, if we need any advice.'

The doctor nodded and looked relieved. He had heard of mothers who refused to care for their own babies but he had not yet experienced such a situation himself. He observed Ewan carefully. He was young to have the responsibility of a wife and baby but at least he seemed happy about his new status.

At first Gerda refused to talk about the baby, but when the nurses kept asking if she had chosen a name for him she suddenly gave them the first thing that came into her head.

119

That evening when Ewan visited, she told him the baby was to be called Ringo. He stared at her in disbelief.

'Ringo! What sort of a name is that to call my son?' he demanded angrily. Gerda's mouth formed the familiar sullen pout that he had come to expect.

'It's after a young man I saw on the television. He's in the Beatles.'

'You can't burden a child with a name like that.'

'Why not? It's different.'

'Of course it's different. Why can't we name him after your father, or my father – or both if you like?'

'No! I'm going to call him Ringo.'

'No son of mine will have a name like that,' Ewan said stubbornly and Gerda recognized the green glitter in his eyes. She knew he meant it. Suddenly she felt too tired to argue and her eyes filled with the tears which came all too readily.

'Choose one of the other names then,' Ewan said more gently, 'if you must have someone famous. What are they all called? Let's see, there's George, and John, and one called Paul . . . At least they are ordinary names. Or your own maiden name, Allan. Don't you like any of them? We shall have to arrange a christening at church and you will be able to wear your smart clothes again.' Ewan was learning how to channel Gerda's thoughts from divisive subjects. True enough, the tears dried and she brightened visibly at the thought of standing up in Lochandee Church before the congregation.

'Mmm . . .' She began to try out each of the names. 'Paul Maxwell sounds all right . . .'

'Yes, it sounds quite good,' Ewan agreed with a flash of relief and resolved to register the birth of his son without delay. In fact, unknown to Gerda he registered the baby as Paul Ross Maxwell and although she was annoyed at the change when he told her on the morning of the christening, she was too absorbed in grooming herself for the role of beautiful young mother to make a fuss. The gravity of the service and the vows she and Ewan made on behalf of their small son washed right over her head, but she accepted the adulation and admiring glances of the congregation as her right.

Afterwards the family gathered at Wester Rullion for a buffet lunch. Even Gerda's father had agreed to come down for the christening, bringing with him a lady friend whom Gerda had never met before. Daisy Wright was a plain, homely woman and did her best to fit in with everyone, but Gerda and her father were wary of each other and Rachel could only guess at the bitter quarrel which must have come between them.

'I don't think we shall be receiving any invitations to visit from Gerda,' he told Rachel wryly before he left. 'But I'd appreciate a wee bit o' news about the wee fellow when ye have a minute to drop a line.' He looked her in the eye and shook his head bravely. 'Dinna let her tak advantage o' your kind heart. The bairn is hers. She should be looking after him, but I can see for masel' that ye're more used tae him than she is.'

'I love him dearly already.' Rachel smiled, looking down at the infant in her arms. 'We both do. I'm just helping out until Gerda recovers her strength.'

'Aye, well that will be a guid while if she's like her mother,' he warned.

Shortly after she had eaten at the christening, Lucy had to make a dash for the bathroom. When she came out Gerda was waiting on the landing.

'I saw you hurrying upstairs,' she said. 'You're looking pale.' She eyed Lucy shrewdly. 'Sick, were you?'

'Just a bit of an upset,' Lucy said lightly. 'I'll be all right in a wee while. Don and I will have to be leaving soon to get back for the milking, but I'm glad we came. You have a lovely baby, Gerda. You must both be very proud of him.' Lucy was sincere but Gerda's pale eyes glittered angrily.

'He might be lovely but just look what he's done to me!' She glared down at herself in disgust.'

'But you're almost back to normal already, Gerda, and surely it was worth it to—'

'Worth it! Just you wait another few months. I guessed

that's what's wrong with you when I saw you rush to the bathroom, not that I ever had that bother. You'll soon look like an overblown balloon and—'

'But that's only for a few months and I'm sure it must be worth any discomfort to have a baby of one's own,' Lucy said.

'It's awful. It's degrading the things you have to suffer in hospital. Do you know what they—'

'I don't want to hear, Gerda,' Lucy interrupted firmly, seeing the malice on Gerda's face and knowing how much she would enjoy recounting all the worst aspects of giving birth. She pushed past her and ran down the stairs to join the others.

Gerda followed her and announced loudly, 'Lucy is going to have a baby!'

Silence fell on the room and everyone looked towards Lucy with Gerda behind her. Lucy's eyes sought Don's across the room and he hurried to her side, putting a protective arm around her shoulders.

'Thank goodness we told your parents,' he whispered softly, then he turned to face the room. 'It is true but we didn't want to steel the limelight from Gerda and Ewan,' he said smoothly. 'Now that you all know, I must say we are delighted and—'

'When, Lucy? When is it due?' Bridie asked excitedly.

'October.'

'Oh, I'm so pleased for you. You and Don will be super parents.'

'I'm pleased for you too, lassie,' Rachel said, giving Lucy a warm hug. 'But I hope you'll take care and not be working too hard . . .'

'She never said that to me,' Gerda muttered angrily to Ewan.

'She knew you did take care,' Ewan said. 'Lucy is further away and there's none of her own family near enough to help.'

'There was none of my family near me!'

'Lucy, Lucy.' The twins tugged at Lucy's hands. 'Can we come and stay in the holidays and help you nurse the baby?

We know how. We help Granny to look after baby Paul, and we rock his pram when he cries.'

'I'm sure I shall be pleased to have your help,' Lucy laughed, 'but we shall not have a baby for ages and ages yet.'

'How long is ages?' asked Alicia.

'Four months at least. That will be after your summer holidays. You will be back at school.'

'But we shall have a week in October for potato picking. We could come then,' Margaret insisted eagerly.

Bridie raised her eyes heavenward. 'We shall have to see how you two behave, and if you have learned to tidy your room by then,' she told her offspring, and received the usual groan in perfect unison as a reply.

Eleven

Ross was secretly delighted when he heard the baby was to take his name, albeit as a secondary name. Peter Forster rejoiced in the news that there would be another generation of Maxwells at Wester Rullion. He had long since decided he would never marry and have a family of his own. The Maxwells had befriended him when he most needed friends and, except for the kindly Mrs Forster, who had treated him as her own son, they were the dearest people in the world to him. So his pleasure in the birth of Ewan's son was sincere. The future of Wester Rullion was assured and he felt deeply satisfied and content with the world. But he rarely saw Gerda so he had no opportunity to express his congratulations in person.

As time passed Peter was surprised to see the baby spending several hours every day with his grandmother, and yet Gerda herself rarely came near the farm. He knew young Billy Smith had neither liking nor respect for her.

'She's a lazy bitch,' he confided to Peter, 'and she thinks she's Lady Muck the things she expects my ma to do. The extra money's useful though, since we bought the cottage, so Ma puts up wi' her queer ways. She drives into Dumfries most days as soon as Ewan brings the bairn up here to his granny. She reckons the bread and the groceries frae the travelling shops are too dear but Ma says it's just an excuse to gang gallivanting. It costs her more in petrol than the odd halfpenny on a loaf. When the bairn is at home Ma always has tae change his nappies. She washes them all tae. She says there's aye a stinking pile waiting for her tae clean after the weekend.' He wrinkled his freckled nose in disgust, then

124

he grinned his infectious, gap-toothed grin. Peter, who was intensely loyal to the Maxwells, instantly forgave him for telling tales. ''Tis a pity bairns are not born like wee calves wi' their clothes already on and just have to lift their tails when they want a pee!'

'We should all be as hairy as cavemen then,' Peter chuckled, 'and that young lady who works at Mr Conan's garage wouldn't fancy you like that,' he teased, laughing at the flare of colour in Billy's cheeks.

One Saturday afternoon a few weeks later, Peter had bathed and changed into his second-best suit, and was preparing to drive into Dumfries for a hair cut. He was surprised to see Gerda pushing the pram towards the farmhouse. The baby was propped against his pillow, chortling merrily to himself and waving his chubby fists at the world in general. Gerda seemed oblivious to his charms but Peter paused to speak, as he always did when he saw Mrs Maxwell pushing Paul in his pram. Paul recognized a familiar face and gave one of his wide, toothless smiles. Peter grinned down at him, pleased that the baby was beginning to remember him. He resolved to carve him a wooden tractor for Christmas, a sturdy toy on little wheels with a pull-along string.

'He's a lovely boy, Mrs Maxwell. I must congratulate you on producing such a fine son,' he said sincerely. Gerda would have walked on by but suddenly she stopped scowling and stared at Peter. She rarely saw him when he was clean-shaven and smart. His black wavy hair was thick and shining. He smiled at her and for the first time she noticed how white and even his teeth were against his tanned skin. Paul crowed and waved his fist and Peter turned to look down at him, poking him with a gentle finger. He loved children and animals. Recently he had acquired a collie pup of his own, which he hoped to train to work the cattle and sheep. But Gerda didn't want him to turn his attention to Paul; she wanted his admiration, even if he was only a worker. Gerda couldn't bear to be in the company of a man if he didn't give her all his attention.

'Are you going into town? I don't suppose I could beg a

lift? There's something wrong with my car and Ewan has gone off to one of the fields – something to do with getting ready for harvest. He wouldn't even take time to bring his own son to visit his grandparents,' she added in an aggrieved tone. There was nothing wrong with her car. It was a sudden whim that had made her ask for a lift from Peter, a determination to make him notice her.

Ewan had refused to waken baby Paul from his sleep just to bring him to his grandparents.

'Surely you can stay at home and look after him yourself for once,' he had said irritably. 'Mother has him far too often as it is. She's not getting any younger, and this hot weather tires her out. '

'She likes having him. It won't do any harm to waken him. I need to go to Dumfries.'

'No you don't, Gerda. You went yesterday, and the day before, and probably the day before that, for all I know. It's just become a habit.' Ewan had not even waited for her to agree. He simply strode away up the track to the fields, expecting her to do as he asked. Gerda scowled, remembering the set of his shoulders. Ewan was no longer a college boy – he was broadening out into manhood, strong and straight like his father – but he had no right to give her orders as though she was one of his workers. She would teach him a lesson and she would use Peter Forster to do it.

'Right then, Peter, I'll just dump the pram up at the farmhouse and call in to Mrs Maxwell. I'll be back in a second.'

'B–but I'm only going in to the barber's. I promised Ewan I'd be back to get the cows in for milking . . .'

'That's fine. You can drop me off at the bottom of Friars' Vennel and pick me up when you're ready,' she called over her shoulder, allowing him no opportunity to protest further.

It did not take Peter long to get his hair cut and buy the few things he needed. He was waiting on the Whitesands, impatient to get back to the farm as he had promised, but there was no sign of Gerda. She was deliberately testing his patience as well as Ewan's. If Peter was late back, Ewan would know she had been with him. She saw him sitting in his little Morris Minor, drumming his fingers on the steering wheel and frowning anxiously.

The windows were wide open and holidaymakers strolled along beside the River Nith, watching the water cascading over the salmon leap. Normally Peter would have enjoyed watching them, but today he felt tense and uneasy. He barely knew Ewan's wife. He had never been alone in her company before. Usually she scarcely passed the time of day when she saw him. So why was she being so different today? Surely it was not just because he had admired her baby . . .

'Here I am! Not too late, I think.' She leaned against him deliberately, drawing in her long legs slowly, taking time to smooth her skirt before she shut the car door. She turned to look at him.

'Mmm, the barber has certainly cut away your lovely curls,' she gurgled throatily, and to Peter's consternation she reached out and ran her fingers seductively through his hair, allowing her fingertips to trail down the side of his neck. He jerked away sharply.

'We're half an hour late,' he said shortly and started the car, driving away with several bumpy jerks. He cursed silently and felt the telltale pulse beating beneath his jaw. He prided himself on his driving. Gerda leaned forward to place a carrier bag on the floor between her feet, showing an expanse of thigh as her skimpy skirt wrinkled up. She made no effort to tug it into place, well aware that Peter had noticed, even though he was making a good show of keeping his eyes on the road.

Once they were out of town and cruising along the Lockerbie road she turned towards him, a smile hovering on her full red lips. He glanced at her and wondered if she had any idea how much more beautiful she looked when she lost her sullen pout. He could understand why Ewan had suffered such a fatal attraction.

Gerda laid a hand on his thigh. He almost swerved into the grass verge.

'Don't do that!' But she did not remove her hand. He brushed it away roughly.

127

'Why, I do believe you're shy, Peter,' she said softly and edged closer so that her shoulder touched his. 'Have you ever had a woman?' She blew gently, right into his ear. He shivered. He could smell her perfume and feel the soft brush of her hair. Her hand moved back to his thigh and this time her fingers splayed out, far too probing for Peter's comfort. He put his foot down on the accelerator and the little car shot forward, but she did not stop her searching fingers and he pushed her away.

'Yes, I've had women!' he told her coldly. 'They are two a penny. A wife is different. Or ought to be,' he added pointedly.'

'Being a wife doesn't mean I'm not still a women,' Gerda murmured. She lifted her hand to brush her fingertips over the newly cut hair at his temple. 'Being married has not changed me . . .'

'Then it should have done!' Peter said harshly, and knocked her hand away, none too gently.

'So what would you want in a wife then, Peter?' Gerda purred, undeterred by the grim set of his mouth and the frown that creased his brown forehead. She knew she was making him feel uncomfortable, disturbing him. She enjoyed teasing. He changed gear as they turned off the main road and he did not answer. Gerda persisted. 'Don't you want to get married? You're getting old,' she taunted.

'Old?' He glanced at her.

'Well you must be at least ten years older than Ewan.'

'Ewan is just a boy.' He snorted. 'He should be enjoying life, not tied down with a wife and children.'

'Tied down!' Gerda was indignant. 'I'm the one who is tied down. I'm the one who has had to bear his brat!'

'It was your choice. No one forced you to marry him.'

'So! You haven't told me what you want in a wife. I think I can guess, though. You'd want a woman who put your slippers to warm every night and did—'

'I can tell you what I wouldn't want in a wife,' Peter said fiercely. They were almost at the cottage now, he realized with relief. He turned to face her as he drew the car to a halt. 'I wouldn't want a slut for a wife, a woman who flirted with every man she met.'

'Why, you . . .' Gerda's pale eyes were like ice as she raised her hand. Peter pushed it down.

'I wouldn't if I were you,' he said quietly, and she saw the contempt in his eyes. Over Peter's shoulder she saw Ewan approaching, a look of surprise on his face at the sight of his wife in Peter's car. Her own car was still standing at the door of the cottage and he had thought she was inside looking after Paul. Suddenly Gerda leaned towards Peter and pressed her mouth to his, then she climbed out of the car.

'Thank you so much for a lovely afternoon, dear Peter,' she said loudly. Peter's eyes widened in shock and he brushed a hand angrily across his mouth. He was unprepared for the door opening on his own side, even less prepared to find Ewan's furious green eyes staring down at him. He knew at once Ewan had witnessed the kiss, knew too that that had been Gerda's intention.

'Sweet Jesu!' he muttered and brushed a hand across his eyes.

'What the hell do you think you're doing with my wife? Who asked you to take her out?'

'She did.' Peter felt at a disadvantage sitting in his car with Ewan standing over him. 'She said her car wouldn't start and—'

'Don't tell me lies! There's nothing wrong with her car. You're using that as an excuse to go jaunting with my wife. My wife! You—'

Peter pushed him away and clamoured out of the driver's seat. He stood straight, the same height as Ewan now. They faced each other. 'I'm talking to you man to man, Ewan,' he said quietly, 'not as your paid employee. If you can't control your wife then don't blame me. I didn't ask her to come with me today, or want her for that matter . . .'

'Oh no?' Ewan gave a harsh laugh. 'That's not what it looked like to me. What would you have done if I hadn't arrived, I wonder.'

'Possibly slapped her face,' Peter said evenly. He sighed

heavily. He had always got on well with Ewan, but in some ways he was still so young, even though he was now a husband and a father. 'I'd hate to see you hurt, Ewan. Surely you must know if I wanted a woman I could get one any Saturday night on the Whitesands in Dumfries.' He saw Ewan's eyes open wide and realized Ewan had probably not known that sad little fact of life. How sheltered his life had been. 'I would never take another man's wife, Ewan, least of all my boss's. I'm happy here. You know that. What you don't seem to know is how to handle a woman like the one you've chosen for a wife – and what's more I can't advise you on that. But I'm telling you now, just keep her away from me in future.'

Ewan stepped back automatically and Peter got into his car and drove away, but he had a sick feeling in the pit of his stomach. Somehow he knew that this would not be the end of the matter.

Ross was tired. It was always a busy time of year but now that they had both silage and hay to gather in, each crop seemed to run into the next without respite. As soon as the sheep were sheared, and sometimes even before, the first of the silage was ready to cut. The state of the grass was important in order to get protein for winter feed for the cows, and the right amount of sugar in the leaf to encourage a good fermentation. Ewan was adamant that it had to be at the right stage. Day after day they carted the heavy loads of fresh grass to the pits, levelling it and rolling it to ensure the ideal conditions – enough heat, but not too much, and no air pockets. They wanted only the beneficial bacteria to multiply. Then the pits had to be covered and weighted to make them as air and watertight as possible. Ewan would have liked to erect roofs over the silage pits to keep them dry, but Ross felt the cost was more than they could afford. As soon as the grass had grown again the routine began once more, topping up the pits so there was plenty of silage for the winter. No sooner was that done than the hay was ready. True, they did not make as much hay since Ewan had left college because he preferred the silage – especially since they already had a milking parlour and cubicle sheds which he had adapted for easier feeding. He had influenced Bridie with his ideas too. She was considering converting the Lochandee byre into a milking parlour, but that meant she would need to build a huge shed for cubicles to house the cows in winter. It would cost thousands of pounds. One of the officers from the government buildings in Dumfries had advised her about getting a grant to help pay for it. Expansion was what the government wanted.

Ross sighed heavily. Everything seemed to move at a pace faster than he could keep up with these days. He frowned. Rachel was tired and irritable these days too. He was sure she was doing too much, looking after Ewan's child every day. It was not as though Gerda went to work, or came to help with the hens or the calves. In fact she did nothing. He wondered how she filled her day.

When they were busy with seasonal work, Bridie always sent Frank Kidd and his father, Sandy, over to help. Sandy was getting too old for hard work now but he still liked to come for the hay and harvest. He always said no one made a harvest tea like Mistress Maxwell, but Ross realized it was all extra work for Rachel. The busier the men became, the busier she was too. Of course Peter went over to help with the hay and harvest at Glens of Lochandee in exchange, but that did not lessen Rachel's workload.

Max and the twins loved to come to Wester Rullion if they were on holiday from school. Max was now twelve and a useful young worker, and already as good with the tractor as Frank, although it made Ross uneasy to see him in charge of the big machines.

'I'm careful, Grandpa,' he insisted. 'I do exactly what Dad has taught me to do, and he says so long as I do that I shall be safe.'

Alicia and Margaret loved to help with baby Paul but that was a mixed blessing for Rachel. They were ten years old and sensible. They helped her collect the eggs and clean and pack them into boxes ready for the packing station. They entertained wee Paul and took him for walks in his pram too. She loved them dearly and enjoyed their company, but they had healthy appetites and enjoyed their granny's cooking, especially her rhubarb pies and gingerbread.

Ross resolved to have a word with Ewan. Gerda was the only member of the family who didn't pull her weight. Ewan was irritable and tired too and there was a tension between him and Peter that Ross had never noticed before. Indeed the whole atmosphere troubled him.

At Skeppiehill Farm Lucy often felt hot and tired as the summer progressed. The baby was not due until October and she did most of the milking herself while Don worked at the hay and harvest. She also fed the calves and hens and made teas to send to the harvest field for Don and his brother and young Richard Green, who had recently left school and become a full-time worker.

Don's father had succeeded in his ambition to buy the neighbouring farm to Home Farm. He had decided it should be for Jake, his youngest and favourite son. Neither Don nor Lucy could feel much enthusiasm. They were afraid it might make Mr Greig even more mean with money. Don had already spoken to his father about needing an increase in his weekly pay now that Lucy had had to give up teaching, and with a baby soon to be fed and clothed. Mr Greig flatly refused. Lucy knew Don's mother had quarrelled with her husband about it. In fact the relationship between Don's parents was decidedly strained and it troubled Don when he felt he was the cause. The only time Mrs Greig spent any time with Chris was when she came over to see Don and Lucy and arranged to meet her mother too.

As soon as Lucy had recovered from the baby's birth, Chris and Adam planned to be married. Her mother was aware of her plans but it grieved her that her only daughter was to be married so quietly and without her father to give her away.

'Oh, Ma, he gave me away the minute he knew I was a lassie!' Chris exclaimed impatiently, then hugged her mother when she saw how hurt she was by the whole affair. 'I'm not bothered about a fancy wedding, Mum, honestly. Adam and I know we love each other. We know we're right for each other. Surely that's what matters.'

'I know it is, ma bairn, but I canna understand your father being so bitter about Adam. He's a hard-working young man and he's a fine stockman. He might even get a farm one day . . .'

'Oh, he will, Ma. He certainly will,' Chris said, pursing her lips with determination. 'We're not doing so bad already, it's just that the land we rent is spread out with a bit here and a bit there, and so the animals take more looking after. But we'll show Dad. One of these days he'll realize Adam is just as good as any of his sons. Except our Don,' she added softly. 'Nobody works as hard as he does, nor for so little. I don't know how he puts up with Dad. Surely he's given them more money now that Lucy has had to give up her job?'

'Not yet he hasn't. If he doesn't, I've told Lucy she must keep as many hens as she can manage to look after, so long as she can sell the eggs. She'll have to keep the money.'

'But then Dad will stop paying Don altogether, or cut down the pittance he allows him.'

'Surely he'll not do that,' Mrs Greig said with troubled eyes. 'He'll drive Don away if he goes on being so mean. You know he has it in his head that if he keeps Lucy short of money she'll go whining to her parents. He thinks they're made o' money and they'll just keep handing over to her.'

'But that's terrible! Lucy would never ask anybody for anything. She's too proud. Anyway, Don would hate that. Besides,' she frowned, 'I don't think the Maxwells are wealthy. They work hard and they seem to be making a success of the tourist buses, but they earn their money, just like farmers do.'

'I know that, and I've tried to tell your father that, but he doesn't want to listen.'

'No, he's getting more thrawn as he gets older. I never

133

remember him being this mean and miserable when we were young.'

'Oh, he's always been a bit tight with money,' her mother said wryly, 'but he never grumbled about me keeping a bit o' egg money to myself, so we always got by. The thing is, he's real proud o' the way Don runs the farm and when the neighbours praise him and Lucy as a pair o' hard workers, he laps up all the praise. "Aye," he says, "I brought up ma lads we–el," and he takes all the credit!'

'Mmm. Well Don's not that soft. You wait; the worm will turn one o' these days if Father doesn't treat him fairly. After all, he's got a farm for each o' his sons now. Willie will get Home Farm, and Jake will have the new place. He can't expect Don to go on handing over all the profits from Skeppiehill so that Jake can act the gentleman. It's time his blue-eyed boy got down to some hard graft, like everybody else.'

Her mother nodded, but her eyes were troubled. She didn't like to hear Chris sounding so bitter, even on Don's behalf. She had always been such a happy, cheerful girl, and she had worked as hard as any of the boys, but her father had taken her for granted.

Twelve

Lucy's baby was born with the minimum of fuss on October 4th, 1965. Don was thrilled with his baby son, and he felt a deep surge of love for Lucy as she looked up at him, pale and tired, but supremely happy, a tender smile curving her soft mouth.

'I do love you, so very much,' he whispered huskily. Silently he vowed he would make their lives happy and provide well for them. Surely now his father must see he had to have his independence, make his own decisions – and mistakes – but above all provide a decent living for his wife and child.

'What shall we call him?' Lucy asked. The birth had been nothing like as bad as Gerda had threatened. She was thankful her baby was so perfect, but for now she was exhausted and relieved it was over.

'Chris wants to come and see you both tomorrow,' Don said. 'She can hardly wait to see her new nephew.' He grinned wickedly. 'We'd better think of a really shocking name before she dreams one up for us. I think we should keep away from family names and then we don't offend anyone. What do you think?'

'We–ell, all right, but I would have liked to call him Harry for a second name. I always thought of Harry Mason as my father, and he did love me. He was a good man.'

'I'm sure he was,' Don said gently. 'Of course we'll call the wee fellow Harry. How about Zacharias for his first name?' he suggested solemnly, making an effort to keep his face serious. Lucy's eyes opened wide.

'You wouldn't!' Then she saw the twinkle in Don's eyes

and knew he was teasing. 'What about Alexander?' she asked. 'Or Niall? Or Fearcher – that's Gaelic for Farquhar, I think. It means very dear one.'

'Mmm,' Don said doubtfully. 'Don't you think it should be short, easy to spell for the wee fellow? What about Ryan?'

'Ryan . . . Ryan Greig . . . Mmm, I think that sounds all right. I'll try it out on Chris if she does manage to visit us tomorrow.'

'Oh, she will. And I think Conan and Fiona and Mrs Maxwell are hoping to drive up to see you on Wednesday if you feel well enough.'

'Oh, I shall be fine once I've had a good sleep. It will be lovely to see them, Don.'

'Yes. I expect mother will pay a quick visit tomorrow. She can't wait to see her first grandchild.' He bent and kissed her tenderly. 'I'll leave you to rest now, my darling. I hate going home without you.'

'I know. I wish I was coming with you. One of the nurses says it will be a week before I can get home.'

'You've done a splendid job. Babies are so helpless,' Don said, looking down at the tiny dimpled fists of his sleeping son. 'When you think how calves and lambs just get up and walk and feed . . .'

'I know.' Lucy smiled. 'That's what I said to the nurse, but she said cows don't have to wash nappies and iron little nightgowns. She's advising me to rest while I get the chance.'

'She's right, and you're almost asleep now, so I'll let you have peace. I'll be back tomorrow night.'

Rachel stared now at the helpless infant, sleeping so peacefully with his hands above his head. She felt tears prick her eyes and had to struggle to keep them back. This was her great-grandson. She could scarcely believe it. She'd had her sixtieth birthday in May but she didn't feel like a great-granny.

'He's a beautiful baby, Lucy,' she said, her voice trembling. She swallowed hard and looked at Conan. He knew exactly what she was thinking. He gave a wry grimace.

'No, I don't feel like a grandad, so don't ask!' But he grinned widely. 'You've done well, lassie,' he said, looking down at Lucy, watching them anxiously.

'You have indeed,' Fiona agreed and Lucy was surprised to see her eyes fill with tears. 'He's so lovely, and he looks so helpless . . .'

'He certainly knows how to feed,' Lucy said with feeling. 'I'd be glad if you could come up and stay for a day or two when I get home.'

'Oh, I'd love that,' Fiona agreed instantly, and looked at Conan. He shrugged.

'It's OK with me. Things are easing off a bit now the summer bookings are over. Of course it would be better still if you could come down and stay with us, Lucy, but I don't suppose there's much chance of that?'

'No,' Lucy said regretfully. 'I'm afraid not. Don could have done with a wee break. He works far too hard, but there's not much we can do about it at present.'

'Your mother's cottage at Lochandee is to sell,' Conan said suddenly. 'Fiona and I thought of buying it . . .'

'Whatever for?' Rachel asked in surprise. 'I didn't even know it was to sell.'

'Oh, it was just a whim. The old couple who were in it have neglected it rather, and the garden is overgrown. It seems sad to see it like that, and I don't think it will make much money, although there's plenty of ground at the back. It's a good site. It would be a good investment if I thought Lucy and Don would ever have any holidays to spend there . . .' He sighed. 'It was just a thought. We really miss you, lassie. I wish I could have afforded to buy a farm nearer to us for you and Don, but we can't manage that.' He looked down thoughtfully at the sleeping child. Rachel followed his gaze. Was he thinking of the baby's future?

She never knew exactly what was in Conan's mind, but so far he seemed to have made the right decisions as far as his own business was concerned. In fact, she had to admit she was proud of Conan and Fiona's achievement, building up a completely new business from nothing. It always gave her a thrill when she saw one of their buses on the road, heading for places she had barely heard of.

Conan was not sure himself why he wanted to buy Beth's old home, except that he knew Lucy had been happy there as a child. Indeed, he had spent many happy hours himself in the bicycle shop with her great-grandfather, old Mr Turner. He just had a gut feeling that he wanted to buy it. Of course, he wouldn't consider it without Fiona's approval. She had agreed it might prove an asset so long as the asking price was reasonable, but she knew it would never be worthwhile as a holiday home for Lucy and Don, much as she would have loved the idea. Don simply didn't have time for holidays.

Back at Wester Rullion, Ross was tired and irritable. He couldn't bring himself to make the effort to go with Rachel to visit Lucy, much as he longed to see her and her baby. Conan had tried hard to persuade him to take a day off and accompany them, but the thought of getting ready, and the long drive, had seemed like a huge effort. Now with Rachel gone and the house quiet he wished he had gone. He felt lonely and dispirited.

In his heart Ross knew it was his own lack of energy that depressed him, but he also knew he must have words with Ewan. Things could not go on as they were. Rachel had too much to do, and Gerda took advantage of her love of children, and baby Paul in particular. He spent so much of his time with them that it was almost as though he was their son instead of their grandson. He was a bright, happy baby and Ross loved him almost as much as Rachel, but he did not have the extra work of caring for him. So, instead of taking his usual rest after lunch, Ross went out to wait for Ewan's return.

'Come into the house, Ewan,' he said as soon as he saw him walking up the track from his own home. 'There's things we need to talk about.'

Ewan's heart sank. He could see by his father's grim expression that there was something serious, and not just the farm, his father wished to discuss.

138

As soon as they were indoors Ewan turned to him. 'If you're wondering about Peter and me—'

'This has nothing to do with Peter,' Ross interrupted, 'but since you mention him, I've noticed he doesn't seem as happy as he was and there's a tension between the two of you which I don't like. I've always run a happy ship and Peter is a grand worker and an honest and reliable man, so whatever is wrong between you, you'd better put it right.'

'I will. It was a stupid misunderstanding on my part anyway.'

'Good. It's Gerda I wanted to talk about. She doesn't pull her weight. It's bad enough that she neither wants to work at her own job or help with anything here, not even the hens. Most farmers' wives are glad to look after the poultry.'

'She's just not used to country life . . . Besides, I didn't think Mother wanted to give up her hens . . .'

'She doesn't, but she can't do everything. You knew Gerda would have to live in the country before you married. We did try to tell—'

'I know! I know!' Ewan snapped, then said quickly,' I'm sorry, Father.' He rubbed a hand over his brow. 'She . . . she doesn't seem to want to adapt . . .'

'Well, she should at least look after her own bairn!' Ross said shortly. 'Your mother has far too much to do.'

'I thought she liked having Paul.' Ewan looked hurt.

'She does. She loves the wee fellow. We both do. I know she'd rather look after him than spend time doing the accounts, but they have to be done as well, and it's too much. And don't tell your mother I've been discussing this with you.'

'Of course not.' Ewan nodded. 'I'd be willing to take over the bookkeeping, if you think Mother would agree. Would that help?'

'We'll ask her. Don't think she's been grumbling about having Paul. She loves him, but he's your bairn. I'd have thought Gerda would have wanted to care for him herself.'

'I expect she'll be better with him when he can walk and talk. She hates changing his nappies . . .'

'From what Billy Smith says, his mother does that as often as Gerda – and she does all the washing. I think if you bring him up here a few hours each afternoon that should be plenty.'

Ewan had expected another quarrel when he conveyed the gist of his father's comments to Gerda. Surprisingly she seemed to consider them seriously and later that evening she offered to help him with keeping the farm accounts. He was surprised and pleased. Maybe she had found an interest in Wester Rullion at last, he thought with relief. Certainly he had more than enough work to do himself, especially in recent months.

Ewan was increasingly aware how easily his father became breathless and how quickly he seemed to tire, even when attempting light tasks. He wondered whether his mother had noticed the changes, and whether it was really his father who was tired of Paul. He had certainly seemed irritable today and that was unusual. Ewan wondered why he had not gone to visit Lucy and the baby.

Gerda was less pleased the following day when Ewan insisted she must take care of their son more often.

'I suppose your mother will only have time for Lucy's baby now!' she snapped.

'Lucy's . . .' Ewan stared at her. 'Don't talk daft.' He laughed. 'Mother only went for the day, to see her and the baby. They're too far away to visit very often, and I can't see Lucy and Don having much time to come down here. Don seems to be even more overworked than I am.'

'That's what you think. I know your mother has been knitting for Lucy's brat. Even the woman who works at Lochandee knitted two pram suits for him.'

'Emmie?'

'If that's her name . . .'

'Emmie is Frank Kidd's wife. She's known me and Lucy all our lives. She and Lucy's mother were close friends. Anyway, she knitted two jackets for Paul when he was born, didn't she? How do you know she knitted for Lucy anyway?'

'Bridie was going on about it.'

*   *   *

140

It was a long winter for Ross. He had several bouts of severe bronchitis and each one seemed to leave him more prone to infection. But he refused to stay in bed.

'People die when they take to their beds,' he insisted stubbornly. 'Anyway, I can breathe better when I'm sitting up.' More than once he had added softly, 'And I like to be near you, Rachel.'

She knew this was true, and indeed she felt easier in her own mind when she could keep an eye on him as she worked, peeling the vegetables, making broth, just cooking and baking or cleaning the eggs. They talked when he had the energy and he dozed when he was tired. She kept the kitchen as cosy as she could, thankful for the constant heat of her Aga cooker. It was rare for the doors and windows to be closed at Wester Rullion but Rachel watched over Ross diligently, constantly afraid of draughts or anything that would give him a chill.

She was thankful she no longer had the responsibility of paying the bills and keeping the books. The government were becoming ever more watchful for things like income tax, especially where they thought businesses avoided it. They had to keep more accounts and obey more regulations than ever before. She had heard Bridie telling Ewan one of the conditions of accepting a government grant was the presentation of her accounts to the Department of Agriculture's inspectors.

'It's to prove we're worthy of the grants we've been given for building the new milking parlour and cubicle shed,' she explained. 'We're supposed to prove we have made Glens of Lochandee more efficient with the money.'

'I'm glad I've kept the hens myself then,' Rachel said as she listened to their discussion. 'I always keep a cash book, just in case any of the inspectors want to take a look.'

'You'd be lost without your hens and chickens, Mum.' Rachel nodded. Ewan said nothing. Gerda and he had had an almighty quarrel when Gerda discovered she was not to handle the cash from the egg sales. He couldn't understand it because she didn't want anything to do with the hens themselves.

141

'I'll be back to see you tomorrow,' Bridie said to her father. She followed Ewan outside and they talked for a little longer before Bridie drove home.

'I think Ewan is a bit worried about the way Gerda looks after wee Paul now that Mother doesn't have him so often,' she said to Nick when they were snuggled up together in bed later that evening.

'Why? I mean, she's nothing else to do and surely even Gerda wouldn't neglect her own baby?'

'You wouldn't think so,' Bridie agreed slowly, but Nick could tell she was frowning, even in the darkness.

'Maybe it's just Ewan being overanxious. He thinks the world of wee Paul. What did he say exactly?' Nick asked.

'O–oh, he was just asking me if babies always got red cheeks when they were getting teeth. They often do, of course . . . But . . . but he seems to think Gerda slaps Paul across his face when he cries. Apparently she hates changing his nappies, so she just leaves him until Ewan gets home, if Mrs Smith isn't there to attend to him.'

'And Ewan changes the nappies?' Nick asked incredulously. 'More fool him then, when Gerda's sitting around all day twiddling her thumbs.'

'Well, what would you do if your baby was crying and miserable and your wife refused to attend to him? You wouldn't just leave him. You're too soft-hearted for that.'

'I'd spank my wife's backside and tell her to get on with it.'

'Oh, would you indeed!' Bridie said. 'You and how many men?'

'Just me, cariad,' Nick said softly and drew her closer. 'The best wife in the whole world, I have.'

And then all thoughts of Ewan and his wife were forgotten.

Ross's health gradually seemed to improve and once or twice he even made the effort to travel into Lockerbie, which surprised Rachel as he rarely went to town except to the market.

The new year had barely begun and Ross had done his

usual work helping with the milking and the calves to relieve Peter and Billy Smith over the holidays. Gerda sulked and grumbled alternately because Ewan could not take a break. 'Even if I could leave the cows to milk themselves, where would either of us want to go in the middle of winter?' he argued.

'I've heard some of the young farmers are going off on a skiing holiday,' Gerda said sullenly, 'but we never go anywhere exciting.'

'We're not exactly young, free and single any more, either. We're a married couple with a son to care for.'

'We could leave him with your mother now that your father is keeping better.'

'Oh, no we couldn't,' Ewan said angrily. 'Paul is our responsibility. Anyway, my mother has him often enough as it is since father's chest improved again.'

'Well we could take him with us then . . .'

'No! I'm not going anywhere at this time of year. All we need is a frosty spell and there'll be frozen pipes to thaw every morning before the animals can drink, not to mention the roads to clear to get the milk tanker in if we get snow. I can't leave my father to cope with all that.'

'I wish I'd never married you, you miserable bastard! Even my father was going abroad for Christmas.'

'Was he?' Ewan's eyes widened in surprise. 'I didn't know you'd heard from him. You said you'd quarrelled.'

Gerda flushed guiltily. 'I haven't heard from him,' she muttered sullenly. 'Nor do ever I want to hear from him again. One of his old neighbours sent me a Christmas card, if you must know. He's gone and married that . . . that woman!' Gerda's red mouth curled contemptuously.

'Daisy? He's married Daisy and never said a word to anyone?' Ewan laughed aloud. 'Well good for them. I hope you've written to wish them happiness. We should send a wedding gift . . .'

'Over my dead body! Anyway, I don't know where they are.'

'What d'you mean?'

'It seems Daisy owned her own house as well and they've both sold up and taken off. According to Mary Docherty they're thinking of settling abroad somewhere warmer. She only sent a card because she'll be crowing over me!'

'Why would she be doing that?' Ewan frowned. 'She probably thought you would want to know . . .'

'Don't be so bloody stupid! She'll be laughing up her sleeve because she knows I'll not get his house now, not when he's got another wife. I'll bet it was her who persuaded him to sell it. She'll be spending the money and enjoying herself . . .'

'They both will, and why not?' Ewan reasoned. 'Your father has worked all his life. Anyway, I liked Daisy.'

Gerda stared at him as though he was mad, then she uttered a stream of oaths and slammed out of the house. He heard the car start and he raised his eyebrows at his small son, playing on the hearthrug at his feet. Paul raised his own dark little brows in perfect imitation and Ewan laughed and scooped him up, cuddling him close.

'You're all the compensation I need for putting up with a bad-tempered wife,' he whispered, knowing Paul was still too young to understand, or to repeat his words.

In the middle of January Ross developed another severe chest infection. There was great anxiety for several days and Fiona telephoned Lucy with news every evening. Suddenly the weather took on a brief, spring-like spell and Ross's health seemed to take a turn for the better too.

'I have a terrible urge to go and visit,' Lucy confided to Don that evening. 'You know he's never seen Ryan yet. Would you mind terribly if I drove down to Wester Rullion now that the weather has improved a little? I thought we could stay overnight with Fiona and drive back again in daylight.'

'All right,' Don agreed. He leaned forward and pulled her close, kissing her gently. 'You know I'd feel happier if I was coming with you both, but I really can't get away at this time of year.'

'Oh, Don, I know that.' She reached up and touched his

144

cheek. 'I wouldn't expect you to go. In fact I'm not sure why I suddenly feel the need to go myself, but I have this sudden urge to see them all . . . Silly, isn't it?'

'No, sweetheart, it's not silly at all. They're your family and we didn't even get to see any of them at Christmas this year. You go while the weather is reasonable.'

'All right, I'll phone Fiona now and we'll go tomorrow if it's convenient.'

Although the days were short, a pale sun broke through the February chill as Lucy drove down the twisty road towards Dumfriesshire. She enjoyed the familiar glimpses of the river and Drumlanrig Castle as she drew nearer Dumfries before cutting across country in the direction of Wester Rullion. There were still pockets of snow behind the hedgerows and on the hills, but Lucy felt a surge of happiness as she approached the familiar countryside and the warmth of welcoming faces.

There were even more welcomes than she had anticipated by the time she reached Wester Rullion. All of Bridie's children attended Dumfries Academy now and she had collected them straight from school and driven over so that they could all see baby Ryan. Rachel hugged her warmly and took the sleeping baby from her, holding him down for Paul to see. Paul was eleven months old now and pulling himself up at every chair or ledge. He poked gently at the woollen bundle in his grandmother's arms and looked up enquiringly. 'Bay-bay?' he said, round-eyed. Margaret and Alicia both wanted to hold Ryan at the same time.

Under cover of the general hubbub, Lucy managed to regain control of her own emotions. She was overwhelmed by their warmth, but she was shocked at the sight of her grandfather's haggard face, so pale and thin. He had always had such a healthy, outdoor look and it smote her heart to see how frail he seemed, how ready he was to take a seat by the fire.

'Tea is ready.' Rachel smiled, reluctant to relinquish her hold on the baby who was smiling at all and sundry after his long sleep in the car.

145

'He'll probably show me up tonight by not sleeping at all.' Lucy smiled ruefully.

'Don't worry about that, lassie, Fiona and Conan will want to make the most of him.'

'Yes,' Bridie agreed, 'and Nick will be popping over there to see you both later this evening.' She glanced towards her father and lowered her voice. 'We thought it better not to have everyone here at once.'

Lucy nodded her understanding and bent to talk to Paul.

Ewan stood in the doorway, silent in his stockinged feet, unobserved. Lucy's love of children, her gentle voice and smiling face were all such a contrast to his own wife, he thought with a touch of sadness. His small son was doing his best to chatter in response to Lucy's baby talk, holding out his favourite toy motor to her.

'You're a beautiful boy then, aren't you?' Lucy laughed and picked him up in her arms, catching sight of Ewan's wistful face as she rose to her feet. Paul saw him too and chortled even more merrily, holding out one chubby arm.

'Da-da, Da-da,' he announced triumphantly. Ewan came forward then and kissed Lucy on the cheek, enquiring after her health and how her journey had been.

'How is Gerda?' she enquired in return, but she could not miss the shadows that darkened Ewan's green eyes, so like her own. It had always been like looking into a mirror image.

'Gerda is . . . she's in good health. She . . . she needed to go into town. She'll be sorry she missed you . . .'

Lucy nodded. She knew Ewan far too well. Gerda had not wanted to be here. And Ewan was not a happy man.

'Conan was telling me Gerda has joined the amateur dramatics club. Is she enjoying it?'

'I reckon so. She was there several evenings a week before Christmas, helping with the pantomime. She works behind the scenes – make-up and costumes and things, I think.' He spoke without rancour and Lucy wondered if he found it a relief to have peace from Gerda's constant company now they were married. She had always found the other girl's carping and criticism very wearing herself, but on the other

146

hand Ewan loved her – or at least he had loved her when they married – and she had no reason to suppose that had changed. She looked at him more closely. There was no doubt he looked strained and tired, but his father's health and the extra responsibilities of Wester Rullion could account for that.

Later, Conan and Fiona welcomed Lucy and baby Ryan just as warmly. Fiona was reluctant to put Ryan down to sleep for the night. She had bought a second-hand cot and Bridie had brought over some baby blankets that had been left over from the twins' baby days.

A little later Nick called in, but when the news and weather came on Lucy saw his laughing face sober dramatically. The announcer was forecasting an end to the brief spell of fine weather with the threat of hard frost and snow in places, particularly Scotland. He and Conan exchanged frowning glances.

'Do you have to return tomorrow, Lucy? Are you sure you couldn't stay a few days with us?' Conan asked, knowing what her answer would be even before he asked.

'I must go home tomorrow,' Lucy said in consternation. 'I promised Don . . .'

'Aye, well I think you should stick to the main road then,' Nick advised solemnly. 'It will be busier, but you'll be less likely to get stranded if there's other traffic about. The gritting lorry will have been out if there's much ice or snow,' he added quickly, seeing Fiona's anxious expression. 'I'll be getting back to Lochandee now then, and let you get a good night's sleep.'

Conan went with him to the door and Lucy could tell by their low voices that they were concerned for her. She turned to Fiona with a reassuring smile.

'We'll leave straight after breakfast and be home by lunchtime, so don't worry. I just had a feeling that I needed to see my grandfather again, especially after he has been so ill. I . . . I got rather a shock though. I'm glad I came. I'm pleased he's seen Ryan.'

'Ye–es.' Fiona looked at her oddly, noting her pensive

face as she stared into the leaping flames. 'We're all truly happy to see you, Lucy, but I'll not rest easy until you telephone to let us know you're safely home.'

Thirteen

Nick returned to Rullion Glen the following morning before Lucy had even started to eat her porridge.

'I know there's no sign of snow here yet, Lucy, but it's been a hard frost and Bridie thinks there could be snow up by Cumnock. I've a spare set of wheel chains here, so I'll pop them in the boot if that's all right with you. Do you know how to fit them?'

'I–I think so.' Lucy frowned. She had not had time to listen to the weather forecast and it was still dark outside but she guessed it was going to be one of those bleak February days when it never seemed to get properly light. She felt her stomach begin to churn. Perhaps she should not have come to visit at this time of year after all. Then she remembered the shock she had felt at the sight of her grandfather and knew she was glad she had made the effort. He had been touchingly pleased to see her and Ryan, his first great-grandson. She thanked Nick for his trouble and summoned a wavering smile. 'You're very thoughtful, Nick. I do appreciate it.'

'A pleasure it is, Lucy,' Nick said gruffly. 'We wouldn't like the car to skid with the baby and you. There's too precious you are.'

'We'll hope the chains aren't needed,' Conan said, 'but they're a big help if the roads are bad. I'll put a shovel in too. I see you've already got a spare travelling rug. If you're prepared, you'll not need anything.' He grinned. 'I think I'm beginning to sound like my mother. Remember how she worried about us, Nick, when we were home on leave from the RAF?'

'Indeed I do. Kind she was too. Packing up food for the journey in spite of the rationing.'

Lucy hastily swallowed her own breakfast, feeling a sudden urgency to be safely home again with Don. She wasted no time in preparing Ryan for the journey, tucking him warmly into his carrycot as soon as he had been fed and changed. He had slept most of the way down, as he usually did when the car was moving, but today he seemed to sense her own tension and he whimpered fretfully. Conan insisted on securing the cot to the back of the rear seat with two raincoat belts, in case the car should skid. Fiona had filled a large flask of hot coffee and packed up some sandwiches.

'Just in case you get delayed.' She smiled wanly, wishing Lucy did not have to make the journey on her own.

'We know you're a careful driver, Lucy,' Conan assured her, 'but you can never be sure what sort of problems other drivers might cause. Best to be prepared, and if you've any doubts, turn round and come back here. I'm sure Don would prefer that rather than have an accident.'

'Yes.' Lucy nodded, swallowing the lump in her throat with difficulty. She hugged them both warmly and climbed into her car, blinking back tears. How blessed she was to have two people who loved her so much, when they could both have resented her. In spite of the bitterly cold morning she felt an inner warmth, kindled by the love of her friends and family.

The house telephone rang at Rullion Glen Garage. Fiona answered and gave the number, feeling a strange quiver in her stomach.

'Hello, it's Don Greig here.' The line crackled abominably. 'Can I speak to Lucy, please?' he shouted.

'Hello, Don. Lucy left here about an hour ago . . .'

'Oh, hell! I didn't expect her to leave so early. Straight after lunch she said yesterday. Should've phoned sooner. Hello? Can you hear me?'

'Yes. Is everything all right?'

'Weather's terrible here . . . I wanted Lucy to wait with

you . . .' A loud crackle drowned the rest of his words.

'Phone us when she gets home!' Fiona called quickly, but she didn't know whether he had heard her or not. The phone in her hand was burring but there was no connection. She tried to call him back, but without success.

She pulled on her coat and boots and made her way down the icy path to the bottom of the garden, oblivious for once to the snowdrops peeping through the sheltering rhododendrons that she and Conan had planted together. As she made her way to the garage to find Conan, the sky glowered sullenly overhead. She shivered. There would certainly be snow before nightfall. How quickly the weather could change at this time of year. She wondered what instinct had urged Lucy to drive down to see her grandfather at this time of year, especially now that he seemed to be recovering at last. Yet it had been like spring yesterday, and the day before. Who could blame her for wanting him to see her son?

Gerda was irritable and short-tempered. She had no excuse to go to the drama club until preparations started for the next play. Some of the players had been given parts but so far the costume and stagehands had not met to discuss their plans for the production. She couldn't wait for the next meeting. Hubert, the new stage manager, thought she had made some good suggestions towards the last production. Although she had been one of the poorest students in the music group at college, her basic training was proving an advantage now and she had discovered a hidden talent for devising dance steps to suit the music. Gerda glowed when he expressed his appreciation so openly.

Hubert Boyd-Hill was relatively new to the area, as she was, and it had forged an additional bond between them. She basked in his admiration. More than once he had offered to drive her home. She had been forced to decline because she had her own car, but she knew from his expression that he was disappointed by her refusal. If he asked again she would explain that she was only refusing because she didn't want to leave her car in town. She shuddered at the thought. Her

151

car was the one thing that made life at the farm bearable. She would feel like a prisoner without it. Besides, what explanation could she give to Ewan? He had been furious with her for begging a lift into town with Peter when there was nothing wrong with her own car. She couldn't use that feeble excuse again.

Even so, she resolved to find some reason for getting better acquainted with Hubert. He was at least five years older than Ewan, maybe more. He had lived in London and was clearly a man of the world. He told her he had come back to Dumfries when his elderly mother was ill, but she had since died, leaving him her house. He had decided to stay in the north for a while until he had sorted out her affairs. Dick Bone, one of the main actors, hinted that it was not true. He said Hubert had lost his job and come to stay with his mother because he was short of money. He said she had been frail for years and Hubert had never been near when she needed him. Gerda preferred to think Dick was jealous. She had seen Hubert driving away in a sleek black Jaguar so that proved he wasn't short of money, didn't it? Most of the women in the little company hung around him, including Dick's girlfriend, so she guessed he resented Hubert's charisma and good looks.

Paul had been playing on the rug in front of the fire but he began to demand attention, and then to cry. Gerda frowned and swore under her breath.

'What's wrong with you now!' she snapped sullenly. 'You've had your dinner. You can't possibly need changing again, you sodden little pee-bag!'

'Gan-gan . . . Want Gan-gan.' The little boy began to cry in earnest. Gerda glared at him, then her eyes narrowed thoughtfully. She glanced out of the windows. Big flakes of snow were still swirling from the leaden sky but they were melting almost as soon as they landed. Why shouldn't she drive into town? If the snow did settle she might be a prisoner here for days. Why shouldn't she grab a little time to herself while she could? That's what she needed to cheer her up, a little jaunt into town. She hated winter and the

152

short, dark days. The idea had no sooner entered her head than she was bundling Paul into his coat and leggings. She would drop him off with his grandmother then she could smarten herself up in peace before she set off for town.

Rachel had stopped asking where Gerda was going or when she would be back, only to have her head snapped off. But today she looked anxiously at the lowering clouds and ventured her opinion.

'The snow is falling faster now. I think we shall have a fair covering before dark,' she said anxiously.

'I need to go into town to get stuff for him,' Gerda muttered sullenly, glaring towards her small son whose chubby arms were clasped around Rachel's neck as though he would never let her go. 'I shall be back before the roads get bad. Send him home with Ewan after he's finished milking his bloody cows.' She turned on her heel and hurried back to the car without waiting for Rachel to agree.

Rachel pursed her lips. She hated to hear Gerda swear, especially now Paul was picking up words and trying them out for himself. She sighed. It never occurred to her daughter-in-law to ask if it was convenient to leave Paul for the afternoon. She hugged him tightly. She loved him, of course she did, and she knew he loved being with her, but today it was too cold and wet to take him outside with her to gather up the eggs. She would have to leave him with his grandfather while she hurried round the hen houses on her own. She frowned briefly. Ross tired so easily still, although his chest was much improved. When he was tired he was easily irritated, even with Paul, much as he loved his small grandson.

Gerda donned the fur coat that had caused such anger and dismay when she had been threatened with the bailiffs. She snuggled into the soft fur and preened herself before the mirror. She had regained her slender figure and she felt elegant in her high-heeled, thigh-length boots. She paused a moment, frowning angrily as she remembered Alicia remarking that she looked like Dick Whittington in the pantomime at Carlisle. It was bad enough when the twins dissolved into giggles, but she'd caught the look that Nick and Conan had exchanged and the suppressed smiles on their faces. She had been furious but now she twirled before the mirror and admired her own reflection. What could they know about fashion? Nothing! She looked good. She felt good. They could snigger as much as they wanted. She arranged the matching fur hat on her blonde head and fixed it at an attractive angle.

The roads were still clear although the snow was coating the fields and hedgerows with white and the windscreen wipers were kept busy clearing snowflakes. The town was quiet but the shops were well lit and Gerda's spirits rose. She would keep away from Barbours today. Her account was already overdrawn and she had a feeling some of the staff had been warned. She had opened accounts at two of the shops in Carlisle recently and when the weather cleared she would go down there to view the new spring fashions. Meanwhile she would have a browse around Binns and perhaps buy herself a new perfume. It was warm and bright inside the department store and her spirits rose. She still couldn't get used to the small country town of Dumfries after she had been used to such a wide choice of department stores in Glasgow. Not for the first time she wondered whatever had possessed her to tie herself down to a life in the country. Ewan's adoration had cooled and she could no longer twist him around her little finger with the promise of sex. There was no excitement in her life.

She dabbed perfume on the inside of her wrist from the sample that the smiling assistant offered.

'Let me buy that for you,' a deep voice said behind her left ear. Gerda spun around, looking up into the dark, handsome face with its shadowy outline of stubble around the jaw.

'Why, Hubert! I didn't expect to see you today.' Her pleasure was evident in her shining eyes and parted lips. If she'd been a cat she would have purred loudly, Hubert thought cynically. 'I can't decide which of these two perfumes to buy.' She dabbed a more expensive perfume on her other wrist and held them out for him. He bent his head and she was surprised to see a faint sprinkling of silver at his temples. It added maturity and increased his attraction, she decided. If he was going to buy the perfume, she would choose the most expensive one. He said he preferred the first one, being wise to the ways of women, and well versed in the price of such fripperies. Gerda was not so kittenish underneath and she insisted she would really prefer the second. She made a good pretence at displaying shock when the assistant stated the price.

'Let me take you for a cup of tea in the restaurant.' She smiled winningly. 'That's the least I can do since you have been so generous.' She linked her arm through his as he tucked his wallet firmly back into the inside pocket of his jacket and buttoned up his overcoat. She drew him, unresisting, towards the lift.

They lingered a long time over tea and cream cakes. The restaurant was quiet, with few shoppers willing to linger longer than necessary in such uncertain weather. The waitress hovered in exasperation. She wanted to clear the table and be ready to leave as soon as the manager gave permission. She glanced anxiously out of the tall windows overlooking the street. The snow was beginning to lie now and the road below was white, even where the car tyres had left tracks. At last she breathed a sigh of relief as the couple rose to go.

Gerda smiled with satisfaction. It had been a profitable afternoon. She had made all her explanations to Hubert Boyd-Hill and he had offered to collect her at home and drive her to the drama club meetings so that he could see her home afterwards.

'Indeed, why wait until the meetings start officially?' he said softly, looking directly into Gerda's pale blue eyes. 'We could start our own discussions as soon as the weather clears. It sounds as though your husband is too busy to ask questions.'

'How right you are! Ewan is far too preoccupied with his cows to bother about my arrangements.' She gave a tiny pout. 'In fact, I'm really looking forward to sharing our mutual interests.'

'And so am I. So am I,' he said as they stepped into the lift. They were the only people in it and as the metal doors slammed shut he turned and drew her into his arms, kissing her expertly, until her lips parted. He lifted his head with a small smile of satisfaction. He wondered if her husband's family was really as wealthy as she pretended. The mink coat she was wearing must certainly have cost a pretty penny. He would see for himself when he collected her.

They were both surprised when they emerged from the warmth and brightness of the store to find snowflakes swirling all around them and the pavements thickly coated.

Gerda drove slowly and carefully. She had no wish to damage either herself or her car. Inside she felt a bubble of excitement as she recalled her meeting with Hubert. It didn't occur to her to wonder why he was not at work in the middle of the day like most other men mid-week.

The snow was thicker as she turned on to the narrower roads where there had been less traffic. She peered through the windscreen. She ought to wear glasses for driving but she hated the thought of anything that would mar her beauty.

She was later than she had meant to be and she wondered whether Ewan would be home before her. She hoped he was attending to Paul. She frowned at the thought of her small son. He was a burden she had dismissed while talking to Hubert. Her mind was going over the afternoon's conversation when the offside front wheel of her car caught a grass verge, hidden by snow. It skidded across the narrow road and tilted sideways, half in a ditch. Gerda panicked. She revved violently but the wheels spun uselessly. It was really dark now. She fumbled in the glove compartment for her torch and switched it on. No response. The battery was flat. Why hadn't she checked? She hated the dark. What was she to do? Should she wait for Ewan to come and search for her? But no, if he was home he would be looking after Paul, and he would probably be angry because she was not there to look after him herself.

She pushed open the car door with an effort and scrambled out. Her feet were already frozen and damp from her short walk in the town. The soles of her fashionable boots were thin and not meant for trudging down a country road where the snow was now well over her ankles. Her fur coat, her beautiful mink, was getting wetter by the second and she tried to hurry, blinking the snow from her eyelashes. Before long she reached the end of the short lane leading up to the two cottages and even from there she could see the light streaming out from Mrs Smith's kitchen window, but her own house was in darkness. She tried to see her wristwatch but it was too dark. Surely it must be after six o'clock, so why wasn't Ewan home and getting Paul his supper, preparing him for bed?

In fact Ewan felt extremely harassed and angry. In her haste not to leave Paul too long with his grandfather, Rachel had hurried round the hen houses as fast as she could, while taking care not to break any of the precious eggs. They were always scarce at this time of year. The days were so short and the weather damp and cold so the hens could not be blamed for wanting to stay inside all day. On days like this they were settling down to roost by three o'clock in the afternoon. Rachel was coming out of the last wooden hut when her foot slipped on a patch of ice beneath the virgin snow. She tried hard to hold on to the basket of eggs but in doing so she twisted her ankle, making her wince with the hot, shooting pain. She could have wept with frustration. At least half the eggs would be cracked or chipped and she had barely enough to keep her regular customers supplied at this time of year. She hated to let them down. Her ankle throbbed painfully as she turned to secure the wooden door, and for the first time in her life Rachel forgot to close the little trap-door that the hens used.

She was hobbling painfully across the farmyard when Peter Forster came round the end of the tractor shed. He hurried to her side at once, his face filled with concern. He took the basket from her frozen fingers and gave her his free arm to lean on as he helped her back to the house. Rachel felt embarrassed as he helped her off with her wet coat and proceeded to ease her wellington boot from her swelling foot. Peter had infinite patience, but in spite of his gentleness Rachel couldn't help but wince.

'Thank goodness it's not broken,' she said shakily.

'This is almost as bad.' Peter frowned anxiously. 'It is swelling rapidly. Sprains need a cold compress and a crêpe bandage for support. You will need to rest it.' He kicked off his own snowy wellingtons. 'Let me help you into the kitchen where it's warm and then I'll bring Ewan to help you and to make a cup of hot tea.'

'Thank you, Peter,' Rachel said faintly. 'You're a good laddie.'

Peter smiled to himself. He would always be a laddie in the eyes of Mr and Mrs Maxwell. He settled her by the Aga and reassured Ross that nothing was broken. Paul would have climbed on her knee to kiss her better but Peter forestalled him, explaining gently that Gan-gan was hurt and couldn't cuddle him just now.

When Ewan saw what had happened, he realized his mother had probably been hurrying too much. His lips compressed. As soon as he had bound up her ankle and placed it on a low stool he made tea for her and his father. Then he hurried out to find young Billy.

'Go down to the cottage and tell Gerda to come up here at once. Tell her my mother has injured her ankle,' he said brusquely.

Billy returned to say there was no reply at Mrs Maxwell's cottage and the car was away.

'Ma would come and help if I tell her what's happened,' Billy suggested. Ewan thought for a moment.

'All right then, Billy. Take the tractor down and bring her on the back of it if she's willing. Explain what's happened. Maybe she could make the evening meal and keep an eye on Paul until I've finished the milking, or until Gerda returns,' he added grimly. 'And Billy . . .'

'Aye?'

'Ask your mother if she would help up at the farm instead of working for my wife at the cottage. My mother will have more need of her until her ankle is better. Gerda can do her own housework – aye, and look after Paul. It'll give her something to do rather than driving off to Dumfries every day,' he muttered angrily, more to himself than to Billy, but the lad had sharp ears and he repeated Ewan's words to his mother.

'Aye, it's time the laddie saw sense.' Her eyes gleamed with satisfaction. 'Time he stood up to that lady wife o' his like the man he is. Spoiled her he has, frae the very beginning. I'd rather help up at the farm any day. At least Mistress Maxwell appreciates what folks do for her, and that's more than ye can say for her ladyship.'

'Hurry up then, Ma. Ewan said I was to give ye a lift on the back o' the tractor. Can ye hold on?'

'Aye, laddie. Better than walking up tae the farm in this snow. Thoughtful laddie he is, Ewan. Just wait while I get ma coat and scarf, son, then I'll be with ye.'

Don tried to telephone Fiona and Conan shortly after two o'clock but he couldn't even get the operator. Why, oh why, wasn't Lucy home by now? He fretted, pacing restlessly around the kitchen, reluctant to go back out to work yet knowing there was nothing he could do if the phone lines were down.

Back at Rullion Glen, Fiona was just as worried. She tried to phone Don for the umpteenth time.

'Lucy will be safely home by now,' Conan reassured her. 'They can't let us know if the phones aren't working.' Even so he had come home early. There was little to keep him at the garage today but his thoughts had been continually with Lucy and his own baby grandson.

'Ours are working,' Fiona said irrationally, and Fiona was never irrational. 'Br–bridie ph–phoned.' To Conan's consternation she began to weep, silent tears rolling down her pale face.

'Hey!' he said softly, dismayed. Fiona never cried. She was always in control of her emotions – well, except for some things, but that was passion and this was real distress. He drew her gently into his arms. 'There's no need to get so upset. Lucy is an excellent driver.'

159

'I–I know. B–but Bridie was worried too. Sh–she had heard the tail end of a radio announcement. The r–roads are bad up above by Sanquhar. Th–there's been an accident some-where near C––Cumnock . . .'

'An accident? When? What did it say?'

'A c–car . . .' Fiona's voice was barely audible and she hid her face against his chest and clung to him. Conan's arms tightened. He felt suddenly tense.

'What did they say?'

'A c–car and two lorries. One . . . one person k–killed. No n–names y–yet. It musn't be Lucy . . . It c–can't b–be Lucy! But . . . b–but . . .'

'Oh, God,' Conan breathed. 'Oh dear God, please don't let it be Lucy . . .' He sank down on to the settee, taking Fiona with him. They clung to each other, each needing the other's comfort and reassurance.

Fourteen

Outside, Don heard a tractor and tugged on his coat and boots. One of the neighbours must need help. He was astonished to see his father chugging slowly into the yard.

'What's wrong?'

'That's a fine way to greet your old man!' He switched off the engine. 'Your mother's been nagging me since eleven o' clock. She can't get through on the phone.'

'It's out of order. Is yours on?'

'Aye. It's only yours, and the few cottages along this road, I reckon. Somebody must've run into the telegraph pole at the junction. The line's down.'

'So it'll be on in the village?' Don asked eagerly. Why hadn't he thought to go down on the tractor and try the call box?

He half turned away but his father asked abruptly: 'Is that wife o' yours back wi' the bairn? That's what I've come to find out.' His face was grim, and Don knew he had not come of his own accord.

'No, they're not back yet. I'm just going—'

'She's a silly bitch going visiting at this time o' year. And you're a silly bugger for letting her go.'

Already tense as a fiddle string, Don's anxiety boiled into anger. Furious anger, suddenly uncontrollable.

'No, Father! I'm a silly bugger for staying here and working for you like a bloody slave. Getting paid a pittance for my trouble. Why should Lucy have to stay away from her family when they're ill? I should have been with her, but I can't leave your bloody farm – yes, yours! It's not mine, is it? Not one blade o' grass, not a single piece o' straw, not even

161

the muck I barrow to the midden every day. Adam and Chris are better off than we are, yet you despise him for not being the son o' a farmer! I've no say in how things should be run. I can't employ a man, I've no money to pay one. And there's Jake, a farm bought for him – in his own name no less! He hasn't a single bloody cow to milk, but he has two men running after him, twiddling their thumbs. Lucy and me, we're slaving here to pay their – yes, their – wages . . .'

More and more words tumbled out of Don's mouth in a fast and furious torrent. He was powerless to stop them. All his pent-up frustrations poured forth, but his anger was fuelled by his anxiety for his wife and son. Even when he paused for breath his father just stared at him, open-mouthed. Don, his eldest, had always been the easiest to manage, the quiet, hard-working son. He had the patience of the true stockman. He rarely swore, never lost his temper . . . Even when Don swung away from him he couldn't speak. Don, white-faced and tight-lipped, stared up at him coldly.

'Now you can bed your own bloody cattle. They are yours after all. Everything's yours! I'm going down to the phone box.' He strove for a calm he could not feel. 'And I'll tell you another thing! Don't send me any more of your dirty-dealing heifers to milk, because I'll send them right back to you!' Yet even as he strode towards his own tractor he noticed one of the lights on his father's needed a bulb. His father was a hopeless mechanic. He would see if he could get a spare bulb at the machinery repair shop on the way back.

Fiona was relieved to hear Don's voice but her spirits sank when he told her he was calling from the call box in the village and that there was still no sign of Lucy.

'I–I'd hoped to hear they had returned to Rullion Glen,' Don said dully, and only now did he realize how much he had pinned his hopes on hearing Lucy was safe.

Lucy drove steadily, negotiating the twists and turns on the road to Thornhill, past Drumlanrig Castle and through Sanquhar, her spirits rising as the miles to home and Don grew fewer. The wipers were still managing to keep the windscreen fairly clear but she could see the snow was getting thicker and faster. Ryan had slept almost all the way down and she hoped fervently that he would do the same most of the way home.

The thought had barely entered her mind when she came upon a line of traffic. The driver of the car two in front got out to pass on the news that another car had skidded on a patch of ice while turning into a farm road.

'We'll not be held up long though,' he said reassuringly, his eye on the carrycot as Ryan began to stir. 'Two young fellows in a van are manoeuvring it out o' the way. There's nobody hurt.'

`Thank you.' Lucy summoned a smile and wound up the window but the cold blast of air and the man's voice had been enough to disturb Ryan and he began to whimper. Lucy sang softly, hoping the sound of her voice would soothe him as it usually did, but she could feel her own tension mounting as the snow blotted out the world while they waited.

Eventually the vehicles began to move again and she breathed a sigh of relief. Surely the movement of the car would put Ryan back to sleep. But her baby son had other ideas. He was nearly five months old now and blessed with a fine pair of lungs when he decided to exercise them. Nothing Lucy could say or do while driving would pacify him and she felt her own tension growing with the noise and his obvious distress. Normally, when the roads were clear, she would have been at least three-quarters of the way home by now. In front of her a large articulated lorry slowed. Another lorry coming in the opposite direction stopped and the two drivers held a brief conversation. Lucy risked a quick glance round at Ryan and saw his small fist waving furiously, one woollen mitten already off. His woolly hat was lopsided, covering half his face at one side and stuck behind his ear at the other as he writhed and struggled.

He couldn't be cold. Fiona had filled a small hot-water bottle and tucked it under the mattress of his carrycot, and he was warmly clothed. Perhaps his struggles and yells had made him too hot, or probably thirsty. Lucy frowned. At least she could give him warm milk and a reassuring cuddle, but where? About five minutes later the lorry in front indicated he was turning off into a lay-by. Instinctively Lucy seized the opportunity to follow its tracks in the smooth white snow. She drew to a halt close behind the lorry.

She squeezed into the back of the car and wrestled with the straps Conan had used to secure the carrycot. Obviously he had reckoned without her needing to undo them before she reached home. Eventually she lifted out her gasping baby son, opened her coat and snuggled him inside before she opened her blouse for him. He sucked greedily and Lucy smoothed his hot little brow with a gentle finger, relieved by the blessed silence.

'Anyone would think I was starving you, little one,' she murmured. She felt her own stomach churning but she knew it was more nerves than hunger. Even so, she wouldn't mind a drink of hot coffee from the flask now she'd thought about it. She glanced at the lorry anxiously, praying he wouldn't leave until she was ready to follow. Another lorry drew in behind her, the bonnet so close to her bumper she knew he must be nearly touching. She felt shut in between the two huge vehicles. She saw the vague shape of the driver going past her window to talk to the driver in front, and was startled a few minutes later when her car door opened and a man's head thrust inside. She stifled a scream.

'Ooh, I'm sorry, lass. Didn't know you was . . . was . . .' He nodded towards the suckling baby, his own face red. Lucy was quite decent but she felt acutely embarrassed.

'What do you want?' she asked tensely.

'Me and my mate there,' he nodded towards the other lorry, 'we just wondered if you're all right, see. Didn't know as y'ad a baby.'

'I'm f–fine. Th–thanks . . .' Lucy stammered.

'I stopped 'cause me mate stopped. Same firm, see.'

'Oh.' Lucy wished he would go. She wanted to move Ryan to her other breast. He began to whimper.

'I've kids back 'ome. Wouldn't let 'em out in this weather,' he ventured with a note of criticism.

'I'm on my way home now. I've been visiting a sick rela-
tive,' Lucy said defensively. 'Now, if you'll excuse me . . .'
Another head appeared. 'Did y'tell 'im, Bill? Ooh! It's a
woman. You all right, love?'
'She has a kid. She's feeding it.'
'Oh. Sorry, love. We wondered if you wanted a hot drink?
I 'ave a flask and a spare cup. Me wife allus sends me off
OK in this weather.'
'Thank you. I have a flask. Will you be staying here long?'
Lucy ventured anxiously.
'Naw, not long. The lorry back there stopped to tell us
there's a bit of an 'old up further up t' road. Lorry slipped
'is load or summat. We'll wait till you're ready. You follow
in my tracks and Bill 'ere'll watch you from behind. Peep
yer 'orn when yer ready t'move on.'
'Thank you. Y—you're v—very kind.'
The journey seemed to Lucy to get slower than ever from
then on. The snow was falling faster now. Suddenly the brake
lights in front flashed urgently and they ground to a halt. After
about five minutes the two lorry drivers climbed from their
cabs and met at the tail of the first lorry. One of them tapped
on her window. She was reluctant to open it in case the cold
air wakened Ryan again. She wound it down the merest crack.
''E's gone to see what's wrong. We'll let yer know, love.'
It seemed ages before the two men came back. It was like
being alone in a white, closed-in world, just her and Ryan.
Lucy grew more and more agitated as the snow piled up
beside the road. She wished she could telephone Don. But
even if she could have reached a phone in this wilderness,
he wouldn't be in the house. He was probably thawing out
water bowls so the cattle could drink, or collecting the eggs
as she should have been doing. Her heart sank even further
when the lorry drivers returned. She could see by their
solemn faces that they were getting anxious too, though they
spoke cheerfully enough.
'Looks like we'll be 'eld up for a good while yet, lass.
There's trouble up ahead. I could bring yer one of me sandwiches . . .'

'No, no, thank you. I have a pack somewhere . . .' Lucy looked round vaguely. 'B–but how long? I mean, why . . .'

'Seems there's an accident. Take a while to clear. You get that rug round yerself, lass.'

'Get your feet up off the floor,' the other driver advised. 'Further away from t' snow. You'll keep warmer snuggled up. Nothing else we can do but keep warm and wait. We're going into the cab in front. Peep if yer want owt.'

''Ave a bit nap if yer can, love. Looks like being a slow journey, even when t' road's clear.'

'Where yer 'eading anyway, love?'

Lucy explained the way she usually took across country to Skeppiehill.

'Ye'd be better staying wi' us, love. Follow me up as far as yon big roundabout, then double back.'

'It's a bit further, but ye'd be safer, lass.' His companion nodded. 'I'll knock on t' window when we're ready t' move. Dun't you worry. D'ye want owt from yer boot?'

'Er . . . no thanks. I've got the baby's things in here. I have chains in the boot. Perhaps I should put them on now the snow is getting deep?' She hoped she could remember Nick's instructions.

'They wouldn't do any 'arm, love. We'll just put 'em on now for yer if yer like.'

Lucy accepted gratefully. 'You've been very kind, but you must be wet and cold, and I don't even know your names . . .'

'Bill Rowbottom.'

'Johnny Greenhough,' they answered in unison and grinned cheerfully.

Don was subdued and deeply troubled as he drove back from the village, but he had remembered to get a bulb for his father's tractor and as soon as he got back he fixed the light. His father appeared at one of the shed doors, fork in hand. He came across and clapped a hand on Don's shoulder.

'Ye're a good lad, Don. I'll think on what ye said and we'll come to an arrangement. About you managing things here.'

'Right.' Don nodded, but his mind was on Lucy. It would be dark in less than an hour, what with the snow and heavy clouds. 'You'd better be getting home. Mother will be worrying about you. Remember to put your lights on.'

'What news o' your wife and bairn?'

'They haven't returned to Dumfries. Lucy must be on the way here.'

His father nodded, and frowned up at the glowering sky. 'Let us know if ye can. We'll report your phone out of order.'

'I did that from the call box. They'll not repair it until the weather improves though.'

When his father had gone, Don collected the egg basket and hurried round the half-dozen hen houses to collect the eggs. Most of the hens were already perching for the night and he shut them all in to save returning later. He had begun to realize what a lot of work Lucy did outside between her hens and rearing a few capons and geese for Christmas, as well as feeding the calves for him. For two summers now she had also kept two hives of bees and done quite well with the honey from them. She and Chris had both decided it would be a worthwhile sideline for a bit of extra cash. He hoped his father would remember and keep his word about making changes, but he knew what a control freak he had become, how reluctant he was to hand anything over. Knowing this had made it all the more of a shock when he had bought the farm for Jake and put it in his name. The hurt had been all the greater because Jake was the youngest of the family and had done the least to build up the family business.

Lucy couldn't believe she had dozed off. It was the sound of tapping on her car window that alerted her.

'We're ready to roll, lass. You OK?'

She nodded, blinking her eyes and stretching her stiff, cramped limbs. She longed to go to the toilet and to stretch her long legs outside but this was neither the time nor the place. She realized the two lorry drivers had been busy shovelling away snow from her car and helping other vehicles in the line. She was tremendously grateful to have met up with such good Samaritans. Mercifully Ryan was still sleeping peacefully, snuggled up in his cot. She wished she had a radio in the car to hear the news and weather. She had forgotten to wind her watch that morning in her haste to get away. She had told Don she would be leaving soon after lunch, so hopefully he would not be too anxious yet.

Both the lorry drivers tooted their horns at her when they reached the roundabout. Lucy tooted back as she veered off on the last leg of her journey home to Don. She had made a note of the name of the Yorkshire firm on the back of the first lorry, already resolving to write and thank both the drivers. She knew this road well but the snow was deeper, with less traffic, and the side roads were always the last to be cleared and gritted. She was glad of the chains that helped to grip the packed surface, but it still took her twice as long as usual to reach Skeppiehill.

As she drove into the yard she could see the lights streaming from the byre, making yellow paths across the snow, illuminating the dancing snowflakes. She gave a huge sigh of relief and thankfulness. Before she went into the house, or even lifted Ryan from the car, she ran to the byre door to tell Don they were safely home.

Afterwards young Richard Green said to his elder brother and Chris, 'I thought he'd never stop hugging and kissing her, he was that pleased to see her.'

'Just you wait until you fall in love, kiddo.' Adam grinned. 'I expect poor old Don was worried sick, having his wife and bairn out on the roads on such a night.' His expression sobered. 'And it was a nasty accident that held them up. It could easily have been Lucy.'

'Thank God it wasn't,' Chris said seriously. 'I was worried sick, and according to Mum, even Dad was relieved when Don phoned from the call box to say they were safely home. I see in the newspaper one of the other people who was injured has died, as well as the driver.' She shuddered. 'Yes, I can imagine our Don just about wetting his breeches with worry. Lucy and young Ryan are his whole world.'

*　　*　　*

Spring came with a flourish of primroses on the grassy banks and beneath the hedgerows. Shy wild violets peeped out from their secret places and Ross was thankful to be alive. He was able to get outside again without fear of the cold, blustering winds that had robbed him of his breath and wrapped iron bands around his chest until he could scarcely move. Rachel was relieved to see him looking so much happier. She knew nothing of his difficulties with the wind and the iron bands, but she had sensed how tense and unhappy he had been. His mind so often seemed to be concentrating on other things as he sat brooding beside the fire, or shooting questions abruptly at Ewan, who came in regularly to keep his father up to date with the progress of the spring sowing, or newly calved cows, the lambing and all the other farming developments. She suspected Ross had had too much time to think and his thoughts had magnified into anxieties during the long periods he had been forced to spend indoors. They had both felt it was a longer winter than usual, though in fact it had been just another season.

Ross had insisted that Ewan should employ another man and Rachel had been concerned, thinking he was giving up on life. Common sense told her he would never be fit enough to do the full day's work of a healthy young man again, but his brooding troubled her, so it was a relief to see him outside again, taking an interest in the stock and in the newborn lambs, and even in the garden. In fact, Ross felt as though he had been away for a long time and was seeing everything through new, appreciative eyes.

Rachel was surprised when he insisted on driving to Lockerbie, even though it was not a market day. Usually they discussed everything connected with the farm and family. She wondered whether these visits had something to do with his health, but she had no doubt Ross would confide in her when he was ready.

Rachel's own spirits rose with the spring sunshine. She had taken delivery of a new batch of day-old chicks and they were chirping merrily in the electric brooder that Ross had bought for her two years earlier. It had taken her some time to get used to buying in chicks ready hatched instead of setting broody hens on clutches of eggs. Now they came in boxes, little balls of yellow fluff, already sexed. She still marvelled at this, and it was a blessing not having twice as many cockerels as she wanted. Even so, she still liked to rear a few ducklings from the odd broody hen.

There were still days of blustery showers, more like March than May, but they did not usually last more than a day or so. Ewan had only a few ewes left to lamb, stragglers that were late for one reason or another. He had penned them in a small field on the other side of the farmyard and taken the rest of the flock to new pastures further away. Ross enjoyed keeping an eye on the few remaining ewes. He felt he was doing something worthwhile as Ewan and Peter got on with other work in the fields.

It was on one of these afternoon checks around the ewes that Ross saw one of them with a lamb hanging. Ewes could be incredibly stupid and the moment she saw Ross she set off at a run across the small paddock with the half-born lamb still dangling, obviously needing a little help to ease it into the world. At the same time Ross was aware of the clouds gathering beyond the barns and he guessed another sharp shower was on the way, and with it the increasing bite of the spring winds so typical of his native south-west Scotland. He sighed. He ought to hurry towards the barn and shelter until it passed, but by then the lamb would be dead and he hated to see the death of any young animal when it could so easily be prevented.

The little group of sheep had gathered together again and were circling closer. He waited, still and silent, feeling the first cold drops of rain on his cheeks. The ewe came with the rest, obviously feeling safer as part of the group. Ross waited until they were near the corner of the little field, then he made a grab for the ewe. He had years of experience of the ways of sheep and he caught her, grabbing her thick fleece and drawing her down, struggling to hold her until he could reach the lamb with his other hand. But the ewe was well grown and heavy, and in her stupidity she resisted and struggled with all her might. Ross hung on grimly and succeeded in helping the lamb, willing it to live as it lay slimy and bedraggled on the ground. He wanted to rub it dry before the wind and rain chilled it, but his breath caught in his throat and the familiar iron band tightened around his chest, holding him down on his knees. He bent forward, gasping against the restriction in his chest. Warily the ewe came closer to investigate the feeble bleating of her offspring. She licked it dry, nudging it to get on to its feet and follow her away from the figure of the man who now lay sprawling on the grass, one hand outstretched.

'Rachel . . .' he breathed on a last, long sigh.

The rain came in piercing silver darts, cutting, wetting, driven by the sharp gusts of wind. Moments later the sun reappeared, and the wind sighed gently. A rainbow arched across the sky.

Fifteen

Only three weeks earlier, Fiona had been rejoicing with Lucy over the news that she was expecting another baby in November. She knew how Lucy had always hoped to have more than one child, being an only child herself. Fiona feared the shock of her grandfather's death, baldly reported over the telephone, might affect Lucy and the baby, so it was a relief when Don's deep voice came over the wires. He would break the news gently and be there to comfort Lucy.

Don himself was shocked to hear of Mr Maxwell's death. They had believed he was making a good recovery. Sixty-four was not so very old, surely. If only the fire had not damaged his lungs. Even in his agitation, Don thanked God that Lucy had followed her instinct to visit him in February. He shuddered, remembering how nearly he had pleaded with her not to make the journey to Wester Rullion. She would never have forgiven herself, or him. At least she could be glad her grandfather had seen their baby son, his first great-grandson.

Rachel was too stunned to fully appreciate all that Ross's death would mean to her, or to those around him. All she knew was that she had lost her lifelong friend and companion, as well as her husband and the father of her children.

At his funeral, the little church at Lochandee had been packed and she was overwhelmed by so many faces. Afterwards the memory was no more than a blur. She could not even recall the reassuring words of Jordon Niven, the young lawyer, who had talked to her after the funeral. In her heart she felt that nothing he, or anyone else, had to say

172

could make the slightest difference. For the present she could think no further than coping with each day and, even worse, each long night.

Ewan now felt the full weight of the burden of running Wester Rullion. He was twenty-five and responsible for the employment and welfare of two men older than himself, as well as young Billy. He must use them well, treat them fairly and pay their wages promptly. This had been his father's maxim, and now it must be his. His mother, his wife and his young son were all dependent on him alone, and the income he must make from farming Wester Rullion.

In response to Jordon Niven's brief letter Ewan had visited the lawyer in his offices in Lockerbie. He was surprised and puzzled by some of the provisions his father had made. It was evident his mother had known nothing of the most recent changes and neither did she want to discuss them. Had his father had a premonition of his own death? What else had he seen of their future as he sat by the fireside? He must have observed more of the minutiae of all their lives than he had ever had time to see when he was out milking cows every day. Ewan felt no resentment about the changes. Indeed he felt an obscure relief.

After some reflection he decided not to tell Gerda the details of the provisions his father had made for his death, nor about his discussion with Jordon Niven. He knew there should be no secrets between a man and his wife, but he sensed she would not understand his father's decision. One thing she would certainly question was the legacy of a thousand pounds to be paid to Lucy. He had not yet brought himself to tell her of Lucy's true relationship to his family. His intuition told him Gerda would then be even more spiteful towards Lucy than she was already.

'A–ah Lucy. . .' He sighed softly. He could not forget her tear-drenched eyes or the way she had clung to him after the funeral, understanding and sharing his memories and his grief. There had always been a close bond between her and his father, even before any of them had understood she was one of the family, even before his father had arranged the music lessons for her when she was still a child. He was glad the bond he himself had shared with her remained as strong as ever in times of trouble. Theirs was a bond forged by more than the ties of blood; they had genuine respect for each other, and shared a true friendship that had grown and strengthened throughout their childhood and teenage years.

How gentle Lucy had been with his mother. In contrast, Gerda had seemed almost callous. Fiona, ever shy of showing emotion, had seemed embarrassed in the face of his mother's grief, while Bridie had been in need of comfort herself. As always she had turned to Nick, as he should have been able to turn to Gerda, but Nick had proved a tower of strength to them all. Gerda had offered no words of comfort to anyone. When he had first broken the news of his father's death, her first words, and her selfishness, had shocked him.

'Now Mrs Smith can return to her proper duties,' she had said.

'What do you mean?' He asked, bewildered by her train of thought.

'She'll be working for me again, of course. Your mother doesn't need her now.' He still felt sick and ashamed for her. 'Mrs Smith will stay where she is.'

'You mean we are moving to the farmhouse?' Gerda's eyes gleamed in anticipation. 'When?'

'No! For God's sake, Gerda, my father died less than three hours ago and you're already wanting changes. Have you no heart? No feelings?' He had not yet heard what Jordon Niven had to say. 'Leave things be. Mrs Smith will be company for my mother in the days ahead, even if she doesn't need her help. Let her decide.'

'All you think about is your bloody family and your animals. Why don't you think about me for a change?'

'Because you're hardly ever here.' Suddenly he was angry and disillusioned and the whole world seemed to be crashing around him. 'All you think about is yourself and your drama group! And that fancy spiv who calls on you – Hubert Hill or whatever he calls himself.'

174

'Hubert Boyd-Hill,' Gerda corrected haughtily. 'At least he's civilized, and he knows how to treat a woman.'

Ewan didn't answer. He felt drained with grief, utterly alone. Only the chubby arms of his small son brought him comfort and hope for the future.

On November 15th, Lucy gave birth to another baby boy, and Don knew he was the result of their passionate loving after the anxieties of the snowbound roads on that February night.

Chris, who was to be godmother, looked down wistfully at her small nephew.

'It's time you had a baby of your own.' Lucy smiled gently at her dearest friend.

'Adam and I would both love to have children, you know that. We're not quite ready for them yet, though. It would mean me giving up teaching. We've nearly paid for the cottage and at least it's habitable now. Maybe next year, when Adam sells his heifers . . .'

'Are they doing well?'

'Very well,' Chris said proudly. 'Bridie thinks they should leave a good profit if they all calve without problems. She has her eye on one of them herself. She likes the breeding of it.'

'You're almost as enthusiastic as Bridie herself and Adam,' Lucy teased.

'Well, it is our bread and butter. If we can't have quantity we must go for quality, Adam says.'

'You've done so much in such a short time, I think you'll soon have quantity as well. At least you own your own home, which is more than we do. I hope your father is proud of you.'

'He'll never admit it if he is. I don't think he'll ever approve of Adam. That's why we need to prove ourselves and get established before we have any children,' she said vehemently.

'Well, to be honest,' Lucy blushed, 'we didn't mean to have another baby quite so soon . . .'

175

'Maybe not, but he's here now and he's lovely,' Chris crooned, giving the white woolly bundle a hug. 'How about you and Don then? Are you managing all right? Is Dad sticking to his agreement? Mum says he still refuses to put the tenancy in Don's name, even though Don pays for the rent.'

'That's true, but at least the rest of the decisions are up to Don now, and I think we shall end up with a small profit this year, and hopefully a better one next year. It's been a big relief since your father stopped sending those lorryloads of cattle from his dealing. We can budget for the feeding and fodder now, and the work is more even. Don was always afraid the dealers' cattle might bring tuberculosis or abortion, or some other disease to infect our own cows. Now we know where we stand, he's grading up some of the better cows to pedigree status and we have started milk recording.' She grinned. 'We shall soon be in competition with you and Adam – and with Bridie and Ewan.'

'You'll need a spare bed for the milk recorder to stay overnight then?'

'Yes. We're going to decorate the back bedroom as soon as I can find the time and energy again. It's a tremendous boon having a regular man to help with the field work, especially now I shall have two wee Greigs to keep me busy. Not that Richard isn't turning into a good lad,' she added quickly lest Chris should think she was criticizing her young brother-in-law.

'Oh, I'm sure he's a good laddie but he's just a boy. He's like Adam though, he prefers working with the cattle rather than tractors. It suits him fine now that Ted Black is working at Skeppiehill. Father should have let Don have a full-time man from the beginning.'

'I know,' Lucy said quietly. 'It was impossible to do all he had to do. He still works too hard, but I don't think he can help himself. There's always another job to do.'

'Aye, Don was always the most conscientious of my brothers.' Chris smiled wryly. 'I can't imagine how Jake will manage a farm of his own. He always managed to slide out

176

of the jobs he didn't like when we were all at home. As for our William, he'll work hard enough when he has to, but he's like Mum, he'll do anything for a peaceful life, even when he knows Dad is being unfair – as he was to you and Don.' She gave Lucy a mischievous smile. 'That's two good things that came out of those awful February storms.'

'Two?'

'Yes, this wee cherub, and Don losing his temper and standing up to Dad at last. He was so worried about you and wee Ryan he didn't care what he said to Dad. Have you decided on a name for this wee one yet?'

'We're considering Cameron Donald. What do you think?'

'Mmm.' Chris repeated the names. 'Yes, I think that will suit you, wee fellow,' she crooned down to the sleeping infant. 'Though you'll probably get Cam or Ron or Don...'

'Oh, don't say that!' Lucy pleaded, chuckling as Chris did a little dance as she sang the names.

The christening was just before Christmas. The weather was usually worse after Christmas anyway, and Bridie had thought it might take her mother's mind off her first Christmas without Ross.

'Mother has always made the Christmas dinner and had all of us around her. This year I've persuaded her to let me make it at Glens of Lochandee. No fuss, just Nick and me and the children.'

'What about the rest?' Lucy asked.

'Oh, Gerda never wants to come to family gatherings. Nick can't stand her anyway, so it's just as well. Ewan will probably enjoy playing Santa Claus this year. I expect Conan and Fiona will be coming to you if the weather is suitable.'

'Yes, I think they will, so long as the rest of the family don't mind.'

'No, better for Mother to have a quiet Christmas this year, I think. But if you're willing to have the christening, Lucy, that would be a good excuse for a family gathering, but without the nostalgia that this Christmas will hold for Mother. I'll make the christening cake if that would help.'

Lucy agreed and the Greigs and the Maxwells were duly invited. At the last minute, Gerda said she felt unwell and decided it would be better if she spent the day at home in bed.

Chris came over early to help. They had arranged a christening luncheon after the morning service at the local kirk to allow the travellers to get home before it was too late if the roads were icy. Rachel found it hard to join in the celebration but she was content to nurse the baby, another great-grandson, and listen to the conversation. She liked Don's mother. She was a homely woman who cared deeply about her family and clearly loved her two small grandsons, but Rachel had never felt easy about Mr Greig. She noticed the way he ignored Chris's husband, although it was obvious that Adam was very knowledgeable about cattle and pedigrees. She could hear Bridie and Ewan having a good discussion with him. Mr Greig's voice rose above the others and she half listened as he quizzed Don about a bull he had bought the previous week.

'That was fair price you paid. Four hundred and eighty guineas, I heard.' Don quirked an eyebrow at Lucy and she smothered a smile. They had guessed his father would criticize.

'Well, he doesn't need your permission any more,' Mrs Greig defended her son. 'And he was always a fair judge o' a good beast.'

'Aye, I'm not doubting that. I'm just wondering where he got that kind o' money.'

'He didn't come and ask you for it anyway,' his wife retorted.

'Not yet he hasn't, but there's time.'

'Don't worry, Father,' Don said drily, 'I wouldn't have bought it if I'd thought I would need to ask you for the money.' He refused to satisfy his father's curiosity.

Afterwards, while Chris helped Lucy with the washing-up, she said quietly, 'I knew Dad would quiz you about the bull. Don told me you'd given him half of the money your grandfather left you. I'm sure you won't regret it though.

Adam says he has a fine pedigree and he should leave some good stock.'

'Yes, that's what Bridie thought. I'd have given Don all the money but he wouldn't take it. It was a struggle to persuade him to use half but he really needed a bull and it is such an important part of the herd. I remember my grandfather telling Bridie a good bull was half the herd, though we do use more artificial insemination now. Don insisted we put the rest of the money in the bank in case of emergencies.'

As soon as Ewan and Paul had left for the christening, Gerda climbed out of bed and enjoyed a leisurely bath, generously perfumed with some new bath salts she had bought. Then she dressed in a new red woollen suit and black suede boots. She flung her mink coat and leather bag carelessly on to a chair to wait for Hubert, but she couldn't resist a last little pirouette before the mirror.

As time wore on, Gerda's anticipation and excitement turned to irritation, and then to anger. Hubert had promised to collect her by eleven o'clock and take her out to lunch. He had promised more than that and she felt a small quiver of guilt and apprehension for he had made his meaning all too plain. Still, she thought, she was taking the contraceptive pill now, so who was to know? There would be no more mistakes as there had been with Paul. She grimaced at the thought. She would rather die than go through all that again.

At last she saw Hubert's car turn into the lane and her annoyance evaporated.

'I had thought we might have a bite of lunch here before we set out,' he said, 'but I saw that old cow next door peeking from behind her curtains so we'd better not linger.'

'But you said you were taking me out to lunch,' Gerda pouted.

'I know. I was waiting for the postman. I expected one of my clients to send me a nice fat cheque this morning but it hasn't arrived, so I'm a bit short of ready cash. I don't suppose you could bring a few pounds? I'll pay you back when I've been to the bank.'

'I'll see how much Ewan has left in the drawer where he keeps the money for the wages,' Gerda said with a little frown. 'Now that bread's gone up I can never make the housekeeping last. And imagine doctors and dentists getting a thirty-five per cent pay rise – they're up to four thousand a year! I keep hinting at Ewan that he should give me more money but he—'

'Oh, don't go on so much about money!' Hubert said irritably. 'Just get some and let's be off.'

Gerda frowned but she rarely argued with him in case he stopped coming. He often mentioned clients these days but she could never quite discover what sort of clients he had, except that they were supposed to be in London.

'I've booked us in for bed and breakfast in a—'

'I can't stay for bed and breakfast!' Gerda gasped. 'Ewan will be back tonight.'

'Well, *we* know it's bed then dinner we really want, but I could hardly book for that, could I?' He sounded impatient. 'Not where we're going anyway. It would be different in London, of course.' Hubert gave her one of those looks that promised so much, and yet made Gerda feel almost gauche. She was a little in awe of his confidence and sophistication. Sometimes she sensed a restlessness in him and wondered if he was bored and yearning for the bright lights of city life. Twice he had returned to London and she had missed his company badly. They often met when Ewan thought she was out with friends, or at an evening class, or curling.

Hubert drove straight back into Dumfries. Gerda was surprised. As soon as they had parked the car he led her into a long, narrow café where they often met. As usual they went right to the back. Hubert ate heartily, then immediately went off to the toilets, leaving Gerda to pay the bill and meet him outside. She was a little put out by this, even though he had warned her he was short of cash. Presumably he would pay for their bed and dinner with a cheque. She hoped so, because Ewan didn't keep much cash in the house these days. She flushed. He must have realized she often helped herself.

180

He had never said anything, but he hated quarrels, especially if Paul was around.

At the thought of actually going to bed with Hubert, Gerda's insides went into spasms of desire and tension. So far they had indulged in some rather heavy petting but she had always called a halt. This time he had made it clear they must seize this opportunity to sleep together while they had the chance. She knew part of the attraction was that Hubert was forbidden fruit, but he made her feel so feminine and desirable. Her stomach clenched with anticipation. Wasn't she supposed to be a respectable married woman? A slight smirk lifted her mouth as she thought how shocked the Maxwells would be if they knew she was dishonouring their name. Things had been grim enough when Ewan's father had had to settle her huge debts. But Mr Maxwell was no longer in charge now, and she could handle Ewan – or rather his finances – since he had entrusted her with the farm accounts. She had found it wasn't too difficult to hide one or two minor expenses, especially now that Ewan was preoccupied with his additional responsibilities. Again she felt a twinge of guilt at her impending betrayal of her husband. Ewan did trust her in spite of their frequent arguments.

She would have been surprised if she had known of the problems and potential scandals each generation of Maxwells had faced and overcome with dignity. She would also have been furious to learn she had been kept in the dark about their family secrets, especially where Lucy was concerned. She had always been jealous of Lucy.

'Where in the world are we going?' Gerda asked, sitting up straighter as they crossed the border into England.

'I've never been to this place myself,' Hubert admitted. 'It was recommended to me as suitably remote, and they serve excellent food apparently.'

'I see . . .' Gerda frowned as the shadows lengthened. 'It will be quite a long drive home. I'd like to be back and tucked up in bed when Ewan returns, remember?'

Hubert gave her a sideways glance. 'Would it be so terrible

if he discovered us? The worst that could happen would be divorce.'

'Divorce? I don't want a divorce!' Gerda sat up straighter.

Hubert's lip curled slightly. No, you little goose, he thought, you want to have your cake and eat it, but I fancy a nice big slice too. However, his voice remained silken-smooth.

'Just imagine the pleasures we could enjoy together, sweet-heart,' he said softly. 'You could spend your money as you wished without having to ask your husband.'

'Ewan never has that much spare money. His family have always ploughed everything back into improving the farm or the stock or the land. It's all tied up. They live well enough when it comes to food – they never skimp on anything in that line – but when it comes to clothes!' She raised her eyebrows and pulled a face. 'Bridie and her mother make a new outfit last about ten years! They've never heard of fashion. Even Fiona Maxwell is growing like them.'

'Fiona? She's the one who lives at Rullion Glen garage?'

'Yes. Ewan reckons she has as much money, and as much influence in running the business, as Conan does, but she—'

'She's very attractive, and she was very smartly dressed the day I saw her. Women like that don't need to follow fashion. They have style.'

Gerda looked at him sharply. Was he trying to make her jealous? No, his admiration seemed genuine, but she still felt put out.

'You wouldn't find her very warm in bed, I'll bet. She's never given her husband a child.'

'Not like you, eh, my pet?' He patted her hand in her lap. Suddenly he frowned. 'There's no chance you'll have more babies, is there?' he asked sharply.

'You bet there isn't! I've taken the pill ever since Paul was born.'

'Good. I wouldn't want that sort of problem.'

'Neither would I! Where in the world are you taking me?'

'I'm beginning to think we're lost. I knew the place was

182

remote, but this is beyond a joke,' he muttered as he negotiated the narrow, twisting roads. There was little sign of habitation anywhere and darkness was falling fast now. Had the supercilious Humphrey Jacobs played a nasty trick on him when he recommended this place? But no, he had telephoned and they had taken his booking, though he had not given his own name. Had he taken a wrong turning?

'There's lights, look! Away down there ahead of us,' Gerda said suddenly.

'A–ah, so there are,' Hubert said with relief. Even so, he had to follow the narrow road around several sharp bends as they wended their way downhill towards the welcoming lights ahead.

'This will be an awful road if it snows,' Gerda said nervously.

'You're telling me!' Hubert's expression was grim, but it soon lightened again. 'But we shall not be here long enough for that. Just don't let on that we don't intend to use the bedroom after dinner.'

'But surely they'll realize . . . I mean . . .' Gerda frowned. She felt unaccountably nervous. She had lived in town most of her life, as had Hubert. She had swiftly learned that if you wanted to do anything secretly, it was easier to do it amongst the crowds of folks who never noticed you than it was in the country where everyone knew everyone else, even in remote places like this. However, she kept silent, sensing that Hubert would not thank her for her opinion.

The building was long and low but already the lights glowed in welcome from almost every window and a spacious courtyard spread out before them. Raised flower beds flanked the entrance, though they were almost bare now except for hebes and some cyclamen.

'Gosh, it's cold.' Gerda shivered as they climbed out of the car. She wondered why Hubert had not parked nearer to the entrance. He was about to lock it, but then he paused.

'You'd better leave your coat in the car.'

'Leave my coat?' Gerda pulled the warm fur closer around her slim figure.

'It will be safe enough locked in the boot. We don't want them to think you're Lady La-la, do we?' He couldn't tell her he had every intention of slipping away without paying the bill. He would say they were coming to collect their luggage, but they would just drive away. 'Just you hand your coat to me and run inside. I'll be with you in a second.'

He suddenly remembered Gerda didn't know what name he had booked under. She might give his real name. He sprinted after her and was in time to usher her indoors. 'You go to the fireside,' he said softly. 'I'll get the room key.'

Gerda obeyed but she couldn't calm her nerves. She had never felt like this before. 'But then you've never cheated on a decent husband like Ewan before.' She almost stopped in her tracks. In her head she could hear those words quite clearly. It was her father speaking them. But when had she ever paid attention to her father's advice? She tossed her fair hair defiantly and seated herself beside the blazing fire in the small lounge that opened off the reception. Moments later, Hubert joined her, swinging a key triumphantly between his thumb and forefinger.

'I told them we'd bring our luggage in later,' he whispered. 'I said we wanted to freshen up before we ate our evening meal. They've agreed to start serving at six thirty tonight because there aren't many other bookings. The young woman on reception says there's snow forecast for the hills and that always makes a difference to their trade at this time of year.

'I see. . .' Gerda said, feeling suddenly breathless. If there were not many people in, they would be more conspicuous, but surely there couldn't be anyone who knew Ewan, or any of the Maxwells, in a place like this? Even so, she hurried up the staircase in front of Hubert, reluctant to be seen for once.

The room was warm and clean and comfortable, but not the sort of elegant place Hubert normally used in London. The chintz curtains and bedspread were pretty, though, and suited the character of the old building, and the small en suite bathroom provided everything they needed for their short stay.

Gerda heard him turn the key in the lock and she turned to face him. He opened his arms wide. She went into them with less urgency than he had expected and he frowned slightly, but he was confident he could rouse in her a passion that she had probably never experienced in her life so far.

Sixteen

E wan often wondered where his day had gone. He missed his father more than he had believed possible, considering Ross had been getting less involved in the day-to-day running of Wester Rullion.

'It's all the little jobs he did,' he confessed to Rachel, 'and the bits of advice I took for granted.' He sighed. 'There were so many things he had accumulated from a lifetime's experience.'

'I know, laddie.' Rachel nodded. It was now three years since Ross died, but she still found herself turning to speak to him, to ask this or that, or to tell him some detail about her day. 'But you are doing all right, aren't you? You're not worried about the farm, are you?'

'No–o, not really.' He frowned. 'The small expenses always seem to add up to more than I expect, but we've a lot to show for our big expenditure. I keep trying to explain to Gerda that the cows have to be fed and kept bedded and warm if we expect them to produce milk and calves. She seems to think I'm being extravagant when the big feed bills come in during the winter, or when the accounts arrive for new grass seed or cereals in the spring. She doesn't understand that nature needs a helping hand and doesn't just produce an abundance unaided.' He grinned ruefully. 'Except for weeds, of course. All the sales representatives are keen to sell sprays to kill this or that, but I'm not so sure they can all be as harmless as they claim.'

'No, nature has its own strengths and weaknesses – though I must say it must make life a lot easier now that you don't have to handle all those thistles in every sheaf of corn.'

'Yes, buying the combine harvester has proved a great benefit, but I'm afraid that's another expense that Gerda doesn't understand. She seems to think that every time I buy something like that for the farm, she should have some luxury or other for herself or the house.'

'I don't suppose she understands that's the way businesses run.' Rachel nodded. 'I must say I'm very glad I still have my few hens to keep my independence. But surely Gerda must be getting used to the way the cash flows in and goes out again at different times of the year, and that it's essential to budget for the lean times? She is still doing the farm accounts for you?'

'Oh, yes, she does them, but she has no interest in what they mean.' Ewan frowned and changed the subject. He didn't want to be disloyal to his wife. 'At least we have moved on a bit. Not like Polish farmers – still milking half a dozen cows in a wee wooden byre.'

'A–ah yes, Peter was telling me about his trip to his homeland. He seemed rather disappointed, I thought.'

'Yes, he was, but then it's such a long time since he lived there, and none of his close family survived after the war. He's glad he's been back to visit, but he says this is where he belongs now. I was relieved to hear it. I don't know what I should do without Peter.'

'He's a good man, but Billy is almost a man now and he must be proving quite useful, isn't he?'

'Oh, he is, but I don't think he's got over the shock of his mother's death yet.'

'Well, it was so sudden, I can't blame him.'

'Are you sure you don't mind giving him his dinner every day? It's not too much work for you?'

'Not at all. I'm glad to do it. He's a nice laddie and it makes it more worthwhile to cook for myself too.'

'But you have Paul most days as well . . .'

'He's a grand wee laddie.' Rachel's face softened. 'And a born farmer. I shall miss him when he starts school. There's not much he doesn't know about what you're doing each day and what all the machines are used for. He loves to talk to Billy over lunch and Billy tells him the names of the cows and which ones have had a calf.'

'Yes, he has a good memory for one so young. I'm often surprised,' Ewan admitted proudly.

'It's a wonder Gerda doesn't miss his company . . .'

'She seems pleased to be rid of him,' Ewan said frankly. He often wondered what his wife did all day at the cottage now that Paul was getting more independent. He had long since accepted she needed a drive in the car every day on some pretext or other. She had joined a badminton club in Dumfries, and she still went to her drama group. She still saw Hubert Boyd-Hill whenever he was up in Scotland, even though she knew he disliked the man intensely.

His name was never mentioned since that December night, three years ago. He had returned from Lucy and Don's after baby Cameron's christening, expecting to find Gerda in bed recuperating from her illness. After dropping his mother off at the farm he had come home to find the cottage cold and dark. Snow had begun to fall on the way and it was settling fast. Paul had fallen asleep not long after leaving Lucy's, worn out by the day's excitement and playing with Ryan. The two little boys were almost the same age and played well together. Even his mother had relaxed a little and smiled at their antics, forgetting her own grief for a little while.

He had carried his sleeping son into the house and put him straight to bed. Then he had lit the fire, made himself a hot drink and settled down to await Gerda's return. He was annoyed that she had ventured out on such a night, especially after claiming she was too ill to attend the christening. She had not even left a note to say where she had gone.

He must have dozed fitfully, for he woke with a stiff neck. It was well past midnight. The minutes ticked into an hour, and then two. Ewan's anxiety grew. Had Gerda gone gallivanting with the actor fellow? Ewan had no idea whether Hubert Boyd-Hill really was an actor or not, but he always seemed to be acting a part any time they had met. Ewan felt an instinctive distrust for the man.

He had been relieved when Gerda joined various evening

classes, but none of them interested her as much as the drama group did. Her father had been right to warn him, he decided sadly; she was born to be restless. He was learning to live with that for the sake of Paul. He shuddered, remembering their confrontation in the early hours of that bleak December morning – and her ultimatum. He had no doubt she would carry out her threat.

His tension and anxiety had grown as the minutes ticked into hours, but it had turned to impotent fury when Gerda eventually waltzed nonchalantly into the house, with Boyd-Hill following as though he belonged there. There was no explanation, no apology. They both looked like the cats that had swallowed the cream. Ewan rose from his chair, white-faced with weariness and anxiety, but at the sound of their empty laughter his anxiety turned to fury. He couldn't help himself. He strode to the door, taking Boyd-Hill with him by the neck of his overcoat. The oily smile died on Hubert Boyd-Hill's face. He was taken aback to find Gerda's husband still up at that hour. At the sight of his green eyes glittering with anger he offered no resistance. He breathed in the frosty night air with a gasp of relief.

Gerda began to sulk but Ewan was too angry to choose his words carefully.

Even now, three years on, he could still see the malice in her pale eyes when he had told her she must choose between himself and her actor friend. When she saw he meant it, she had used her trump card. She knew Ewan and she knew what would hurt him most.

'If I go, I take the boy!' Her voice was a whining screech, filled with sullen venom. She did not love Paul. She did not even want him. But the child was the best weapon she could have wished for. His love for his son was Ewan's Achilles heel, and she knew it. She exploited her advantage to the full. It was emotional blackmail.

Ewan had no love left for Gerda. She had destroyed it. But he loved Paul with all his heart and he could not bear to be parted from him. Even less could he consign his child to Gerda's callous treatment. As time passed they developed an uneasy truce. On his part it was for Paul's sake alone. As far as he was concerned his marriage was over and he no longer cared. He threw himself into his farming, striving for success and an inheritance that Paul would be proud to own.

It surprised him that Gerda continued doing the farm accounts when she steadfastly refused to do anything else to co-operate. She didn't like cooking or mending; she hated housework; she was not fond of children and had no desire to go back to teaching. She showed not the slightest interest in the farm or the animals. Yet the only time she grumbled over doing the accounts was when he remonstrated with her over her extravagant household expenses, and that was becoming a serious bone of contention. She never failed to remind him of the huge bills for the farm.

'Will you never understand, Gerda? That is the way business works. You have to spend a little to make a little. The things *you* spend money on don't earn us anything.'

Ewan appreciated any help, but not at any price. He had become more involved in the British Friesian Cattle Society and the National Farmers' Union. Attending the meetings took up precious time, but still he was seriously considering taking over the accounts himself. He and Bridie also gave a fair amount of time and help to the local young farmers' club with their competitions and coaching evenings. They had benefited themselves in the past, and felt they owed something in return.

Gerda grumbled incessantly about any activities that took him away in the evenings, but he knew it was only because she wanted to go out herself and he was not always available to look after Paul.

On top of everything, there were the records to be kept for the pedigrees and the milk recording. He wished Gerda would agree to take over the registrations of the pedigree calves. Each one had to be sketched meticulously within a month of birth, and its pedigree registered, and all in duplicate. As with the Lochandee herd, the good breeding and pedigrees added a substantial bonus when selling the surplus heifers. All this he explained patiently to Gerda, trying to capture her interest, if only for the benefit of their son. Ewan still held a glimmer of hope that Gerda might settle down and be a worthy mother, even though he knew beyond doubt that she could never be the wife he had dreamed of.

At Skeppiehill Farm, Lucy and Don were expecting their third child and Don longed for a little girl.

'You're the best thing that ever happened to me in my whole life.' He smiled, squeezing Lucy's thickening waist. 'I love our wee laddies, but I hope this one is a wee girl just like you.'

Lucy smiled down at him from her perch on the arm of his chair. She stroked the hair back from his temple.

'We'll just take what God sends us and love the wee mite just the same. I think Christine and Adam are hoping for a wee boy though.'

'I can't say I blame them. Adam has done well since he got the tenancy of Wester Hall. It was a good move buying the cottage and doing it up. Selling it gave them the capital to stock the farm just when they needed it. Even Father must be impressed with his son-in-law, but I'll bet he'll never admit it.'

'No, I don't suppose he will.' Lucy frowned, tracing the lines etched prematurely on Don's craggy face. 'You work far too hard, my love,' she murmured softly. 'If you have any more sleepless nights you'll be worn out.'

'I know. But it's only toothache.' Don yawned hugely. 'Anyway, you'll be pleased to hear I've made an appointment to see Mr Munro, the dentist, on Friday morning.'

'Oh good! At last.' Lucy grinned, standing up and stretching wearily. 'I'll make us a drink of cocoa, then we'll get to bed. This little person may have been kinder to me over the morning sickness business, but he's making up for it now the way he kicks! I think he's going to be a rugby player.'

'No. I'm sure this one will be a wee girl and she's already practising her piano scales,' Don quipped, but his smile was weary and he smothered another yawn.

Later, when Fiona telephoned to enquire how Lucy had got on with her check-up at the clinic, Lucy told her Don had made an appointment to see the dentist.

'I don't know whether his teeth can be solely responsible, but Don is so exhausted by night time I'm getting really worried about him.'

'You shouldn't be worrying, Lucy,' Fiona said. 'It's not good for you, or the baby.'

'I know, but Don works so hard . . .'

'He always has. That's why he's making such a success. Bridie is really proud of you two. She was just telling Conan what a good stockman Don is proving to be.'

'Well, he loves his cows, but I don't want him to kill himself over them.'

'He won't. I'm sure he has more sense than that, Lucy,' Fiona comforted.

Even so, Lucy stared hard at the phone when she had returned it to its rest. She shuddered. Maybe tuberculosis was less common these days, but it could still happen, and Don's father had been one of the last to get his dairy herd attested. Don and his brothers had all drunk milk when they were children . . . Oh, stop it, Lucy! She admonished her inner self sternly. Your imagination is running riot!

Strangely enough, Don was more cheerful and less exhausted than he had been for weeks when he set off for town. Lucy sighed with relief. It had just been her imagination – and of course Don had not the faintest sign of a cough, as Chris had been swift to remind her.

On Friday evening, as Fiona cleared up after their evening meal, she put a hand on Conan's shoulder.

'You wouldn't phone Lucy would you, darling, and ask how Don got on at the dentist?'

'The dentist!' Conan laughed. 'Don's a big strong man and as tough as they come! Of course I'm not phoning. Anyway, you usually enjoy any old excuse for a chat with Lucy . . .'

'I know. I don't want her to think I'm fussing, though. It's just that she seemed extraordinarily worried about Don

192

the other day, and it's not like Lucy to exaggerate or get things out of proportion. Of course I tried to brush her worries aside, but after I put the phone down I couldn't help wondering . . .'

'You're worse than Lucy,' Conan teased. 'Hurry up and clear up, then we'll take a run over to see Mother – unless there's anything else you want to do?'

So it was that the telephone rang in an empty house when Lucy tried to contact Fiona later that evening. By the next morning, in the bright sunshine of a new day, she had succeeded in calming her fears. She decided not to bother Fiona. After all, Mr Munro had probably sent Don to the doctor simply because there was nothing wrong with his teeth.

'He just said it was a medical matter,' Don had said.

'But why did he insist you see the doctor immediately? I mean, he didn't even give you a chance to come home first.'

'He probably guessed how much I hate wasting time getting changed into my good suit just to see the likes o' him.' Don grinned. 'Anyway, he telephoned Doctor Mackenzie himself so I didn't have much option but to go straight over to the surgery. At least it saved me waiting. Doctor Mackenzie saw me straight away. He asked how you were keeping, by the way.'

'Did he say what your blood tests were for? Maybe you're anaemic, like I was before Ryan was born. Maybe that's why you're so tired . . .'

'Maybe.' Don frowned. 'Let's forget about it, sweetheart. Just you worry about yourself and that wee princess o' mine.'

'All right.' Lucy nodded. But she didn't find it so easy to set aside her concerns over her family, and especially Don. He was the light of her life, her reason for being. Every instinct told her something wasn't right. But what?

Rachel was always pleased to see her family and that night she welcomed Conan and Fiona warmly.

'How is Lucy keeping? Did she say when the baby is due?'

'She seems to be keeping well.' Fiona smiled. 'The baby isn't due until August. But she seemed more concerned about Don than herself. He's getting ready to start making silage next week, but she thinks he's far more tired than he ought to be.'

'Mmm, well this is a busy time of year, especially when he does the milking himself as well as working in the fields all day.'

'Lucy says young Richard is an excellent man,' Conan intervened, 'and Don gets help from his neighbours when he's busy with silage.'

'That's true,' Fiona conceded, 'but then he has to help them in return, so that makes it last twice as long.'

'Would you like to take a run up to visit Lucy next week, Mother?' Conan asked. 'We could take young Paul with us, if you like. He and Ryan seem to get on well. I suppose it's because they're about the same age.'

'And both crazy about cows and tractors!' Fiona chuckled.

'Would you have time to go?' Rachel asked doubtfully. 'I mean, isn't this the start of your season? And with the tours and everything. . .People keep telling me they see your coaches wherever they go.'

'We have to take a day off now and then, and midweek suits us better than weekends, especially if we're both away from the depot.'

'All right, that would be lovely,' Rachel agreed, 'so long as Lucy is not too busy. I could do a good lot of baking for her to put in the freezer,' she added with enthusiasm.

'Oh, mother! You never stop looking after us all, do you?' Conan laughed.

'But I'm sure Lucy would appreciate that,' Fiona added quickly. 'Especially if she is providing extra food for the men at the silage. I'll give her a ring tomorrow night and see whether it will be convenient. I . . . er . . . I'd like to see her for myself.' Fiona couldn't dispel her feeling of uneasiness, yet neither could she explain it.

There had still been no word from the doctor about Don's blood tests when the family arrived for their visit the

194

following Tuesday, but as Don said, with the weekend in between, there hadn't been much time. He didn't mention the phone call from the surgery, asking him to go in. He was glad he had taken the call himself. He didn't want to worry Lucy, or to spoil her time with her family. Such occasions were rare enough for her. Even so, he could have done without wasting precious time going down to the surgery so soon and at such short notice, especially when they were just getting the silage under way, but the doctor had phoned himself and he had been insistent. Maybe it would be worth it if he could prescribe something to dispel his awful feeling of lethargy.

Seventeen

It was a beautiful day, so typical of early summer with the fields and hedges a verdant green. Ryan and Paul played happily together in the garden at Skeppiehill with three-year-old Cameron tagging along behind them, joining in when he could. Rachel had brought a bountiful supply of scones, fruit pies and buns for the freezer, as well as gingerbread and a fruit loaf. Lucy appreciated her grandmother's thoughtfulness.

'You must have been busy preparing for a week!' she smiled, giving Rachel a spontaneous hug in a way none of the rest of Rachel's family ever quite managed.

'It's a pleasure, lassie. I remember what it used to be like when there were extra men to feed at Lochandee. Of course we had no freezers then, so we couldn't prepare in advance, but your mother was always there to lend a hand.' She sighed. 'Poor Beth. I don't know what we'd have done without her.'

'She certainly made lovely apple pies,' Fiona agreed. 'She used to bring me one regularly when I first moved to Lochandee.'

Looking back afterwards, Lucy felt that that was her last day of true, carefree happiness.

Fiona immediately knew there must be something seriously wrong when Lucy telephoned in the middle of the following afternoon. She could hear the tension in her voice and knew she was striving to hold back tears. Then it was Fiona's turn to sink on to the hall seat in shock. She felt like someone had hit her in the chest.

'Leukaemia! Oh, Lucy! I–I c–can't believe it . . .' Fiona knew her own face had drained of colour and she wondered how Lucy must be feeling, and in her condition too. 'What . . . How . . .' She couldn't even frame the questions tumbling around her brain. 'Sh–shall I come up? Could I . . .'

'Don has to see a consultant,' Lucy said dully. 'Doctor Mackenzie is arranging it. He . . . he said there would be no delay.'

'How is Don taking it?'

'Well, he only heard this morning. I–I think he's blocking it out. He's gone outside to organize the silage team. Oh, F–Fiona . . .' Lucy could no longer stifle her tears. 'I'll ph–phone when there's more n–news.' She put the phone gently back on its rest, knowing Fiona would understand.

Fiona did. She clearly recalled how stunned and frozen she had felt when she heard the doctor's diagnosis of her own mother. This was far, far worse. Don was a young man, father of two young sons – and another child not yet born. She pulled on a jacket and ran to the office at the depot to find Conan. He saw at once that something had upset her. He dismissed the young man who was taking his instructions. Even so, he was as stunned as Fiona by Lucy's news.

'I pray to God they can do something for Don,' he breathed raggedly. 'They're so young . . . There are different kinds of leukaemia, aren't there?'

'I–I believe so.' Fiona nodded, her voice little more than a whisper. 'Poor Lucy. They were doing so well together since Don's been running the farm, a–and w–with their little family and everything . . .' She bit back a sob. Conan strode round the desk and took her in his arms. Fiona rarely showed her emotions and he knew how deeply distressed she must be, and how much worse Lucy must feel.

'We must wait and see what the consultant says, what sort of treatment they can offer. If only . . .' Conan bit his lip. He felt small and helpless in the face of this problem. No amount of hard work, or even money, could help, even supposing he had thousands of pounds to spare.

*   *   *

The consultant explained to Lucy, as gently as he could, that this form of leukaemia was particularly virulent and especially so in the case of younger patients. Moreover, he suspected that Don had probably been fighting against it longer than they realized.

In the days and weeks that followed, Lucy maintained an outward calm, but inside her heart and mind rebelled against the unfairness, the cruelty of life. In that summer of 1969 the world was holding its breath, waiting for one man to set his foot upon the surface of the moon. In Britain, it was almost four o'clock in the morning on July 21st when Neil Armstrong uttered his famous words, 'One small step for man, one giant leap for mankind.' While the world rejoiced for this momentous achievement, all Lucy asked of God was one small miracle to help Don overcome the disease that was eating away at his life's blood.

The silage was finished and the grass had grown again. Ill though he was, Don organized the men to bring home the second cut. Only when both the silage pits were full and stored for the winter did he give in. Don's remaining strength ebbed away.

He was laid to rest in the cemetery beside his grandparents. Lucy knew she had to be brave for the sake of her two small sons, but at the end of August she gave birth to a baby girl, the little princess Don had yearned for and would never see. Lucy's control snapped as she gave way to the well of grief. Fiona was with her, watching helplessly, her own heart heavy. There was nothing, absolutely nothing, she could do to comfort Lucy at a time like this. All she wanted was her husband at her side.

Following Don's death, all the neighbours rallied round to help at Skeppiehill, well aware of Lucy's burden and the need for her to regain her strength. Surprisingly, Don's brother Willie came over most days to help Richard with the milking and feeding the calves and sheep. But Lucy knew she could not go on accepting charity. She had to organize the work now. She needed to employ another man to help

Richard. When she was stronger, and the baby more settled, she would do the milking herself if the two men were busy with other work, especially now that their neighbour's daughter, Biddy Norman, had agreed to lend a hand with the children for a year.

Don had insisted on discussing the future with her and Lucy knew they could just about afford to pay another man now and still eke out a living for herself and the children. She was not afraid of hard work – indeed it would be a relief to throw herself into labours that would send her to sleep at night. She would plan for the future of her children. Adam would advise her about breeding and which bulls to choose in order to keep the pedigrees.

Having thought through her plans, she told Willie, expecting him to be relieved. She asked him, as she had also asked Richard, if he would keep a look out for a good, trust-worthy man she could employ. Willie avoided her eyes and scuffed the ground with the toe of his boot.

'I'll mention it tae Faither,' he muttered.

The following morning Mr Greig himself arrived. He didn't beat about the bush, but neither could he look Lucy in the eye. His tone was brusque.

'Farming's no sort o' a life for a woman on her own,' he said. 'There's no need for ye tae hire a man. The wages are going up to thirteen pounds and three shillings a week. Ye'd never manage. I've decided oor Willie will take over Skeppiehill. It's time he'd a place o' his ain. There's a wee cottage in the village that would do for you and the bairns.'

Lucy stared at him. The colour drained from her pale face and for an awful moment she thought she might faint.

'B–but Don and I. . .We talked it over, planned the future, before . . . before . . .'

'Och, he wasna weel. He wouldna be thinking right.'

'His mind was very clear, as you would have known if you'd bothered to visit him.'

'Now don't ye get on your high horse wi' me, woman! If ye ken which side your bread's buttered, ye'll no' be causing any trouble in Don's family. The cottage will need a bit o' decorating, but I expect ye'll manage that.' He looked beyond her and his eyes travelled around the kitchen. 'Aye, ye made a fair job o' decorating this place.'

'I won't move! I c–can't. I promised Don . . .'

'Now listen tae me.' Mr Greig's eyes hardened and Lucy shivered at the coldness she saw there. This was the grand-father of her children. 'The cows are mine. Don didna pay for them and—'

'But he earned them! Six times over! All the work he did for you, ever since he left school, and here at Skeppiehill, and you never paid him wages . . . You promised to set him up in a farm instead. Even then you took the profits as long as you could get away with it!'

'That's all i' the past. Remember, I'm the tenant here. It's my name on the rent book. I pay the rent.'

'D–Don paid the rent!' Lucy gasped. 'He . . . he gave it to you . . .' Lucy's voice tailed away. She stared at her father-in-law incredulously, shocked to the core of her being.

He nodded his head slowly as he saw understanding dawn. 'That's right,' he said triumphantly. 'The tenancy is in my name. I'll say who lives here, who farms it, and it'll no be a widow-woman. I'll give ye a few weeks to get gathered up, then oor Willie will move in. We'll help ye move your wee bits and pieces o' furniture, the things that belong to you, mind. The likes o' that useless piano . . .'

Lucy sank on to a stool and buried her face in her hands. There were no tears. Her eyes felt hot and dry. Her whole being was in shock and she began to shake uncontrollably.

'There's nae need tae upset yoursel'. Ye're young and pretty enough. Ye'll be taking another husband before we ken where we are, but I'm damned sure he'll get naething frae this place.' The baby began to cry. 'I'd best be going then. I'll arrange for ye tae rent the cottage. Think on. A couple o' weeks then we'll bring a tractor and trailer to move your stuff.' He turned on his heel and strode away. Lucy was thankful because she had a terrible desire to seize the kettle from the hob and fling it at him. She knew how heartless he had been with Chris and Adam, but she had never dreamed he would take everything she and Don had worked for. As she fed the baby she pondered her situation. It was true she had no claim to the tenancy of the farm. She had nothing to prove that the cows were Don's. All she could claim was the machinery Don had bought. She had receipts for that. But machinery lost its value the moment it was delivered. All she had was the new tractor and trailer, a second-hand buck rake and a few small tools. She still had five hundred pounds in the bank from her Grandfather Maxwell. Thank God Don had insisted she must keep it, but it would not last long . . . Already the new decimal coins were beginning to appear in circulation – five new pence for a shilling and a ten-pence piece for two shillings. Soon the new fifty-pence coin to replace ten-shilling notes was to be in use. Conan and Fiona were convinced these changes, along with the threat of more strikes and the high interest rate of eight per cent, would render money in the bank almost worthless before long.

All day her mind went round and round. This was a problem she must solve herself. She couldn't run back to Fiona for some magic solution this time. Automatically she attended to the children and washed and cooked and tidied the house, but her mind was seething with problems. Should she try to get a teaching job again? Who could she trust to look after the children? Biddy Norman was too young to be left alone with them. How much would it cost to look after them?

Lucy had barely put the boys to bed when there was a tap on the back door. Christine came in, closely followed by Adam. Wordlessly, Chris opened her arms and embraced Lucy, hugging her tightly, rocking her as though she was a child herself.

'Mother told me what he's done! I can't call him Father any more.'

For the first time that day Lucy allowed the tears to fall. 'I know it's no g–good crying,' she sobbed.

'He's a fiend! A miserable, greedy swine!' Chris raged.

'Oh, Chris . . . p–please d–don't say that. I d–don't want—'

'Trouble?' Chris laughed harshly. 'He has brought the trouble on himself. When Mum phoned to tell me what he had done, she was all for walking out on him.'

'Oh, no! Don would have hated that to happen, Chris!'

'I know. Anyway, she's worked all her life to keep the farm going and rear my father's beloved sons!' Chris growled sarcastically. 'And she has nothing in her own name. He controlled everything. I've persuaded her to stay but she wants you to know, Lucy, that she will never, never forgive him for the way he's treating you and the wee bairns, their own grandchildren. She's moved into a different bedroom. She says she'll never sleep with him as his wife again. That's the only way she can show him how disgusted she is – but that doesn't help you.' Chris slumped dejectedly on to a stool.

'Aye, well that's for them to decide,' Adam interrupted gently. 'Listen, Lucy, Chris and I want to help you salvage whatever you can from this sorry mess – for Don's sake, and the bairns, as well as yourself. The bull he bought with the money you gave him – you should be able to sell him and claim the proceeds. Do you know how he was registered with the Friesian society?'

'Oh, yes, it was my job to do the accounts and register all the pedigrees,' she gave a wan smile, 'and anything else that involved using a pen. It was Don who insisted we should build up the herd together, in our joint names. That's why he chose Donluc for the herd prefix.'

'Good for him!' Adam's eyes lit up, then narrowed thoughtfully. 'So–o,' he whistled softly, 'does that mean the calves from the bull are registered under your own herd prefix?'

'Yes, of course. All the calves and young stock born since we've. . .s–since we thought we were f–farming on our own, have been registered, including two young bulls that Don planned to sell as stock bulls at the next Paisley pedigree sale.'

'Well, well!' Adam sighed with relief. 'That's better than we'd dared to hope, isn't it, Chris?'

'I–I don't know what you mean,' Lucy said dully.

'It means my miserable pig of a father can't claim any of the stock registered in yours and Don's name. Some of the heifers from the bull you bought must be pretty near the calving by now. Right?'

'Six of them are due to calve any time now.' Lucy nodded. 'Richard is really good at watching them. I–I had thought of asking him if he would like to stay here, in the house. He's very conscientious. He's getting up at nights to see them calved safely, just as Don used to do.'

'Aye, he'll be sorry when he hears the place is being taken over by Will,' Adam agreed. 'It would be a lot easier for him to stay here, and for you, if you've a spare room.'

'Oh, there's plenty of rooms,' Lucy nodded. 'You ask him, Adam. Then if he wants to refuse it will be easier for him.'

'Right then. So the thing to do is arrange a sale of all the stock with your herd prefix, Lucy. Considering the bull's pedigree, plus the way he seems to be breeding, I reckon you'll get a reasonable sum. When folks hear the reason you're selling, that'll add a bit too. Farmers are pretty good at rallying round with support and Don was always popular and willing to lend a hand to neighbours. I'd like to offer for the bull myself. Maybe Bridie would buy a half share with me . . .'

'B–but. . .' Lucy looked from one to the other. 'Your father, Chris? He'll never allow—'

'He can't stop us!' Chris declared firmly. 'The trouble is it takes time to arrange a pedigree sale. It can't be done in five minutes. There's all the pedigrees and milk records to be assembled and the auctioneers need to get them printed in the sale catalogue.'

'If we act quickly, we should be in time for the next sale. I could phone the auctioneers in the morning and let them know how many to expect,' Adam offered.

'Good idea,' Chris said firmly. 'And if Richard stays here with you, Lucy, until after the sale, he'll make sure there's none of the calves and stirks slyly find their way to Home Farm courtesy of Will.' Chris's mouth set in a determined line.

'I–I don't know what to say . . .' Lucy began.

'I know it's not what Don had planned for you, Lucy,' Adam said gently. 'But I promised him I'd give you all the support and help you wanted. This seems to be the best we can do to salvage something of Don's for you and the bairns. But we'll make the most of what we can get. Some of the neighbours will lend a hand with washing and grooming the day before the sale, and I'll come over myself and help Richard milk them very late the night before so they look their best on sale morning.'

'Y–you're very kind, both of you. But, Chris, your father will be furious with you and Adam . . . He'll never stand for it. I can't let you—'

'Chris's father will not be pleased,' Adam said grimly, 'there's no doubt about that.' He grinned suddenly, a faintly malicious grin. 'Wait until he sees the prices I'm expecting you to get, Lucy. And there's damn all he can do about it when they are in your name.'

'Serves him right. Don earned every penny you'll get, and more besides. The whole lot should have been yours, Lucy. What did Fiona and Conan say?' Chris asked doubtfully. 'I don't know how I'm going to face them at the christening.' She bit her lip anxiously.

'I haven't told them,' Lucy said. Her voice trembled. 'I–I can't. I have to make my own decisions over this. You've cheered me up a bit though. At least it sounds as though I shall have a bit longer to decide what to do. I–I hate the thought of living so near and having to watch Will making changes here . . . D–Don had so many plans . . .'

'I can understand that,' Chris said gently. 'Don't think about it. Not until after the sale. Father will just have to wait a bit longer for his bloody farm. Some other solution might turn up. Just tell him firmly that you'll move out in your own time. Remember you have our support – and Mum's. I can't tell you how much this has upset her.'

Later that night, as Richard and Chris prepared for bed, she said, 'I know I shouldn't interfere, but I think I shall feel better if I can explain to Fiona and Conan what Father has done. I want to let her know how much we, and Mum, despise him for it.'

'Do you think you should?' Adam asked doubtfully. 'I had a feeling Lucy didn't want them to know until she had come to terms with yet another change in her life. It's certainly been turned upside down.'

'Yes, it has, but Lucy's family might have other suggestions – or at least a better solution than that old cottage. I wouldn't be surprised if they want her to move back down to Dumfriesshire when they hear she can't keep the farm on.'

'They might,' Adam said doubtfully, 'but Lucy is very proud and independent.'

'I know, and Fiona knows that too. She'll be tactful, I'm sure. Anyway, there may not be anything they can do . . .'

'Well, if you're telling them, perhaps you should telephone Bridie too and see whether she would be interested in buying a half share in the bull. I think he'll make more at auction than Don paid for him, especially when his progeny will be there to show how well he's breeding. We have to do the best we can for Lucy, even if it means we don't get him ourselves.'

'You're a good man, Adam,' Chris said warmly. 'I know Don would willingly have given you the use of the bull for a season if he'd known you wanted to try him on your own cows.'

Eighteen

Fiona's instinctive reaction to Chris's news was shock and indignation on Lucy's behalf, then even more so on Don's. He had worked so hard and been loyal to his parents. But Fiona learned to exercise control over her own feelings and she listened intently as Chris went on to explain how she and Adam planned to help Lucy get as much as possible of what was rightfully hers.

'You're proving a true friend, Chris. I understand how hurt and angry you must feel, but I fear it will make things even more difficult for you and Adam with your family.'

'They can't get any worse. I'm ashamed to call him my father. We shall do everything we can for Lucy. I just wanted you to know that neither Mother nor I condone what he is doing to Lucy.'

Conan was away overnight inspecting a hotel that he hoped to use for one of their tours. When he returned the following evening, she told him what Mr Greig proposed to do. He was furious. He was all set to drive up to Ayrshire and confront him on Lucy's behalf.

'She's in no condition to stand up to a heartless sod like that! I'll speak to him myself. Surely she must have some legal rights.'

'You can't do that,' Fiona reasoned. 'You might spoil the friendship between Chris and Lucy. Remember we're not supposed to know yet. Chris wanted to let us know how she felt herself, but she probably guessed how we would react and is giving us time to come to terms with it. Knowing Lucy as we do, I don't think she will want a legal battle with Don's family. We must wait until she confides in us. She'll probably tell us after the christening on Sunday. I've been thinking about it half the night.'

'Ah, sweetheart! I'm sorry I was away when you needed me. No wonder you look tired.' Conan was contrite.

'Well, now I've had more time to consider, I can't help wondering if Mr Greig might be right—'

'Right? He's a miserable, money-grabbing—'

'Hush!' Fiona put a finger over his lips. 'He's doing it for all the worst possible reasons, and he's behaved abominably, but for all that, it may be for the best in the end. It would be a hard life for Lucy, trying to keep the farm going and bringing up three small children on her own. You must admit farming is hard work, even with a husband.'

'We–ell, yes, that's true enough,' Conan conceded with a frown. 'But I still think . . .'

'We can't do anything to help until Lucy tells us herself. Meanwhile we could find out if there are any suitable cottages around here. I know it's selfish of me, but now that this has happened . . .'

'You mean we should encourage Lucy to move back?' Conan said slowly as understanding dawned.

'Well, at least we would all be nearer if she does need help. And she will need to earn a living one way or another to keep three children. She is going to need all the support she can get.'

'That's true . . . The trouble is, Lucy is so proud and independent.'

'And who does she take that from, I wonder?' Fiona teased gently.

'I suppose you're right; she does take after me in lots of ways. But I'd feel happier, too, if she was living nearer. We could give her a job organizing the booking and payments for the tours. She would be ideal with her intelligence and her integrity . . .'

'We could, and it would be to our benefit, but Lucy would never believe us. I doubt if she would accept. I think the best we could hope for at present is to persuade her to move back down here. Would it be worth ringing Jordon Niven to see if he has any houses coming up for sale?'

'It's worth a try, but I doubt if Lucy would accept help in that direction either. She'll want to wait till she sees how much money she can spare. Even a cottage to rent would do temporarily.'

'That's true. I . . . er . . . I don't suppose we could ask Jordon Niven if he has anything suitable? I think he would agree to co-operate with us if there was something afford-able, especially if we explain Lucy's circumstances.'

'How d'you mean?' Conan asked, looking at his wife intently.

'Well, Chris thinks Lucy will easily get back the price of the bull Don bought, and maybe more. She already has five hundred pounds in the bank. If there's a house to sell for something like fifteen hundred to two thousand pounds, perhaps we could ask Jordon to offer it to her for a thou-sand. We could pay the rest to him and Lucy need never know. We could easily afford that, couldn't we?' There was pleading in Fiona's eyes and Conan suddenly realized how much she would love to have Lucy and her children living nearby. Come to think of it, so would he.

'You're a witch of a woman!' He chuckled. 'I don't know where you got such a devious brain.'

'I'm not devious! Anyway, when you deal with city slickers, as I used to, you have to use all your wits to stay one step ahead.'

'All right, I'll telephone your Mr Niven tomorrow,' Conan promised and prayed silently they could reach some arrange-ment without ever hurting Lucy. At least Jordon Niven was trustworthy and discreet, and Conan had a feeling he would do almost anything to please Fiona, so long as it was legal.

The following morning Bridie telephoned Fiona. She sounded unusually diffident.

'I had a phone call from Adam Green, Chris's husband, last night. He . . . I . . . He says Lucy will be selling the bull and he wants to know whether I would buy a half share,' Bridie said carefully.

'And would you?' Fiona asked. 'Or would you be doing it as a favour to Lucy?'

208

'Oh, Fiona!' Bridie burst out, unable to keep up a pretence. 'I'm so terribly sorry this has happened after all Lucy has come through recently. Mr Greig must be a monster of a man . . .'

'Yes, I think so too. Do you want the bull, Bridie?'

'Oh, yes, but Don knew that before he died, so Lucy would know I'm not bidding as a favour. He has excellent breeding behind him and he's leaving nice young stock. I reckon he'll make at least eight hundred guineas. That's why Adam thinks he can only afford a half share. We'd have to have him insured and draw up a proper agreement of course. I shall certainly go to the sale and bid up some of his progeny. I'll rally round some of the other breeders too. They'll make sure Lucy gets a good sale when they know the circumstances. It makes my blood boil when I think how shabbily Mr Greig is treating her.'

'Yes, I know. We're not supposed to know yet, but Chris phoned to explain. I expect Lucy will tell us at the christening. But, Bridie . . .' Fiona frowned at the phone. 'Perhaps it wouldn't be such a bad thing if you telephoned Lucy and told her you would like to buy a half share of the bull, and mention the price you are willing to pay. It might reassure her to know she has at least a thousand pounds or more. According to Chris the cottage Mr Greig is procuring for her isn't up to much and Lucy hates the idea of living there. Conan and I would love to have her living down here. She may insist on renting a cottage, of course, but if there was one to sell at an affordable price, Conan thinks it would be more secure, and a good investment for her and the children.'

'Yes, I'd agree with him on that. I wonder whether Lucy would fancy moving back to her old home in Lochandee? Rumour has it that the man who bought it has run short of money. He raised the roof to make bedrooms and he knocked out a downstairs wall and took out a fireplace. I haven't seen it, but Carol told me it's been empty for months and she's quite upset about it. She stayed there with Beth, you know, when she first came to Lochandee with Wendy and Joanne as evacuees.'

209

'I didn't know it was still unoccupied. It has a lovely big garden at the back. Conan thought about buying it the last time it was to sell.'

'Maybe you should mention Chestnut Cottage to Lucy, see what she thinks? She would certainly tell you if the idea didn't appeal.'

'Yes, she would. I wonder whether we could take a look from the outside before we go up for the christening? It might be cheaper when it needs things doing.' Privately she thought it might be easier to persuade Lucy that it was cheaper than it really was if it looked half derelict. At least they knew it was soundly built and it had potential. Fiona's heart ached for Lucy and she wondered whether it was sensible to suggest returning to the home where she had spent her childhood.

'Carol would let you see it. She has a key for the tradesmen getting in but they told her they weren't coming back until they got some money.'

'Oh dear, as bad as that? Still, the owner might be glad to sell in that case. It's an ill wind if it doesn't blow somebody some good. Thanks for that bit of information, Bridie.'

'You're welcome. I'd love to have Lucy living in Lochandee again myself, and I'm sure Mother would too. Adam says his brother, Richard, is terribly upset about the upheaval. He'd been with Don since before he left school. Apparently he's made up his mind to leave Skeppiehill as soon as Lucy and the children move out.'

'Oh, I didn't know. Chris didn't mention him, but I know it's distressing to everyone concerned.'

'I'd offer him a job here, at Glens of Lochandee, but I've no spare room. He'd have to find digs. Of course, I haven't mentioned that to anyone else,' she added hurriedly. 'Frank and Emmie are getting older though, and neither of them like the new milking parlour. They preferred when the cows were in the byre and tied in their own stalls.' She sighed. 'You can't please everyone, but there's always changes. Some folks have a worse deal than others. It makes me think how lucky Nick and I are.'

'I know what you mean. My life with Conan seems like heaven compared with Lucy's.'

'I feel so sorry for her. Do let me know if you think there's anything we can do.'

'Will do. If we do persuade her to move down here, I expect we would be glad of Nick and his lorry to move her furniture, but we must let Lucy make her own decisions.'

At the christening Lucy looked pale and drained. Chris and her mother were tense and ill at ease and Fiona knew how difficult it must be for them. The boys' christenings had been a celebration and the minister and his wife had joined the family for a meal afterwards. This time it was a short, simple ceremony at home, and then the minister took his leave. Baby Kirsten cried all the way through but Lucy knew it was not the christening, or the people, that had upset her. She was hungry and fretful all the time and Lucy blamed herself. She was constantly tired and worried and her mind was in turmoil. Kirsten seemed to sense her mood and she sought constantly for her breast whenever Lucy picked her up.

At the last minute Rachel had decided she would like to be present at her great-granddaughter's christening. Now she rose from her chair and moved across the room to Lucy. Gently she lifted the crying infant into her arms and rocked her. For a little while she was quiet but soon she was nuzzling into Rachel, clearly searching for food. She caught Lucy's eye and moved into the kitchen. Lucy followed.

'Please don't wear yourself out,' Lucy said wearily.

Rachel smiled. 'I may be a great-grandmother, lassie, but I'm only sixty-seven and I don't feel like one.' Then her expression grew serious. 'If Beth had been alive she would have advised you to put this wee bairnie on the bottle and stop wearing yourself out with fretting over her. I had to put Bridie on the bottle – or at least the nurses at the fever hospital did. They took Conan and wee Margaret away because of the diphtheria, and they had to take Bridie into isolation too. It didn't do her any harm in the end. Wee Kirsten will be more content if you give her what you can then top her up with a bottle.'

'Do you think so? Really?' Lucy stared at her grandmother in disbelief. 'It must have been awful seeing your children being taken away, then . . . then losing one of them . . .'

'It was,' Rachel said quietly. 'Now, you take my advice and preserve your own health and strength, Lucy. You've three bairnies depending on you, not just Kirsten. If you would like me to come and stay any time, lassie, you only have to say the word. Fiona or Ewan would drive me up. I'd be glad of the company and I can always keep an eye on the laddies and nurse this wee treasure.' She looked down at the tiny figure, sucking her thumb as though her life depended on it. Lucy looked at them and her eyes filled with unexpected tears. They came too readily these days. She knew it was because she was exhausted.

'I hardly know what I want,' she said, striving for control.

'I can understand that, lassie,' Rachel said softly. 'One minute all you want is your own company – a wee bit space, some solitude. And the next you're feeling angry because you are alone and the world seems so unfair.'

'Yes.' Lucy stared at her grandmother. 'That's exactly how I am. You really do understand . . .'

'Of course I do, Lucy.' Rachel put her free arm around the thin shoulders and squeezed gently. 'So remember that when you need help. I'll do my best not to add to your troubles.'

'You would never do that,' Lucy said.

They returned to the room in time to hear Conan and Chris discussing houses.

'I was just telling Chris and Adam that your mother's house is to sell again, Lucy,' he said with deceptive casualness. 'The man who bought it had all sorts of grand plans but he's run short of money before he's finished half of them. I believe it looks pretty awful. I expect it will be a bargain for whoever buys it, though.'

'Have you any idea how much it will make?' Chris asked.

'I shouldn't think it'll make more than a thousand to twelve hundred pounds the way it looks. Of course, it will cost a few hundred to make it habitable.'

'Would you fancy going back there to live, Lucy?' Chris asked. 'Or, if not to the same house, would you like to go back amongst your friends and all the people you know?'

Her mother looked startled and stared at her daughter in dismay. 'Oh, no!' she protested. 'You shouldn't suggest such a thing, Chris.' She sounded hurt and her mouth trembled at the thought of losing her grandchildren. 'You wouldn't move so far away, would you, Lucy?'

'Now, Mother, it has to be Lucy's decision where she lives,' Chris said firmly. 'And there's nothing to attract anybody to that old cottage that my father is expecting Lucy to rent.' She turned to look Lucy in the eye. 'You know how much I'd miss you, Lucy, if you moved away, but I believe you need all your friends around you, and all the help you can get while the children are so young.'

'But I would help if she needed me . . .' Mrs Greig began.

'You couldn't, Mother. Things are strained enough for you at home as it is. You would feel even more torn in two. It's not good for you.'

'If Lucy did decide to move back home,' Fiona said, deliberately using the word home, 'we should all be relieved and delighted, of course, but Mrs Greig,' she reached out and patted the older woman's work-worn hands as they twisted on her lap, 'Adam and Chris would bring you down to visit Lucy and the children. You might even manage to stay for a weekend now and then if Lucy has a spare bedroom.'

'Even if she hasn't room, there's plenty of us to give you a bed,' Rachel suggested. 'But of course it will depend on what Lucy decides to do.'

'I expect there'll be other cottages to sell eventually,' Conan said. 'Maybe not such a bargain as Chestnut Cottage, of course. It has such a good-sized garden at the back. Ideal for children.' He smiled reminiscently. 'I seem to remember getting into hot water for trying to climb the old tree and falling into the burn.'

'That's right, you did!' Rachel recalled accusingly. 'You were often late home from school, but that day I remember you were very late and you were wearing somebody else's trousers.'

Lucy listened quietly. All her memories of Lochandee had been happy ones until her mother's death. Even then Fiona had welcomed her so warmly, and she had known everyone in the village. She had never felt alone or left out of things. Not like she did now.

'I'll think it over,' she said quietly, and they all knew the matter was closed. But the seeds had been sown. In time Lucy would make her own decision. Conversation turned to the coming sale and Bridie's and Adam's desire to buy the stock bull, and then inevitably to Ewan.

In the end it was Mr Greig who precipitated Lucy's decision. He arrived at the house two evenings later, clearly expecting to find Lucy alone and the children in bed.

'Oor Will tells me ye're planning tae sell my stock and make off wi' the money,' he accused without any preliminary greeting. Lucy looked back at him. There was nothing in him that reminded her of Don. For a fleeting second she wondered whether he really was Don's father. 'I'll sue ye if ye sell anything!'

'I shall sell nothing that belongs to you, Mr Greig.' Inside she was trembling but outwardly she looked cool and her green eyes held his furious gaze unflinchingly.

'Then what's all this nonsense about entering cattle for the pedigree sale?'

'Don's cattle, you mean? The young stock he bred and reared? I shall sell none of the milking cows you claim as yours.'

He saw the contempt in her face and his eyes narrowed. 'They're all mine. You can sell the old bull if you like, but ye'll get nothing for him by the time ye've paid the haulage.'

'I expect to get back every penny we paid for him,' Lucy said. 'He is a proven stock bull now and his progeny will show his real value.'

'Somebody's been advising ye!' he growled. 'But I'll make sure ye dinna try selling anything else frae here. I'll—'

214

'Good evening, Mr Greig.' Richard said as he came through from the kitchen. He was only twenty-one but he held himself erect and addressed Don's father with cold politeness. Lucy knew he must have heard their conversation and she was relieved by his appearance. Mr Greig was disconcerted.

'What are ye doing here at this time o' night?' he demanded.

'Doing my job as stockman,' Richard answered levelly. 'I'm lodging here to keep an eye on the stock for Mrs Greig, just as I promised your son I would do.'

'What d'ye mean, "keeping an eye"? There's nae need for ye tae be staying here—'

'I think there is, Mr Greig. We have heifers due to calve. Fine pedigree heifers, registered in Mr and Mrs Greig's name and with their own prefix.' He paused, letting the information sink in. He saw the anger glinting in Mr Greig's eyes and went on, 'They are too valuable to risk losing any. I shall be staying at Skeppiehill until after the sale, but now that you are here, I may as well tell you I shall be leaving here as soon as Mrs Greig and her children move out.'

This was an exceptionally long speech for Richard and Lucy now looked at him in astonishment. He caught her eye and saw a little twitch at the corner of her mouth. He knew he had her approval and felt a surge of relief, but Chris had warned him he might need to stick up to her father. The older man stared at him.

'And good riddance, I say!' he growled furiously. 'You and that bloody upstart of a brother, ye're nothing but trouble. Ye'll get no reference for another job frae me. I'm warning ye, naebody will employ ye.'

'Oh, you needn't concern yourself, Mr Greig. I've had two offers of work already.'

Mr Greig opened his mouth and snapped it shut again. He turned on his heel and strode away without a word. Lucy went into the kitchen and sank weakly on to a chair. Richard followed.

'Shall I put the kettle on, Mrs Greig? Make us a cup of tea?'

'Yes please, Richard. Thank goodness you were here.'

'I'm glad if I was a help.' Richard frowned. 'Do you think they would move any of our young stock away before the sale?' he asked.

'Willie and his father? I don't think they would dare, not now they know you are staying here too, but we'll move the dog kennel round to the yard and Tim will be sure to bark and warn us if anyone comes snooping.'

'Yes, that's a good idea,' Richard said with relief. 'I sleep like a log, or so my mother says.' He grinned.

'You need your sleep when you're up so early to milk. Anyway, I'm a light sleeper so don't worry. The only problem is I wouldn't be surprised if Willie stops coming to help us.'

'I'm not bothered. He's more hindrance than help half the time. It's the way he cuts corners. I'll manage with a bit o' help from Walter Blake.'

'Yes.' Lucy nodded. 'I shall be glad if Willie stays away myself. All he seems to do is eat. Chris is buying my hens and the two smaller huts so she will be taking them away soon and that will be another job less.'

When Richard had gone to bed Lucy sat on in the warm kitchen, mulling over Mr Greig's visit. He seemed to have no love at all for his grandchildren. In fact he almost seemed to hate her because she would not do exactly as he wanted. Chris was right; there was nothing to keep her in this district now – in fact it would be an impossible situation. She glanced at the clock. It was late but she didn't think Fiona would be in bed yet. Before she could change her mind she dialled the numbers.

'I'm still not sure what I want to do, Fiona,' she said carefully, 'but I'd like to know what price the man wants for Chestnut Cottage and how much you think it would take to make it habitable – or at least enough room for us to manage. The children could share a room for now and maybe I could do some of the rooms when I can afford it.'

'Sounds a good idea,' Fiona agreed calmly, but inside she was cheering madly. She didn't tell Lucy that Conan already knew the price of Chestnut Cottage. 'I'll phone Jordon Niven tomorrow and ask him to send you particulars.'

'Thanks, Fiona. Goodnight.'

Lucy slept better that night than she had done since Don's death. Even Kirsten seemed more content now that she was getting supplementary feeds. Perhaps she would ask Grandma Maxwell to come and stay while she helped Richard prepare for the sale. Then there would be the packing to do.

Ewan increasingly had worries of his own, but beside Lucy's troubles he knew his problems with Gerda and her spending paled into insignificance. Even so, he couldn't put it out of his mind forever, especially now he knew that he could no longer trust her.

Usually Gerda opened the mail as soon as the postman arrived, and she was diligent about checking the used cheques and the bank statement, mainly so that she could remove the personal ones she didn't want drawn to Ewan's attention. Quite by chance they had a relief postman one day. He was not familiar with the rural run, so he didn't know the regular postmen had their favourite houses where they stopped for coffee. As a result he arrived at the cottage much earlier than usual. Ewan was just finishing his breakfast so he opened the letters while he drank another cup of tea. One of the letters was the bank statement. He flipped through the used cheques then sat up, alert now. He paid greater attention. He drew out six. The names of the firms were totally unfamiliar to him. The amounts were not huge, but two of them were nearly a hundred pounds each, so not trivial either when added up.

Gerda came down for breakfast late, yawning, still in her dressing gown. She stared when she saw the opened letters and Ewan scrutinizing the returned cheques. She tried to snatch them from him.

'I'll check them when I've had my breakfast. Isn't it time you were back at the farm?'

'I'm in no rush. I was up half the night calving a cow. There's some cheques I don't recognize . . .'

'Oh? Maybe the bank has sent them here by mistake.'

'I don't think so. They all have your signature on. Who

217

is P. M. Wilson and Son, and what have we bought from them?'

'Oh, that. It was just a little household account – paraffin or something, I think.'

'And R. Carlyle Ltd.?'

'You've been checking up on me!' Gerda accused, her pale face flushing angrily.

'It seems I need to check up on you, then?' Not for the first time Ewan wondered whether his trust in his wife had been misplaced. His heart sank. She was supposed to be his life's partner, mother of their son. If he couldn't trust Gerda, whom could he trust? There was nothing else she was willing to do to help. His father had always left the accounts to his mother as long as he could remember. He couldn't ever remember them falling out about money. After all, they were working to the same end, weren't they? He looked up at Gerda with a frown. Perhaps not. Perhaps Gerda wouldn't care if the farm didn't pay, or if there was nothing for Paul to inherit.

'What are you staring at me like that for?' Gerda snapped.

'I wasn't staring exactly, just wondering . . .'

'Well, stop wondering then and get on with your precious farming. You're always wanting me to help with your bloody book work.'

Paul came through, trailing his favourite teddy and rubbing his eyes. 'Why are you shouting, Mummy? Are you cross?'

'Of course not!'

But Paul knew when his mother was angry. 'C–can I c–come with you, Daddy?'

'You're not dressed,' Gerda snapped.

'I'll wait for you, wee chap,' Ewan promised. 'You can have breakfast with Granny. I'm going to be busy moving some calves to new pens.'

'Can I see them?' Paul asked eagerly.

'If Granny will bring you outside. Now get dressed quickly.'

Gerda flounced away, her mouth set and sulky. Ewan sighed. It was not the money that bothered him so much. It was the fact that Gerda refused to tell him the truth. She had gone behind his back, and he knew it was not the first time. He also knew instinctively that her deceit might grow if he did not confront her. He resolved to say no more for the present, but he would make a point of checking the bills from now on so that she knew he was not blind to her overspending. He should have remembered her father's warning. He sighed heavily. He really had enough to do outside without wasting time on accounts.

Meanwhile Gerda sulked. One of the bills had been for a pair of satin sheets at seventeen pounds. She knew that was more than any of Ewan's men earned in a week, but she didn't care. She had taken them to Hubert's house. They were heavenly, sensually indulgent when they made love and they earned Hubert's total approval.

Nineteen

L ucy was glad of her grandmother's help with the children. There was far more work to preparing the stock
for the sale than she had realized and she was extremely
grateful to Richard and Adam, and two of the neighbours
who had volunteered to clip and shampoo the six newly
calved heifers.

When she saw them, gleaming black and white in the
sunlight, their neat udders clean and powdered, she knew
Don would have been truly proud. Tears sprang to her eyes
and she dashed them away. Crying helped no one.

'You've worked hard and made an excellent job of them
all, Richard,' she praised warmly. Richard's youthful face
flushed with pleasure.

'D'you think Mrs Jones will think so too?'

'I'm sure she will, Richard. Are you seriously thinking of
moving down to Dumfries to work at Glens of Lochandee,
then?'

'I'd like to work with a pedigree herd, and with a boss
who cares about stock.' He nodded. 'But Mrs Jones says I
ought to drive down and see the herd and the place for myself
before I make up my mind. If I decide to move she said I
could stay with one of the men and his wife for a month
until I find digs. Frank . . . I've forgotten his name.'

'Frank Kidd and Emmie. I know them well. I'm sure you
would get on with them. I'm driving down myself the day
after the sale to look at the house where I used to live. I
believe it's in an awful mess but my grandmother says we
could stay with her until some of the rooms are ready for us
to move in.'

'She's a fine old lady, Mrs Maxwell. Chris says all your family are nice folks – well, all but one.' He flushed guiltily but Lucy smiled.

'Don't worry, Richard, I can guess who Chris had in mind, and I don't get on very well with her either.'

He looked relieved.

The sale was an even greater success than Adam had forecast and Richard was proud and pleased by his elder brother's approval. Lucy felt overwhelmed. She knew some of the young stirks had made more than their real market value, even for pedigree cattle. One or two had been bought by neighbours who were not remotely interested in pedigrees and had bought as a kindly gesture. Even those who had not purchased had helped by adding to the bidding.

The biggest surprise of all had brought some disappointment to Bridie and Adam, but their joy for Lucy was greater. One of the men who selected bulls for the English Milk Marketing Board's bull-breeding station had attended the sale especially to see Don's bull, and to inspect his progeny. Adam, with Bridie's full support, had bid to the maximum they could afford but they had been outbid. The bull had made more than three times what Don had paid for him. Lucy couldn't believe her ears. Ewan was standing beside her and he turned to give her a spontaneous hug of congratulations just as one of the farming press photographers clicked his camera.

'Now I'll go and have a word with the buyer and book some semen to inseminate some of my cows.' Ewan grinned.

'Yes, we'll come with you and book some for ours too,' Bridie agreed as she and Adam joined Lucy at the ringside. 'It will be cheaper at first, but if he breeds as I think he will, it will get dearer, especially once production figures for his progeny become available.'

It was the report of the sale that enlightened Mr Greig, since he had refused to attend the market in person. He was furious. He had never fully appreciated Don's careful stockmanship, or his eye for selection.

221

Mr Greig did not come to offer a helping hand on the day Lucy was due to move, much to her relief. She didn't want to see him again but she felt tearful when Don's mother came to say goodbye and wish her well. She pressed three ten-shilling notes into her hand, one for each of the children.

'I needna have worried about you needing help with the furniture, lassie. I see you family are taking good care o' ye.'

'Yes, they're all very kind.' Lucy sighed, watching Ewan, Nick, Conan and Adam manoeuvring the piano into Nick's lorry. 'Chris and Adam have done everything possible to help me. Christine is a true friend. I shall never forget her kindness, or yours. Please come to see us when we are settled in.'

'I'd like that, lassie, though I don't know how you can ever forgive the way you've been treated by the rest o' my family.'

'You've always done your best for us,' Lucy said sincerely, 'and you must get to know Don's children and keep in touch. He would have wished it.'

'Aye, I'll do that,' Mrs Greig said through her tears.

Lucy was dismayed at the state of her old home and her heart sank. Had she been too hasty in her desire to get away from Skeppiehill? It would be several weeks before she and the children could move to Chestnut Cottage. Rachel assured her she was delighted to have their company, but Lucy worried in case the invasion of herself, a young baby and two boisterous toddlers would prove too much for her grandmother. Perhaps she should have stayed with Fiona . . . But her grandmother had offered first and she would have been hurt.

'I miss Paul now he's started school,' Rachel confessed. 'I expect he'll want Ewan to fetch him up to play with Ryan as soon as he gets home in the afternoons. We've always given him strict instructions not to come up the lane and through the farmyard by himself. You can never tell what might distract a young boy's attention and make him wander off. Or one of the tractors could be working and children are almost invisible from a tractor cab. He's always been quite obedient so far.'

'Paul's a lovely little boy. He's like Ewan used to be, don't you think?'

'Yes, he is. And his mind is set on being a farmer, though he might change as he gets older.'

'I must try to teach Ryan his letters and numbers so that he's not too far behind when he starts school at Lochandee,' Lucy said anxiously.

'He'll be fine. He's a bright wee fellow. It's better for him not to have too many changes all at once, although he does seem to have accepted all the upheavals in his young life very well so far. Peter and Billy seem pleased to have him around when it's safe for him to watch them at work.'

When Ewan realized Lucy had been in the habit of sketching the calves and handling the pedigree registrations and milk records, he was quick to ask if she would take over the Wester Rullion records.

'It would be a great help to me. There's always things to see to around the farm. I'd be glad to pay you, Lucy, if you could manage to do them.'

'Oh, I don't want any money! But doesn't Gerda take care of all the bookwork?' she asked in surprise.

'She pays the bills and enters them in the book for the accountant, but nothing more. She doesn't do the PAYE for the wages and she hates anything to do with animals or the farm.'

Lucy saw the shadows in his green eyes and her heart ached for him. She guessed he had been sadly disillusioned since his marriage to Gerda. 'I'll be glad to help, so long as your mother doesn't mind. I could sketch the calves while Cameron and Kirsten have their afternoon nap and Ryan can come with me as he used to do at home.' Home! She scarcely knew where home was any more. All her furniture was stored at Fiona's. She swallowed hard, banishing the melancholy that threatened to swamp her. 'I'll fill in the pedigrees in the evenings if you show me where you keep the files and schedules, Ewan. Do you attach the Register of Merit certificates?'

'No, I keep them separate but write it on each registration. Everything is still at Mother's, so there's no problem there. Gerda said she didn't want the filing cabinet cluttering up her house.'

Lucy nodded. At least she would be doing something useful. She had enough money to pay for the essential renovations to Chestnut Cottage and, thanks to the success of the farm sale she should have enough to manage until Kirsten was a year old if she was careful. By then Cameron would also be ready for school and she would look for work. Conan had offered her a job. Business seemed to be growing fast but she shied away from anything that might be contrived for her convenience. She needed to be independent.

She had enjoyed teaching and Carol had already volunteered to look after the children when she was settled at Lochandee again. It would be a great relief to know Kirsten was in the care of someone she could trust. Her mind returned to Harry Mason, the man she had believed to be her father. She had loved him as a father, too. He had been so keen for her to train to be a teacher. Neither he, nor her mother, had lived to see her qualify, she thought sadly, but she was grateful for their influence now – and for Fiona's help and generosity. In spite of Don's death she knew she had been fortunate in her family and friends and she felt a surge of thankfulness.

Surely Harry and her mother would have approved of her moving back to Lochandee and her early roots. Everyone else seemed to approve. Everyone except Gerda, she thought. It was unfortunate that she had seen the photograph in the paper of Ewan giving her a congratulatory hug at the sale. Gerda had no reason at all to be jealous, and yet she always gave that impression. Certainly her tongue was as spiteful as always whenever they met. Thankfully that was not often. Gerda seemed to go into town most days, returning just in time to get Paul off the school bus. Since Paul started school, Ewan had fallen into the habit of having his midday meal at the farm, along with Billy Smith. Already Ryan and Cameron looked forward to spending lunchtimes with him and Billy. As for herself, Ewan was the nearest she could have had to a brother and it was comforting to slip back into their old easy friendship.

Rachel continued to insist she didn't need peace and quiet. 'I enjoy having people around and preparing meals. It reminds me of the old days and it keeps me young.'

Even so, Lucy and the children spent most Sundays with Conan and Fiona. Bridie's twins often joined them there, but they still pleaded with Lucy to come over to Glens of Lochandee on Saturdays. Alicia and Margaret were fourteen now and they both loved children and wanted to teach. Paul usually accompanied them to Glens of Lochandee but he and Cameron followed Max around the farm whenever possible. At sixteen, Max's heart was already set on farming and he was reluctant to leave Lochandee, even for agricultural college. He was remarkably patient with his young cousins and often pushed them around in the hay barrow as he bedded the calves, making them squeal with delight when he went fast.

'You're just like your mother, Bridie,' Lucy said pensively. 'You seem to thrive on having people around you.'

'Oh, I enjoy it when you bring the wee ones. Besides, Lucy, you fit in as though you'd never been away. You're never afraid to lend a hand. Your mother was just the same. Actually, I look forward to your visits. It's lovely to have a womanly chat.'

'Yes,' Lucy smiled. 'I know exactly what you mean.'

'As for Paul, he's a grand wee laddie,' Bridie reflected. 'I could love him any time, which is a wonder considering how peevish Gerda is.'

'Yes, he's not a bit like her, but your mother says Gerda's father was a nice man, and of course Paul reminds me so much of Ewan.'

'Yes, he even has the same green eyes, and they sparkle like the devil when he's up to mischief. He has such an impish grin.'

225

'Yes, you should see the list he's made for Santa. It's hard to believe it will be Christmas in three weeks.' Lucy sighed heavily.

'I don't suppose you feel much like rejoicing,' Bridie sympathized. 'I'm not so sure it's a good idea of Mother's to want us all at Wester Rullion for Christmas dinner. Don't you think it might be too much of an ordeal for you this year, Lucy?'

'No.' Lucy's mouth trembled but she bit her lower lip hard. 'I have to make an effort for the sake of the boys. I shall be glad to be busy. Anyway, your mother has set her heart on having everyone at Wester Rullion again.'

'Mmm, well at least Gerda is near enough home to make her excuses if she wants to leave when the washing-up starts,' Bridie said drily.

'Of course! The washing-up!' In spite of her own melancholy Lucy gave a spurt of laughter. 'Gerda was always, but always, like that, even when we were at college. At least she can't make the drama group her excuse on Christmas Day. Exactly what does she do there? Do you know? She seems to go into Dumfries every single day. I asked Ewan but he just looked glum and said she isn't employed by anyone, or at least she doesn't earn any money.'

'No, she just spends it!' Bridie said grimly before she could help herself. She frowned thoughtfully, then looked Lucy in the eye. 'There's lots of rumours going the rounds about Gerda. You're sure to hear them now you're back. I'm sure they can't all be true, but there's usually something . . . I'd hate Ewan to get hurt.'

'So would I. I've always felt responsible for introducing Gerda to Ewan at our twenty-first birthday party. But, Bridie . . .' Lucy bit her lip. 'I got the impression that Ewan is already disillusioned with his marriage anyway. I think the only thing that would really hurt him would be if she ever took Paul away from him.'

'Took Paul away!' Bridie scoffed. 'She could never look after him. She doesn't even like children. He has spent more time with my mother than he has ever spent with Gerda. She seems to think it's a grandmother's duty. Mind you, my mother loves Paul's company.'

'I know, and he adores her, and Ewan of course.'

'Let's change the subject.' Bridie shuddered. 'Gerda's bad news. What did you say to Conan's proposition for Chestnut Cottage, Lucy?'

'A–ah!' Lucy pursed her lips. 'I haven't decided yet.'

'I thought it was a splendid idea, if Conan can loan you the money, but then it would be to my benefit too.'

'Your benefit, Bridie?' Lucy glanced up in surprise.

'We–ell, yes, though it was Fiona's idea originally,' she added quickly. 'She thought if you added a downstairs cloakroom – in the alcove between the hall and the room that used to be your grandfather's shop – you could let out that room without a lodger disturbing you too much. I had hoped you might agree to take Richard in. . .I mean, you do know him. And he's looking for digs. I'd hate to lose him now. He really is a grand young stockman. He and Max get on really well.'

'Yes, I can believe that. He's very conscientious.' Lucy frowned. 'Isn't he getting on with Frank and Emmie then?'

'Oh, yes. Emmie says he's a really pleasant lad to have around and always thanks her for his meals. But the arrangement was only meant to be for a month and that's passed already.' Bridie looked thoughtful. 'To tell you the truth, Lucy, I don't think it's a good thing having two men working together and sharing the same house. Frank and Emmie are excellent workers, as you know, but Frank is very set in his ways. Richard could almost be their grandson and he has more modern ideas, both for work and for leisure. Did you get on all right with him when he lodged with you at Skeppiehill?'

'Oh, yes. He's easy to feed, and clean and tidy around the house. He was really good with the boys too . . .'

'Well then? Wouldn't you consider doing up that room and giving it a go?' Bridie pleaded. 'The going rate for board and lodging is about three pounds, according to the agricultural workers' schedule. Of course, he gets his two quarts of milk a day and a dozen eggs a week. I usually have more chipped eggs than I can use myself, so you could have as many as you like. I'd be really pleased if I thought Richard was happily settled.'

'I hadn't thought about it like that . . .' Lucy said slowly, wondering whether this was a family conspiracy of some sort. Then she tossed her head in annoyance. She was becoming paranoid about keeping her independence. It was all because of Don's father. She had vowed she would never allow herself to be in anyone's power again. 'I jibbed at the idea of borrowing the money,' she confessed. 'Conan and Fiona paid all the legal fees, you know. They've done so much already . . .'

'Well, Conan should help you! It's still hard to think of him as being your real father, Lucy, but he is. Even so, he wouldn't offer you the money if he couldn't afford it. I think he and Fiona are making a real success of the buses and all the tours they organize. Fiona has such a good sense of business and she's so efficient. I've never known her make a bad suggestion.'

'I know you're right, of course. It's just that I hate being beholden to anyone. I'm hoping to have enough money to keep us until Cameron starts school and Kirsten is a bit older. It would probably make things a bit easier if I had Richard as a lodger, especially with the free eggs and milk.'

'Well I don't suppose Conan is in a hurry for you to repay the small loan it would take to make a cloakroom and decorate the downstairs room. In fact, I'll bet Richard would do the decorating for you when it's for his benefit. He could let himself out by the side door so he wouldn't disturb you or the children when he leaves early in the mornings. He has his breakfast with Nick and me anyway, after we've finished milking.'

'I see . . .' Lucy wrinkled her brow. 'I'll think about it and let you know. Richard would need to buy a bike if he was living in the village though.'

'Oh he's got one already. He's eager to explore the district. He met up with Billy Smith one Saturday night in Dumfries.

Billy has introduced him to some of the local folks and promised to meet up with him for the Christmas Eve dance. I'm really hoping he will settle down here.'

It was a beautiful afternoon in May but Lucy felt unusually depressed. Last year she and Don had been together. Never in their wildest dreams had they thought his constant tiredness had a sinister cause. She longed to share all the small achievements of their children with him, the trivial anxieties, the joy of spring. Half her life had been cruelly torn away. She didn't believe the ice around her heart would ever melt completely, despite the warmth and kindness of her friends and family.

As if she was telepathic, Rachel called to see her that afternoon and Lucy welcomed her grandmother with real gratitude. Now Rachel sat in a wooden armchair in the tiny back porch, sleepily watching the boys while Kirsten sat up in her pram, waving to the birds or to anyone in sight.

Richard had become almost a part of the family by now, and he had set himself the task of making a vegetable plot in part of the long-neglected garden. Frank Kidd had been delighted to advise the younger man on double digging and getting some manure into the ground, making drills for potatoes and generally supervising. Richard surveyed his long, straight rows with pride and moved across to help Ryan dig his own small patch to plant some radishes and carrots, while Cameron insisted on having a plot to plant pretty flowers for Mummy.

'I'd forgotten what a lovely big garden this is for children,' Rachel said when Lucy brought out a cup of tea and a plate of newly baked shortbread.

'Yes, it is. I never played in it much myself though. I spent most of my time with Ewan at Glens of Lochandee.'

'Did I hear someone using my name in vain?' A deep voice called from the corner of the path leading from the front of the house and the main street.

'Ewan? What are you doing here?' Rachel asked in surprise. A small figure darted from behind Ewan.

'Boo! I made you jump, Aunty Lucy. Can I play with Ryan and Cameron? Mum didn't come home, did she, Daddy?' Without waiting for a reply from his smiling elders he ran off to where Richard was showing his young assistants how to clean their tools before putting them in the shed.

'I'm going to the farm to milk now, boys, so you can play Cowboys and Indians, but don't you dare run over my vegetables!' he growled fiercely.

'We won't!' they all shouted, grinning mischievously.

'I must get back to the milking too,' Ewan said. 'Gerda promised to be back by half past one, but it's after three and she's still not home. Is it all right if I leave Paul here?'

'Of course it is, Ewan. The boys will be pleased to have him to play,' Lucy assured him.

'And will you bring him back with you, Mother?'

'Of course I will.'

'You look deadly tired, Ewan,' Lucy said, eyeing him with concern. 'I've just made some tea. Come on in and have a cup with Richard before he goes to Glens of Lochandee.'

'Thanks. I could do with a cup to waken me up.'

'Peter said you had been up half the night,' Rachel remarked. 'He said you had a bad calving?'

'Yes, we lost the calf. I'm hoping the cow will be all right. The calf was coming hind feet first – big, too. I think the cow may have hurt her back but she was on her feet and drinking when I looked in after dinner. She's one of our best animals, too.' He grimaced wearily.

'Aye, that's farming though,' Rachel sympathized. 'It's not all straightforward. Away and have a cup of tea, laddie. I'll look after Paul.'

Ewan's pickup truck was parked on the side of the village street, outside Chestnut Cottage. Lucy walked beside him to the front of the house.

'You really do look exhausted, Ewan.'

'Nothing a good night's sleep willna cure,' he said wearily. 'I had intended to rest this afternoon, but Paul didn't believe in giving me any peace.'

'You should have brought him over earlier—' Lucy broke off at the sound of car tyres screeching to a halt.

Gerda didn't usually drive home through Lochandee but there had been a minor accident on the main road and she hated waiting, so she had made a detour. The sight of Ewan's truck outside Lucy's home came as a shock. She drew to a furious halt.

'I might have known you'd be here!' she called angrily. Ewan's eyebrows rose in surprise. 'I've just brought Paul. It's time I was at the milking, but you didn't come home to look after him.'

'Where d'you think I'm going now? Timbuktu?'

'You promised to be back more than two hours ago. I'd no way of knowing when you would come.'

'Oh, that's right, blame me!' Gerda sounded bitter. 'You just can't wait to come round here to see her at the first excuse!' She glared at Lucy.

'I . . . I . . .' Lucy stepped back, shocked by Gerda's insinuation.

'Just ignore her,' Ewan said quietly. 'She always gets unreasonable when she knows she's in the wrong.' He squeezed Lucy's shoulder reassuringly. 'You go in now—'

'Don't you dare stand there whispering to your beloved Lucy in front of me!' Gerda almost screamed.

'For heaven's sake, calm yourself!' Ewan muttered, glancing up and down the street, knowing how swiftly gossip travelled in any village. 'I'm on my way home. If there's anything to say, then say it there.' He strode to the truck and drove quickly away. Lucy had already disappeared and Gerda was left open-mouthed in frustration. But she wasn't finished yet. She had more to say about her husband paying secret visits to his little widow. He would never expect her to see his truck outside Lucy's cottage.

Gerda was moody and taciturn when Ewan returned to the cottage after the milking was finished that evening. He felt too tired to humour her.

'Lucy is the last person you should be jealous of,' he said in a sharp retort to her stupid innuendoes. 'If you'd

231

come home on time I would never have been there.'

'I've every reason to resent her. You all treat her as though she's made of delicate china and—'

'For goodness' sake, Gerda. She's lost her husband. She needs her family—'

'A–ah, and you're not slow to get in there now she's a widow, are you? You can't wait to get your hands on her now she's free, can you!'

'Don't talk filthy rubbish!' Ewan muttered. He was tired and fed up with her carping.

'It's not rubbish. You've always loved Lucy . . .'

'Of course I have. She's one of the kindest, nicest people you could find – which is why she befriended you.'

'So! Now we're getting to the truth. You admit you love her!'

'Of course I do. We were brought up together, almost like the twins . . .'

'Don't take me for a fool, Ewan Maxwell.'

'Well, that's what you are!' Ewan jumped to his feet. 'I'm going to bed.'

'No you don't!' Gerda grabbed his arm. 'Don't walk away from me! If you and Lucy . . .'

'Lucy is my *niece* for heaven's sake!' Ewan forgot caution. He was irritated and exhausted. 'There's little enough to keep me here, with you, but Lucy would be the last person I would go to if I wanted to commit adultery.'

'She's what? What did you say? Y–your niece . . .'

Ewan rubbed a weary hand across his eyes. 'Paul is nearly asleep in the chair. Get him ready for bed and stop acting like a fishwife.'

'Your niece, you said! How can she be your niece?' Gerda's eyes narrowed. Suddenly she knew – knew what she should have guessed all along. 'Conan! He's her father, isn't he? Her real father.'

'Yes, yes, yes. Are you satisfied now?'

'No, I'm not bloody well satisfied.'

'Well you'll have to be. I'm going to bed.' He left her fuming and frustrated.

Well! The perfect Maxwells were not so perfect after all. Ewan had just provided her with another weapon, as well as the son he adored. Why should she worry about sullying their precious name? They had already done that themselves. From now on she would consider nobody but herself.

Twenty

E ven after four years of clandestine meetings with Hubert Boyd-Hill, Gerda still felt the same excitement whenever they were together. She told herself she had done her duty to Ewan when she gave him an heir to take over his farm and his beloved cows.

Hubert moved from his dingy digs into a delightful small cottage on the outskirts of town. They had more privacy and they spent a lot of time there whenever Hubert was not in London. The disadvantage was that Hubert constantly told her he had bought the cottage for her sake.

In his own mind, perhaps he had, she conceded, but she was the one who was finding payments for the mortgage. She had paid for the furniture and the furnishings too. Hubert had good taste, but it was expensive. He seemed to think she could get her hands on never-ending supply of money. He thought farmers reaped gold from their fields instead of grain.

Neither he nor Ewan had any idea of the debts that were piling up with stores in Dumfries and Carlisle, and even further away – not to mention all the mail order companies that had recently grown in number and popularity, selling jewellery and shoes, clothes and even furniture. Gerda found mail order catalogues irresistible and nearly all of them offered credit.

Ever since Ewan had discovered the discrepancies in the firm's bank statements, he had checked them frequently. He could barely summon the energy to quarrel with Gerda unless the sums were large and she had learned to mask her more lavish purchases when using the farm account. She frequently asked stores to make out invoices for two, and sometimes three, smaller amounts, instead of one large one that would draw his instant attention. The payments were becoming more and more numerous and Ewan knew they could not go on. Every month he queried the number of items on the bank statements. They quarrelled bitterly when he criticized her extravagance.

Ewan was no longer the easy-going boy she had married and twisted around her finger. He had grown stern, almost grim, and his responsibilities were heavy. In defending herself, Gerda always resorted to sniping at his family or accusing him of lavishing all his time and attention on the farm and cattle. Illogically she always ended up venting her resentment and spite on Lucy, sensing this provoked Ewan even more than criticism of his mother and Bridie.

It had been a shock, seeing him with Lucy, so friendly and affectionate. She rarely saw that look of tenderness on her husband's face, except when he talked to Paul. Gerda could not forget the anger and jealousy she had felt. She didn't love Ewan, but she was determined no one else would have him. Even if Lucy was related, she was a widow now and she was young and pretty. More importantly she shared all Ewan's interests in the farm. Even Paul had learned to love her. Jealousy and anxiety combined to make Gerda more vicious and unreasonably demanding than ever.

'I have an appointment in town at five o'clock,' she said on Monday morning when Ewan came in for breakfast. 'I shall be leaving here by half past four. You'll have to look after Paul yourself.'

'You know very well that's the worst possible time, Gerda! I shall be right in the middle of milking. Couldn't you change your appointment? Is it with the dentist?'

'No, I could not change it. You change your routine for once. I always have to be here when the school bus brings him back,' she said sullenly. 'He's your son. You look after him.'

'Oh, very well.' Ewan sighed wearily. 'I'll come down

and collect Paul before you leave. He'll stay with my mother until I finish milking. In fact, you could take him to Mother's yourself for once. It would save me having to leave the milking parlour in the middle of milking.'

Gerda turned away, ignoring the weariness on Ewan's face, the shadows in his green eyes. 'You know I never go near the farm, or the house, if I can help it. You'll have to fetch him yourself. Half past four. Don't be late.'

Gerda's appointment was only with Hubert. He had returned from a trip to London and they were going out for a meal and then to a film, but there had been no specific time. Gerda simply wanted to assert her own importance. As it happened Hubert arrived in the early afternoon. Gerda was surprised and pleased until she realized he was in one of his irritable and impatient moods.

'I can't leave until Paul gets home,' she protested. 'Ewan's coming to take him to his granny at half past four. I'll make some tea, shall I?'

'Tea! I need something stronger than tea! Surely he can wait here on his own? Lots of kids do. He's six years old, for God's sake. Don't pamper him.'

Gerda bit her lip doubtfully. Hubert was angry about something and she hoped it was nothing she had done, or forgotten to do, like paying one of the many demands for money he kept receiving.

'I suppose he'll be all right,' she said doubtfully. 'I'll leave the door unlocked so that he can get in out of this horrid rain.' She snatched up her raincoat. 'I expect he'll be all right for once.' She slammed the door and ran after Hubert. 'It's been a filthy day,' she panted. 'You'd think it had turned from spring back to winter overnight the way it's raining . . .' She stopped short, her pale blue eyes widening. 'You've changed the car! It's lovely, but . . .'

'Had a bit of a smash when I was in London,' he said curtly. 'I need a car of some sort if I've to live in this god-forsaken place.' He had no intention of telling her the other car had been hired and had been called in because he was so far behind with the payments. It had taken him all his time to raise the first payment for this one from another company. Things were getting tight all round.

Back at the farm, Ewan and Peter gently guided a cow into the milking parlour. She had had milk fever and had been given calcium into her blood. She was one of their best milkers.

'We'll get her in first so that the rest don't push her around,' Ewan said.

'Aye, she's certainly needing some relief,' Peter agreed. 'It's fairly streaming from her udder.'

'Bella is one of the best milkers we've got. We'll take off enough to ease her.'

The cow obviously appreciated their ministrations, as well as the cake in the parlour trough. Suddenly the cow behind gave a violent push. She had finished her own ration of cake and was determined to shove past Bella to eat from her trough. The weakened cow had no resistance against the strength and determination of the one behind. Her feet slipped, legs buckled. Down she went with a sickening thud. Ewan rarely swore, but he did so now. The concrete of the parlour floor was kept spotlessly clean for the sake of hygiene but on a day like this he could have wished for a thick, soft layer of manure to protect Bella. Swiftly he opened the rear gates of the parlour and drove the other cows backwards until the run was empty except for the prone animal.

'That will give her as much space as we can manage,' he said to Peter, but as she struggled and slipped he knew she would never get up on her own.

'She's not going to manage it, poor beast,' Peter said glumly. 'What'll we do? We can't milk the rest of the cows until we get her out of the parlour.'

'No, you're right.' Ewan frowned and bit his lip. The space was so confined. 'Bring Billy. Between the three of us we shall have to drag her clear of the parlour, then we'll lift her on a wooden pallet with the tractor forks and get her into the shed with plenty of straw.'

It took a tremendous effort for the three men. Bella was

a heavy cow and she did her best to struggle to her feet, but that only made the operation more difficult. Ewan received a nasty kick on his shin bone from one flailing leg. At last they pulled her clear of the passage. Billy ran to bring the tractor. It was a slow job to manoeuvre the cow to the loose box with Peter and Ewan holding her safely on the wooden pallet. They managed it eventually and breathed a sigh of relief. It was only when they turned to go back to the milking parlour that Ewan remembered the time.

'Heavens, it's nearly five o'clock already. I was supposed to fetch Paul at half past four. I expect Gerda will have brought him up to Mother's herself, but I'd better check. Take over the milking, will you, Peter? Just until I get back.'

He ran to the farmhouse but Rachel had seen nothing of Paul. Head down against the driving rain, Ewan ran to the pickup truck. Before he could drive out of the yard he saw two bedraggled figures plodding up the narrow lane from the cottages. One was Mr Smith, Billy's father. Clinging to his hand was Paul. Ewan jumped from the truck and ran to meet them but even before he got close he could see Paul was crying. Shuddering sobs were shaking his small frame. Mr Smith's face was grim.

'I've just got home frae work. I was early today on account o' the weather. Good job tae!' He looked down at Paul. 'This poor wee bugger was huddled on t'doorstep. He couldna reach up tae the latch tae open the door.'

'But . . . but isn't . . . Paul? Surely Mummy didn't put you outside to wait in the rain?'

'She's not at hame,' Mr Smith said abruptly. 'Door's unlocked. I shouted in. The hoose is empty. Thought I'd best bring the wee fellow up here. Sodden he is. Cold tae. He must hae bin cowering there ever since he got off the school bus, I reckon.'

'B—but . . . Thank you for bringing him up.' Ewan was bewildered. Surely Gerda had not left the house before Paul arrived home at three fifteen. She must have known he was not tall enough to reach the old-fashioned door latch himself. His overalls were filthy from working with the cow, but he lifted Paul's shuddering little body in his arms and hugged him close. He felt like crying himself as he felt the soft, cold cheek against his own, saw the frightened tear-drenched eyes and fine wet hair plastered darkly against his small head.

'Will you come on inside for a hot drink, John? I can't thank you enough for bringing him.' He turned towards the house.

'I'll get awa' hame, but thank ye anyway.'

'Oh, but...' Ewan turned, pushing the door ajar with his shoulder just as Rachel appeared. He set Paul on his feet. He ran into his grandmother's arms, sobbing unrestrainedly now.

'M–mummy wasn't there. Nobody was there...c–couldn't open the d–door...' Rachel drew him inside, soothing him gently as she peeled off his wet clothes. Ewan looked at John Smith.

'It was partly my fault,' he said. 'I knew my wife was going away at half past four, but we've had a problem with—'

'She must hae left the house long before then – before the wee fellow even got off the bus. He said she wasna there to meet him. The puir wee devil said he shouted and shouted but she didna come. Scary for a wee laddie, specially on such a day. He'd tried dragging a log to the door to stand on but it had wobbled. He fell and scraped his knee.'

'Thank you for rescuing him,' Ewan said gratefully, but he was trying hard to control his anger at Gerda. He was not blameless either and guilt made him feel worse than ever. But even if he had gone promptly at half past four, Paul would still have been waiting in the rain, cold and alone, for over an hour. He hoped fervently that his small son would not catch a chill or, even worse, pneumonia. Panic claimed him and he dashed back to the house.

Rachel already had Paul in a warm bath. She reassured Ewan as best she could.

'He's a sturdy wee fellow. I think he'll be all right as far as chills go.' Her eyes met Ewan's. 'I'm not so sure what other effects it might have on the wee soul, though,' she said in a low voice, her eyes grave. 'Even now he keeps giving little shuddering sobs. He thought everyone had run away and left him all alone.'

Rachel was right. Physically Paul was a sturdy, healthy boy and he was none the worse for his soaking. Unfortunately Gerda had already sown many seeds of doubt in his young mind about his security with her frequent rages. He had often heard her shouting that she had never wanted a child, and that she didn't see why she should have to stay home and look after him. As he waited alone in the pouring rain, growing colder and hungrier, his childish imagination had grown into a conviction that no one wanted him and he had been left to starve like the boy in the fairy story. He could find the way to the farm and Granny Maxwell, but he had promised her he would never go there alone.

Rachel succeeded in distracting his attention from his ordeal. It was later than usual before Ewan finished milking and he stayed to share the hot meal that his mother had prepared for them. But when it was time to go home to bed, Paul refused to return to the cottage. Eventually Rachel agreed he should stay the night with her until Ewan had sorted out his problems with Gerda and extracted a promise that she would never neglect Paul again.

There was nothing she could do to prevent the nightmares that haunted her grandson's sleep and kept her awake for long hours during the night. When Ewan arrived to drive Paul to school the following morning, he saw at once that both his mother and his son were pale and tired.

'I think he should have a day away from school today,' Rachel said.

'A day off!' Ewan stared at her. His mother had never believed in giving in to weakness. Was she going soft with her grandson?

'We both need a quiet day after the night we've had,' she said firmly. 'I think Paul is going to take a lot of reassuring. It's more than just being left out in the rain. A lot of.other fears surfaced during the night. He's a very troubled wee

240

boy and he has a vivid imagination, which makes his fears worse.'

'I don't want to go back there!' Paul whispered hoarsely. He clung to Rachel in a way he had never done before, his small chin wobbling, his green eyes dark with nameless fears. 'I want to stay with Granny for ever and ever.'

Rachel gave him a reassuring squeeze then sent him outside to feed one of the kittens. She turned to face Ewan. 'Did Gerda say why she had left him?' she asked sternly.

'Not exactly, but I have a fair idea of the reason.' Ewan sat down and stared at the floor, then he raised his head and looked his mother in the eye. 'My marriage to Gerda has been a failure,' he said dully. 'I can't give her the sort of life she craves. The only good thing to come out of it is Paul.'

'Oh, Ewan. . .' Rachel looked helplessly at her son's bowed head and her heart ached for him. But it was not her way to pretend. She had suspected for a long time that things were not right between him and Gerda. She had known he was unhappy, but it had never been her policy to ask questions or interfere. She had done her best to talk to Gerda, to be friendly, but there had never been any response.

'She's been seeing some actor fellow for a long time. When I talked of a divorce she threatened . . .' He bit his lip.

'Wh–what did she threaten?'

'She said she would take Paul with her and she'd make sure I'd never see him again.'

'Oh, Ewan! B–but . . .'

'I know, I know,' Ewan said wearily. 'I've put up with a lot from her for Paul's sake. It would have been bad enough if she had taken him away because she loved him, or even wanted him, but it's even worse to know she doesn't like children, even her own son. She would have done it purely out of spite. I'm convinced she would have neglected him.'

'She's certainly never cared for him much,' Rachel said slowly. 'So what can you do?'

'Last night I told her Mr Smith was a witness to her conduct and her neglect of Paul and that I would fight for him in the courts if necessary. I think I've shaken her conviction that she holds the trump card, but I wouldn't like to put it to the test, at least not yet. If you are willing to keep Paul here for a few weeks I thought we could see whether he changes his mind and wants to return to his mother.'

'Of course he can stay for as long as he likes, but . . .'

'I'll ask the bus driver to drop him at the farm road end. There's just one thing though, Mother. If you have Paul to care for, I insist on getting you some help.'

'Oh, but . . .'

'It could be an indefinite stay. I'm fairly certain Gerda will not leave of her own free will, if only because she wants the money,' he added bitterly. 'So I shall leave the cottage. If you have both Paul and me to look after, would you consider having Joanne to help?'

'Joanne?'

'Carol's daughter, Joanne Williams. You know she nearly had a nervous breakdown after she was jilted?'

'Yes, I knew that, but it wasn't only because he left her for a young girl. She had helped him build up his business from nothing. It was her whole life and she was left with nothing.'

'Well Lucy says she's much better now and she's thinking of doing something entirely different, even if it's only temporarily. When Lucy starts teaching again she will not have time to help me with the pedigrees. She thought Joanne might take it on. I'm going to stop Gerda paying the bills and doing the accounts too. She's cost me far too much already. Keeping the peace at any price will not be important if Paul is not in the house.' Ewan was speaking as much to himself as to her, Rachel knew. She noticed how grim he looked when he mentioned his wife. 'Anyway, can I ask Joanne if she would work two days a week helping you and another day doing the farm's office work? Lucy thinks she'll find it well within her scope after running the business for her ex-fiancé, and Joanne wants something easy until she gets her confidence back.'

'Well, I certainly like Joanne, and her sister, Wendy.'

Rachel said slowly. 'I remember when they came to Lochandee as evacuees with their mother. Carol's husband was lost at sea not long after. They've not had an easy life. If you're sure Joanne will not mind housework then we could give it a trial.'

'I'll have a word with her this afternoon,' Ewan promised. 'I expect Gerda will kick up a fuss when I take the farm accounts out of her keeping. Well, the cheque book anyway.' He grimaced bitterly. 'But that's just too bad. I've had enough.'

Ewan's look of resolve reminded Rachel of his father.

Afterwards she wondered whether she should have tried to influence him. Should he have given his marriage one more chance? Would things have turned out less tragically if he had?

Twenty-One

E wan had tolerated four years of Gerda's neglect, so he decided a few more weeks made little difference to him now. His main concern was to make certain Paul would not suddenly change his mind and want to return to the cottage and his mother. Strangely enough, he rarely mentioned Gerda and he didn't seem to think of the cottage as home. Was it possible she had made so little impression on his young life? Ewan found it even more extraordinary that Gerda never expressed the slightest desire to see her own child.

Without his son, Ewan found the cottage held no attraction for him either. He spent more and more time at the farm, usually only returning to the cottage after he had read Paul a bedtime story and tucked him up for the night. Gerda was rarely at home.

So far Ewan had not made any other changes, but Joanne seemed more than willing to help his mother and it soon became apparent that they got on well together. Lucy had shown her how to deal with the birth registrations for the calves. Once she got used to donning wellingtons and trousers and going into the pens she was very efficient. She didn't seem to mind the calves trying to suck her fingers and she understood how important it was to observe even the smallest marking. She began to take an interest in the animals as individuals too, and she asked questions about the various cow families and their records. Ewan was delighted and relieved.

'I have been invited to judge some herds in Ireland for a competition, Joanne. I had begun to think I ought to cancel because I should be away for several days. I do believe you and Peter will probably manage perfectly between you.'

'We'll certainly do our best, and Billy Smith is very conscientious too, if he has some responsibility.' Joanne nodded. 'It would do you good to get away, Ewan.'

'Yes, I believe you're right. About the accounts – will you be ready to cope with them when I return?'

'That will be no problem.' Joanne smiled. 'After all, I was used to that sort of work . . .' She was amazed to find she could talk about it without flinching now. Lucy was right. She was making a new life and putting the past behind her. Mrs Maxwell's soothing presence and cheerful manner had helped enormously, as had the complete change of environment. She enjoyed walking around the farmyard, seeing the animals and poultry, often taking Paul with her when he was not at school. His questions were endless.

'You'll find a few discrepancies between the bank and the accounts to begin with, I expect,' Ewan said. He met her eyes squarely and gave a wry grimace. 'Gerda has been making use of the business cheque book. She's taken advantage and I've let her get away with it for too long.' He sighed. 'It seemed worth it for Paul's sake. Recently the amounts have grown in size and number and it's got to stop . . .'

'Oh. I see.' Joanna nodded uncomfortably but she gave him a sympathetic glance. So she was not the only one who had been disappointed in her choice of partners, she realized. It must be worse to have been married and find it was all a dreadful mistake.

A few evenings later Ewan waylaid Gerda on her way out.

'Perhaps you'd like to move in permanently with Hubert Boyd-Hill,' he suggested. 'You spend so little time here anyway.' She looked at him sharply but she was dismayed to find he was neither bitter nor upset. He was quite matter-of-fact. She realized it was what he wanted her to do. He no longer cared. She stared at him.

'You can't get rid of me so easily,' she snapped. 'This is my home.'

'In that case I'll move out myself,' Ewan said evenly. He was determined to remain cool and unprovoked. He knew exactly what he wanted to do now and the sooner he could get Gerda out of his life, and Paul's, the happier he would be.

'Makes no difference to me.' Gerda shrugged. 'You're hardly ever here anyway.'

'Then that makes two of us. We'll agree to go our separate ways. You can keep the contents of the cottage. They're all your choosing anyway. Just one thing. . .' His green eyes narrowed. 'Don't imagine I'll put up with Boyd moving in here. I've subsidised you both long enough. As soon as enough time has passed we'll get a divorce.'

'Divorce!' Gerda's voice rose. 'I never said anything about divorce. I'll not agree . . .'

'My dear Gerda.' It was Ewan who showed his contempt now. 'You can't seriously believe I want to keep you as my wife the way things are.'

'We can go on as we are . . .' she began. Ewan thought he detected something like fear in her pale blue eyes, but there was hardness too.

'I think not. I only put up with you playing around with your fancy man and helping yourself to money for Paul's sake. But you're the most unnatural mother I've ever come across.'

'You never met mine!' Gerda snorted. 'At least I stayed. She didn't!' Ewan didn't answer. There was no point in prolonging things.

'I'll get the rest of my things from my room, then I'll collect the box with the accounts and the cheque book and take them with me up to the farm. Joanne Williams will handle all the books from now on.'

Gerda stared after his retreating figure, her face paling. The cheque book! He was taking it away with the accounts . . . What would she do? What would Hubert say when she couldn't get the extra money he kept demanding?

She had never been able to manage on her allowance, though she knew it had been a generous one after she gave up teaching. Would Ewan even continue to pay it? Swiftly, without any clear thought, she slipped the new cheque book under a cushion. The old one had only a few cheques left and the postman had brought the new one yesterday. She would say the bank had forgotten to send a replacement if Joanne asked.

She would probably never notice a few extra cheques so long as the amounts were inconspicuous. Even if she did, Ewan might ignore them. She slumped in a chair. He was not a bad man. He had been more tolerant than she deserved, even though it was only for the sake of his brat. Had she ever loved him? Truly loved him? In her heart Gerda had to admit she had not. All she had wanted was his adulation. That and someone who could keep her in pretty clothes and buy her jewellery.

The sound of a car horn brought her to her feet. That would be Hubert. She would not tell him tonight.

Ewan set off for his trip to Ireland with a lighter heart than he'd had for some time. He felt he had reached a major turning point in his life. He had made his mistakes but he had a lot of life ahead of him and he would make the best of it, especially as far as Paul was concerned.

He signed some cheques ready for Joanne.

'Pay the biggest bills first and if you see Gerda, ask her if the bank have sent out the new cheque book. I'll sign the rest when I return and I'll tell them to send all communications to this address from now on. I must ask them to cancel Gerda's signature on the business account too.' He frowned. He hadn't thought about that. Still, he had no time to do anything about it until he came back from Ireland and Gerda would have no access to his account anyway without a cheque book.

Joanne did as he asked and posted off the cheques to the various businesses. Resolving to have everything up to date and ready for Ewan's return, she decided to walk down to Gerda's cottage and ask whether the new cheque book had arrived.

Gerda frowned at the sight of Joanne but she did not invite her in. Joanne was pleasant and businesslike. It never occurred to her that Gerda would be totally dishonest in her dealings with Ewan.

'Oh, I did fill in the form for the new cheque book but the bank must have forgotten to send one. They often make mistakes,' Gerda said airily. 'You'll have to go in and ask for it next time you're in town.'

Joanne thanked her and turned away, unsuspecting. She was just turning away from the cottage when a gleaming Jaguar pulled up. Joanne's eyebrows rose and she eyed it appreciatively.

'Who was that?' Hubert Boyd-Hill asked abruptly. Gerda frowned but she explained why Joanna had called. He had been furious when he heard Ewan had left the cottage and taken away the accounts and cheque book.

'You should have played him along better. Surely you could have used your feminine charms on him!'

Gerda had remained sullen and silent. He obviously didn't mind sharing her with another man so long as she got her hands on plenty of spare cash for his benefit. She hadn't told him then that she had kept the cheque book, but she told him now.

'Well, well!' he chuckled. 'My clever little goose!' Then he sobered. 'It's only a matter of time before they find out you have it. I think we'd better put it to use right away.'

'There's no hurry . . .'

'Of course there is. Your husband will cancel your signature – if he hasn't done so already,' he said, jerking upright at the possibility. 'You should have told me. The sooner we clear him out the better.'

'Clear him out?'

'How much does he usually keep in his business account?'

'He always likes to make sure there is enough to pay the monthly bills, cattle cake, the vet, tractor fuel, the wages, things like that . . .'

'How much spare does he keep, for God's sake?'

'He's trying to accumulate enough to change one of his big machines just now. I suppose he could have about five thousand if the milk cheque is in and the bills aren't paid yet . . .'

'Five grand!' Hubert's small eyes gleamed. 'Right. Make

out a cheque to yourself for that amount and we'll go in right away and cash it.'

'We can't do that!' Gerda gasped.

'We have to, before that woman goes in and alerts the bank, and before the firms present the cheques she's sending out. You always paid the bills at the end of the month, didn't you?'

'Y–yes. But in any case they would never give me that much in cash. We only ever drew about a hundred pounds to pay wages and petrol . . .'

'All right. Make it two thousand then. I'll drive you in right away. And while you're at it you can make out a cheque to me for the other three thousand. I'll put it into my account until we need it.'

'I c–can't!' Gerda stared at him. The amounts she had fiddled herself had been hundreds, but never thousands – apart from the fur coat. She frowned. If she added up all her debts it would take two thousand to pay them off. She had no idea how much Hubert's own debts might be. She was pale and irritable. She had not slept for thinking about them since Ewan left.

'Can't or won't?' Hubert demanded angrily. 'Either you do it now while we have the chance or that's the end for us.'

'You don't mean that, Hubert . . .' Gerda stared at him. She felt like bursting into tears. He looked back at her and turned on his old charm, speaking softly, persuasively. He knew she would do as he wanted in the end, and once the money was in his possession Maxwell would never get his hands on it.

It was another two days before Joanna went into town. She called at the bank but, as she had anticipated, they refused to hand over Ewan's cheque book without his authority. He would be home by midnight if he caught the evening ferry. He could sort things out in person.

There was a small pile of letters waiting for Ewan the following morning but he pushed them aside until he had eaten his breakfast.

'Joanna couldn't pay the rest of the bills but she said she would call in tomorrow morning and do them after you've had time to go to the bank for a new cheque book,' Rachel said as she sipped a cup of tea.

'Mmm, all right. Did she ask Gerda if it had been delivered to the cottage?'

'Yes, she did, but Gerda told her she would have to collect it. She said the bank often made mistakes, but I don't remember them being careless.'

'No... Yes! What the...' Ewan swallowed the last of his tea in a gulp and waved a letter at his mother. 'They've made one now! This says my account is overdrawn!'

'Overdrawn...' Rachel looked at him in concern. 'Could Joanne have made a mistake, do you think?'

'I don't know...' Ewan scraped back his chair and went towards the bureau. He frowned as he looked at the invoices Joanne had just paid and then at the cheque book stubs, all neatly filled in and in order. 'I can't see any mistake here. Joanne's meticulous. I'll telephone the bank.'

He returned a few minutes later, his face pale and strained. 'They put me through to the manager. I'm going in to see him now. As soon as I've washed and changed.'

'But...' Rachel shook her head. Ewan was already taking the stairs two at a time. She went into the hall and brought out his mackintosh and fine leather boots. It was still raining heavily.

'I'll tell you all about it, Mother, when I know myself.'

'Yes, I know that. I was going to say concentrate on your driving and forget about the bank—'

'Forget! There was more than six thousand pounds in my account, more than enough to pay all this month's bills and change the combine harvester!'

'Think about that when you get there. There will be floods on some of the back roads after the rain we've had ...' Rachel frowned and bit her lip. Ewan had already closed the door behind him. He was so worked up about it, but surely the bank would put matters right.

*   *   *

250

Ewan stared across the desk incredulously. 'You paid out two thousand pounds? In cash?'

'Well, your wife does have your authority to sign the cheques, Mr Maxwell,' the bank manager said levelly.

'Not any more she doesn't!'

'I . . . er . . . I see. You mean you want us to cancel that authority?'

'Certainly I do. Even so there was well over two thousand pounds in my account. So why is it overdrawn?'

'One moment while I get the particulars of your account and recent drawings, please.'

Ewan waited, drumming his fingers impatiently. He could barely control his agitation, or his fury. He should have guessed Gerda would do something like this. He should have cancelled her authority immediately. In fact he should never have given it in the first place.

'Here we are, Mr Maxwell.' The man was frowning down at the papers in his hand. He read out one or two of the amounts – cheques that Joanne had paid and which Ewan recognized as legitimate monthly accounts for cattle cake, another for detergents and sundry dairy items. 'A–ah, this is the one that made you overdrawn. Three thousand, two hundred and forty pounds, ten shillings and sixpence.'

'Three thousand. . . Three! Then it's definitely a mistake.'

'A new tractor? A car?'

'No! Who is the cheque made out to?'

'Messrs H. Boyd-Hill—'

'What! Why the . . . Stop the cheque! You must stop the cheque!'

'It's too late for that, Mr Maxwell.' The manager's sandy eyebrows rose. 'The cheque was dated more than a week ago.'

'That doesn't mean anything. It could have been back-dated. It probably was. Has it gone through?'

'Yes. It was presented four days ago.'

Four days. Ewan's mind calculated furiously. That must have been the day after he left for Ireland.

'Do you wish me to see who signed the cheque.'

251

'No.' Ewan slumped in his seat. 'The man's a swindler! And she's just as bad. Can't you get the money back? Is there nothing you can do?'

'I'm afraid it's too late for us to do that.'

'I see. Thank you.' Ewan rose, his face grim, his mouth set. At the door he turned back to the bank manager. 'Be sure to cancel my wife's authority. In fact, to make doubly sure, you can cancel my account and open a new one.'

'We can certainly do that, Mr Maxwell, but meanwhile you are over—'

'Set up the new account. I'll come back tomorrow and sort this mess out. Meanwhile if you could arrange an overdraft to cover this month's cheques . . .'

'We—ell . . . Very well, I'll see what I can do, Mr Maxwell. I shall need your signature and . . .' He looked at Ewan shrewdly. 'Your family have dealt with us for many years and we have never had anything like this happen before.'

'Nor ever again, I hope!' Ewan muttered as he went out.

At that moment, if he had known where to find Hubert Boyd-Hill he knew he would have been capable of murder. As it was he did know where he could find Gerda at this time on a pouring-wet morning. She was probably not even out of bed. He yanked on his mackintosh and ran across the street to his car.

His mind was seething with some way to make the two of them pay for their treachery. It wasn't just money. He was a fool. He had been tolerant too long, overlooked too many things for the sake of peace in his home.

He would turn Gerda out of the cottage. She could live with her actor. She could starve by the roadside for all he cared now. What a fool he'd been. His thoughts went round and round. His brain made plans and as quickly rejected them. He had to keep within the law.

In front of him a car drew to a halt. Ewan stepped frantically on the brakes. Tyres squealed on the wet road. For the next mile he concentrated his attention on the traffic, but once out of town he put his foot down automatically, his jaw clenched. Mentally he pulverized Hubert Boyd-Hill's cunning face.

Ewan knew the road like the back of his hand. Had he been thinking, he would have remembered the hollow between Waterside and Stoneybrae would be flooded in this weather. But his thoughts were far from the roads, or driving. The car hit the water at speed and skewed out of control.

Twenty-Two

G erda heard the knocking on the cottage door. She groaned and turned over, snuggling even further beneath the blankets. She was not expecting anyone and she never answered the door looking a mess, still in her nightgown and without make-up.

The knocking ceased. The two people conferred and decided to drive on up to the farm.

Rachel stared in shocked silence at the policeman and woman. Afterwards she couldn't remember inviting them in, or the kindly policewoman making tea for her. She must have given them Bridie's number, and Conan's.

'We think the car must have spun out of control when it hit the water,' the policeman was explaining to Conan. 'It appears to have rolled over the banking and into the field. The doctor believes your brother was killed instantly.'

Rachel was only vaguely aware of the burr of voices. She couldn't take in the meaning of the words. Ewan! Her son. The youngest of her family. Paul's father. He couldn't be dead. He couldn't!

It was Bridie who stayed to care for her mother and look after Paul in the days that followed. The little boy couldn't understand that he would never see his daddy again. His earlier nightmares returned.

'Let him stay with us for a few nights,' Lucy suggested the second weekend after the funeral. 'It might take his mind off things and it will be good for Paul and Ryan to play together. Besides, Bridie, you look all in. You can't go on helping Peter at Wester Rullion and running Glens of Lochandee, as well as having broken nights with Paul. You have all helped me such a lot. I'd like to do something in return.'

'Thank you, Lucy,' Bridie agreed gratefully. 'There's worse news though. I haven't told Mother yet. She's been so quiet and withdrawn. Not at all like herself. I don't want to add to her troubles.'

'Yes, it was a terrible shock for all of us and it must have been far worse to find the police at the door. Surely things can't get any worse.'

'Mr Niven asked me to go into his office. Conan too. You'll not believe this, b–but Gerda went to see him the day after the funeral and instructed him to sell Wester Rullion immediately, and everything connected with it. She told him she would arrange for the cows to be sold at the local market next week.'

'But she can't do that, surely! Even if she could, it would be a stupid thing to do!'

'She seems to think pedigrees are just worthless bits of paper . . .'

Lucy gasped. 'In a fine herd like Wester Rullion they would treble the value, and more. I can't believe even Gerda could be stupid enough to want to sell a herd like this as ordinary commercial cattle. How could she possibly throw away everything your father and Ewan have worked for all these years?' Lucy felt anger boiling up in her on Ewan's behalf. 'Joanne and I could find all the information for a catalogue if the herd has to be sold. But does it? Has she the authority? Had Ewan made a will? What about Paul's inheritance? He must have rights too.'

'Ewan hadn't made a will, but yes, Paul does have legal rights. Gerda insisted she had the right to handle everything. She is his mother and responsible for Paul.'

'Responsible!' Lucy gasped in disbelief.

'Mr Niven said his interview with her was the most unpleasant he has ever experienced. She insisted he should put the houses on the market immediately – Mother's and Peter's, as well as the cottage.'

'Surely she wouldn't. . .She can't do that! Can she? Ewan

was intending to apply for a divorce when they'd been apart long enough. He . . . he told me so himself.' Lucy took a deep breath to steady the welter of emotions she felt. 'I know it's not Christian of me to say so, b–but all that show of the grieving widow, dressed impeccably in black from head to toe . . . it was all a pretence. Sh–she never loved Ewan . . .'

She couldn't bring herself to tell Bridie the words Gerda has hissed in her ear at the funeral. Lucy had just given her grandmother a comforting hug and stepped away. Gerda leaned towards her on the pretext of exchanging sympathetic platitudes. Instead she hissed, 'You needn't pretend. I know now you're Conan's bastard.' Lucy knew she would never forget the venom behind the words, nor the look of triumph in Gerda's pale eyes as she muttered, 'The Maxwell money is mine now. You're nothing!' She couldn't suppress a shudder as she recalled the look on Gerda's face.

'Are you all right, Lucy?' Bridie asked in concern. 'You're terribly pale.'

'Y–yes, I'm fine. It was just talking about the funeral and r–remembering . . .'

'Well, Nick would certainly agree with you about the grieving widow bit. He thinks Gerda is the biggest hypocrite on earth. He thought she was trying to imitate Jackie Kennedy.'

'He may be right.' Lucy nodded with a wan smile.

'Mr Niven thinks there's someone advising Gerda, or at least influencing her. He got the impression she wants money in a hurry. Whoever it is, he says neither of them under-stands much about the ways of business, especially farming, or about the legal aspects.'

'I can imagine.'

'Apparently she was dismayed, almost alarmed, when Mr Niven told her it could take twelve months or more before Ewan's affairs were settled. That was bad enough, but when she heard the provisions my father had made before his death she flew into hysterics and cursed him. He threatened to put her out of the office.'

'That's typical of Gerda when she doesn't get her own way.'

'I thank God that Father had the wisdom to seek Jordon Niven's advice, and to act on it. Not long before he died he gave instructions for Wester Rullion to be put in trust for Paul. He made a provision for Mother and Peter Forster to occupy their respective farmhouses for as long as they live.'

'Oh, thank goodness for that!' Lucy let out a long breath she didn't know she had been holding. Again Gerda's venomous words echoed in her head. 'What a shock she must have got. Obviously Ewan must never have told her what your father had done.'

'It was certainly a shock. She threatened to get another lawyer. Jordon Niven told her she would be very welcome to do so but he would carry out his duties and there was nothing she could do to get her hands on any of the land or property, including the cottage. She could live in it, but it belongs to the farm and she can't sell it.'

'Gosh, I'll bet Gerda was furious.'

'Shocked speechless,' Mr Niven said. 'Then she flew into a furious rage. Before she left the office he got the impression she was almost afraid . . . though I can't think why.'

'Perhaps she's in some kind of trouble. Maybe in debt. She used to overspend when we were at college, but her father always came to the rescue then.'

'I never thought of that. She ran up big debts before Paul was born. I remember she bought a mink coat and the firm was going to sue her for the money.' Bridie frowned suddenly. 'I wonder if that has anything to do with Mr Niven having difficulty with the bank . . . As executor, he was arranging for the business to carry on as usual until everything gets sorted out, but they're refusing to give permission for anyone to sign cheques. Apparently Ewan had been in and given instructions to that effect just before he was killed. I think they are going to open a new account. All the bills will have to go through Mr Niven as executor. As you'll know, Lucy, the existing bills have to be paid and

257

new ones keep coming. I ordered a load of cattle cake yesterday but we have to keep the farm running. The cows don't suddenly stop eating.'

'No, of course they don't. Do you think Peter will be able to carry on here with Billy Smith if you hire another man? I know no one can replace Ewan and everything he did, of course . . .'

'I think Peter would manage most things. Joanne seems very competent with the pedigrees already and she was just taking over the accounts. I can't understand why there should be a problem.' Bridie frowned.

'It does seem strange that the bank should stop all the payments,' Lucy agreed. 'That will certainly worry your mother if she finds out.'

'I hope she doesn't hear about it until we get things sorted out. Peter is a conscientious stockman. He knows we'll all be working for Paul's sake and he thinks the world of him. I think we shall manage until Paul is old enough to decide if he really wants to farm.'

'He's so young.' Lucy sighed sadly. 'But he does love animals.'

'Well, I shall do everything I can to give him his chance, poor wee soul,' Bridie said. 'One thing's for sure, we must never let Mother know Gerda was planning to turn everything into cash – even the house.'

'You're right.' Lucy shivered. 'She would take Paul away without a second's thought if it meant she could get control of his inheritance.'

'Lucy! I hadn't thought of that! It would break Mother's heart to lose both Ewan and Paul! That would be worse than losing her home.'

'We can't let that happen, Bridie.' Lucy's usually gentle expression hardened. 'I know Gerda's attitude to children. She would never love and care for Paul as a mother should.' Nor even as any normal, compassionate human being, she thought silently.

'I pray it will never come to that,' Bridie said anxiously. 'Ewan was chief trustee, but it's Conan and myself now,

258

with Mr Niven. Father must have had some sixth sense that Paul might need protecting from his own mother.'

Gerda was nervous about seeing Hubert after her interview with Jordon Niven, but he had known she was going to the lawyer's office and he couldn't wait to hear how quickly she could get her hands on Ewan's fortune, even if it meant having the brat tagging along with them.

He was waiting for her at the cottage, pacing the floor and smoking. He had already arranged for her furniture to be removed and sent to the saleroom in two days' time. Some of his own items were antiques, although it was her money – or rather Ewan's – that had paid for them. They were going to a specialist sale. Sometimes she felt resentment at Hubert's high-handed actions but he always seemed to have good reason for them and he always charmed her out of her moods.

The question now was, could she keep his attentions without the regular cash handouts he had grown to expect? Could she soothe his temper when he heard her news? In spite of his charm, Gerda was aware of his faults, but many of them were her faults too, so she understood and forgave them.

'We're two of a kind, you and I,' he had often remarked, and she knew he was right.

Now she faced him across the living room. She reported the steps that Ross Maxwell had taken to protect his grandson's inheritance, but Hubert seemed unperturbed.

'You're the boy's mother. You'll have control of him and his fortune. You must tell them all you're selling the property in the boy's best interests. Once you have the cash—'

'No! You don't understand, Hubert. I can't touch any of the property, not even this cottage. Oh, I can live in it,' she said bitterly, 'for as long as I like, but I can't sell it. Bridie and Conan are the trustees now that Ewan is dead. I can't even have the cheque book to go on paying the bloody bills!'

'That's ridiculous!' Hubert swore profusely. 'Somebody will have to pay out the money!'

'The lawyer says it could be a year or more before

Ewan's affairs are wound up because he was in business. Meanwhile I get the same pitiful bloody allowance. I can't even have that until he has sorted out the "problems with the bank". We both know what the problems are! There's no money left in the account to pay the monthly bills. I shall get nothing!' she wailed. 'What am I going to do? I've had two letters threatening to take me to court. I haven't enough money to pay a fraction of what I owe, even if I use all of the two thousand pounds I drew in cash. Can't you lend me some? I don't want to go to jail, Hubert. Hubert!'

She watched as his face paled. He slumped down on to the nearest chair.

'This is a fine bloody pickle we're in! I thought spouses got a better deal these days when husbands died without a will.'

'That's what Mr Niven said. Scottish law changed in 1964. God knows how bad it was before that! I could have inherited up to five thousand of moveable assets if I hadn't had the brat. As it is I'm only entitled to two and a half thousand. If the cottage had belonged to Ewan, instead of his father tying the deeds into the bloody farm, it would have been mine. I could have sold it, so long as it was not worth more than fifteen thousand! Imagine what I could do with fifteen thousand . . .' She sank down on to the settee and closed her eyes.

'You thought there'd be no problem,' Hubert said accusingly. 'I've already sent for the airline tickets, but we both know the cheque will bounce unless you put some money into the account.'

'You'll have to use some of the three thousand pounds I gave you. Have you cashed the cheque?'

'Of course I have!' he said scornfully. 'Your dearly beloved husband would have stopped it the minute he returned from Ireland.'

'Yes. I think he'd probably been to the bank. He must have been on his way back when he was killed.'

'And we thought we were home and dry! I thought we'd

be better off when we heard he was dead, but we're going to be a hell of a lot worse off. Unless we think of something pretty quickly . . .'

'I've already used some of the two thousand pounds I drew in cash . . . Don't look at me like that! I had to, to keep the local shops quiet until we got out of the area. You'll have to draw the money from that cheque I gave you.'

'Not on your life! I've banked that in the new name we agreed to use once we go abroad. Mr and Mrs Fritz. You said that was your mother's maiden name.'

'It was, and much good it ever did me,' Gerda muttered bitterly.

'Never mind the past,' Hubert said irritably. 'Who is handling the creditors? Paying the bills for the farm to keep going?'

'Mr Niven is the executive. He said that paying creditors was the first priority. Only after that can I get anything. I should be due up to two and a half thousand of the moveable estate. But don't you see? We took all the cash out of the account. I think that's what he meant by "moveable estate"! There won't be any. There isn't even enough to pay this month's bills! Ewan would probably have sold some cows or something if he'd been alive. He'd have been furious when he found out, but I knew he'd find the money to pay the bills somehow. That's the Maxwell way – pay what you owe.'

'To hell with the Maxwell way!'

'I'm afraid, Hubert. The bank is sure to be looking into things to find out what happened to Ewan's capital. Mr Niven will find out who drew the cheques . . . They might even think we killed Ewan to get his money!'

'It was an accident, for God's sake. Calm down, Gerda. Niven won't know anything until he starts poking his nose in, and lawyers always take forever.' Hubert's small eyes narrowed as he considered various plans and rejected them. Eventually he said, 'I'll tell you what we'll do. You said the first priority was for Niven to pay the creditors, didn't you?'

261

'Yes, but . . .'

'Listen, you goose! You're still Maxwell's wife, or rather his widow. Your creditors are his responsibility. This is what we'll do. Listen carefully, and don't argue. It's the only way.'

Twenty-Three

'Gerda, make a list of all the firms that are demanding money from you,' Hubert ordered. 'Then you'll have to use my old typewriter. I'll help you compose an official-sounding letter. It will inform all creditors of Mr Ewan Maxwell's death and instruct them to send their accounts to his solicitor for settlement.'

'We can't do that! Mr Niven will—'

'He'll not know. We'll post the letters when we're ready to leave here, and preferably when we're about to leave the country too, if we play our cards right.'

'But some of them are threatening to take me to court now. Now, I tell you!'

'I'm not intending we should hang about! It will keep them quiet for a few days if they get a response to their demands and some hope of eventual settlement. By the time they all send their demands to Niven we shall be long gone.'

'But what about your own bills?'

'Don't you worry your head about them, my sweet,' Hubert said smoothly. 'You don't think I use my own name all the time, do you? The most recent bills are already in Maxwell's name. Things like the car and the London tailor who made my suits.'

'Hubert! How . . . how . . .' Gerda was lost for words. 'Supposing Ewan had found out?'

'I only used his name after things were getting pretty hot for me. I knew the crunch was coming one way or the other. Now, let's get going. I have another little plan, if I can contact the man we need to carry it out. I'll need to make a few calls around the pubs to find him though.'

'What sort of plan?' Gerda asked suspiciously.

'I'll tell you when I find out whether it can be done or not. By the way, does Mrs Maxwell still go to church every Sunday? Back to Lochandee?'

'Yes, but why do you want to know that?'

Hubert tapped the side of his nose, a gesture that always infuriated Gerda, but she was too tense to tell him so right now. She was in a mess. They both were. She didn't know how to get out of it on her own. She didn't even know where her own father was living now, she thought bitterly. He should be here to help her. Typically, Gerda managed to blame everyone except herself for her predicament.

It was a further two nights before Hubert managed to contact the man he believed would help them carry out his plan. The cattle dealer gave every indication of being a slow, simple sort of fellow. Smugly, Hubert thought he handled the whole thing pretty smartly himself.

He related a fine story about Gerda's pathetic state since she had been widowed, and the unfair treatment she was receiving at the hands of the Maxwells, but Hubert knew nothing about the world of farming, a fact which the cattle dealer had been quick to grasp.

'Is the herd free frae brucellosis?' he asked gruffly.

'Brucellosis?' Hubert frowned. 'I expect so. They're all pedigree anyway.'

'Brucellosis is a disease, man! Nothing to do with the way the animals are bred. They're worth more all round if the herd is accredited.' He eyed Hubert shrewdly from under the shadow of his cap and smothered a smirk of satisfaction. 'You'll need a permit for each animal you want to sell. Take the ear numbers to the government offices. They'll fix you up with the paperwork.'

'I–I can't do that!' Hubert frowned. He had no idea what ear numbers were, or where to find them. 'I told you this whole operation has to be carried out as soon as possible and with the minimum of fuss. We don't want everybody knowing . . .'

'I see. . .Right ye are, guvnor.' The dealer's eyes narrowed, watching the suave man closely, seeing the nervous way he fiddled with his beer glass. 'You'll understand the cattle are worth a lot less then,' he suggested slyly, 'if I can't sell them on as accredited – free frae tuberculosis and brucellosis?'

'Oh, but they will be. It's one of the best herds in Scotland!'

'Maybe it is, but man, ye must ken even the best herds get breakdowns in health. Then they have to dispose of their reactors. Nobody's going to take your word, or mine, that they're free frae disease, not without all the bits o' paper frae the government.'

'B–but you can still sell them?'

'Aye. I'll send them down to a dealer pal o' mine in Cheshire. There's still demand for cattle down there after the bad outbreak o' foot-and-mouth. As I said, I canna pay ye as much for them without the permits.'

'We'll take what we can get,' Hubert declared, unused to the way dealers operated and bargained over the last sixpence. The man raised his eyebrows and bit back a grin. 'But you have to move them on a Sunday morning while the women-folk are at the church,' Hubert reminded him. 'We don't want to cause them more . . . er . . . distress than they've suffered already,' he added smoothly.

'You said they were pedigree cattle. I'll need the regis-trations.'

'Oh, forget about the formalities, my man,' Hubert said haughtily and waved his hand. He was totally unaware he was brushing aside more than half the value of most of the cows, or that well-bred pedigree animals from an attested herd would bring four times what a dealer would pay if they were sold at a pedigree auction.

'But you did say they were pedigree? I've heard o' the Rullion herd. They're pretty good by all accounts.'

'Oh they are. They've won at some of the agricultural shows . . .'

'Pedigree breeders dinna need the likes o' me tae sell their cattle as a rule,' the dealer said drily. He looked searchingly at Hubert. There was something fishy about this transaction. It was like taking sweets from a baby. But so long as no one accused him of stealing the cattle it was all right by him. He could make a pretty sum out of men like this Mr Fritz – if that was his real name. 'Ye dinna have the pedigree registrations to hand then, I take it?'

'Er . . . no. The paper work has been . . . er . . . neglected.'

'Well, so long as ye understand they're only worth the price o' commercial cattle without them.'

'Very well. How many could you load in an hour? And when can you remove them?' Hubert asked eagerly – too eagerly.

'Let's see.' The dealer lifted his cap and scratched his head as though wrestling with a major problem. 'I could send my two big lorries. Say twenty animals in each . . .' He frowned at Hubert, eyeing his well-polished brown shoes and the cut of his jacket. 'I take it ye'll no be there tae help load them on to the lorry.'

'Oh no!' Hubert stared back at him. 'Don't you send a man with the lorry?'

'Well it doesn't bloody well drive itself!' he retorted sarcastically. 'But two drivers canna load forty cows on their ain! Not in an hour.' He was dealing with a right ninny here. He frowned. 'I'll need a letter o' authority frae the widow who wants tae sell them. Ye'll need tae hand it over before any o' the cows are loaded on to my lorries.'

'You will have it.' Hubert assumed an air of superiority. The dealer was hard pressed not to burst out laughing. 'In return I request payment in cash.'

'What? For the whole bloody lot!' The man's eyebrows almost disappeared beneath his cap.

'That's what I said.' Hubert nodded officiously.

'Proper cocky wee feller he was,' the dealer remarked later to one of his drivers, 'and as ignorant as a pig in a sty about selling livestock. If the cows are as good as I've heard then we'll try and squeeze an extra one on each lorry. If I'm any judge o' silly buggers, he'll be none the wiser. In fact we'll tell him we could only load thirty-nine and that's what I'll pay him for.'

He had promised Hubert he would send extra men to load

the animals and he certainly kept his word on that score. Instinct told him the sooner he had his cargo loaded and off the premises the better it would be.

When Bridie came out of church the following Sunday morning she was astonished to find Peter Forster waiting for her. She could see he was agitated even before she reached him, and his face was white. Her first thought was for the sick cow he had been attending. She knew he had been up most of the night with a difficult calving, but they had both thought the cow would survive, even though the calf had been born dead. That was one of the hazards of farming and had to be accepted. It was not something to get so worked up about. But her own philosophical attitude deserted her when he greeted her.

'I never go to bed in the daytime! They came while I was sleeping! They've taken half of the milking herd! Maybe more. They said they had written authority . . .'

'Peter,' Bridie said faintly, 'I don't know what you're talking about.' She took his arm and gently steered him out of the churchyard, away from curious glances. Nick and her mother and the children were talking to Lucy as they came out of church, but seeing her with Peter they all moved to join them before Bridie could get Peter to explain coherently.

'This is not the place to discuss things.' Nick frowned, seeing the groups of people eyeing them.

'Come to my house,' Lucy suggested. 'It's only up the street, Peter. Whatever is wrong, you look as though you need a drink of something.'

'But Mrs Jones!' Peter almost wailed, snatching at Bridie's arm. 'The longer we wait, the further away the lorries will be . . .'

Once inside Lucy's house the children obediently went to change out of their Sunday clothes and scampered outside to play.

'Now, Peter, start at the beginning,' Nick said quietly while Lucy brewed a pot of strong tea.

'I never go to bed during the day . . .' Peter looked pleadingly at Bridie.

'You must have been tired out after last night.' She nodded. 'And it is Sunday, after all. No one could blame you for that. Go on, Peter. You said there were two lorries . . .'

'Yes. I did not hear them come. I was sleeping deep. I heard cows making much noise. Looked out of the window and I saw men rounding them into the yard. Bringing the cows in from the field! So early in the day. Other men were chasing them into a lorry – the biggest lorry I have seen. Another big lorry was in the yard. I dress quickly and run downstairs. Pull on my boots and outside. I ask, "What are you doing?" One man – he seemed to be boss – said he had instructions to remove the cows. "Whose instructions?" I say. Mrs Maxwell, he tell me. I say he must stop until I bring you, Mrs Jones. He laugh. They filled the first lorry, moved it away and start filling the next lorry. I note down the numbers and come straight for you.' That was the longest speech Peter had ever made and he paused for breath, then added urgently, 'We must get back the cows! We must go after the men!'

'I can't believe this!' Bridie had not realized she was standing over Peter, willing him to tell them exactly what had happened, yet not wanting to know what her brain was telling her. She flopped on to a kitchen chair. Her eyes moved to Nick, silently beseeching him to find a solution. Then her gaze settled on her mother's face. Rachel looked white and drawn. She caught Bridie's eyes on her.

'This must be Gerda's doing,' she said. 'She is determined to get what she can, while she can. I've known for a long time that she's been spending more money than she should. Ewan put up with it for Paul's sake. Now he is dead and she knows there must be an end to the money. The day he was killed he had been at the bank. I overheard him speaking on the telephone before he left. I . . . I think his account was overdrawn. He said that was impossible. There should have been at least five thousand pounds in it.'

'Mother! You never mentioned this before.' Bridie stared

at her mother in dismay. They had believed they were protecting her but she had guessed how things were all along.

'It was money,' Rachel said dully. 'Ewan is dead. Dead.' She suppressed a shudder. 'All the money in the world can't bring him back.'

'Oh, Mother.' Bridie moved to her side and put an arm round her shoulders. Suddenly even the theft of their cattle seemed relatively unimportant beside the enormity of Ewan's death. 'Drink your tea. Please, Mother. All this time you've been trying to protect us and we've been trying to shield you. Mr Niven said there were problems with the bank. But why should Gerda instruct someone to remove the cows? And who? Peter's right, we must try to get them back. Shall we inform the police, Nick?' She looked helplessly at her husband.

'I think that's the only thing we can do. At least Peter got the numbers of the lorries involved.' He gave Peter a reassuring pat on the back.

'You're sure the man said he had Mrs Maxwell's authority to remove the cows, Peter?' Bridie asked.

'He said so. He waved a letter at me. He did not let me read it though.'

'Could it be that Gerda believes the cows are hers now, to dispose of how she likes?' Nick asked with a frown.

'She knows they're not!' Bridie said. 'I told you she'd been in to the solicitor's office the day after Ewan's funeral. She couldn't wait to get her hands on everything. He told her she had no claim to anything until all the creditors had been paid. If it's true that the money had all been taken out of the farm account without Ewan's knowledge, then it must have been Gerda who withdrew it! She would know there was none of the moveable estate that Mr Niven talks about. She would know there was nothing to pay the creditors or her.'

'I'll phone the police. They'll track down the owner of the lorries,' Nick said.

'Use my phone,' Lucy said, indicating the door to the hall. 'It will save time.'

'I suppose we should notify Mr Niven but that will have to wait until his office opens tomorrow. Gerda should be charged with theft.'

'She has left her home,' Peter announced suddenly. 'It is empty since a few days ago. Billy Smith told me. A furniture lorry came and removed everything. The removal men said they were taking it to the salerooms at Carlisle.'

Bridie stared at him in disbelief. 'I didn't know that. But where will she live?'

'The postman told Billy's father he had brought a letter from the office of . . . er . . . passports, is it? It was addressed to Mrs Fritz, but it was the address of Mrs Maxwell's house on the envelope. Mr Smith promised to hand the letter in to Mrs Maxwell. She laugh when she take it from Billy's father. She said the government office was stupid to put wrong name on the envelope.'

'Perhaps she's going abroad for a holiday.' Bridie frowned. 'Maybe she's going to see her father.'

Rachel sat up, suddenly alert. 'She doesn't know where her father is. He asked me not to pass on his address to anyone, especially Gerda. He did not want her to cause trouble for his new wife. Twice each year he sends a gift for Paul and asks for news of him. I send the reply to a post office box, but I know it is in Portugal.'

Bridie stared at her, amazed that her mother managed to share so many confidences and always keep them to herself.

Nick came back into the kitchen. 'The police say it will be easy enough to find out who owns the lorries and to track them down. They praised your prompt action, Peter,' he added, giving the still agitated Peter a reassuring smile. 'Apparently if Gerda has authorized the sale of the cows, and she is not the rightful owner, then it is tantamount to theft.'

'It is Paul's inheritance. She has stolen from her own son,' Bridie said indignantly, 'especially if she has already claimed all the available cash from Ewan's account.'

'What good would his inheritance be if Gerda took him away from here?' Rachel asked. Her voice trembled and sank to a whisper. 'It was bad enough when she neglected him at the cottage. I couldn't bear what it might do to him.'

'Oh, Mother,' Bridie said gently. 'Is that what's been troubling you? Is that why you have been so quiet – so withdrawn?'

'It is my greatest fear,' Rachel said clearly. 'To lose Ewan, and then for his mother to claim Paul . . .' She shuddered. 'She threatened to take him away from Ewan once before, if he divorced her. Ewan told me so himself. Since Gerda has neglected Paul more and more, Ewan was prepared to leave her and to fight for his son. With Ewan gone, who but his own mother would have charge of him, if she wants him? Let her take the cows, if that will get her away from here, if she will leave Paul in peace, here where he belongs. Don't you see?' Rachel pleaded, looking round the circle of faces. 'If Paul inherits anything of value, Gerda would claim him so that she could control whatever he has. She would turn everything into cash, and she would spend it. Her father warned us. It is a weakness with her, a flaw in her character. I'm sixty-five now. I may not be here long enough to see him grow to manhood, but I'm not thinking of myself. I c–couldn't bear what it might do to Paul if Gerda took him away. He never asks for her or wants to go to her. If he has nothing she will not want him. He would only be a burden to her.'

'I see.' Bridie looked up and met Lucy's troubled eyes. Lucy gave a faint nod.

'It seems dreadful to steal from her own son, I know, but your mother is probably right about her motives, however harsh it sounds.'

'But she will have no idea of the real value of Ewan's cattle,' Bridie said glumly. 'A dealer would never pay their true worth. Should we really let her get away with it, Mother? I . . . I don't know whether we can afford to. Mr Niven seemed to think we would have to sell some of the stock just to settle creditors – and there's no wonder if all the capital has been taken from the bank already. Now we know why. Perhaps we should see what he says – and Fiona and

271

Conan too. Conan is a trustee, after all. He must be consulted.'

'Then I must speak to Mr Niven too,' Rachel said. 'I would do anything, make any sacrifice, to keep Paul here with us. No cows or money in the world are worth a little boy's happiness – and safety.' She shuddered.

Bridie looked at her mother doubtfully. 'What she's done is . . . is criminal!'

'I know it is. I know it's wrong to take the cows like that – and such a waste of fine animals too. She will pay for her sins one day, I'm sure of it. All I ask is that Paul should not be made to pay too.'

Twenty-Four

The police tracked the cattle to three farms in Cheshire, all belonging to the same farmer and cattle dealer. He had purchased them quite legitimately and readily gave the particulars of his Scottish contact. There again the dealer had proof that he had been given authority by Mrs Gerda Maxwell to remove the cattle from her premises. The deal had been initiated by a Mr Fritz and he had requested payment in cash. The dealer had insisted on having a signed receipt and proffered this to the police as proof that he had conducted the transaction in good faith. All this they reported to Conan, Mr Niven and Bridie.

'But so far they have not been able to track down either Gerda or this Mr Fritz,' Bridie reported to her mother. Rachel looked white and strained. She could not rid herself of the terrible fear that Gerda would retaliate by taking Paul away if she found herself trapped in a nasty situation.

'I expect they have moved to another house.'

'You've kept Paul away from school again, Mother?' Bridie frowned as she watched the little boy walking across the farmyard, his hand in Peter's as he chattered happily about the animals.

'Yes. I know it's wrong, but I'm afraid Gerda might steal Paul away like she did the cows,' Rachel said tensely. 'I couldn't bear to lose him too, Bridie. Or at least I would bear it, if I believed he would be better off with his own mother. But Gerda resented him from the day he was born. She never made any effort to care for him. It would break his heart to leave Wester Rullion and all his family. He often talks about Ewan, even though I explained his daddy had gone to live with the angels.'

Bridie nodded, unable to reply for the lump in her throat. So far she hadn't told anyone except Nick, but Mr Niven was becoming seriously concerned about the growing list of creditors. He felt many of them were not genuine business creditors. He was requesting more details from the firms concerned. Some of them were long overdue and demanding immediate settlement. If the missing capital could not be replaced soon he could see no way out except to sell the remaining cattle. It was up to her to prepare her mother, but she scarcely knew how to begin.

Mr Niven felt strongly that Gerda should be traced and made to repay the money she had taken from Ewan's estate, both in cash and by selling so many of the dairy herd, especially since it was impossible to generate income from the farm without them.

'You must make your mother understand that many of these later accounts are for expenses incurred by your brother's widow,' Mr Niven had said that morning when Bridie kept her appointment at his office.

'I–I'll try to explain and get her to change her mind.'

'I can understand her reasoning.' Jordon Niven sighed. 'If the child is happy where he is it would be cruel to take him away, especially if, as you say, his mother does not look after him well.'

'She never has! There's no place in Gerda's life for a child – except to use as a pawn,' Bridie said angrily. She felt thoroughly frustrated. She felt Gerda should be made to pay, and that could mean going to jail, but she knew she could never go against her mother's wishes. And anyway, it was true it would probably break Paul's heart to leave Wester Rullion and the animals and the people who loved and cared for him.

'If we leave things the way they are now,' Jordon Niven said slowly, making his fingers in to a steeple as he always he did when considering a serious situation and finding no satisfactory solution, 'it looks as though the boy is going to lose his inheritance whatever we do. Only today we have had two creditors contact us – one from London demanding payment for a car supposedly hired by a Mr Maxwell and never returned. The firm has reason to believe the car has since been sold. It is clear to me your sister-in-law is not alone in this . . . this treachery. If we settle all these additional creditors there will nothing left to run the farm as a viable business . . .'

'B–but surely . . .' Bridie's face went white as she stared across the desk.

'It is true.' He tapped a sheaf of papers with a long finger. 'Some of these accounts have been accumulating over several years. It looks as though Mrs Gerda Maxwell has never paid her way. Then again, if we do manage to trace her and to press charges, would she still have the cash she withdrew from the bank? And supposing we sue her, if she claims legal custody of her son, as you fear, she will no doubt use whatever meagre income can be raised from Wester Rullion on his behalf. All in all it would appear the child would reap no benefit from renewing his relationship with his mother.'

'No, he would not!' Bridie said robustly. 'She must have been bleeding Ewan dry for years. He'd have done anything to protect Paul, I know he would.'

'He had made an appointment to see me to discuss divorce proceedings,' Jordon Niven said thoughtfully. 'I am not breaching client confidentiality by divulging that information. Your brother is dead and the knowledge that he had reached such a decision may help us all decide what is best for his son. If you don't mind, Mrs Jones, I think I would like to call on your mother tomorrow afternoon. I have always found her a woman of wisdom. Will you make sure it is convenient, please? After that I will arrange to see yourself and your brother again as trustees for the land and buildings. Fortunately the creditors would have no claim on them, only on the stock and the machinery.'

Bridie frowned. What good were the land and buildings if there were no cattle and no capital to replace them? Land, labour and capital – her father had always declared they were the three limiting factors to successful farming. Paul would inherit the land, but there was no capital to buy the stock or to pay the wages, and without wages there would be no labour. She brushed away sudden tears as she thought of all the years and hard work her parents had put in to buy and improve Wester Rullion and to build up the dairy herd. Maybe she should drive over to the garage later and discuss everything with Conan and Fiona. They all owed it to Ewan to do whatever was best for his son, and Paul was such a lovely little boy.

Jordon Niven was surprised to find Rachel looking calm and dignified, but with a determined set to her soft mouth. Ross Maxwell would have told him that meant that there was no way she would change her mind. He noted the lines of strain and her unusual pallor. Even since he had seen her last, her thick, dark hair seemed to have turned almost white, but her green eyes held a determined gleam as she set a tray of tea before him and pulled up a small table.

'I must tell you, Mr Niven, nothing you can say will persuade me to pursue my son's widow and to raise a court action against her. If cornered she is capable of retaliating ruthlessly and viciously. I will not allow my grandson to be sacrificed in the name of justice.'

Jordon Niven sipped his tea slowly, regarding Rachel over the rim of the china cup. He set it carefully in its saucer. 'Did your daughter explain how deeply in debt your son's estate is?'

'Ewan was never in debt!'

'No, not personally, nor his business, but with the bank account depleted and the addition of creditors we knew nothing about—'

'Yes, Bridie explained all of that.' Rachel leaned forward. 'It is a nasty business to be landed with someone else's debts. I agree it is most unjust and that the persons responsible should be punished, but . . .' She shook her head vigorously. 'Not at any price. Not all the money in the world is worth my grandson's happiness and peace of mind, Mr Niven.'

'I understand your point of view, Mrs Maxwell, but I firmly

believe some of the creditors were not even your daughter-in-law's. Do you know the name of her . . . her friend?'

'Ewan mentioned a Mr Hubert Boyd-Hill . . .'

'But no one called Fritz?'

'Fritz was the name of Gerda's mother. And Gerda's maiden name was Fritz-Allan.'

'A–ah! I see. It seems to me that our Mr Boyd-Hill used several different names. The police appear to think a Mr and Mrs Fritz travelled to Portugal by air the day after the cattle were stolen. According to your daughter, Mr Fritz was the name of the man who negotiated the trumped-up sale with the cattle dealer.'

'Yes, that's correct. But, Mr Niven, before we go any further there is a question I would like to ask you.'

Jordon Niven bit his lip. He had a growing feeling that Mrs Maxwell was taking charge of this interview. 'Go ahead. What do you wish to know?'

'Supposing we settle the farm creditors, plus the debts that Gerda and her . . . her friend have accumulated.' She held up her hand to brook any interruption. 'Once my son's estate is settled, finally settled, is there any way that dreadful pair could use the Maxwell name again to run up more debts for us – or later for Paul – to settle?'

'There are ways of preventing such a situation occurring again, but—'

'And if we decide not to pursue Gerda for theft of the cattle, is there any way we can make sure she cannot claim custody of Paul? The child's welfare, Mr Niven, is my over-riding concern.'

Again Jordon Niven sipped his tea, giving himself time to decide the best course of action and the best advice.

'Let me get this straight, Mrs Maxwell. Even if it means selling off the remaining cattle to pay all – I do mean all – the people claiming from your son's estate, you would be willing to do that so long as the boy's mother had no claim on him?'

'Exactly that. Gerda must never get custody of Paul.'

For the first time Jordon Niven allowed himself a small

277

smile. 'I think we could make sure of that, Mrs Maxwell. If the Fritzs have gone abroad to live we could issue a warrant in the various names they are known to have used . . .' Now he held up a hand to prevent Rachel's protest. 'This would not be with a view to pursuing them for the money at all costs, so much as making them less likely to risk returning to this to this country and possibly going to jail. In view of her past neglect, I believe we could also make a case ensuring Mrs Gerda Maxwell cannot claim custody of Paul, so long as yourself, or other family members, are prepared to take on that responsibility.'

'I am, but I realize at my age I may not live for as long as he needs me. I will discuss it with my family, but I am sure Bridie or Lucy would care for Paul.'

'In that case, Mrs Maxwell, I think I can handle things to your satisfaction. But that still leaves the creditors. How could you continue to live here, and to feed, clothe and educate your grandson, if there is no income from the dairy herd?'

'Ah . . .' For the first time Rachel's eyes clouded and her expression was one of deep sadness. 'It is not what I would have wished for Paul, and certainly not what my husband would have done, but during the night I decided on a solution that will suffice until Paul is of age to take over the running of Wester Rullion himself and decide his own future. It will not be as easy for him as my late husband had intended, but at least it should protect the land.'

'May I ask what this solution might be?' Jordon Niven asked with some unease. After all, Mrs Maxwell was an elderly woman now. Was she capable of making such major decisions on behalf of her grandson?

Almost as though she read his thoughts she said, 'I am sixty-five, Mr Niven. I will admit that recent events have rather shaken me, but now there is a challenge to be faced for Paul's sake.' She gave a faint smile. 'My late husband would have told you I thrive on challenge. I hope to live at least another ten years, but that is in God's hands. Since the rest of the stock must be sold, we must prepare for the best

278

pedigree sale we can arrange. That should clear the creditors, I believe. After that, most of the arable fields will be sown with grass and all the fields will be let for seasonal grazing. It is not ideal,' she said sadly, 'or what any of us would have wished, but I know several of our neighbours will be glad of the opportunity to rent extra grass so close to home. Renting grass parks, we call it around here. My daughter will no doubt rent some of it to supplement the Glens of Lochandee land. I believe she will also supervise the cropping of two or three fields each year to keep the grass in rotation, with the help of Peter Forster. We employ three men and I shall be sorry to lose Billy Smith, but one man will be sufficient to take care of the farm in its new form. Peter will not be happy either, but I think he will prefer to stay here. He will check the cattle belonging to the neighbours each day, fertilize the grass and mend the fences, drains and ditches. Yes, there will be plenty for him to do.' She sighed. 'He will still be able to keep a couple of pigs and I shall have my hens. We may even be able to keep two or three calves for Paul in the small paddock beside the house ... As far as the cottage is concerned, it could be sold if the debts are not settled by the sale of the cattle. Otherwise we will rent it out to give a little extra income.'

'It sounds to me as though you've got it all worked out, Mrs Maxwell,' Jordon Niven said with a note of respect.

'Yes, I lay awake most of the night thinking things through.' Rachel sighed, feeling suddenly weary. 'I believe income from grass lets is treated differently for tax purposes, but Fiona will advise us about that.'

'She will indeed,' Jordon Niven agreed readily. 'Fiona and Conan have built up an excellent business with their coach tours. Did I hear they have taken over a hotel too, somewhere on the south coast? You must be very proud of them.'

'Yes, I've been blessed with a good family.' Rachel nodded, but she gave an unconscious sigh of weariness and Jordon Niven rose to take his leave. He hoped everyone would agree to this new strategy for Wester Rullion. It was not at all what Ross Maxwell had had in mind when he tried so hard to protect his life's work for his son and grandson. But it seemed to be the best that could be salvaged in the circumstances. Paul was luckier than many to have such a family to love and care for him. He hoped with all his heart that Mrs Maxwell would be blessed with many more years to guide her grandson towards manhood.

Twenty-Five

R achel remained firm in her decision to sell off the remaining cattle, pay off all the debts and clear the Maxwell name once and for all. In her heart she knew she would make almost any sacrifice to protect Paul and keep him amongst those who loved him.

Inevitably the day of the sale came round and Rachel's courage and determination almost failed her when she saw how it upset Paul. Had she made the wrong decision? Yet what alternative had there been? None that she could have explained to a six-year-old boy. She could never tell him his mother had run away with all the available cash and stolen the animals that would have brought in income. No, it was enough to have Mr Niven's assurance that Gerda Maxwell would have no claim on her son, or his inheritance in future.

Bridie had explained as gently as she could that the remaining animals would have to be sold but it had taken three months to finalize the arrangements, fix a date for a pedigree sale on the farm, and to get all the milk records and pedigrees ready for the auctioneers to print the catalogue. Perhaps it had been a mistake to hold the sale at Wester Rullion, yet she knew it was better, especially for the animals. It would have been a mammoth task to transport the young cattle to the auction, and they would have had a second journey by lorry to various parts of the country after the sale.

Paul simply couldn't understand why they had to go anywhere and he sobbed into his grandmother's lap.

'I'll keep him indoors,' Rachel whispered above his head, but her eyes were troubled as they met Bridie's stricken gaze. Both Bridie and Lucy had done their utmost to make this sale a success. Every spare minute had been used to search out records and pedigrees, getting the animals into the very best condition and, over the past few days, washing and grooming them for the big day. Peter Forster and Billy Smith had worked hard too and had spent the intervening weeks cleaning and painting any surplus machinery that would no longer be needed. After the sale, even the milking parlour would be dismantled and sold. This had been Nick's suggestion.

'There will be no use for it without cows. It will deteriorate and the rubber parts will perish. There are more modern systems being developed anyway. It's better to get whatever cash is available now.'

Reluctantly Rachel had agreed, knowing that Nick spoke good sense.

There was as much bustle inside the house as there was outside. A small room near the back door had been cleared for the buyers to come and pay their money to the auctioneer's clerks. The dining room had been cleared and set with trestle tables to feed the people attending the sale, especially those breeders who had travelled several hundred miles to buy some of the Wester Rullion bloodlines. When she saw the crowds in the yard, Rachel worried whether there would be enough cold meats to feed them all.

'Don't worry,' Fiona said calmly. 'If you think we are running short just give me a signal and I'll pop into town to the butchers.'

'There's piles of food,' Lucy said reassuringly. She had hired the tea urns from Lochandee village hall and Joanne and her mother had volunteered to help keep the teacups filled.

'I've never seen so much food in a house before!' Carol exclaimed. Although she had lived in Lochandee ever since the war, her roots were in the city and she had never got into the habit of having a big baking day every week as most country people did. Bridie and Lucy had baked pies and scones and Rachel had been baking fruit loaves for the past few weeks. It was a tradition to give the purchasers a good feed at a farm sale, though Nick had told them the farmers' wives often refused to cater these days. Many of the farm sales arranged for a van to come and sell food to those who needed it.

'We'll cater the old way,' Rachel said with quiet determination. 'I would hate the neighbours to think we were mean, or so short of money we couldn't feed them.' She was well aware of the rumours circulating in the district. The sales representatives travelled from farm to farm selling machinery, feeding stuffs, seeds and fertilizers, dispensing the gossip of the countryside along with their sales patter.

It had often amazed her that news spread so rapidly. Most of the salesmen would have known Gerda was seeing another man, even if they didn't know who he was. They would also be aware that following Ewan's death there was insufficient cash to pay for all the products their respective firms had supplied to Wester Rullion. Jordon Niven had reached agreements with the major farm suppliers, assuring them their accounts would be settled in full if they would agree to wait until after the sale. The Maxwells had a good reputation for prompt payment as a rule so there had been only one firm that had raised objections. Rachel felt saddened and embarrassed by the whole affair.

As the buzz and air of excitement increased, Paul ran upstairs to his bedroom. Alicia promised to keep an eye on him. The twins were almost sixteen now and they had pleaded with Bridie to take a day off school to help their granny at the sale. Rachel was glad of their young legs to fetch and carry and keep the teacups and saucers washed and replaced ready for the constant stream of hungry farmers.

'Paul has cried himself to sleep, lying face down on top of his bed.' Alicia said quietly.

'It will be a blessing if he sleeps until most of the business is by,' Lucy said, overhearing. She had arranged for Kirsten to stay with an old friend in Lochandee and she had insisted Ryan and Cameron should go to school as usual, much to their disappointment. She needed to be free of

283

parental duties if she was to help her grandmother today. She knew Paul was to have gone to school too, but the auctioneer and his clerks had arrived early and shortly afterwards the cars of early viewers began to arrive. Paul, Nick, Max, Alicia and Margaret had been at Wester Rullion since the crack of dawn getting animals fed and bedded and giving them a last-minute brush-up. They were gathered around the kitchen table eating a big breakfast, preparing for the long day's work ahead. The air of tension and excitement increased. Paul could sense it. He looked at the strangers. He listened intently as the auctioneer discussed the arrangements for getting the cattle into the sale ring. With dawning horror he began to realize what his elders had really meant when they had talked about a sale.

Already dressed in his school shoes and uniform he had dashed out of the house and into the yard, narrowly missing a carfull of prospective buyers that was edging its way to the field where the cars were to park. Rachel panicked, fearing for his safety.

'Wait here, I'll get him, Mother.'

Bridie found Paul in one of the calf pens with his arms around the necks of two small calves. They were twins and had been very small when they were born. Paul had helped to care for them. Although they were two months old they were still small for their age. They were his favourites. His teeth were chattering and racking sobs shook his small shoulders as he whispered into their ears. Bridie's heart ached for him. A memory of herself as a child flashed into her mind. She had felt ill with grief when the dreaded foot-and-mouth had come to Lochandee, and her father had tried so hard to explain why all her beloved animals had to be slaughtered. But these animals were not being killed. She tried to tell Paul they would be going to a lovely new home, but nothing she could say would comfort him. Bridie remembered the awful silence in the farmyard at Lochandee when all the animals had gone. It had felt eerie and deserted, so empty . . . so lonely . . .

Against her better judgement Bridie found herself kneeling

beside Paul, promising to keep these two small calves out of the sale. For a moment his sobs ceased. He looked searchingly into her face, but then his face crumpled again. 'B–but their friends will be l–leaving. They'll be l–lonely . . .'

'No they won't, they'll have each other. And they'll have you.' She stood up. 'Come back to the house with me, Paul. I promise to keep these two calves specially for you, but I do have a lot of work to do today.' Silently Paul shook his head and buried his wet face against the neck of one of the calves. It tried to lick his hair. In desperation Bridie picked him up and carried him back to the house, still sobbing as she handed him over to her mother for comfort.

Bridie made a large card saying WITHDRAWN FROM SALE and went out to find Peter. He had promised to organize the animals ready for going into the ring. He was as pleased as a small boy himself when Bridie told him what she had done.

'I will look after them with Paul,' he said solemnly. Bridie knew how upset Peter had been when he first heard about the sale, but he had been relieved to learn he would still have a place at Wester Rullion, albeit not so interesting to him. Billy Smith had been upset too, but Bridie had given him an excellent reference and he had got a job on a farm near enough for him to continue living at the cottage with his father. He was to start immediately after the sale.

A fortnight earlier Chris and Adam had come down to visit Lucy and to get a preview of the Wester Rullion stock. Bridie had shown them round, telling Adam which animals she would like to buy for her own herd at Lochandee.

'I shall have to stand beside the auctioneer to answer his queries as the animals come into the ring,' she said. 'I wondered whether you would bid for me, Adam? I want it to be all fair and honest.'

'I'll be pleased to do that, Mrs Jones,' Adam said, regarding Bridie with respect. He knew lots of breeders would have taken advantage of the relationship and taken their pick before the sale.

'As a matter of fact, I would like to keep two or three of

the cow families going with the Rullion prefix. One day I hope they will provide a small nucleus for Paul to build up a herd of his own, if he decides farming is what he wants to do. These are the ones my father started with,' she indicated the names in the catalogue, 'and I know Ewan was pleased with the way the Ruby family was breeding, so perhaps you could put in a bid for either of these two.'

Adam grinned as she pointed to the lot numbers. 'I have a fancy for one of them myself. Now I know I'm really on the right track.'

When Paul woke up, the actual selling of the animals was almost over but the house was full of strangers telephoning for cattle lorries to transport their purchases. Nick's two lorries were fully booked and so were several others that had come to the sale in the hope of getting work. The dining room was full of men, all discussing their purchases.

'It's almost time for me to meet Ryan and Cameron from school,' Lucy said to Rachel. 'Shall I take Paul with me and keep them all at Lochandee until the lorries get loaded and on their way?'

'Oh, Lucy, if you would!' Rachel agreed with relief. 'It might take his mind off things if he and Ryan can play together.'

'Yes. They are in the same boat now,' Lucy said sadly. 'Neither have a father and neither have a farm. Well, Paul will have a farm, but he will still have to struggle to buy the stock and make it a proper farm again.' Her tone was wistful. Conan gave her a speculative look, biting his lip as thoughts went round and round in his head.

At this stage, he decided, there was nothing he could do to help his grandsons. They had the love and care of their mother and that was what they needed most. In a few weeks Lucy would be starting teaching full-time in one of the local village schools a few miles from Lochandee. She seemed to be looking forward to it. She already had several pupils for piano lessons. She could have had more but she preferred to spend some time after school with her own children. She continually assured Fiona they were all right for money, but

Conan knew about and approved of his wife's generosity with little gifts of shoes for the boys or a dress for Kirsten.

He smiled as he looked across at Fiona now, calmly refilling plates of scones for the hungry men and returning their quips with a wit and humour of her own. Neither of them would have wanted Lucy to be widowed so tragically young, but Lucy's loss had been their gain. It was lovely having her live so near. They truly enjoyed their grandchildren. Fiona was inordinately proud of Cameron's way with numbers, although he had not been at school very long. Ryan was different. Already he was reliable and steady, not as quick to learn as his younger brother, but acutely observant and he had an excellent memory. As for Kirsten, Conan thought she was the most beautiful little girl in the world with her green eyes and red-gold hair, not to mention the wide, toothy smile that could charm the heart out of him. Lucy was always remonstrating with him for spoiling her.

Rachel came and sat in an empty chair beside him.

'You're looking pleased with yourself, Conan.'

'Was I?' He looked startled. 'I was just daydreaming and thinking how lucky we are to have Lucy living near us now.'

'Yes, she's a grand lassie. Ever ready to lend a hand, and full of sound common sense.' She sighed heavily. 'It's an ill wind if it doesna blow some good to somebody, I suppose.' She bit her lower lip hard and her voice held a faint tremble. 'Though I find it hard to see what good can possibly come out of this day's toil.'

Conan looked at her sharply. 'But Bridie said it had been an excellent sale. Better than her expectations.'

'Oh, yes, it will pay off all the creditors, and a bit besides. But just think what a waste it was to sell the very best of the dairy herd as commercial stock – and maybe not even a fair price for commercial cattle. Gerda knew nothing about cows. It was criminal really . . .'

'Mother! You're not regretting your decision not to prosecute, are you?' He looked at her in consternation. She had been so certain.

'No . . . No, I'd have sacrificed anything, everything, just

287

to make sure Paul is loved and cared for. There was no telling what Gerda might have done with him – maybe even put him in a home if she felt he was preventing her enjoying her life.'

'I'm glad to hear you've no regrets,' Conan said in relief. 'If it's any consolation to you, Fiona thought you had made the wisest decision possible and Lucy most certainly did. She knew what Gerda was like when it came to caring for children.'

'Oh well, I'm glad Fiona agreed with me. Your father had great faith in her advice, you know. I have often wondered if she had anything to do with him putting the land into a trust for Paul, and making all those provisions for Peter and for me to stay in our houses. That must have been a shock to Gerda when she found out.'

'I'll bet it was, but then Father would never have done it if he had not mistrusted her motives. He was pretty shrewd himself.'

'Yes. He certainly did his best to provide fairly for each of you, but I don't know what he'd have thought to this day's work. I shall feel as sick at heart as Paul does when I go out in the morning and see all the empty sheds. It will not be like a farm at all.'

'Did Bridie tell you she had kept back twin calves for Paul to rear? And one of the heifer stirks hurt its leg trying to jump out of the sale ring, so she withdrew it as well.'

'Ah, I didn't know that.' Rachel's face brightened a little.

'Then Peter has his pigs and you have your hens, and the old collie,' Conan comforted. 'I know it will not be the same as before, but at least the fields are still yours and soon there will be other cattle to graze them. Bridie said she was bringing some from Glens of Lochandee.'

'Aye, you're right, laddie. We should be thankful for what we have left, and especially that Paul will be safe and loved.'

Twenty-Six

'You know, Mother, you look really smart in that new outfit. I can't believe you're seventy-nine,' Bridie said in all sincerity as she eyed Rachel's emerald-green dress with its matching jacket and a hat that toned in as though it had been made for it.

'Hush!' Rachel's green eyes sparkled with humour. 'I don't feel a day above fifty, so don't tell anyone.'

Bridie smiled back at her and sat down on a vacant chair. 'I hope I look as well when I'm your age.'

'I think you make an exceedingly lovely mother of the groom,' Rachel assured her. 'Indeed I heard Nick telling you so, and he's still a handsome man himself. I'm sure Max is very proud of you both, but then he always has been.'

'Yes, we've been very lucky with our children, and Megan is a lovely girl. She shares all Max's interest in the farm and the cattle. I'm looking forward to taking things a bit easier once they come back from their honeymoon.'

'Yes, Nick was telling me he has booked a holiday abroad on one of Conan's tours. You'll need to get passports . . .'

'Did I hear someone mention my name?' Conan chuckled as he joined them and took a seat on the other side of Rachel. 'My word, Mother you get younger every day!'

'And you've inherited your father's silver tongue, laddie. Are you wanting to ask a favour?'

'Not at all!' Conan said indignantly, then he saw the twinkle in her eye and grinned. 'I imagine you're very proud of all your grandchildren today?'

'I am indeed, and my great-grandchildren,' said Rachel.

'Yes, those two wee flower girls almost stole the show.

Alicia and Margaret needn't have worried about their offspring misbehaving. They looked and acted like angels during the ceremony.'

'Kirsten makes a beautiful bridesmaid, and she is so patient with the little ones. You and Fiona must be very proud of her, Conan.'

'We are,' Conan said simply. 'Lucy has made a good job of bringing up her family on her own. I often wondered whether she would get married again when she was widowed so young, but I don't think she will now.'

'No, I don't think she'll ever love anyone but Don. Conan?'

'I know what you're going to say, Mother.' Conan smiled down at her.

'You do? You always were a mind-reader. Maybe that's why you've done so well in that business of yours. It's not everyone who can deal with the public. Someone told me you make them feel you are doing them a real favour by organizing a wonderful holiday so they quite forget you're relieving them of their money while you're doing it.'

'Well that's part of the secret of running a successful tourist business.' Conan grinned then his green eyes grew serious. 'I couldn't have done it without Fiona though. We've been a team in every way from the very beginning.'

'I know. You were very fortunate. So, does Fiona approve of the offer you have made to Ryan? And are you sure about it? It would be a dreadful disappointment to him if you changed your mind after he gets through agricultural college. He reminds me so much of your father . . . and yet he's like Don too. Bridie says you couldn't get a better stockman anywhere.'

'Yes, she said the same to us but we accepted years ago that all Ryan wanted to do was farm. He's never shown any interest in the buses.'

'Not like Cameron does.' Rachel smiled.

'Fiona agrees we should give all three of our grandchildren an equal chance and Cameron has already decided for himself. He wants to go to university and then join us in the tourist business. Fiona is pleased but she does understand how desperately Ryan wants to farm.'

'It's bred in him, on both sides.'

'Yes, I realized that when he and Paul were quite small. Mentally I think I made plans to help him a long time ago. I always knew it was Lucy's deepest regret that she would never be able to help him into a farm as Don would have tried to do. But I wouldn't have suggested putting up the capital for Ryan and Paul to go into partnership at Wester Rullion without getting Bridie's agreement first. That's right, isn't it, Bridie?'

'It is. Of course, we are both trustees for Paul so it's a big responsibility. Now, I think I'd better circulate amongst the wedding guests.' Bridie smiled. 'I'll talk to you again later, Mother.' Rachel and Conan watched her go towards another group of wedding guests, her feet light, her figure still neat in her dusky-pink suit.

'Fiona has agreed to draw up a proper legal partnership for the boys,' Conan said, 'so you have no need to worry, Mother, and Bridie will supervise the farming side of things until they are twenty-five.'

'Yes.' Rachel nodded seriously. 'It is better to have an agreement in case they decide to split up, as you and Nick did.'

'Well, Paul will have the Wester Rullion land out of trust by then and if we provide Ryan with the capital to stock it and install a modern milking parlour, they should have a good start. After that it will be up to the pair of them to work hard and make a success of things. Neither Bridie nor I expect them to farm in partnership forever. They're both ambitious. I think they will expand until they can afford a farm each. At least they will have a decent start.'

'Yes, that's more than I dared to hope when Ewan was killed,' Rachel reflected. 'I'm sure they'll both work hard.' Her eyes moved to Paul, tall and slim-hipped, with an infectious smile and light brown hair. 'Meanwhile, having something to work for will give them an incentive to get through their course at agricultural college,' Rachel agreed.

'Yes.' Conan grinned. 'They both thought they should rush into farming straight away but Bridie has insisted they must work on another farm for a year at least to broaden their experience before they go to college. I agree with her. After all they're only nineteen,' he added sternly.

'Oh yes.' Rachel smiled at his tone. 'And you and Nick were fighting a war at their age. Remember?'

'So we were. Our view of the world changed completely. No doubt theirs will too.'

'You think one of them might decide to do something else other than farming?' Rachel asked in surprise. Ever since they were old enough Ryan and Paul had spent their weekends and school holidays at Glens of Lochandee, trailing after either Max or their Aunt Bridie. There was only six months between them and they had always been the best of friends.

'They probably both know more about livestock and breeding than their college lecturers will ever know,' Bridie had said, 'but farming is changing rapidly, especially since decimalization came in and after all the strikes the price of everything seems to have doubled. Then the Common Market has brought so many new regulations. I can't teach the boys everything, and I can see great changes ahead.'

The boys had protested vigorously. 'You can teach us all we want to know, Aunt Bridie,' Paul said, and Ryan had heartily agreed.

'No I can't. You need to learn about economics and the science behind animal diseases and hygiene. Bacteriology can be very interesting and it helps you understand why I make you do some of the things when you think I'm fussing.' She grinned at them. 'Oh yes, I know what you think! Anyway, there's accounts to do, and a lot to learn about seeds and managing grass, making silage, using the correct fertilizers and getting the soil analysed. I know lots of people think nature sees to all these things but you two should know better and you need to learn to combat the problems as they arise, and even see them coming. You might both decide to be arable farmers . . .'

'We shall not!' they had echoed in unison.

'Well I often think it must be easier than milking cows

seven days a week. But if you go to college the choice will be yours.'

Conan and Fiona had agreed with Bridie on this and reluctantly the boys had also agreed.

'Look, Max and Megan are starting the dancing,' Conan said, drawing Rachel's attention back to the wedding reception. 'They make a lovely couple, don't you think?'

'I do indeed. I pray with all my heart they'll be happy together at Glens of Lochandee.'

'I think they will. They seem well matched. Would you like to dance, Mother?'

'Won't Fiona be waiting for you?'

'She's too busy chatting to Mrs Greig, Lucy's mother-in-law. Now there's a woman who looks ten years younger since she was widowed.'

'She does look well,' Rachel agreed. 'But no wonder. Mr Greig was such a crotchety old man. Christine is like her mother. She and Lucy have remained close friends over the years. Look, there's Cameron asking one of the bridesmaids to dance!' Rachel said in delight. 'He's just like you, Conan, with his green eyes and roguish grin. He has your build too, tall and slim. Ryan is more like Don was, sturdier built. Is Fiona pleased Cameron will be joining you in the business?'

'Yes, she is, and she's delighted he's studying accountancy. She feels we shall need one in the firm when she retires, and I think she's right about that. Cameron is already pretty useful around the offices, and he doesn't mind getting his hands dirty either if one of the buses needs attention. I thought at one point he was going to be a mechanic, but I believe he'll be more useful as an administrator, especially if he takes over the business some day.'

'And Kirsten?'

'She's like Bridie. And Fiona says Lucy was the same – excels at languages. She's only fifteen yet but she talks about going to university. Fiona has already told her we could use someone who can speak a couple of foreign languages to deal with the problems we get now we send tours abroad.

Whatever she decides we shall see she gets a share in the business too. Fiona has already put some shares into Lucy's name. We want to keep it in the family.' He grinned down at Rachel. 'I'm getting as bad as Father, except that he wanted to make us all into farmers at Glens of Lochandee.'

'Yes.' Rachel sighed. 'But you each made your own way in life in the end.'

Conan saw the shadow that passed over her face. 'You're thinking of Ewan?' he asked softly.

'I was. He thought Gerda was the love of his life. He was so young . . . We should have been firmer, made them wait . . .'

'Things might have been worse if you had. I suppose we were both a bit headstrong – each in our own way,' Conan reflected.

'You were indeed!' Rachel agreed. 'You can't imagine how we worried about you when we knew you'd joined the RAF.'

'I think I can understand now,' Conan said, leading her back to a seat as the dance finished. His eyes moved to Lucy, and then to her children, his own grandchildren. He hoped and prayed their paths through life would be happy. His gaze moved to Paul, his nephew.

'Paul looks just like my father,' he said involuntarily.

'I've often though so too.' Rachel smiled. 'Except he has green eyes, like yours and mine. He has a lovely nature and that's the biggest blessing of all. He and Ryan could almost pass for brothers. I'm sure they will make a great success of bringing Wester Rullion back to the farm it used to be.'